1ᵉ

B. C. É.

DROWNED HOPES

By Donald E. Westlake

NOVELS

Sacred Monster • A Likely Story • Kahawa
Brothers Keepers • I Gave at the Office
Adios, Scheherazade • Up Your Banners

COMIC CRIME NOVELS

Trust Me on This • High Adventure
Castle in the Air • Enough • Dancing Aztecs
Two Much • *Help* I Am Being Held Prisoner
Cops and Robbers • Somebody Owes Me Money
Who Stole Sassi Manoon? • God Save the Mark
The Spy in the Ointment • The Busy Body
The Fugitive Pigeon

THE DORTMUNDER SERIES

Drowned Hopes • Good Behavior
Why Me • Nobody's Perfect
Jimmy the Kid • Bank Shot • The Hot Rock

CRIME NOVELS

Pity Him Afterwards • Killy • 361
Killing Time • The Mercenaries

JUVENILE

Philip

WESTERN

Gangway (with Brian Garfield)

REPORTAGE

Under an English Heaven

SHORT STORIES

Tomorrow's Crimes • Levine
The Curious Facts Preceding My Execution and Other Fictions

ANTHOLOGY

Once Against the Law (edited with William Tenn)

DONALD E. WESTLAKE

DROWNED HOPES

THE MYSTERIOUS PRESS

New York • London
Tokyo • Sweden • Milan

The Mysterious Press, 129 West 56th Street, New York, N.Y. 10019

Printed in the United States of America

Library of Congress Cataloging-in-Publication Data

Westlake, Donald E.
    Drowned hopes / by Donald E. Westlake.
        p.   cm.
    ISBN 0-89296-178-3
    I. Title.
PS3573.E9D76   1990   89-35859
813'.54—dc20   CIP

Bibliomystery

Dortmunder and I received more than our normal share of help in this piece of work. Here is where our worthy assistants receive the warm handshake ILOS: In Lieu of Salary.

Through the fine efforts of New York Is Book Country, whose auction of usually useful objects aids the New York Public Library, Doron Levy came along to assist with a drive-through at a semicrucial point. Justin Scott accepted a phone call from my characters when *I* could help them no more, thus assisting both us guys here and the Mystery Writers of America. Batesville's Bob Smith kept us all warm and dry. And Joe Gores even sent a fella from his own crowd to help out. To them, to the more usual suspects, and to you, my thanks.

Why to you? Because, unless you read this novel, all of these efforts will remain incomplete. You close the circle. Peace.

FIRST DOWN

CHAPTER ONE

As gray dawn crawled over the city, Dortmunder went home to find May still up, dressed in a baggy sweater and green plaid slacks. She came out of the living room into the hall when she heard him open the door, but instead of asking, as she usually did, "How'd it go?" she said, sounding nervous but relieved, "You're back."

He answered the usual question anyway, being tired and out of sorts and not at his most observant. "Not so good," he said, opening the closet door. With slow and tired motions, he took tools from the many inside and outside pockets of his black jacket, placing them with muffled clanks on the closet shelf. "The jeweler's gone, moved to Rhinebeck; there's a pasta restaurant in there now. The antique guy's switched to Disney collectibles. And the check-cashing place got a dog." Taking his jacket off, he held it up and looked at the new ragged tear at the bottom in the back. "Mean goddamn dog," he said.

"John," May said. She sounded tense. Her left hand pretend-smoked, fiddling with an imaginary cigarette, flicking ghost ashes on the floor, something she hadn't done since just after she'd quit.

But Dortmunder was full of his own problems. Hanging up his torn jacket, he said, "It's almost enough to make you rethink a life of crime. I did get a *little*, though, after I locked the dog out and he ran away." He began pulling crumpled money from inside his shirt, putting it on the hall table.

"*John*," May said, her eyes very round and white, "there's somebody *here*."

He paused, hand over the money. "What?"

3

"He says—" May glanced at the doorway to the living room, apprehension and mistrust defining her features. "He says he's an old friend of yours."

"Who does?"

"This man."

"Al?" The voice, hoarse and ragged but somehow self-confident, came from the living room. "Is that you, Al?"

Dortmunder looked bewildered, and then startled. "No," he said.

A man appeared in the living room doorway. He was as gray and cold as the dawn outside, a thin gristly bony old guy of just over six feet tall, dressed in a gray windbreaker over a faded blue workshirt, and baggy gray pants and black worn shoes. He had a craggy rectangular head sitting up on top of his stony body like a log redan full of guards. His eyes were bleak, cheeks ravaged, brow furrowed, hair gray and thin and dead and hanging down over his large leathery ears. "Hello, Al," he said, and when he spoke his lips didn't move; but what ventriloquist would use *this* for an alter ego? "How you doin, Al," the hoarse gray voice said through the unmoving lips. "Long time no see."

"Well, I'll be goddamned," Dortmunder said. "They let you out."

CHAPTER TWO

The gray man made a sound that might have been meant for a laugh. "A surprise, huh?" he said. "Surprised me, too."

May said, "So you do know him." She sounded as though she wasn't sure whether that was good news or bad news.

"Tom and I were inside together," Dortmunder told her, unwillingly. "We were cellmates for a while."

The gray man, who looked too flinty and stringy and knotted to be named anything as simple and friendly as Tom, made that laugh sound again, and said, "Cellmates. Pals. Right, Al? Thrown together by the vagaries of fortune, right?"

"That's right," Dortmunder said.

"Why don't we sit in the living room," Tom suggested, his lips a thin straight line. "My coffee's gettin cold in there."

"Sure," Dortmunder said.

Tom turned away, going back into the living room, walking rigid, like a man who's been broken and then put back together a little wrong, using too much Krazy Glue. Behind his stiff back, May waggled eyebrows and shoulders and fingers at Dortmunder, asking, *Who is this person, why is he in my house, what's going on, when will it end?* and Dortmunder shrugged ears and elbows and the corners of his mouth, answering, *I don't know what's going on, I don't know if this is some kind of trouble or not, we'll just have to wait and see.* Then they followed Tom into the living room.

5

Tom sat on the better easy chair, the one that hadn't sagged all the way to the floor, while Dortmunder and May took the sofa, sitting facing Tom with the look of a couple who've just been asked to think seriously about life insurance. Tom sat on the edge of the chair, leaning forward, lifting his cup from the coffee table, sipping with deep concentration. He looked like the background figure in a Depression movie, a guy hunkered over a small fire in a hobo encampment. Dortmunder and May watched him warily, and when he put the cup down he leaned back and sighed faintly, and said, "That's all I drink now. Lost my taste on the inside."

Dortmunder said, "How long were you in, Tom, all in all?"

"All in all?" Tom made that sound again. "All my life, all in all. Twenty-three years, this last time. It was supposed to be for good, you know. I'm habitual."

"I remember that about you," Dortmunder said.

"Well, the answer is," Tom said, "while I been eating regular meals and getting regular exercise and a good night's sleep all these years on the inside, the world's managed to get worse without me. Maybe I'm not the one they should of been protecting society from all along."

"How do you mean, Tom?"

"The reason I'm out," Tom said. "Inflation, plus budget cuts, plus the rising inmate population. All on its own, Al, without any help from yours truly, society has raised up a *generation* of inmates. Sloppy ones, too, Al, fourth-rates you and me wouldn't use to hold the door open."

"There is a lot of that around," Dortmunder agreed.

"These are people," Tom went on, "that don't know a blueprint from a candy wrapper. And to pull a job with a *plan*? When these bozos take a step forward with the right foot, they have no really *clear* idea what they figure to do with the left."

"They're out there, all right," Dortmunder said, nodding. "I see them sometimes, asleep on fire escapes, with their head on a television set. They do kinda muddy the water for the rest of us."

"They take all the fun outta prison, I can tell you that," Tom said. "And the worst of it is, their motivation's no damn good. Now, Al, you and me know, if a man goes into a bank with a gun in his hand and says gimme the money and a five-minute start, there's only *two* good reasons for it. Either his family's poor and sick and needs an operation and shoes and schoolbooks and meat for dinner more than once a week, or the fella wants to take a lady friend to Miami and party. One or the other. Am I right?"

"That's the usual way," Dortmunder agreed. "Except it's mostly Las Vegas now."

"Well, *these* clowns can't even get that much right," Tom said. "The fact is, what they steal for is to feed their veins, and they go right on feeding their veins inside, they buy it off guards and trusties and visitors and each other and probly even the chaplain, but if you *ask* them why they ignored the career counselor and took up this life of crime for which they are so shit-*poor* fitted, they'll tell you it's political. They'll tell you *they're* the victims."

Dortmunder nodded. "I've heard that one," he said. "It's useful in the sentencing sometimes, I think. And in the parole."

"It's a crock, Al," Tom insisted.

Gently, Dortmunder said, "Tom, you and I've told the authorities a couple fibs in our time, too."

"Okay," Tom said. "Granted. Anyway, the result is, inflation makes it cost more to feed and house a fella in the pen in the manner to which we've all become accustomed, and budget cuts— Did you know, Al," he interrupted himself, "that health-wise, long-term cons are the healthiest people in America?"

"I didn't know that," Dortmunder admitted.

"Well, it's the truth," Tom said. "It's the regularity of the life, the lack of stress, the sameness of the food intake, the handiness of the free medical care, and the organized exercise program. Your lifers are the longest-lived people in the society. Any insurance company will tell you so."

"Well," Dortmunder said, "that must be some kind of consolation, I guess."

"Yeah." Tom made that laugh sound again. "Just knowing if you were out somewhere having fun you'd die sooner." Tom slurped coffee without apparently opening his lips, and said, "So, anyway, with all of those things coming together, with its costing more to house me and feed me, plus you've got these budget cuts so they got *less* money to do this housing and feeding, plus you've got the entire male population between seventeen and twenty-six clamoring to come in to be housed and fed, the governor decided to give me a seventieth birthday present." Grinning closed-mouthed at May, he said, "You wouldn't think I was seventy, would you?"

"No, I wouldn't," May said.

"I look younger than Al here," Tom told her.

May frowned at Dortmunder. "John," she said, "why does he keep calling you Al? If you do really know him, and if he really knows you, and if you really lived in the same cell together, and if your name is John—and it *is* John—why does he call you *Al*?"

Tom made a sound that might have been meant for a chuckle. "It's a kind of an inside joke between Al and me," he said.

Dortmunder explained, "It's Tom's idea of comedy. He found out my middle name's Archibald, and I don't much love that name—"

"You hate it," May said.

"It's one of the worst things about being arrested," Dortmunder said. "When they look at me and say, 'John Archibald Dortmunder, you are under arrest,' I always cave in right away, and that's why."

May said, "And when this man found out how much you hated that name, that's what he decided to call you from then on?"

"That's right," Dortmunder said.

"And his idea of a nickname for Archibald is Al?"

"Right again," Dortmunder said.

"Inside joke," Tom said, and made the chuckle sound again.

"That," May said, "is his idea of humor."

"You're beginning to get the picture," Dortmunder told her.

"Al," Tom said, "are you really close with this woman? I mean, can I talk in front of her?"

"Well, Tom," Dortmunder said, "if you plan on talking much in front of *me*, you'll be talking in front of May. I mean, that's the way it is."

"That's okay," Tom said. "I got no problem with that. I just wanted to be sure you were secure in your mind."

Dortmunder said, "Tom, you want something."

"Of course I want something," Tom told him. "What do you think I am? You think I do *reunions*? You think I make my way around the country, drop in on old cellmates, cut up a lot of old jackpots? Al, do I look to you like a guy sends out *Christmas cards*?"

"Like I said, Tom," Dortmunder answered patiently, "you're here because you want something."

"Yes," Tom said. "I want something."

"What?"

"Help," Tom said simply.

"You mean money?" Dortmunder asked him, though he didn't think that could be it. Tom Jimson was not a borrower type; he'd rather shoot you and rob the body than be reduced to begging.

"Well, it's money in a way," Tom said. "Let me explain, okay?"

"Go right ahead."

"You see," Tom said, "it's like this. What I always did when I made a good-sized haul, I always stashed some or all of it, hid it somewhere so I'd have it if I needed it later on. I learned that when I was just a kid, from Dilly."

May said, "Dilly?"

Dortmunder told her, "John Dillinger. Tom started out with Dillinger, and that's what he called him."

May said, "To his face?"

"Lady," Tom said, "I never had a lot of trouble gettin my own way. I want to call this fella here Al, I call him Al. I wanted to call Dilly Dilly, that's what I called him."

"All right," May said. The wary look in her eyes was on the increase.

"So anyway," Tom said, "Dilly and I kind of come out together, in a way of speaking. What I mean, he got out of the pen in Indiana in 'thirty-three, and that's when I was just gettin started myself. I was fourteen. I learned a lot from Dilly that year, before he pulled that fake death of his, and one of the things I learned was, always stash some of it away for a rainy day."

"I remember that," Dortmunder said. "I remember, while we were cellmates, every once in a while you had to tell some lawyer where another of those stashes was so he could go dig it up and pay himself what you owed him."

"Lawyers," Tom said, his voice rasping more than usual, and his lips moved slightly, just enough to give a glimpse of small, white, sharp-looking teeth. "They got their hands on a lot of my stashes over the years," he admitted, "and they never gave me a thing for it all. But they didn't get the *big* stash, and they weren't going to. That one I held out, even from the lawyers. That one's my retirement. There's a place in Mexico I'm goin, way down below Acapulco on the west coast. That money's gonna get me there, and once I'm there that money's gonna keep me happy and healthy for a good long time. I'm gonna be an *old* man, Al, that's the one ambition in life I got left."

"Sounds good," Dortmunder said, wondering why Tom didn't just get on that southbound plane. Why come *here*? Why tell this story to *Dortmunder*? Where was the part he wasn't going to like?

"What it was," Tom was saying, "it was an armored car on the Thruway, taking money from Albany on down to New York. We had a nice clean hit, but then my partners ran into some trouble later on, and it wound up I had the whole seven hundred thousand."

Dortmunder stared at him. "Dollars?"

"That's what they were using back then," Tom agreed. "Dollars. This was a year or two before I went up the last time. I was pretty flush, and what with one thing and another I didn't have any partners to share the stuff with, so I got me a casket—"

"A box, you mean," Dortmunder said.

"A *casket*, I mean," Tom told him. "The best kind of box there is, Al, if you want to keep something safe. Airtight, watertight, steel-encased."

"Sounds great," Dortmunder said.

"It is," Tom said. "And, you know, you can't just go out and *buy* one of those. The company that makes them, they keep those babies under very tight control."

Dortmunder frowned. "They do?"

"They do. See, they don't want you to take it into your head to buy a box and stick old granny in it and shove her in a hole in the back yard. Free-lance burial, you see. The law doesn't like that."

"I suppose not," Dortmunder said.

"So it happened," Tom went on, "I happened to know this undertaker around that time. We did business together—"

Dortmunder and May exchanged a look.

"—and he slipped me a box out of his inventory. Sunnyside Casket Company's best, and worth every penny of it. It's a crime to waste those boxes on dead people."

"Uh-huh," Dortmunder said.

"There was a little town up there," Tom went on, "not far from the Thruway. Called Putkin's Corners. I went in there one night and went out behind the library to a spot where you couldn't be seen from any windows where anybody lived, and I dug a hole four feet deep, and I shoved the casket in and covered it up, and I drove away, and nobody in the entire world—except now you two—ever knew I was ever *in* a town called Putkin's Corners in my entire life."

"And that's what you need help with?" Dortmunder asked. "Getting that casket full of money back out of Putkin's Corners?"

"That's where I need help, all right," Tom agreed.

"It doesn't sound like it should be that much trouble," Dortmunder assured him, thinking Tom meant that, now he was seventy years old, he wasn't up to all the digging and lifting required.

But Tom shook his head, saying, "A little harder than you might think, Al. You see, about four years after I went up, a while before you come in to be my cellmate, the state of New York condemned all that land and houses and four villages up there, including Putkin's Corners, and made everybody move away. And then the city of New York bought up all that land, and they threw a dam across partway down the valley, and they made themselves another reservoir for all you people down here."

"Oh," Dortmunder said.

"So that's why I need help," Tom explained. "Because as it stands right now, that stash of mine is under three feet of dirt and fifty feet of water."

"Ah," Dortmunder said. "Not easy."

"Not impossible," Tom said. "So here's the deal I'd like to offer. You got a head on your shoulders, Al—"

"Thanks," Dortmunder said.

"So you come into this with me," Tom finished. "We get that box of mine out of Putkin's Corners, you and me and whoever else it takes, and when we get it we split down the middle. Half for me, and half for you, and you share your half how you like with whoever else you bring in. Three hundred fifty thousand. I can live to be an old man on that much, especially down in Mexico. What do you say?"

"Interesting," Dortmunder said, thinking he'd like to know more about the problems that had afflicted Tom's partners in the original robbery, leaving him sole possessor of the seven hundred thousand dollars. But thinking also that at seventy Tom was probably not quite as dangerous as he'd been at forty-three or forty-four, when the robbery had taken place. And thinking beyond that to the amount of money itself, and the hassle he'd just gone through tonight for petty cash out of a check-cashing place with a bad-tempered dog. He didn't know exactly how you went about digging up a casket from fifty feet down in the bottom of a reservoir, but let's just say he had to bring in two or three other guys, say three other guys; that still left nearly a hundred thousand apiece. And there are no dogs in a reservoir.

Tom was saying, "Now, you probably want to get some sleep—"

"Yeah, I'm due," Dortmunder admitted.

"So maybe this afternoon, early afternoon, we could drive on up and I could show you the place. It's about two hours up from the city."

"This afternoon?" Dortmunder echoed, thinking he'd like to sleep a little longer than that. The check-cashing place's dog had kind of taken it out of him.

"Well, the sooner the better, you know," Tom said.

May said, "John? Are you going to do this?"

Dortmunder knew that May had taken an aversion to Tom Jimson— most human beings did—but on the other hand there were all those advantages he'd just been thinking about, so he said, "I'll take a look at it anyway, May, see how it seems."

"If you think you should," May said. The air around her words vibrated with all the other words she wasn't saying.

"I'll just take a look," Dortmunder assured her, and faced Tom again to say, "Where are you staying now?"

"Well," Tom said, "until I get my stash out of Putkin's Corners, that sofa you're sitting on's about as good a place as any."

"Ah," Dortmunder said, while beside him May's cheekbones turned to concrete. "In that case," Dortmunder said, "I guess we better drive up and take a look this afternoon."

CHAPTER THREE

After the Thruway exit, the road took them through North Dudson, a very small town full of cars driven with extreme slowness by people who couldn't decide whether or not they wanted to make a left turn. Dortmunder didn't like being behind the wheel, anyway, and these indecisive locals weren't improving his disposition much. In his universe, the driver drives—usually Stan Murch, sometimes Andy Kelp—while the specialists ride in back, oiling their pliers and wrapping black tape around their screwdrivers. Putting a specialist behind the wheel and making him drive through little towns hundreds of miles from the real city—well, tens of miles anyway, around a hundred of miles—meant that what you wound up with was a vehicle operated by someone who was both overqualified and nervous.

But the alternative, this time, was even worse. If Tom Jimson had ever known how to drive a car, and had ever cared enough about humanity to try to drive it in a nonlethal fashion, both the skill and the caring had disappeared completely in the course of his latest twenty-three-year visit inside. So Tom had rented the car—a *rental*, not even something borrowed from the street, another nervous-making element—and now Dortmunder was doing the driving, regardless.

At least the weather was good, April sun agleam on the white aluminum siding sheathed around all the quaint old houses that made North Dudson so scenic a place that a city boy could get a migraine just by looking at it. Particularly when he hadn't had enough sleep. So Dortmunder concentrated on the few familiar reminders of civilization along the way—traffic lights, McDonald's arches, Marlboro Man billboards—and just kept driving forward, knowing that sooner or later North Dudson would have to come to an end. Beside him, Tom looked around, smiled ironically without moving his lips, and said, "Well, *this* place is still the same piece of shit, anyway."

"What do I do when I get out of town?"

"You keep driving," Tom said.

A taco joint with a neon sign in its window advertising a German beer made in Texas was the last building in North Dudson, and then the fields and forests and farms took over. The road began to wobble and to climb, and here and there horses looked up from their grazing in rock-littered fields to give them the fish eye as they passed by.

About four miles out of town, Tom broke a fairly long silence by conversationally saying, "That was the road."

Dortmunder slammed on the brakes, sluing to a stop on the highway and giving the old fart in the pickup truck tailgating him yet another infarction. "Where?" Dortmunder demanded, staring around, seeing no intersection, his question blotted out by the squawk of the pickup's horn howling in outraged complaint as the truck swung on by and tore away down the road. "Where?" Dortmunder repeated.

"Back there," Tom said, and gave him a look. "You can't take it *now*," he said. "Putkin's Corners is gone, remember? That's the whole problem here."

"You mean the *old* road," Dortmunder said. "Not any road I'm supposed to take now."

"You can't take it now," Tom said. "It's all overgrown. See it?"

Dortmunder still couldn't see any road, so Tom must have been right about it being overgrown. "When you said, 'That was the road,'" Dortmunder told him, "I thought you meant I was supposed to turn or something."

"When you're supposed to turn or something," Tom said, "I'll tell you so."

"I thought you *did* tell me so," Dortmunder explained.

"Well, I didn't."

"Well, it just *sounded* that way," Dortmunder said, as a station wagon went by, yapping its horn at them for being stopped in the middle of the road. "When you said, 'That was the road,' it *sounded* like you meant that was the road."

"It *was* the road. Twenty-three years ago it was the road." Tom sounded snappish. "*Now* what it is is a lot of trees and bushes and hills."

"It was just confusing, what you said, is all," Dortmunder explained, as a big truck full of logs gave them the air horn on its way by.

Tom half turned to look full at Dortmunder. "I understand what you're saying, Al," he said. "So don't say it anymore. Drive on, okay? I'm seventy years old. I don't know how much longer I got."

So Dortmunder drove on, and a mile or so later they came to a sign that said: ENTERING VILBURGTOWN COUNTY. "This is the county," Tom said. "When they did the reservoir, they covered almost this whole county. There's no towns left here at all. Putkin's Corners was the county seat. There's the road."

A two-lane blacktop road went off to the right. Dortmunder nodded at it and kept going straight.

Tom said, "Hey!"

"What?"

"That was the road! What's the matter with you?"

This time, Dortmunder pulled off onto the gravel verge before he stopped. Facing Tom, he said, "Do you mean I was supposed to turn there?"

"That's what I said!" Tom was so agitated his lips were almost moving. "I told you, 'There's the road'!"

"The last time you told me 'There's the road,'" Dortmunder said icily, getting fed up with all this, "you didn't *mean* 'There's the road,' you meant something else. A history lesson or some goddamn thing."

Tom sighed. He frowned at the dashboard. He polished the tip of his nose with a bent knuckle. Then he nodded. "Okay, Al," he said. "We been outta touch with each other awhile. We just got to get used to communicating with each other again."

"Probably so," Dortmunder agreed, ready to meet his old cellmate halfway.

"So *this* time," Tom said, "what I meant was, 'Turn here.' In fact, I'm sorry that isn't the way I phrased myself."

"It would have helped," Dortmunder admitted.

"So I tell you what you do," Tom said. "You turn around, and we go back, and we'll try all over again and see how it comes out. Okay?"

"Good."

Dortmunder looked both ways, made the U-turn, and Tom said, "Turn here."

"I already knew that, Tom," Dortmunder said, and made the turn onto the new road.

"I just wanted to practice saying it right."

"I'm wondering," Dortmunder said as they drove through the forest along the new road, "if that's some more of your famous humor."

"Maybe so," Tom said, looking out the windshield, watching the road unwind toward them out of the woods. "Or maybe it's concealed rage," he said. "One time, inside, a shrink took a whack at me, and he told me I had a lot of concealed rage, so maybe that's some of it, coming out in disguised form."

Dortmunder, surprised, gave him a look. "You got *concealed* rage?" he asked. "On top of all the rage you *show*, you got *more*?"

"According to this shrink," Tom said, and shrugged, saying, "But what do they know? Shrinks are crazy, anyway, that's why they take the job. Slow down a little now, we're getting close."

On the right, the forest was interrupted by a dirt road marked NO ADMITTANCE—VILBURGTOWN RESERVOIR AUTHORITY, with a simple metal-pipe barrier blocking the way. A little later, there was another dirt road on the same side, with the same sign and the same pipe barrier, and a little after that a fence came marching at an angle out of the woods and then ran along next to the road; an eight-foot-high chain-link fence with two strands of barbed wire angling outward at the top.

Dortmunder said, "They put barbed wire around the reservoir?"

"They did," Tom agreed.

"Isn't that more security than most reservoirs get?" Dortmunder waved a hand vaguely. "I thought, most reservoirs, you could go there and fish and stuff."

"Well, yeah," Tom said. "But back then, the time they put this one in, it was a very revolutionary moment in American history, you know. You had all these environment freaks and antiwar freaks and antigovernment freaks and like that. . . ."

"Well, you still do."

"But back then," Tom said, "they were *crazed*. Blowing up college buildings and all this. And this reservoir became what you call your focal point of protest. You had these groups threatening that if this reservoir went in, they'd lace it with enough chemicals to blow every mind in New York City."

"Gee, maybe they did," Dortmunder said, thinking back to some people he knew down in the city.

"No, they didn't," Tom told him, "on account of this fence, and the cops on duty here, and the state law they passed to make this reservoir off limits to *everybody*."

"But that was a long time ago," Dortmunder objected. "Those chemicals are gone. The people that had them took them all themselves."

"Al," Tom said, "have you ever seen any government *give up* control, once they got it? Here's the fence, here's the cops, here's the state law says everybody keep out, here's the *job to be done*. So they do it. Otherwise, they wouldn't feel right taking their paycheck every week."

"Okay," Dortmunder said. "Complicates things for you and me, but okay."

"Not a real complication," Tom said, but unfortunately at that point it didn't occur to Dortmunder to follow through and ask him what he meant by that.

Besides, here came the reservoir. The fence continued on, and through it water gleamed. A great big lake appeared, smiling placidly in the afternoon sun, winking and rippling when little playful breezes skipped over it. Pine trees and oaks and maples and birch trees surrounded the reservoir, growing right down to the water's edge. There were no houses around it, no boats on it, no people in sight anywhere. And the road ran right along beside it. On the other side of the road, past another fence, was a big drop-off, the land falling away to a deep valley far below.

"Stop along here somewheres," Tom said.

There was a very narrow shoulder here, and then the fence. If Dortmunder pulled right up against the fence, Tom wouldn't be able to open his door, and anyway the car would still be partly on the road. But there hadn't been any traffic at all along this secondary road, so Dortmunder didn't worry about it and just stopped where they were, and Tom said, "Good," and got out, leaving his door open.

Dortmunder left the engine running, and also climbed out onto cement roadway, but shut his door against the possibility of traffic. He walked around the car and stood beside the fence with Tom, looking out at the serene water. Tom stuck his gnarly old tree-twig finger through the fence, pointing as he said, "Putkin's Corners was right about there. Right about out there."

"Be tough to get to," Dortmunder commented.

"Just a little muddy, is all," Tom said.

Dortmunder looked around. "Where's the dam?"

Tom gave him a disbelieving look. "The dam? Where's the dam? *This* is the dam. You're standing on the dam."

"I am?" Dortmunder looked left and right, and saw how the road came out of the woods behind them and then swung off in a long gentle curve, with the reservoir outside the curve on the right and the valley inside the curve on the left, all the way around to another hillside full of trees way over there, where it disappeared again in among the greenery. "This is the dam,"

Dortmunder said, full of wonder. "And they put the road right on top of it."

"Sure. What'd you think?"

"I didn't expect it to be so big," Dortmunder admitted. Being careful to look both ways, even though there had still been no traffic out here, Dortmunder crossed the road and looked down and saw how the dam also curved gently outward from top to bottom, its creamy gray concrete like a curtain that has billowed out slightly from a breeze blowing underneath. Beyond and below the concrete wall of the dam, a neat stream meandered away farther on down the valley, past a few farms, a village, another village, and at the far end of the valley what looked like a pretty big town, much bigger even than North Dudson. "So that," Dortmunder said, pointing back toward the reservoir, "must have looked like this before they put the dam in."

"If I'd known," Tom said, "I would of buried the goddamn box in Dudson Center down there."

Dortmunder looked again at the facade of the dam, and now he noticed the windows in it, in two long rows near the top. They were regular plate-glass windows like those in office buildings. He said, "Those are windows."

"You're right again," Tom said.

"But— How come? Does a dam have an inside?"

"Sure it does," Tom said. "They got their offices down in there, and all the controls for letting the water in and out and doing the purity tests and pumping it into the pipes to go down to the city. That's all inside there."

"I guess I just never thought about dams," Dortmunder said. "Where I live and all, and in my line of work, things like dams don't come up that often."

"I *had* to learn about dams," Tom said, "once the bastards flooded my money."

"Yeah, well, then you got a personal stake," Dortmunder agreed.

"And I studied *this* dam in particular," Tom told him. Again pointing through fence, this time at an angle down toward the creamy gray curtain of the dam, he said, "And the best place to put the dynamite is *there*, and over *there*."

Dortmunder stared at him. "Dynamite?"

"Sure dynamite," Tom told him. "Whadaya think I got, nuclear devices? Dynamite is the tool at hand."

"But— Why do you want to use dynamite?"

"To move the water out of the way," Tom said, very slowly, as though explaining things to an idiot.

"Wait a minute," Dortmunder said. "Wait a minute wait a minute wait a minute. Your idea here is, you're gonna blow up the dam to drain all the water out, and then walk in and dig up the box of money?"

"What I figure," Tom said, "the cops and all are gonna be pretty busy downstream, so we'll have time to get in and out before anybody takes much of an interest." Turning away to look across the road (and the dam) at the peaceful water in the sunshine, he said, "We'll need some kind of all-terrain vehicle, though, I think. It'll be pretty goddamn muddy down in there."

Dortmunder said, "Tom, back up a bit, just back up here. You want to take all that water *there*, and move it over *here*."

"Yes," Tom said.

"You want to blow up this dam here, with the people inside it."

"Well, you know," Tom said, "if we give them the word ahead of time, they might get upset. They might want to get in our way, stop us, make problems for us or something."

"How many people work down in there?" Dortmunder asked, pointing at the windows in the dam.

"At night? We'd have to make our move at night, of course," Tom explained. "I figure, at night, seven or eight guys in there, maybe ten at the most."

Dortmunder looked at the windows. He looked downstream at the farms and the villages and the town at the end of the valley, and he said, "That's a lot of water in that reservoir, isn't it?"

"Sure is," Tom said.

"Everybody asleep down there," Dortmunder said, musing, imagining it, "and here comes the water. That's your idea."

Tom looked through the chain-link fence at the peaceful valley. His gray cold eyes gleamed in his gray cold face. "Asleep in their beds," he said. "Asleep in *somebody's* beds anyway. You know who those people are?"

Dortmunder shook his head, watching that stony profile.

Tom said, "Nobodies. Family men hustlin for an extra dollar, an extra dime, sweatin all over their shirts, gettin nowhere. Women turnin fat. Kids turnin stupid. No difference between day and night because nobody's goin anywhere anyway. Miserable little small-town people with their miserable little small-town dreams." The lips moved in what might have been a smile. "A flood," he said. "Most excitin thing ever happened to them, am I right?"

"No, Tom," Dortmunder said.

"No?" Tom asked, misunderstanding. "You think there's a *lot* of excitement down there? Senior proms, bankruptcy auctions, Fourth of July parades, gang bangs, all that kind of thing? That what you think?"

"I think you can't blow up the dam, Tom," Dortmunder said. "I think you can't drown a whole lot of people—hundreds and hundreds of people—in their beds, or in anybody's beds, for seven hundred thousand dollars."

"Three hundred fifty thousand," Tom corrected. "Half of it is yours, Al. Yours and whoever else you bring in on the caper."

Dortmunder looked frankly at his old cellmate. "You'd really do that, Tom? You'd kill hundreds and hundreds of people for three hundred fifty thousand dollars?"

"I'd kill them at a dollar apiece," Tom told him, "if it meant I could get outta this part of the world and get down to Mexico and move into my goddamn golden years of retirement."

Dortmunder said, "Tom, maybe you were inside too long. You can't do things like that, you know. You can't go around killing hundreds and hundreds of people just like snapping your fingers."

"It *isn't* just like snapping my fingers, Al," Tom said. "That's the problem. If it was like snapping my fingers, I'd go do it myself and keep the whole seven hundred. If I learned anything on the inside, you know, it's that I can't be a loner anymore, not on something like this. Except at the very beginning, with Dilly and Baby and them, I was always a loner, you know, all my life. That's why I talked so much when we were together in the cell. Remember how I used to talk so much?"

"I don't have to remember," Dortmunder told him. "I'm listening to it." But what he did remember was how odd he used to find it, back in the good old days in the cell, that a man who did so much talking was (a) famous as a loner, and (b) managed to get all those words out without once moving his lips.

"Well, the reason," Tom went on, "the reason I'm such a blabbermouth is that I'm mostly alone. So when I got an ear nearby, I just naturally bend it. You see, Al," Tom explained, and gestured at the sweet valley spread out defenseless below them, "those aren't real people down there. Not like *me*. Not even like you."

"Yeah?"

"Yeah. If I go hungry three, four days, you know, not one of those people down there is gonna get a bellyache. And when the water comes down on them some night pretty soon, *I'm* not gonna choke at all. I'm gonna be busy digging up my money."

"No, Tom," Dortmunder said. "I don't care what you say, you just can't do it. I'm not a real law-abiding citizen myself, but you go too far."

"I just follow the logic, Al."

"Well, I don't," Dortmunder told him. "I can't do something like this. I can't come out here and deliberately drown a whole lot of people in their beds, that's all. I just can't do it."

Tom considered that, looking Dortmunder up and down, thinking it over, and finally he shrugged and said, "Okay. We'll forget it, then."

Dortmunder blinked. "We will?"

"Sure," Tom said. "You're some kind of goodhearted guy, am I right, been reading the *Reader's Digest* or something all these years, maybe you joined the Christophers on the inside, something like that. The point is, I'm not too good at reading other people—"

"I guess not," Dortmunder said.

"Well, none of you are that real, you know," Tom explained. "It's hard to get you into focus. So I read you wrong, I made a mistake, wasted a couple of days. Sorry about that, Al, I wasted your time, too."

"That's okay," Dortmunder said, with the awful feeling he was missing some sort of point here.

"So we'll drive back to the city," Tom said. "You ready?"

"Sure," Dortmunder said. "Sorry, Tom, I just can't."

"S'okay," Tom said, crossing the road, Dortmunder following.

They got into the car, and Dortmunder said, "Do I U-turn?"

"Nah," Tom said, "go on across the dam and then there's a left, and we'll go down through the valley and back to the Thruway like that."

"Okay, fine."

They drove across the rest of the dam, Dortmunder continuing to have this faintly uneasy feeling about the calm, gray, silent, ancient maniac seated beside him, and at the far end of the dam was a small stone building that was probably the entry to the offices down below. Dortmunder slowed, looking at it, and saw a big bronze seal, and a sign reading CITY OF NEW YORK—DEPT. OF WATER SUPPLY—CITY PROPERTY, AUTHORIZED PERSONNEL ONLY. "City property?" Dortmunder asked. "This is part of New York City up here?"

"Sure," Tom said. "All the city reservoirs belong to the city."

A New York City police car was one of three vehicles parked beside the building. Dortmunder said, "They have city cops?"

"The way I understand it," Tom said, "it's not duty that's given to the sharpest and the quickest. But don't worry about it, Al, you wanted out and you're out. Let the next guy worry about New York City cops."

Dortmunder gave him a look, feeling a sudden lurch in his stomach. "The next guy?"

"Naturally." Tom shrugged. "You weren't the only guy on the list," he explained equably. "The first guy, but not the only. So now I'll just have to find somebody with a little less milk in his veins, that's all."

Dortmunder's foot came off the gas. "Tom, you mean you're still gonna do it?"

Tom, mildly surprised, spread his hands. "Do I have my three hundred fifty grand? Has something changed I don't know about?"

Dortmunder said, "Tom, you can't drown all those people."

"Sure I can," Tom said. "*You're* the one can't. Remember?"

"But—" Just beyond the stone building, with the reservoir still barely visible behind them and the forest starting again on both sides of the road, Dortmunder came to a stop, pulling off onto the gravel verge and saying, "Tom, no."

Tom scowled, without moving his lips. "Al," he said. "I hope you aren't going to tell me what I can do and what I can't do."

"It isn't that, Tom," Dortmunder said, although in fact it *was* that, and realizing it, Dortmunder also realized how hopeless this all was. "It's just," he said, despairing even as he heard himself say it, "it's just you can't *do* that, that's all."

"I can," Tom said, colder than ever. "And I will." That bony finger pointed at Dortmunder's nose. "And you are not gonna queer the deal for me, Al. You are not gonna call anybody and say, 'Don't sleep at home tonight if you wanna stay dry.' Believe me, Al, you are not gonna screw me around. If I think there's the slightest chance—"

"No, no, Tom," Dortmunder said. "I wouldn't rat on you, you know me better than that."

"And *you* know *me* better than that." Looking out his side window at forest, Tom said, "So what's with the delay? How come we aren't whippin along the highway, headin back to the city, so I can make the call on the second guy on my list?"

"Because," Dortmunder said, and licked his lips, and looked back at the peaceful water sparkling in the sun. Peaceful killer water. "Because," he said, "we don't have to do it that way."

Tom looked at him. "We?"

"I'm your guy, Tom," Dortmunder said. "From the old days, and still today. We'll do it, we'll get the money. But we don't have to drown anybody to do it, okay? We'll do it some other way."

"What other way?"

"I don't know yet," Dortmunder admitted. "But I just got here, Tom, I just came aboard this thing. Give me some time to look the situation over, think about it. Give me a couple weeks, okay?"

Tom gave him a skeptical look. "What are you gonna do?" he demanded. "Swim out with a shovel and dive and hold your breath?"

"I don't *know*, Tom. Give me time to think about it. Okay?"

Tom thought it over. "A quieter way might be good," he acknowledged. "If it could be done. Less runnin around afterward. Less chance of your massive manhunt."

"That's right," Dortmunder said.

Tom looked back at the reservoir. "That's fifty feet of water, you know."

"I know, I know," Dortmunder said. "Just give me a little time to consider the problem."

Tom's gray eyes shifted this way and that in his skull. He said, "I don't know if I want to stay on your sofa that long."

Oh. Dortmunder stared, agonized. The thought of May came into his mind but was firmly repressed, pushed down beneath the hundreds and hundreds of drowned people. "It's a comfortable sofa, Tom," he said, his throat closing on him as he said it but managing to get the words out just the same.

Tom took a deep breath. His lips actually twitched; a visible movement. Then, the lips rigid again, he said, "Okay, Al. I know you're good at this stuff, that's why I came to you first. You want to find another way to get down to the stash, go ahead."

"Thank you, Tom," Dortmunder said. Relief made his hands tremble on the wheel.

"Any time," Tom told him.

"And in the meantime," Dortmunder said, "no dynamite. Right?"

"For now," Tom agreed.

CHAPTER FOUR

Joe the mailman came whistling down Myrtle Street in the bright sunshine, his tune blending with the songs of birds, the hiss of sprinklers, the far-off murmur of a lawn mower. "Myrtle!" shouted Edna Street, turning away from her regular spot in the upstairs front bedroom window. "Here comes the mailman!"

"I'll get it, Mother!" Myrtle Street called, and went skipping down the well-polished mahogany staircase toward the front door. A pretty person of twenty-five—no longer really a pretty girl but somehow not quite a pretty woman either—Myrtle had lived most of her life in this old sprawling beautiful clapboard house here in Dudson Center, and was barely conscious anymore of the oddity of having the same name as her home address. At least some of the mail Joe would be bringing up onto the porch this afternoon would be addressed:

Myrtle Street
27 Myrtle Street
Dudson Center, NY 12561

A few things, such as *Modern Maturity* and *Prevention* magazine, would be addressed to Edna Street, plus a ton of stuff addressed to somebody named CAR-RT SORT, or to Current Resident.

Joe the mailman smiled roguishly as he climbed the stoop to the wide front porch of 27 Myrtle Street and saw Myrtle Street pushing open the

24

screen door. He liked the way her legs moved inside her loose cotton dresses, the demure but lush swell of her breasts within the gray cardigan she always wore, the pale softness of her throat, the healthy animal sparkle in her eye. Joe the mailman was forty-three years old, with a family at home, but he could dream, couldn't he? "Lovely as ever," he greeted Myrtle as she smiled hello and reached for today's messages from the world. "We must run away together one of these days."

Myrtle, who had no idea of the actual depth of depravity lurking within Joe's plain-to-lumpish exterior in his badly fitting blue-gray uniform, laughed lightly and said, "Oh, we're both much too busy, Joe."

"What's he want?" screeked Edna's voice from upstairs. "Don't you give him anything for postage due, Myrtle! Make him take it back!"

Myrtle indulgently rolled her eyes and laughed, saying, "Mother."

"She sure is something," Joe agreed. He was imagining his head between those legs.

"See you tomorrow," Myrtle said, and went back inside, the screen door slamming on Joe's creative study of her behind.

Climbing the stairs, Myrtle went quickly through the mail. Myrtle Street, Myrtle St. She and her mother had been Myrtle and Edna Gosling when Edna had inherited the place from her mortician father and moved in with her not-yet-two-year-old baby. To be Myrtle Gosling of Myrtle Street would have been perfectly ordinary and unremarkable, but she hadn't remained that for long. She'd been not-yet-four when Edna met Mr. Street—Mr. Earl Street, of Bangor, Maine, a salesman in stationery and school-and-library supplies—and not-yet-five when Edna married Mr. Street and decided to give her only daughter her new husband's name. Myrtle had been not-yet-seven when Mr. Street up and ran away with Candice Oshkosh from down at the five-and-dime, never to be heard from again, but by that time Edna had firmly become Mrs. Street, and her daughter was just as firmly Myrtle Street, and that was simply the way it was.

Entering the front bedroom, Myrtle found her mother putting on one of her many black hats at the oval pier-glass mirror, staring with suspicion and mistrust at her own hands as they jammed the hat in among her steel-gray knotted curls. "Here's the mail," Myrtle said, unnecessarily, and Edna turned to snatch the thin sheaf of circulars and bills from her hands. It was required that Edna look at *all* the mail, that Myrtle not throw away the most pointless sale announcement or congressional report before her mother had seen it, looked at it, touched it, possibly even smelled it. "We have to go soon, Mother," Myrtle said. "I don't want to be late for work."

"Pah!" Edna said, greedily fingering the mail. "Make them wait for you. They waited for *me* when *I* worked there. *Watch* him, will you?"

So Myrtle hurried to the front window to stand watch while her mother examined the mail. Out there, Joe the mailman was just crossing the street down at the corner to start his delivery to the houses across the way. A Mrs. Courtenay, a fiftyish widow, lived over there, just two doors from the corner. A woman who wore bright colors and hoop earrings, she had thus earned Edna's utter condemnation. Edna was convinced that some day Joe the mailman would enter that house—and that widow, no doubt—rather than merely drop off the mail there, thus committing—among other things—a gross dereliction of his sworn Federal duty to deliver the mail, and Edna would at *once* phone the main post office downtown and have Joe the mailman dealt with. It hadn't happened yet, but it would, it would.

Well, of course, Myrtle knew it would never happen at all. Joe wasn't like that. True, on occasion Mrs. Courtenay would appear at her door when Joe arrived, decked in her bright colors and her hoop earrings, and she and Joe would chat a minute, but the same identical thing sometimes happened between Joe and Myrtle herself—today, for instance—which didn't mean Joe would ever come in *here* and perform . . . anything. It was all just silly.

But it was better, in the long run, to go along with Mother's little idiosyncrasies. "He's on Mrs. Courtenay's porch now," she reported to the rattling sound of Edna tearing open an electric company bill. "He's putting the mail in the box. He's leaving."

"She didn't come out?"

"No, Mother, she didn't come out."

Edna, hatted and still clutching the mail, scampered over to glare out the window at Joe the mailman taking a shortcut across Mrs. Courtenay's lawn to the next house on his route. "Probably having her period," Edna commented, and switched her glare to Myrtle. "Are you ready or not? You don't want to be late for work, you know."

"No, Mother," Myrtle agreed.

The two went downstairs together and out the back door and over the gravel to the unattached garage containing their black Ford Fairlane. This part of their day was such a foregone routine they barely even thought about it while going through the motions: Myrtle opened the right-hand garage door, while Edna opened the left. Myrtle entered the garage and climbed into the Ford and backed it out while Edna stood to the left, hands folded in front of her. Myrtle made a backing U-turn on the gravel while Edna closed both garage doors. Then Edna walked around the car, got in beside Myrtle, and they left home.

Myrtle was going to work. She was an assistant (one of three) at the North Dudson branch of the New York State Public Library. Edna was going to her Senior Citizens Center down on Main Street, where she was something of a power. At sixty-two, Edna was three years too young to even be a member of the Dudson Combined Senior Citizens Center, but there was nothing else doing all day in this dead town, so she'd got herself in by lying about her age.

Myrtle was a good, if cautious, driver; cautious mostly about her mother, who was not reticent about remarking on any flaw she might find in Myrtle's judgment or performance skills along the way. She was quiet today, however, all the way from Myrtle Street to Spring Street to Albany Street to Elm Street to Main Street, where they had to stop and wait for the light to change before making their left turn. While they were waiting there, a car drove wanderingly by from left to right, with two men in it; they didn't seem to know exactly where they were going.

And suddenly Edna's bony sharp hand was clutching Myrtle's forearm and Edna was crying, "My God!"

Myrtle immediately stared into the rearview mirror; were they about to be crashed? But Elm Street was empty behind them. So she stared at her mother, who was gaping after that car that had just gone by. The whites were visible all around the pupils of Edna's eyes. Was she having some sort of attack? "Mother?" Myrtle asked, firmly burying that first irrepressible instant of hope. "Mother? Are you all right?"

"It couldn't be," Edna whispered. She was panting in her anxiety, mouth hanging open, eyes staring. Voice hoarse, she cried, "But it was! It was!"

"Was what? Mother?"

"That was your *father* in that car!"

Myrtle's head spun about. She too stared after the car with the two men in it; but it was long gone. She said, astonished, "Mr. Street, Mother? Mr. Street's come back?"

"Mr. *Street*?" Edna's voice was full of rage and contempt. "*That* asshole? Who gives a fuck about *him*?"

Myrtle had never *heard* such language from Edna. "Mother?" she asked. "What is it?"

"I'll tell you what it is," Edna said, hunching forward, staring hollowly out the windshield, all at once looking *plenty* old enough to be a member of the Senior Citizens Center. "It couldn't happen, but it did. The dirty bastard son of a bitch." Bleakly Edna gazed at the sunny world of Dudson Center. "He's back," she said.

CHAPTER FIVE

They should never have let him out of prison," May said.

"They shouldn't have let him out of the cell," Dortmunder said. "As long as I'm not in it with him."

"You are in it with him," May pointed out. "He's living here."

Dortmunder put down his fork and looked at her. "May? What could I do?"

They were in the kitchen together, having a late lunch or an early supper, hamburgers and Spaghetti-Os and beer, grabbing their privacy where they could find it. After the run back from Vilburgtown Reservoir, after they'd actually given the rental car back to its owners (yet another new experience today for Dortmunder), Tom had said, "You go on home, Al, I'll be along. I gotta fill my pockets." So Dortmunder had gone on home, where May had been waiting, having come back early from her cashier job at the supermarket to meet him, and where, with a hopeful expression as she'd looked over Dortmunder's shoulder, she'd said, "Where's your friend?"

"Out filling his pockets. He said we shouldn't wait up, he'd let himself in."

May had looked alarmed. "You gave him a key?"

"No, he just said he'd let himself in. May, we gotta talk. I also gotta eat, but mostly and mainly we gotta talk."

So now they were eating and talking, sometimes simultaneously, and May wasn't liking the situation any more than Dortmunder. But what were

28

they to do about it? "May," Dortmunder said, "if we leave Tom alone, he really will blow up that dam and drown everybody in the valley. And for three hundred and fifty thousand dollars, he'll find guys to help."

"John," May said, "wherever he is right now, your friend Tom, filling his pockets—"

"Please, May," Dortmunder interrupted, "don't do that. Don't keep calling him my friend Tom. That's unfair."

May thought about that and nodded. "You're right, it is. It's not your fault who they put in your cell."

"Thank you."

"But, John, still, what do you think he's doing right now? Filling his pockets; how do you suppose he does that?"

"I don't even want to know," Dortmunder said.

"John, you're a craftsman, you're skilled labor, a professional. What you do takes talent and training—"

"And luck," Dortmunder added.

"No, it doesn't," she insisted. "Not a solid experienced person like you."

"Well, that's good," Dortmunder said, "since I've been running around without it for quite a while."

"Now, don't get gloomy, John," May said.

"Hard not to, around Tom," Dortmunder told her. "And, as for what he's doing outside right now, that's up to him. But I was *at* that dam, I looked down the valley at all those houses. It's my choice, May. I can try to figure out something else to do, some other way to get Tom his money, or I can say forget it, not my problem. And then some night we'll sit here and watch television, and there it'll be on the news. You know what I mean?"

"Are those the only choices?" May asked, poking delicately at her Spaghetti-Os, not meeting Dortmunder's eye. "Are you sure there's nothing else to do?"

"Like what?" he asked. "The way I see it, I help him or I don't help him, that's the choice."

"I wouldn't normally say this, John," May said, "you know me better than that, but sometimes, every once in a great while, sometimes maybe it's just necessary to let society fight its own battles."

Dortmunder put down his fork and his hamburger and looked at her. "May? Turn him in? Is that what you're saying?"

"It's worth thinking about," May said, mumbling, still not meeting his eye.

"But it isn't," Dortmunder told her. "Even if it was—even if it *ever* was, I mean—even then, it isn't worth thinking about, because what are we gonna do? Call up this governor with the birthday presents, say take him

back, he's gonna drown nine hundred people? They *can't* take him back."
Dortmunder picked up his fork and his hamburger again. He said, "A crime isn't a crime until it happens."

"Well, that's stupid," May said. "With a character like that walking around loose—"

Dortmunder said, "May, some famous writer said it once: The law's an asshole. For instance, what if I was still on parole? Tom Jimson's *living* here, no matter what we think. If I was still on parole, and that parole officer of mine, what was his name? Steen, that was it. If he found out a guy with Tom Jimson's record and history was living here, they'd put *me* back inside. But him they can't touch."

"Well, that's crazy," May said.

"But true," Dortmunder told her. "But let's say I do it anyway, I'm feeling this desperation or whatever it might be, and I go and do it. And then it's done. I've gone and told the law all about Tom and his stash under the reservoir. So what happens next? At the very *best*, what they can do is go tell him they heard he had these dynamite plans and he shouldn't do it. And he'll take about a second and a half to figure out who's the blabbermouth. You want Tom Jimson mad at you?"

"Well," May said carefully, "John, it's you he'd be mad at, actually."

"People who play with dynamite don't fine tune," Dortmunder said. He filled his mouth with hamburger and Spaghetti-Os, and then composted it all with beer and chewed awhile.

May had finished. She sat back, didn't light a cigarette, didn't blow smoke at the ceiling, didn't flick ashes onto her plate, didn't cough delicately twice, and did say, "Well, I just hope you can come up with something."

"Me, too," Dortmunder said, but his mouth was still full of food and drink, so it didn't come out right. He held the fork up vertically, meaning *just a second*, and chewed and chewed and swallowed, and then tried again: "Me, too."

She frowned at him. "You too what?"

"Hope I come up with something. To get the money out from under the reservoir."

"Oh, you will," she said. "I'm not worried about you, John."

"Well, I wish you would be," he said. Gazing across the room, frowning at the perfect white blankness of the refrigerator door, he said, "I think it's time I got some help on this."

CHAPTER SIX

Andy Kelp, a sharp-featured, arrow-nosed skinny kind of guy in soft-soled black shoes and dark gray wool trousers and a bulky pea coat, tiptoed through the software, quietly humming "Coke, It's the Real Thing." Hmmmmm, he thought, his fingers skipping among the bright packages. *WordPerfect, PageMaker, Lotus, dBaseIII, Donkey Kong.* Hmmmmm. From time to time a package was scooped up into his long slim fingers and stowed away in the special pocket in the back of his pea coat, and then he would move on, humming, eyes darting over the available wares. The exhibit lights left on all night in the store gave him just enough illumination to study the possibilities and make his choices. And shopping three hours after the store had closed was the sure way to avoid crowds.

Blip-blip-blip. The faint jingling sound, like Tinkerbell clearing her throat, came from the left side of Kelp's bulky pea coat. Reaching in there, he withdrew a cellular phone, extended its antenna, and whispered into its mouthpiece, "Hello?"

A suspicious and bewildered but familiar voice said, "Who's that?"

"John?" Kelp whispered. "Is that you?"

"What's goin on?" demanded Dortmunder's voice, getting belligerent. "Who is that there?"

"It's me, John," Kelp whispered. "It's Andy."

"What? Who is that?"

"It's *Andy*," Kelp whispered hoarsely, lips against the mouthpiece. "Andy *Kelp*."

"Andy? Is that you?"

"Yes, John, yes."

"Well, what are you whispering about? You got laryngitis?"

"No, I'm fine."

"Then stop whispering."

"The fact of the matter is, John," Kelp whispered, hunkering low over the phone, "I'm robbing a store at the moment."

"You're *what*?"

"Ssssshhhhhhh, John," Kelp whispered. "Sssshhhhhh."

In a more normal voice, Dortmunder said, "Wait a minute, I get it. I called you at home, but you aren't home. You've done one of your phone gizmo things."

"That's right," Kelp agreed. "I put the phone-ahead gizmo on my phone at home to transfer my calls to my cellular phone so I wouldn't miss any calls—like this one from you, right now—while I was out, and I brought the cellular phone along with me."

"To rob a store."

"That's right. And that's what I'm doing right this minute, John, and to tell you the truth I'd like to get on with it."

"Okay," Dortmunder said. "If you're busy—"

"I'm not busy *forever*, John," Kelp said, forgetting to whisper. "You got something? You gonna meet with the guys at the OJ?" He was remembering to whisper again now.

"No," Dortmunder said. "Not yet, anyway. Not until I figure the thing out."

"There's problems?" In his eagerness, Kelp's whisper went up into the treble ranges, becoming very sibilant. "You want me to drop over there when I'm done, we can talk about it?"

"Well," Dortmunder said, and then he sighed, and then he said, "Yeah. Come on over. If you feel like it."

"Sure I feel like it," Kelp whispered, in falsetto. "You know me, John."

"Yeah, I do," Dortmunder said. "But come on over anyway." And he hung up.

"Right, John," Kelp whispered into the dead phone. Then, retracting his antenna, putting the phone away in its special pocket inside his pea coat, he looked around again at the various counters and shelves and product displays here inside Serious Business, that being the name of the store. Most of the exhibit lighting was in pastel neon, giving the place a fairytale quality of pink and light blue and pale green, washing faint color onto the gray industrial carpet and off-white shelves. In the fifteen minutes since effecting entry in here via the men's room of the coffee shop next door, a window to the basement of this building and a brief squirm through an air-conditioning duct (pushing his pea coat ahead of himself), Kelp had pretty well browsed completely among all the treasures available here. Time to call it a night, probably.

John should have a personal computer, Kelp thought, but even as he thought it, he knew just how hard a sell John was likely to be. Tough to get him to accept anything new; like his attitude toward telephones, for instance.

But a personal computer, a good PC of your very own, that was something else. That was a *tool*, as useful, indeed as necessary, as a Toast-R-Oven. Wandering back over to the software displays, Kelp picked up a copy of *Managing Your Money*. Surely, even John would be able to see the advantage in a program like that. If he seemed at all interested, they could go out together tomorrow, or maybe even later tonight, and shop for a PC and a printer and a mouse. Maybe come back here, in fact. Kelp, so far, had enjoyed doing business with Serious Business.

CHAPTER SEVEN

May brought in three more beers and they popped the ring opener on the cans: *Pop. Pop. Splop.* "Well, hell," said Dortmunder.

"Oh, John, that's too bad," May said. "Should I get a towel?"

"Naw, that's okay, it didn't spill much," Dortmunder told her, and turned to Kelp to say, "Well? Whadaya think?"

"Hmmmm," Kelp said, and swigged beer. Then he said, "If it isn't bad manners to ask, John, what was this pal of yours in for?"

"He's not my pal."

"Sorry. Ex-cellmate of yours. What was he in for, do you know?"

Dortmunder drank beer, thinking back. "As I remember it," he said, "it was murder, armed robbery, and arson."

Kelp looked surprised: "All at once?"

"He wanted a diversion while he pulled the job," Dortmunder said, "so he torched the firehouse."

"A direct sort of a fella," Kelp said, nodding.

May said, "Like with this dam."

Kelp nodded, thinking, frowning. "You see, John," he said, "I don't really follow how you're involved here. The guy says come help me blow up a dam, you say I don't want to kill a lot of people in their beds, you say good-bye to each other."

"He'll find somebody else," Dortmunder said.

"But isn't that up to him?"

"John doesn't see it like that," May said, "and I agree with him."

Dortmunder finished his beer. "I know," he admitted. "It ought to be that way; I say no and it's done with. But I just have this feeling, there's got to be some way to get at that money without killing everybody in upstate New York."

"And?"

Dortmunder frowned so massively he looked like a plowed field. "This is gonna sound egotistical," he said.

"Go for it," Kelp advised.

"Well, it's just I think, if there's any way at all to get to that money without emptying the reservoir, I'm the guy who should think of it."

"The only one who *could*, you mean," Kelp said.

Dortmunder didn't want to go quite that far in his egotism: "The only one who'd put in the effort," he amended.

Kelp nodded, accepting that. "And what have you come up with so far?"

"Well, nothing," Dortmunder admitted. "But this is still the first day I'm on this thing, you know."

"That's true." Kelp sloshed beer in his can. "You could tunnel, maybe," he said.

Dortmunder looked at him. "Through water?"

"No, no," Kelp said, shaking both the beer can and his head. "I don't think there's a way to do that, really. Tunnel through water. I meant you start on shore, *near* the water. You tunnel straight down until you're lower than the bottom of the reservoir, and then you turn and tunnel across to this casket, or box, or whatever it is."

"Dig a tunnel," Dortmunder echoed, "under a reservoir. Crawl back and forth in this tunnel in the dirt under this reservoir."

"Well, yeah, there's that," Kelp agreed. "I do get kind of a sinus headache just thinking about it."

"Also," Dortmunder said, "how do you aim this tunnel? Somewhere out there under that reservoir is a casket. What is it, seven feet long? Three feet wide, a couple feet high. And you gotta go right *to* it. You can't go above it, you can't go below it, you can't miss it to the left or the right."

May said, "You *particularly* can't go above it."

"That's the sinus headache part," Dortmunder told her, and to Kelp he said, "It's too small a target, Andy, and too far away."

"Well, you know," Kelp said thoughtfully, "this kind of connects in with something I meant to talk to you about anyway." Casually glancing around the living room, he said, "You don't have a PC yet, do you?"

Dortmunder bristled. He didn't know what this was going to turn out to be, but already he knew he didn't like it. "What's that?" he demanded. "Another one of your phone gizmos?"

"No, no, John," Kelp assured him. "Nothing to do with phones. It's a personal computer, and it just may be the solution to our problem here."

Dortmunder stared at him with loathing. "Personal computer? Andy, what are you up to *now*?"

"Let me explain this, John," Kelp said. "It's a very simple thing, really, you're gonna love it."

"Uh-huh," Dortmunder said.

"There must be maps," Kelp said, "old maps from before the reservoir was put in. We use those to do a program for the computer, see, and it makes a model of the valley. Your pal shows us—"

"He's not my pal," Dortmunder said.

"Right," Kelp agreed. "Your ex-cellmate shows us—"

Dortmunder said, "Why don't you just call him Tom?"

"Well, I don't really know the guy," Kelp said. "Listen, can I describe this thing to you?"

"Go right ahead," Dortmunder said.

"The maps I'm talking about," Kelp explained, "I don't mean your gas station road maps, I mean those ones with the lines, the whatchacallit."

"Topographical," May said.

"That's it," Kelp said. "Thanks, May."

Dortmunder stared at her. "How come you know that?"

"Why not?" she asked him.

Kelp said, "I'm *trying* to explain this."

"Right, right," Dortmunder said. "Go right ahead."

"So the computer," Kelp said, "makes a model of the valley from before the water went in, with the towns and the buildings and everything, and we can turn the model any way we want—"

"*What* model?" Dortmunder demanded. He was getting lost here, and that made him mad. "You wanna make like a model train set? What is this?"

"The model in the *computer*," Kelp told him. "You see it on your screen."

"The television, you mean."

"Very like television, yes," Kelp agreed. "And it's this detailed three-dimensional model, and you can turn it around and tilt it different ways—"

"Sounds like fun," Dortmunder said acidly.

"*And*," Kelp insisted, "you can blow up part of it bigger, to get the details and all, and then your, uh, this, uh, this fella who buried it, he shows us on the model where he buried the box, and then we input the reservoir and—"

"You what?"

"Input the reservoir," Kelp repeated, unhelpfully, but then he added,

"Our first model in the program is the valley from when the towns were there. So we can pinpoint the box. *Then* we tell the PC about the reservoir, and put in the dam, and fill the water in, and probably tell it how much water weighs and all that, so it can tell us what might be different down there at the bottom now." A shadow of doubt crossed Kelp's eager face. "There's a lot of data we're gonna have to get," he said, "if we're gonna do this right. Guy-go, you know."

"No," Dortmunder told him. "Guy-go I don't know."

"You never heard that expression?" Kelp was astonished.

"May probably did."

"No, I don't think so," May said.

"Guy-go," Kelp repeated, then spelled it. "G, I, G, O. It means 'Garbage In, Garbage Out.'"

"That's nice," Dortmunder said.

"It means," Kelp amplified, "the computer's only as smart as what you tell it. If you give it wrong information, it'll give you wrong information back."

"I'm beginning to see," Dortmunder said. "This is a machine that doesn't know anything until I tell it something, and if I tell it wrong it believes me."

"That's about it, yes," Kelp agreed.

"So this machine of yours," Dortmunder said, "needs me a lot more than I need it."

"Now, there you go, being negative again," Kelp complained.

May said, "John, let Andy finish about this. Maybe it *will* help."

"I'm just sitting here," Dortmunder said, and tried to drink from an empty beer can. "I'm sitting here listening, not making any trouble."

"I'll get more beer," May decided.

As she got to her feet, Kelp said, "I'll wait for you to come back."

"Thank you, Andy."

While May was out of the room, Kelp said, "Actually, if we could work this out, that's a lot of money."

"It is," Dortmunder agreed.

"I'm not saying necessarily a tunnel," Kelp said, "but whatever, probably wouldn't take a lot of guys. Your old— This, uh, guy, he's seventy years old, huh?"

"Yeah."

"How strong is he?"

"Very."

"Well, that's fine," Kelp said. "So he can carry his weight. Then you and me. And a driver, probably."

"Absolutely," Dortmunder said. "I drove up there once already. That's enough. We'll call Stan Murch, if it looks like we've got something."

"And maybe Tiny Bulcher, for the lifting and the moving around," Kelp suggested as May came back with three more beers. "Thanks, May."

May said to Dortmunder, "I already opened yours, John."

"Thanks."

"You know," Kelp said, popping open his beer can with casual skill, "your old— This guy, uh . . ."

"Tom," Dortmunder said. "His name is Tom."

"Well, I'll try it," Kelp said. "Tom. This Tom sounds a lot like Tiny. In fact, I'm looking forward to meeting him."

Dortmunder muttered, "Better you than me."

"*Anyhoo,*" Kelp said, "we were talking about the PC."

Dortmunder looked at him. "'Anyhoo'?"

"The PC," Kelp insisted. "Come on, John."

"Okay, okay."

"It's true," Kelp said, "we have to get a lot of information to put into the computer, but that's nothing different. You always want the best information you can get anyway, in any job. That's the way you work."

"That's right," Dortmunder said.

"And when we put it all in the computer," Kelp told him, "then we say to it, 'Plot us out the best route for the tunnel.' And then we follow that route, and it takes us right to the box."

"Sounds easy," May said.

"Whenever things sound easy," Dortmunder said, "it turns out there's one part you didn't hear."

"Could be," Kelp said, unruffled. "Could be, we'll give the model to the computer and ask it about the tunnel, and it'll say the tunnel doesn't work, too much water around, too much mud, too far to go, whatever."

"Be sure to put all that last part in," Dortmunder told him, "when you're putting in the rest of the garbage."

"We're not *going* to put garbage in," Kelp corrected him. "We're going to input quality data, John, believe me. In fact," he said, suddenly even more peppy and enthusiastic, "I know just the guy to work with on this program."

"Somebody else?" Dortmunder asked him. "One of us?"

Kelp shook his head. "Wally's a computer freak," he explained. "I won't tell him what we're trying for, I'll just give it to him like as a computer problem."

"Do I know this Wally?"

"No, John," Kelp said, "you don't travel in the same circles. Wally's kind of offbeat. He can only communicate by keyboard."

"And what if he communicates by keyboard with the law?"

"No, I'm telling you that's all right," Kelp insisted. "Wally's a very unworldly guy. And he'll save us *weeks* on this thing."

"Weeks?" Dortmunder said, startled. "How long is this gonna take?"

"Just a few days," Kelp promised. "With Wally aboard, just a very few days."

"Because," Dortmunder pointed out, "until we have this figured out, we have Tom Jimson *living* here."

"That's right," May said.

"And if he decides to stop living here," Dortmunder went on, "it's because he's gone back upstate to make a flood."

"The Jimson flood," said a cold voice from the doorway. They all looked up, and there was Tom, as cold and gray as ever, standing in the doorway and looking from face to face. A wrinkle in his own face might have been intended as an ironic smile. "Sounds like an old folk song," he said, his lips not moving. "'The Famous Jimson Flood.'"

"I think that was Jamestown," Kelp said.

Tom considered that, and considered Kelp, too. "You may be right," he decided, and turned to Dortmunder. "You spreading my business around, Al?"

Getting to his feet, Dortmunder said, "Tom Jimson, this is Andy Kelp. Andy and I work together."

Tom nodded, and looked Kelp up and down. "So you're gonna help me realize my dream of retirement," he said.

Kelp grinned; he acted as though he *liked* Tom Jimson. Still comfortably sprawled on the sofa, "That's what I'm here for," he said. "John and May and me, we've been talking about different approaches, different ways to do things."

"Dynamite's very sure," Tom told him.

"Well, I don't know about that," Kelp said. "That water's been in place there twenty years, more or less. What happens when you make a sudden tidal wave out of it? Think it might roil up the bottom, maybe mess things up down there, make it *harder* to find that box of yours?"

Dortmunder, standing there in the middle of the room like somebody waiting for a bus, now turned and gazed on Andy Kelp with new respect. "I never thought of that," he said.

"*I* did," Tom said. "The way I figure to blow that dam, you won't have no tidal wave. At least, not up in the reservoir. Down below there, in East Dudson and Dudson Center and Dudson Falls, down *there* you might have yourself a tidal wave, but we don't give a shit about that, now, do we?"

No one saw any reason to answer that. May, also getting to her feet, standing beside Dortmunder like an early sketch for Grant Woods' *Urban Gothic* (abandoned), said, "Would you like a beer, Tom?"

"No," Tom said. "I'm used to regular hours. Good night."

Kelp, still with his amiable smile, said, "You off to bed?"

"Not till you get up from it," Tom told him, and stood there looking at Kelp.

Who finally caught on: "Oh, you sleep *here*," he said, whapping his palm against the sofa cushion beside him.

"Yeah, I do," Tom agreed, and went on looking at Kelp.

May said, "Let me get you sheets and a pillowcase."

"Don't need them," Tom said as Kelp slowly unwound himself and got to his feet, still smiling, casually holding his beer can.

"Well, you need *some*thing," May insisted.

"A blanket," he told her. "And a towel for the morning."

"Coming up," May said, and left the room, with alacrity.

"Well," Dortmunder said, having trouble exiting, "see you in the morning."

"That's right," Tom said.

"Nice to meet you," Kelp said.

Tom paid no attention to that. Crossing to the sofa, he moved the coffee table off to one side, then yawned and started taking wads of bank-banded bills out of his various pockets, dropping them on the coffee table. Dortmunder and Kelp exchanged a glance.

May came back in, gave the money on the moved coffee table a look, and put an old moth-eaten tan blanket and a pretty good Holiday Inn towel on the sofa. "Here you are," she said.

"Thanks," Tom said. He put a .32 Smith & Wesson Terrier on the coffee table with the money, then switched off the floor lamp at one end of the sofa and turned to look at the other three.

"Good night, Tom," Dortmunder said.

But Tom was finished being polite for today. He stood there and looked at them, and they turned and went out to the hall, May closing the door behind them.

Murmuring, not quite whispering, Dortmunder said to Kelp, "You wanna come out to the kitchen?"

"No, thanks," Kelp whispered. "I'll call you in the morning after I talk to Wally."

"Good night, Andy," May said. "Thanks for helping."

"I didn't do anything yet," Kelp pointed out as he opened the closet door and took out his bulky heavy pea coat. Grinning at Dortmunder, he said, "But the old PC and me, we'll do what we can."

"Mm," said Dortmunder.

As Kelp turned toward the front door, the living room door opened and Tom stuck his gray head out. "Tunnel won't work," he said, and withdrew his head and shut the door.

The three looked wide-eyed at one another. They moved away in a group to huddle together by the front door, as far as possible from the living room. May whispered, "How long was he listening?"

Dortmunder whispered, "We'll never know."

Kelp rolled his eyes at that and whispered, "Let's hope we'll never know. Talk to you tomorrow."

He left, and Dortmunder started attaching all the locks to the front door. Then he stopped and looked at his hands, and looked at the locks, and whispered, "I don't know why I'm doing this."

CHAPTER EIGHT

You roll aside the two giant boulders and the tree trunk. You find the entrance to a cave, covered by a furry hide curtain. You thrust this aside and see before you the lair of the Thousand-Toothed Ogre.

Wally Knurr wiped sweat from his brow. Careful, now; this could be a trap. Fat fingers tense over the keyboard, he spat out:

```
Describe this lair.
```

A forty-foot cube with a domed ceiling. The rock walls have been fused into black ice by the molten breath of the Nether Dragon. On fur-covered couches loll a half-dozen well-armed Lizard Men, members of the Sultan's Personal Guard. Against the far wall, Princess Labia is tied to a giant wheel, slowly rotating.

```
Are the Lizard Men my enemies?
```

Not in this encounter.

```
Are the Lizard Men my allies?
```

Only if you show them the proper authorization.

Hmmm, Wally thought. I'll have to do a personal inventory soon, I'm not sure how much junk I've accumulated. But first, the question is, do I enter this damn cave? Well, I've got to, sooner or later. I can't go back down through the Valley of Sereness, and there's nothing farther up this mountain. But let's not just leap in here. Eyes burning, shoulders rigid, he typed:

```
Do I still have my Sword of Fire and Ice?
```

Yes.

```
I thrust it into the cave entrance, slicing up and
down from top to bottom, and also from side to side.
```

Iron arrows shoot from concealed tubes on both sides of the entrance. Hitting nothing but the opposite wall, they fall to the ground.

Aha, Wally thought, just what I figured. Okay, Ogre, here I come.

```
Enter
```

Bzzzzzztt.
Doorbell. Drat. Is it that late? Leaving Princess Labia to twist slowly slowly in the lair, Wally ran his fingers like a trained-dog act in fast forward over the keyboard, changing the menu, bringing up the current Eastern Daylight Time—

15:30

—and his appointment book for today, which was blank except for the notation: 15:30—Andy Kelp and his friend to view the reservoir. Oh, well, that could be fun, too.

Lifting his hands from the keyboard, withdrawing his eyes from the video display, pushing his swivel chair back from the system desk, and getting to his feet, Wally felt the usual aches all through his shoulders and neck and lower back. The pains of battle, of intense concentration for hours at a time, of occasional victory and sudden crushing defeat, were familiar to him, and he bore them without complaint; in fact, with a kind of quiet pride. He could stand up to it.

At twenty-four, Wally Knurr was well on his way to becoming a character in one of his own interactive fictions. (He wrote them as well as consuming them, and so far had sold two of his creations: *Mist Maidens of Morg* to Astral Rainbow Productions, Mill Valley, California; and *Centaur!* to Futurogical Publishing, Cambridge, Massachusetts.) A round soft creature as milky white as vanilla yogurt, Wally was four feet six inches tall and weighed 285 pounds, very little of it muscle. His eagerly melting eyes, like blue-yolked soft-boiled eggs, blinked trustingly through thick spectacles, and the only other bit of color about him was the moist red of his far-too-generous mouth. While his brain was without doubt a wonderful contrivance, even more wonderful than the several computer systems filling this living room, its case was not top quality.

From infancy, Wally Knurr had known his physical appearance was outside the usual spectrum of facades found acceptable by the majority of people. Most of us can find *some* corner of the planet where our visages fit more or less compatibly with the local array of humankind, but for Wally the only faint hope was space travel; perhaps elsewhere in the solar system he would find short, fat, moist creatures like himself. In the meantime, his was a life of solitude, as though he'd been marooned on Earth rather than born here. Most people looked at him, thought, "funny-looking," and went on about their business.

It was while doing a part-time stint as a salesman in the electronics department at Macy's as a Christmas season extra four years ago that Wally had at last found his great love and personal salvation: the personal computer. You could play games on it. You could play *math* games on it. You could talk to it, and it would talk back. It was a friend you could *plug in,* and it would stay at home with you. You could do serious things with it and frivolous things with it. You could *store* and *retrieve*, you could *compose music, commit architectural renderings*, and *balance your checkbook*. You could *desktop publish*. Through the wonders of interactive fiction, you could *take part in pulp stories*. To Wally, the personal computer became the universe, and he was that universe's life form. And in there, he didn't look funny.

At the New School, where Wally had once taken a basic course in computers, he now sometimes taught a more advanced course in the same thing, and it was in that course he first met an enthusiast as open to the possibilities of this new marvel of the age as himself. The fellow's name was Andy Kelp, and Wally was delighted they'd met. In the first place, Andy was the only person he knew who was willing to talk computer talk as long and as steadily as Wally himself. In the second place, Andy was one of those rare people who didn't seem to notice that Wally looked funny. And in the third place, Andy was incredibly generous; just mention a new piece of software, a program, a game, a new printer, *anything*, and the first thing you knew here was Andy, carrying it, bringing it into Wally's apartment, saying, "No, don't worry about it. I get a special deal." Wally had no idea what Andy did for a living, but it must be something really lucrative.

Five days earlier, Andy had brought him this problem of the reservoir and the ring—just like an episode in interactive fiction!—and he'd leaped to the challenge. Andy gave him before and after topographical maps of the territory, and Wally's software already included a number of useful informational programs—weights and measures, physical properties, encyclopedia entries, things like that—and all he had to do to get whatever other software he needed was to look it up in the manufacturer's catalogue, give Andy the name and stock number, and the next day there Andy would be, grinning as he took the fresh package out of that amazing many-pocketed pea coat of his. (Wally had been trying recently to figure out how to make an interactive fiction out of a journey through that pea coat.)

In any event, late last night Wally had finished the reservoir program and was really quite pleased with it. Andy had already told him, "Call me any time, day or night. If I'm asleep or not around, the machine'll take it," so Wally had phoned the instant the program was ready, expecting to leave a message on the machine. But Andy himself had answered the call, whispering because, as he said, "My cat's asleep."

Andy had been *very* pleased to hear the reservoir program was ready and had wanted to come over and see it as soon as possible. Wally himself, of course, was available at any time, so it was Andy's own complicated schedule that had kept him away until three-thirty this afternoon. "I'll be bringing a couple of pals of mine," he'd said. "They're very interested in this project. From a theoretical point of view." So this would be him. Them.

Nice. Wally buzzed his guests in through the downstairs door, and went off to get the cheese and crackers.

CHAPTER NINE

Dortmunder and Tom followed Kelp up the dingy metal stairs three flights to a battered metal door, where Kelp cheerily poked another bell button. Looking at the scars and dents on the door, Tom said, "Why do people bother breakin into a place like this?"

"Maybe they forgot their keys," Kelp suggested, and the door opened, and one of the Seven Dwarfs looked out. Well, no; a previously unknown Eighth Dwarf: Fatty.

"Come on in," Fatty said, smiling wetly in welcome and gesturing them in with a stubby-fingered hand at the end of a stubby arm.

They went on in, and Kelp said, "Wally Knurr, these are my pals John and Tom."

"Nice to meet you," Fatty said. (No; *Wally* said. If I think of him as Fatty, Dortmunder told himself, sooner or later I'll *call* him Fatty. Sure as anything. The best thing is, get rid of the risk right now.)

Wally's living room looked like a discount dealer's repair department, with display terminals and printers and keyboards and memory units and floppy disks all over the place, sitting on tables, on wooden chairs, on windowsills, on the floor. One little space had not as yet been invaded, this space containing a sofa, a couple of mismatched chairs, a couple of lamps, and a coffee table with a tray of cheese and crackers on it. Pointing to this latter, Wally said, "I put out some cheese and crackers here. Would you all like a Coke? Beer?"

"I want," Tom Jimson told him, "to see this reservoir thing you did."

Wally blinked, undergoing the normal human reaction to the presence of Tom Jimson, and Kelp moved in smoothly, saying, "We're all excited to see this, Wally. We'll sit around afterward, okay? I mean, to do all this in *five days*. Wow, Wally."

Wally ducked his head, giggling with embarrassed pleasure. Looking at him, Dortmunder wondered just how old the little guy was. In some ways he was a grown-up, if not very *far* up, but in other ways he was like a grade-school kid. However old he was, though, Kelp sure knew how to handle him, because Wally immediately forgot all about his cheese and crackers and said, "Oh, sure, of course you want to see that. Come on."

He led them across to a complete PC system on its own desk, with a worn-looking cushioned swivel chair in front. Seating himself at this, he massaged his pudgy fingers together for an instant, like a concert pianist, and then began to play the machine.

Jesus, that was something. Dortmunder had never seen anything like it, not even at a travel agency. The little man hunched over the keyboard, eyes fixed on the screen while his fingers led their own existence down below, poking, sliding, jumping, tap-dancing over the keys. And after a preliminary few displays of columns of numbers, or of masses of words that went by too fast to be read, here came a picture.

The valley. The valley as it was before the dam was built, seen from just above the highest hilltop to its south. The picture wasn't realistic, was very cartoony, with dividing lines that were too regular and right-angled, perspective that was just a little off, and all primary colors (mostly green), but it was damn effective anyway. You looked at that TV screen and you knew you were looking at an actual valley from the air. "Hmm," Dortmunder said.

"Now, your town," Wally said, his sausage fingers moving on the keys, "was Putkin's Corners. The big one."

"County seat," Tom said.

Dortmunder, turning his head to look at Tom's profile, realized that even he was impressed, though, being Tom, he'd rather kill than admit it.

On the screen, the valley was in motion. Or the observer was, moving in closer and lower, the valley turning slightly as they descended, showing squared-off bits of red and yellow that were becoming the buildings of a town. The predominant green of the valley made no effort to imitate trees, but was simply a green carpet with topographical markings faintly visible on it.

I've seen this kind of thing on television, Dortmunder thought, as the screen showed the town growing larger and larger, the buildings all turning slowly at once as the perspective altered. As though they were in a cartoon helicopter over this cartoon landscape, circling lower, coming in on the town from above.

"That's pretty much what it looked like, all right," Tom said. "Only cleaner."

Keeping eyes on the screen and fingers on the keys, Wally explained, "I input photographs from the local newspaper. I think I got just about everything we need in your part of town. You're the one who hid the treasure, I bet."

Tom, cold eyes flashing, said, "Treasure?"

Smiling easily, Kelp said, "*You* remember, Tom. The treasure hunt."

"Oh, yeah," Tom said.

Kelp had explained his scam before they'd come here. The idea was, an unnamed friend of Kelp's—now revealed to Wally as Tom Jimson—had been involved in a treasure hunt with friends in upstate New York years and years ago and had buried a clue to the treasure in that spot behind the library. The treasure hunt was completed and the treasure itself found, but nobody had come up with that one clue, which was forgotten all about at the time.

Soon afterward, as the yarn went, Tom had gone away—cough, cough—and had not been back to this part of the world for many years. On his recent return, finding the reservoir now in place where Putkin's Corners had once stood, Tom had remembered that unfound clue—a valuable diamond ring around a rolled sheet of cryptic doggerel poetry hidden in a box—and was amused (*Tom Jimson! Amused!*) at the idea of its still being hidden there, beneath so much water.

When Tom had told Kelp the anecdote of the buried clue, as Kelp's cover story continued, Kelp had bet him that the new wonder of the time, the PC—our age's genie-out-of-the-bottle—could show how the clue might be salvaged. Tom had accepted the bet, with a two-week time limit to come up with a solution. If Kelp—and Wally—solved the problem, and the diamond ring was actually salvaged from its watery grave, Tom would sell it and share the proceeds with Kelp, who would share with Wally. If Kelp—and Wally—failed, Kelp alone would have to pay Tom an unspecified but probably pretty substantial sum of money. Before accepting the bet, Kelp had talked it over with Wally, who had assured him the PC was every bit as magical and useful as Kelp believed. In fact, Wally had volunteered (as Kelp had expected he would) to do the reservoir program himself. And so here they all were.

In a cartoon helicopter hovering over a cartoon town. Wally said, "That's County Hall, isn't it?"

"Right," said Tom. "With the library next to it."

The cartoon helicopter *swooped* around the wooden dome of County Hall, and Dortmunder's stomach did a little lurch, as though he were on a roller coaster. "Take it a little slower, okay?" he said.

"Oh, sure," Wally said, and the cartoon helicopter slowed, hanging in the air over the County Hall dome, looking toward the low red brick library building. "It's behind that?"

"Right," said Tom.

Wally's fingers moved, and so did the cartoon helicopter, approaching the library. "I couldn't find any photos of that area back there," Wally explained apologetically, "so I didn't put any details in. I have the size of the field, though, from surveyor's plats."

"It was just a field," Tom said. "The idea was, they were supposed to blacktop it for a parking lot for the library, but they didn't."

Dortmunder said, "Tom? What if they'd changed their mind later? Water; blacktop; you'd still be under something. And they would have dug everything up first before they made a parking lot."

"I knew somebody at the library," Tom said, lips not moving and eyes not turning from the terminal screen, where the cartoon helicopter rounded the side of the library building and looked at a blank tan rectangle of field, with the backs of stores across the way. "She told me," he went on, "they gave up the parking lot idea. Spent the money on books."

"Huh," Dortmunder said. "All of it?"

Wally, hovering his helicopter over the expanse of blank tan, said, "Do you know exactly where the clue was buried?"

"I can show you," Tom said, "if you put in the streetlights."

"I put in everything," Wally told him, "that was in the photos."

"Okay, then. There's one spot back there where you can't see any of the three streetlights. The one next to the library, the one in front of County Hall, and the one on the other block by the stores."

"Oh, that's easy," Wally said, and eased the helicopter down onto the tan field for a landing, where it swiveled upward over a span of ninety degrees and altered itself into the eyes of a person standing on the field, looking at the rear of the library. Wally's fingers moved, and the person turned slightly to the right to look past the library toward County Hall.

"There's the streetlight," Tom said. "Move forward a little."

The person did, at Wally's direction, and the thin pole of the streetlight— a cartoon streetlight, just sketched in—disappeared behind the corner of the library.

"This is some goddamn piece of work," Tom said, leaning closer over Wally's head. "Let's take a look to the left." The angle of vision moved leftward, past the library. "Good," Tom said. "No streetlight. Now the other way."

The person in the field turned all the way around, buildings sliding past in distorted perspective, as in a funhouse mirror, while Dortmunder's stomach did that lurch again. And there was the low row of stores, facing the other way, and between two of them appeared another stick-figure streetlight.

His grim voice hushed, Tom said, "Back up a little, and to the right."

Wally did it. The stores shifted; the streetlight disappeared.

"Right *there!*" Tom crowed, his mouth all the way open for once. "Right goddamn *there!*"

CHAPTER TEN

Was I right?" Kelp demanded, grinning from ear to ear as he and Dortmunder and Tom Jimson walked east on West Forty-fifth Street, away from Wally Knurr's decrepit apartment building—loft building, really, semiconverted to human use—half a block from the river. "Was I right? Is Wally the genius we wanted?"

"He says," Tom Jimson answered, his thin lips immobile, "the tunnel won't work."

"I know that, I know that," Kelp admitted, brushing it aside, or at least trying to brush it aside. "That isn't the—"

"Them graphics looked pretty good," Tom Jimson added, nodding with satisfaction.

The graphics, as a matter of fact, had looked far too graphic. Wally, his fingers scampering like escaped sausages over the keys, had described to them how he'd presented the salvage operation problem to the computer, and how he'd input the tunnel option, and then he'd shown them what the computer thought of the various potential tunnel routes.

Not much. In beautiful blue and brown and green, the computer thought the routes were watery graves, every last one of them. Down would angle the tunnel, a beige tube eating its way into existence through the milk chocolate beneath and beside the baby-blanket-blue cross-section of the reservoir, inching cautiously but hungrily toward that tiny black cube of "treasure" placed just beneath the center of the blue mass like an abandoned novel under a fat man in a blue canvas chair, and sooner or later,

51

at some horrible point in the trajectory, a crack would appear above the tunnel, a fissure, a seam, a funnel-shaped crevice, a swiftly broadening yawn, and in no time at all that ecru esophagus would fill right up with blue.

At that point, despite himself, Kelp's throat would close. Every time. Which had made it difficult to take much part in the immediately ensuing conversation about non-tunnel alternatives, so that it was only now he could say, casually, throwing it away, "Forget the tunnel. The tunnel was never a big deal. That was just to feed the old creative juices, get us thinking about ways that *will* work."

"Like," said Tom Jimson.

"Like we'll find it," Kelp assured him. "We didn't come up with anything *yet*, that's perfectly true, but old Wally and his computer, they'll—"

"Hmp," said Dortmunder.

Whoops; another precinct heard from. They had just stopped at the curb at Eleventh Avenue to wait for the light to change, so Kelp leaned forward to look past the stone outcropping of Tom Jimson's face at the rubble outcropping of Dortmunder's face, and what he saw there told him his old friend John was not entirely happy. "John?" Kelp said. "What's the problem?"

"Nothing," Dortmunder said, and stepped out in front of a cab that, up till then, had thought it was going to beat the light. As the cabby stuck his head out his side window and began to make loud remarks, Kelp and Tom Jimson stepped off the curb after Dortmunder, Tom pausing to look at the cabby, who at once decided he'd made his point and, with dignity, retracted his head back inside his vehicle.

Meantime, Kelp, pursuing Dortmunder, said, "John? I don't get it. What's wrong?"

Dortmunder muttered something. Kelp hurried to overtake him and heard the last part: "—was the planner."

"The planner?" Kelp echoed. "Yeah? What about it?"

Reaching the far corner, Dortmunder turned and said it all over again, out loud: "I was always under the impression, myself, that *I* was the planner."

"Well, sure you are, John," Kelp said, as Tom Jimson joined them and they resumed their walk east. "Sure you're the planner. None better." Kelp even appealed to Tom: "Isn't that right?"

"That's his rep," Tom agreed.

"I've put together a lot of jobs in my time," Dortmunder said.

"Of course you have, John," Kelp said.

"Sometimes things go wrong, a little wrong," Dortmunder said. "I freely admit that."

"Luck, pure luck," Kelp assured him.

"But the *plan* is good," Dortmunder insisted. "I defy you, show me once when I put together a string of events that wasn't the *best* when it comes to you get in, you get the goods, you get out."

"I can't," Kelp admitted. "You win that one, John, I can't come up with even one."

"And all without a computer," Dortmunder finished, with heavy emphasis.

"John, John," Kelp said, while Tom looked a little confused by this turn of events, "the computer doesn't take your *place*, John. The computer's a *tool*, that's all, like a pair of pliers, like a jimmy, a lockpick, a, a, a . . ."

"Over-and-under shotgun," Tom suggested.

"Okay," Kelp said, though reluctantly. "A tool," he repeated to Dortmunder. "There's some safes, you know? You drill a little hole next to the combination, you know the kind?"

"I know the kind," Dortmunder agreed, though still stony-faced.

"Well, the drill," Kelp said, "the drill doesn't take your *place*, John, it's just an aid, kind of. I mean, it's easier than poking a hole through a half inch of steel with your finger, that's all."

"Back there right now," Dortmunder said, "where we just came from, this drill of yours with the TV screen attached to it is thinking up *plans*."

"For your consideration, John," Kelp said. "For you to say yes or no. *You're* the guy in charge."

"In charge of what? A machine and a guy that isn't even on the inside, this Wally of yours that we can't even trust with the right story."

"Oh, you can trust Wally," Kelp assured him. "You can trust Wally to be very involved in the *problem*, and not worry his little soft head about what's going on in the real world at all."

"He better not," Tom said.

"I'm the guy who does the plan," Dortmunder insisted.

They were at Tenth Avenue already; you walk faster when you're arguing. Stopping, waiting for the light to change, they all took a little breather, and then Tom said, "So we're ahead, right? We got three people doin plans, so that's even more chance to come up with the right one."

Kelp, convinced there were quagmires ahead, but unable to keep from following the trail Tom had just indicated, said, "Three people, Tom?"

"Well, two people and a thing," Tom amended. "Al here's gonna think about plans—"

"You're damn right I am," Dortmunder said.

"And your little round fella's machine is gonna think about plans—"

"Hmph," said Dortmunder.

"And, of course, there's me," Tom said with an almost pleasant look. "But I've already got *my* plan."

"That's right," Kelp said with a meaningful look at Dortmunder. "Wally and his computer aren't the problem, John," he said.

CHAPTER ELEVEN

The one called Tom was angry when I said I knew he was the one who hid the treasure. Comment.

A secret is revealed.

But why is it a secret? The treasure is hidden, but it isn't a secret. Comment.

Tom plus treasure is the secret.

That's right. So it matters to Tom that he has a secret. Comment.

One secret means more secrets.

Tom is a man with many secrets. Also, Andy and the one called John were both afraid of Tom, but they tried to hide that. Comment.

Tom is the warlord.

Does Andy work for Tom?

The warlord stays in his castle, surrounded by his minions.

Are Andy and John minions?

Yes.

What are the roles of minions?

Guard. Soldier. Knight. Spy.

So Andy is a knight, employed by Tom. Andy does knight errands for Tom. Andy is a knight-errand. What of John?

John is the spy.

No. The characteristic of spies is that they look trustworthy but are not. John does not look trustworthy. Comment.

Tom is the warlord. Andy is the knight. There is nothing to guard, so John is the soldier.

But what do they want?

The treasure beneath the water.

The cascade of doom, yes. But why do they want it? What is it?

More information is necessary.

They changed the description of the treasure when we needed precision for the tunnel models. First it was a small box, one foot per side, containing a ring. Then it was a large box, eight feet long, three feet wide, three feet high. The second version must be the truth, so the contents must be something other than the ring. What is eight feet by three feet by three feet?

A telephone booth.

No.

A bathtub.

No.

A Zog spaceship.

No.

A refrigerator.

No.

A voting booth.

No.

A coffin.

Yes! The coffin of doom! But what is in the coffin
of doom?

A dead person.

No. It isn't in a cemetery, it's behind a library.
Comment.

A book. The book of the history of the race/planet/encounter.

No. Too big for a book. Comment. What could be in
the coffin of doom?

Valuables.

Yes. Valuables hidden before the reservoir was
made. What are valuables?

Rubies. The blue rose. The defense plans. Pirate gold. The cloak of invisibility.
The kingdom. Bearer bonds. The letters of transit. The princess. The Maltese falcon.
The crown jewels. Money.

Yes! Stolen money?

One secret means more secrets.

Tom and Andy and John buried stolen money in the
coffin of doom. Then the reservoir was made. Why
didn't they save the coffin of doom before the
reservoir was filled?

The warlord was on a journey.

Andy said Tom had been away for a long time, but he
didn't say where. The journey must be for more than
eighteen years because the reservoir was made eighteen
years ago. What journey takes more than eighteen
years?

The return to the planet Zog.

Is that all?

There is no more information on that topic.

There must be something else that takes eighteen
years. Comment.

Tom is the warlord.

Comment further.

Tom is not the hero.

No. I am the hero. Comment further.

The hero is put in prison for eighteen years with the magic tablecloth. Every time he spreads the tablecloth, another meal appears on it. But Tom is not the hero. Wally is the hero. Tom is the warlord.

If Tom did not spend those eighteen years returning to the planet Zog, could he have been the prisoner, even though he's the warlord?

An interesting variant. Possible.

Could Andy and John have been in prison with him?

The knight and the soldier can do nothing without the warlord.

So they didn't have to be in prison. Only Tom had to be in prison. Comment.

Tom is the warlord.

Tom hid the money in the coffin of doom in the field behind the library more than eighteen years ago. Then Tom went to prison. Then the reservoir was made. Where did Tom get the money that he buried?

The warlord raids the peaceful villages.

Tom stole the money. Then he buried it. Then he went to prison. Then they made the reservoir. Then he came out of prison. Then he asked Andy and John to help him get the money back from under the reservoir. Then Andy asked me to help but didn't tell me the truth because there are crimes in it. I have helped. I can go on helping. Should I go on helping?

The warlord is dangerous when defied.

So I should go on helping. Is there anything else I should do?

The hero is impregnable. The hero waits and is patient. The hero gains more knowledge. When the hero knows everything, he will know how to proceed.

Wally pushed back from the keyboard. Right. Time to ask the *New York Times*. Not rising from his wheeled swivel chair, Wally propelled himself diagonally across the room to another table bearing another keyboard and terminal, this one his primary contact with the real world.

The word is *access*, and Wally had it. The computer age could not exist without the telephone lines that tie all the massive brilliant idiot mechanical brains together, and the telephone lines are accessible to us all. To some of us, to a gifted few Wallys among us, the accessibility of the telephone lines means access to the world and all the riches within it. Wally now had the capability to roam at will inside the computers belonging to the Defense Department, United Airlines, American Express, Internal Revenue, Citicorp, Ticketron, Toys-R-Us, Interpol, and many more, including, most significantly at this moment, the *New York Times*. Tapping into that fact-filled know-it-all, Wally typed out his request for information on all robberies, thefts, burglaries and other illegal removals of cash in Vilburgtown County, New York, beginning eighteen years from the present date and extending backward in time through the twentieth century. Then he sat back and watched an unreeling string of *New York Times* items on that subject, in reverse chronological order, crawl upward across his terminal at an easy-reading pace.

Vilburgtown County, even before the city of New York drowned it, had been a quiet, peaceful, law-abiding sort of territory. Tom Jimson's armored car heist on the Thruway stood out against all that rustic quiet like a spaceship from Zog.

CHAPTER TWELVE

What made it the worst for May was the things Tom chose to laugh at on TV. They were never the things other people laughed at—never the things the laugh track, for instance, laughed at—things like people getting confused about who's supposed to go through the doorway first, things like men with strange pieces of clothing on their heads, things like parrots; never anything normal and predictable like that. No, what Tom laughed at was the soldiers getting blown up by the booby trap, or the one-legged skier vowing not to let his handicap keep him from competing on the slopes, or almost anything on the news.

But what else was May to do with herself? At the end of a long day standing at the supermarket cash register, she wanted to *sit down*, in her *living room*, with her *television set*. She wasn't going to cower in the kitchen or the bedroom with a lot of old magazines just because this pathological killer happened to be infesting the apartment at the moment.

Actually, if truth be told, under other circumstances May might have found any number of things to keep her occupied in the kitchen during this Jimson siege, but John was out there right now, the kitchen table covered with maps and charts and lists and photos and lined yellow pads and pencils and pens of different colors and compasses and protractors, the floor around John's and the table's feet littered with crumpled sheets of yellow paper, the expression on John's face thunderously intent. Somehow, May wasn't sure how, it had become some kind of contest, a duel between John and the computer, like those early-nineteenth-century races between a locomotive and a horse, or John Henry trying to beat the spike-driving machine.

Was this a good idea? May was pretty sure it wasn't.

On the television screen, a lost infant crept up onto the railroad tracks; a distant train whistle was heard. Tom's nasal chuckle was heard. May sighed, then looked up as the living room doorway filled with the hulk of John, his face the grim picture of a man determined to outrun the hounds of hell. And the locomotive, too, if need be. "Tom," he said, his voice hoarse, as though he hadn't spoken in days, maybe weeks.

Tom reluctantly looked away from the infant on the tracks. "Yeah?"

"Those stashes of yours," John said.

"The ones the lawyers got," Tom said.

"They didn't get them all, Tom, did they?" John asked. He asked it as though he really and truly wanted the real and true answer.

May was also reluctant to look away from the baby in peril, for quite different reasons, but she just had to turn her head and observe Tom's face. And what *was* that expression? It seemed to be part dyspepsia, part migraine, part the after effects of knockout drops. Showing John this astonishing face, Tom said, "Well, they didn't get the one under the reservoir, no, that's why we're all here." And May realized this was Tom's idea of innocence.

Which John wasn't buying. "There's others, Tom," he said. "Maybe not *big* stashes, but stashes. The lawyers didn't get them all."

"They sure tried," Tom said.

"But they failed, Tom," John pursued.

Tom sighed. "What is it, Al?" he asked. "What's the problem here?"

"We may need some equipment," John told him. "You want to go fifty feet underwater, it's probably gonna mean you're gonna need equipment of some kind."

Tom, his words very careful, his voice sounding as though there were some sort of constriction in his throat, said, "You want *me* to pay for this equipment?"

"We'll divvy at the end," John said, "after we get the big stash, divide the expenses equal. But in front, ahead of time, what do you want to do? Go to somebody that charges a hundred percent interest? You're not gonna take out a bank loan on this, you know, Tom. Filling in the form would already be a problem."

"How about a permanent bank loan?" Tom asked, lifting his eyebrows slightly to show he was being a good sport about all this.

"One job at a time, Tom," John said. "I'll work with you on this reservoir thing, but I don't want to go in with you on any bank jobs."

Tom spread his hands. "You're above robbing banks, Al? You've never spent the bank's money?"

"We got different ways of doing things, that's all," John told him.

"You don't like my methods, Al?"

John sighed. "Tom," he said, "they lack . . ." He looked around, looked at May, looked back at Tom. "Delicacy," he said.

Tom made that chuckle sound. "Okay, Al. If we got equipment we gotta get, expenses, within reason, you know, I mean, I'm not rich, but maybe I could come up with a little of the necessary here and there."

"Good," John said. He nodded at May, as though remembering now she was someone he'd met somewhere once before, and turned away. His feet could be heard thudding back to the kitchen.

May and Tom looked back at the television screen, where now two grown men tried to sell the audience a lot of bad wine mixed with a lot of bad fruit pulp. Tom said, "What happened to the kid?"

"I don't know," May admitted.

"Doesn't matter," Tom said, sounding disgusted. "On TV, somebody always manages to grab the kid in time. Ever notice that?"

"Yes," May said.

"That's just the way they do it," Tom said. Then, brightening slightly, he said, "Well, of course, there's still real life."

CHAPTER THIRTEEN

Dortmunder came back from the library with a copy of *Marine Salvage* by Joseph N. Gores under his coat. He took it out from his armpit as he walked past the living room doorway and Andy Kelp's cheerful voice said, "Reading a book, huh? Anything good?"

Dortmunder stopped and looked in at Kelp seated at his ease on the sofa, holding a can of beer. Knowing May was at work at the supermarket and being in something of a bad mood anyway, Dortmunder said, "You just walked right in, huh?"

"No way," Kelp told him. "Took me at least a minute to get through that lock of yours."

Unwillingly looking around the room, Dortmunder said, "Where's Tom?"

"Beats me," Kelp said. "Somewhere in a coffin of his native earth, I suppose."

"He doesn't have a native earth," Dortmunder said, and walked on to the kitchen, where his work area had overflowed the table and now also covered all but one of the chairs, plus part of the counter space next to the sink. Maps were taped to the wall and the front of the refrigerator, and the crumpled papers under the table were knee deep.

Kelp had trailed Dortmunder into the kitchen. He stood watching as Dortmunder pointedly sat at the messy table and opened *Marine Salvage* to the facing pictures of the *Empress of Canada* lying on her side in Liverpool harbor in 1953 and the *Normandie* lying on her side in New York harbor in 1942. The Chrysler Building and the Empire State Building were both visible in the background of the *Normandie* picture. This East Nineteenth Street building where Dortmunder lived and had to put up with Andy Kelp wouldn't be in the picture because it was too far downtown, the *Normandie* having fallen over at Forty-eighth Street. Dortmunder made a show of becoming very absorbed in these pictures.

But Andy Kelp was not a man to be deterred by hints. "If you aren't busy . . ." he said, and gestured in a friendly fashion with the beer can.

Dortmunder looked at him. "If I'm not *busy?*"

"I thought we'd take a little run over to Wally's place," Kelp said, unruffled. "See how he's coming along."

"*I'm* coming along," Dortmunder told him. "Don't worry about it, I'm coming along fine."

Kelp nodded and pointed at the messy table with his beer can, saying, "I took a look at some of that stuff while I was waiting."

"I see that," Dortmunder said. "Things are moved around."

"You got some very tricky ideas in there," Kelp said.

"Both," Dortmunder told him. "Simple ideas and tricky ideas. Sometimes, you know, a simple idea's a little too simple, and sometimes a tricky idea's too tricky, so you got to concentrate on it and give it your attention and work it out."

"Then after that, what you have to do," Kelp suggested, "is take a break, walk away from it, come back refreshed."

"I just went to the library," Dortmunder pointed out. "I *am* refreshed."

"You don't look refreshed," Kelp said. "Come on, I'll give Wally a call, see if this is a good time to come over."

Dortmunder frowned at that. "Give him a call? What do you mean, give him a call? Did you give *me* a call?"

Kelp didn't get it. "I came over," he said. "That's what I do, isn't it?"

"You come over," Dortmunder said, gesturing at the table, "you go through the plans, you don't give *me* any advance warning."

"Oh, is that the problem?" Kelp shrugged. "Okay, fine, we won't call, we'll just go over." He took a step toward the doorway, then stopped to look back and say, "You coming?"

Dortmunder couldn't quite figure out how that had happened. He looked around at his table covered with half-thought-out plans. He had things to *do* here.

Kelp, in the doorway, said, "John? You coming? This *was* your idea, you know."

Dortmunder sighed. Shaking his head, he got slowly to his feet and followed Kelp through the apartment. "Me and my ideas," he said. "I just keep surprising myself."

Chapter Fourteen

Kelp, leading the way up the battered stairs toward Wally Knurr's battered door, said, "Anyway, the advantage, just dropping in like this, Wally won't have a chance to bring out that cheese and crackers of his."

Dortmunder didn't answer. He was looking at the little red plastic crack-vial tops lying around on the steps, wondering what the letter *T* embossed on each one meant and how come crack producers felt it necessary to add a little styling detail like that fancy *T* to the packaging of their product. Also, as they climbed nearer and nearer to the wonder computer, Dortmunder was feeling increasingly surly, not so much because he'd been double-shuffled into coming here, but because he still couldn't quite figure out how it had been done.

Well, it didn't matter, did it? Because here they were. Kelp, to cut even further into Wally's cheese-and-cracker foraging time, had let them into the building through the downstairs door without bothering to ring Wally's apartment, so now, when they reached the top of the stairs, would be the first the computer dwarf would know of their visit. "I hope I don't scare the little guy," Kelp said, as he pushed the button.

"HANDS IN THE AIR!" boomed a voice, deep, resonant, authoritative, dangerously enraged. Dortmunder jumped a foot, and when he came down his hands were high in the air, clawing for the ceiling. Kelp, face ashen, seemed about to make a run for the stairs when the voice roared out again, more menacing than ever: "GET EM UP, YOU!" Kelp got em up. "FACE

THE WALL!" Kelp and Dortmunder faced the wall. "ONE MOVE AN—*tick*— Oh, hi, Andy! Be right there."

Hands up, facing the wall, Dortmunder and Kelp looked at each other. Slowly, sheepishly, they lowered their arms. "Cute," said Dortmunder, adjusting the shoulders and cuffs of his jacket. Kelp had the grace to look away and say nothing.

Chiks and *clonks* sounded on the other side of the battered door, and then it swung open and the eighth dwarf stood smiling and bobbing in there, gesturing them in, saying, "Hi, Andy! I didn't know you were coming. You didn't ring the bell."

"I guess I should have," Kelp said, walking into the apartment, Dortmunder trailing after.

Wally looked around Dortmunder's elbow at the hallway, saying, "The warlord didn't come?"

Dortmunder frowned at Kelp, who frowned at Wally and said, "Huh?"

But Wally was busy closing and relocking the door, and when he turned to them, his broad moist face wreathed in smiles, he said, "I hope I didn't scare you."

"Oh, heck, no," Kelp assured him, brushing it away with an easy hand gesture.

"This is a bad neighborhood, you know," Wally said confidentially, as though there might be some people around who didn't know that.

"I'm sure it is, Wally," Kelp said.

"There are people out there," Wally said, pointing at the closed door, and he shook his head in disbelief, saying, "I think they live in the hall, kind of. And sometimes they want to, you know, move in here."

Dortmunder, who wasn't feeling any less out of sorts for having been made a fool of, said, "So what do you do when you've got them lined up against the wall out there? Give them cheese and crackers?"

"Oh, they don't line up," Wally said. "It's animal psychology. They run away."

Kelp said, "*Animal* psychology? I thought you said it was people living out there."

"Well, kind of," Wally agreed. "But animal psychology's what works. See, it's kind of like a scarecrow, or blowing whistles at blue jays, or like when you shake a rolled-up newspaper so your dog can see it. They don't stick around to see what you *mean*, they just run away."

Dortmunder said, "But don't they catch on after a while?"

"Oh, I've got all different tapes," Wally explained. "On random feed. I've got one that sounds like a woman with a knife having a psychotic attack, one that sounds like Israeli commandos, Puerto—"

"I'm glad we didn't get the woman with the knife," Kelp said. "Then I *might* have been a little scared. Just for a minute."

Dortmunder said, "Still and all. Sooner or later, they got to figure it out, every time they push that bell button, somebody starts yelling at them."

"But they don't," Wally said, "that's why it's animal psychology. All they know is, every time they come up here and push the bell button to see if anybody's home, something happens that makes them all nervous and upset. So it's conditioning. These people live kind of on the edge of their nerves anyway, so they don't like things that make them *more* nervous, so after a while they stop coming up here. It's what you call association."

Unwillingly, Dortmunder got the point. "You mean," he said, "they associate coming up here with feeling nervous and upset."

"That's right," Wally said, nodding and grinning and patting his pudgy little fingers in the air.

Kelp, rubbing his hands together in anticipation, his own recent nervousness and upset completely forgotten, said, "Well, when *I* come up here, what I feel is great! You been working on the old reservoir problem the last two days, Wally?"

An odd evasiveness, almost shiftiness, appeared in Wally's eyes and demeanor. "Kind of," he said.

Dortmunder became very alert. Was there a flaw here in the computer wizard? "Andy was telling me," he said, "you probably had all kinds of ideas to show us by now."

"Well, we're working on it," Wally assured him, but still with that same indefinable sense of holding something back. "We're working on it okay," he said, "but it's kind of different for us, not our . . . not the regular kind of stuff we do."

Dortmunder frowned at him; somebody else was in on this now? It was becoming a goddamn cast of thousands. "We?" he echoed. "Who's we?"

"Oh, the *computer*," Wally said, beaming, pleased at the confusion. "We do everything together."

"Oh, you do?" Dortmunder smiled amiably. "What's the computer's name?" he asked. "Compy? Tinkerbell? Fred?"

"Oh, I wouldn't *name* it," Wally said. "That would be childish."

"Well," Kelp said, "let's see what you've got, Wally."

"Oh, sure." Wally continued to exhibit that strange reluctance; but then he beamed around at them and said, "How about cheese and crackers? I can run—"

"We just ate, Wally," Kelp said. Moving toward one of the PC setups scattered around the room, he said, "This is the one, isn't it?"

"Well, kind of," Wally admitted, moving reluctantly after him.

"So let's fire it up."

"Yeah," Dortmunder said. "Let's see what the computer thinks." He was beginning to enjoy himself.

"You see," Wally said, squirming a little, "the computer's used to kind of different inputs. So, you know, some of the solutions it comes up with are pretty wild."

"You should see some of the stuff *John's* come up with," Kelp said, laughing. "Don't worry about it, Wally, let's just see what you've got."

Kelp was so absorbed in Wally and the computer that he didn't even notice Dortmunder glare at him, so Dortmunder had to vocalize it: "Tricky, yes. Wild, no."

"Whatever," Kelp said, dismissing all that, his attention focused totally on Wally as the genius butterball reluctantly settled himself at the PC. His stubby fingers stroked the keyboard, and all at once green lettering began to pour out onto the black screen of the TV from left to right. "He's selecting the menu now," Kelp explained to Dortmunder.

"Sure," Dortmunder said.

More greenery on the screen. Kelp nodded and said, "He's asking it to bring up the catalogue of solutions."

"Uh-huh," Dortmunder said.

On the screen, a new set of green words appeared:

1) LASER EVAPORATION

"Well, I don't think," Wally stuttered, in obvious confusion, "we don't have to worry about that one, we can—"

"Wait a minute, Wally," Kelp said. "Is that the first of the solutions? Laser evaporation?"

"Well, yes," Wally said, "but it's not a good one, we should go on."

Kelp was apparently feeling some confusion, and potential embarrassment as well, since this was, after all, his champ at bat here. "Wally," he said, "tell me what that means. Laser evaporation."

Wally looked mournfully at the words on the screen. "Well, it just means what it says," he answered. "Evaporation, Andy, you know? Evaporating water."

Dortmunder said, "Wait a minute, I think I get it. This computer wants to get at the box by getting rid of the water. Same as Tom. Only the computer wants to *evaporate* it."

"Well," Wally said, hunched protectively over his keyboard, "this was just the first thought it had."

"Take a laser," Dortmunder went on, enjoying himself more and more, "take a very big laser and *burn off* all the water in the reservoir."

"Wally," Kelp said. "Let's take a look at solution number two, okay?"

"Well, there were still problems," Wally said. Turning to Dortmunder, he explained, "You see, John, the computer doesn't actually live in the same world we do."

Dortmunder looked at him. "It doesn't?"

"No. It lives in the world we *tell* it about. It only knows what we tell it."

"Oh, I know about that," Dortmunder said, nodding, looking over at Kelp, saying, "That's that word you were using the other day, right? What was that?"

"Guy-go," Kelp said, looking wary.

"That was it," Dortmunder agreed. "Garbage in, garbage out."

"Well, sure," Wally said, his defensiveness more plain than ever. "But actually, you know, sometimes garbage in isn't garbage, depending on what you want the computer *for*. You tell the computer something, and sometimes it isn't garbage, and then other times maybe it is."

Over Wally's head, Dortmunder gave Kelp a superior look. Kelp caught it, shook his head, and said, "Come on, Wally, let's see solution number two."

So Wally's sausage fingers did their dance over the keyboard, and a new set of green words ribboned across the middle of the black screen:

2) SPACESHIP FROM ZOG

There was an uncomfortable silence. Dortmunder tried his absolute best to catch Kelp's eye, but Kelp would have none of it. "Zog," Dortmunder said.

Wally cleared his throat with a sound like a chipmunk gargling. Blinking at the words on the screen, he said, "You see, there's this story—"

"*Don't* explain," Kelp said. He put a hand on Wally's shoulder, part protectively, part warningly. "Wally, okay? Don't explain."

But Wally couldn't help himself: "The computer thinks it's real."

"You know," Dortmunder said, feeling that unfamiliar ache in his cheeks that probably meant he was grinning, "I'm kind of looking forward to solution number three."

Wally did the gargling chipmunk again. "Well," he said, "there's kind of a solution two-A first."

Kelp, sounding fatalistic, said, "Wally? You mean, something that goes along with the spaceship?"

"Well, yeah," Wally agreed, nodding that round brilliant silly head. "But," he added, with a forced hopefulness, "it could have an application maybe, kind of, with some of the other solutions."

"Fling it at us, Wally," Kelp said. Even his cheekbones were refusing to look at Dortmunder.

So Wally did his keyboard dance again, and SPACESHIP FROM ZOG was swept away into oblivion, replaced by:

2A) MAGNET

"Magnet," Kelp said.

Wally swung around in his swivel chair, facing away from the computer for the first time, looking up eagerly at Kelp, saying, "But it isn't wrong, Andy! Okay, the first idea was, the spaceship *finds* the treasure. Or *whatever* finds the treasure. But then the magnet attaches to it, and you pull it *up* out of the water."

"Wally," Kelp said gently, "what we figure, roughly figuring, the treasure weighs somewhere between four hundred and six hundred pounds. That's gotta be a pretty big magnet you're talking about."

"Well, sure," Wally said. "That's what we thought."

"You get it the same place you got the spaceship," Dortmunder told Kelp.

Wally swiveled around to look up at Dortmunder, his expression earnest, moist eyes straining to be understood. "It doesn't have to be a spaceship, John," he said. "Like, a submarine, you know, a submarine's just like a spaceship."

"Well, that's true," Dortmunder admitted.

"Or a boat," Wally said. "Once you find the treasure, you know exactly where it is, you can lower the magnet, pull the treasure up."

"Yeah, but, you know," Dortmunder said, more gently than he'd intended (it wasn't easy to be hard-edged or sardonic when gazing down into that round guileless face), "you know, uh, Wally, part of the problem here is, we don't want anybody to see us. You put a boat, a big boat with a big magnet, out on the reservoir, they're just gonna see you, Wally. I mean, they really are."

"Not at night," Wally pointed out. "You could do it at night. And," he said more eagerly, getting into the swing of it, "it doesn't matter about it being dark, because it's going to be dark down at the bottom of the reservoir anyway."

"And that's also true," Dortmunder agreed. He looked over Wally's soft head at Kelp's grimacing face. Kelp seemed to be undergoing various emotional upheavals over there. "We'll do it at night," Dortmunder explained to Kelp, benignly.

"Wally," Kelp said, desperation showing around the edges, "show us solution number three, Wally. Please?"

"Okay," Wally said, eager to be of help. Turning right back to his computer, he tickled the keyboard once more, and away went **2A) MAGNET**. In its place appeared:

3) PING-PONG BALLS

Kelp sighed audibly. "Oh, Wally," he said.

"Well, wait a minute," Dortmunder told him. "That's not a bad one."

Kelp stared at him. "It isn't?"

"No, it isn't. I get the idea of that one," Dortmunder said, and explained, "That's like one of the things in that book I brought back from the library, that *Marine Salvage* book. Of course, I only read a little of the book on the subway coming home, before Andy said let's go see what you have on all this."

Kelp said, "John? Ping-Pong balls are in the *book*?"

"Not exactly," Dortmunder admitted. "But it led me to the same kind of thought. There's sunken ships where to get them up they fill them with polyurethane foam or polystyrene granules, and it's really just plastic bubbles of air taking the place of all the water inside the ship—"

"That's right!" Wally said. He was so excited at the idea of actual brain-to-brain contact with another human being at this level that he positively bounced in his chair. "And what is a Ping-Pong ball?" he asked rhetorically. "It's just a ball of air, isn't it? Enclosed in a thin almost weightless skin of plastic!"

"It's a way to get a lot of air down to the ship in a hurry without a lot of trouble," Dortmunder went on, explaining it all to Kelp. "So I was thinking, maybe you could fire them down through a length of hose."

Kelp stared at his old friend. "John? This is *your* kind of solution?"

"Well, no, because the problem is," Dortmunder said, and looked down at Wally's gently perspiring face, "the problem is, Wally, this isn't a ship. It's a closed box, and if we open it to put the Ping-Pong balls in, we're gonna get water in there and spoil all the, uh, treasure."

"Well, that's solution three-A," Wally said, and his fingers played a riff on the keyboard, and now the screen said:

3A) PLASTIC BAG

"Oh, sure," Dortmunder said. "That makes sense. We're down there, somehow, probably in our spaceship, and we find this six-hundred-pound box and we dig it up, probably with our giant magnet, and then we put it in our giant plastic bag, and then we fill *that* with Ping-Pong balls, and it just floats right to the surface. Easy."

"Well, kind of," Wally said, his feet shuffling around among the casters of his swivel chair. "There's still some bugs to be ironed out."

"Some bugs," Dortmunder echoed.

"Wally," Kelp said desperately, "show us solution number four."

"Well, Andy, there isn't one," Wally said, swiveling slowly in Kelp's direction.

Kelp looked aghast. "There isn't one?"

"Not yet," Wally amended. "But we're working on it. We're not finished yet."

"That's okay," Dortmunder told him. "Don't worry about it. This has been a very educational experience."

Kelp looked warily at Dortmunder to see if he was trying to be sardonic. "Educational?" he asked.

"Oh, yeah," Dortmunder said. "It clears up my thinking a lot, between tricky and simple. I know which way I'm going now." Patting Wally's soft shoulder—it felt like patting a mozzarella cheese—Dortmunder said, "You've been a great help, Wally. Just like Andy said."

CHAPTER FIFTEEN

W*alk* in?" Kelp demanded.

They were at that moment strolling through Paragon Sporting Goods, on Broadway and 18th Street, heading for the underwater department up on the second floor. "That's the simplest way I can think of," Dortmunder answered, as they trotted up the wide steps. "And, after that little song and dance from your pal and his computer—"

"Wally was a great disappointment to me," Kelp said. "I must admit it. But still, the original model he did was something terrific."

They reached the second floor and turned right. "Wally's a great model maker," Dortmunder agreed. "But when it comes to *plans*, just like I was telling you from the beginning, I don't need help from machines."

"Sure you don't, John," Kelp said. "But just to *walk* in? Are you sure?"

"What could be simpler?" Dortmunder asked him. "We put on underwater stuff so we can breathe down there. We get a flashlight and a shovel and a long rope, and we go to the edge of the reservoir and we *walk in*. We walk downhill until we come to the town, and we find the library, and we dig up the box, and we tie the rope to it. Then we walk back uphill, right along the rope, and when we come out on dry land we pick up the other end of the rope and we pull. Simple."

"I don't know, John," Kelp said. "Walking down fifty feet under water never struck me as exactly *simple*."

"It's simpler than spaceships from Zog," Dortmunder said, and stopped. "Here we are."

There they were. For reasons best known to management, the underwater equipment at Paragon is upstairs; top floor, off to the right of the wide staircase. When Dortmunder and Kelp walked into this section and stopped and just stood there, looking around, they did not at first glance seem as though they belonged here. At second glance, they *definitely* didn't belong, not in this department, not in this store, probably not even on this block. One was tall, stoop-shouldered, pessimistic, walking with a shuffling nonathletic jail-yard gait, while the other was shorter, narrower, looking like the sort of bird that became extinct because it wouldn't ever learn to fly.

The flightless bird said, "So what are we looking for?"

"Help," said the pessimist, and turned around to see a healthy young woman approaching with many questions evident on her face.

The one she chose to begin with was, "Looking for anything in particular, gentlemen?"

"Yeah," Dortmunder told her. "We wanna go underwater."

She studied them with doubt. "You do?"

"Sure," Dortmunder said, as though it were the most natural thing in the world. "Why not?"

"No reason," she said, with a too-bright smile. "Have you gentlemen ever done any diving before?"

"Diving?" Dortmunder echoed.

"You *are* talking about diving, aren't you?" the girl asked.

"Going underwater," Dortmunder repeated, and even made a little parting-the-waves gesture to make things clearer: putting the backs of his hands together, then sweeping them out to the sides.

"In the ocean," the girl said dubiously.

"Well, no," Dortmunder said. "In a kind of lake. But still, you know, under. *In* it."

"*Fresh*water diving," the girl said, smiling with pleasure that they were communicating after all.

"Walking," Kelp said. Sticking his oar in, as it were.

So much for communication. Looking helplessly at Kelp, the girl said, "I beg your pardon?"

"We're not gonna jump in it," Kelp explained. "Not diving, walking. We're gonna walk in it."

"Oh," she said, and smiled with great healthy delight, saying, "That makes no difference, not with the equipment." Turning slightly, to include Dortmunder in her smile, she said, "I take it you gentlemen haven't gone in for diving before."

"There's a first time for everything," Dortmunder told her.

"Absolutely," she said. "Where are you taking your instruction?"

"Instruction?" Kelp said, but Dortmunder talked over him, saying, "At the lake."

"And what equipment will you be needing?"

"Everything," Dortmunder said.

That surprised her again. "Everything? Won't you be able to rent anything at all from the pro?"

"No, it don't work that way at this particular lake," Dortmunder said. "Anyway, right now we're just looking to see what we'll need, what kinda equipment and all."

"Tanks and air and all that," Kelp added, and pointed toward a number of scuba tanks displayed on the wall behind the glass counter full of regulators and goggles and waterproof flashlights.

The girl lost her smile for good. Frowning from Dortmunder to Kelp and back, she said, "I'm not sure what you gentlemen are up to, but it isn't diving."

Dortmunder gave her an offended look. "Yeah, we are," he said. "Why would we want the stuff?"

"All right," she said crisply, either giving him the benefit of the doubt or choosing brisk explanation as the quickest way to get rid of these noncustomers. "Clearly," she said, "you don't know anything about the world of diving."

"We're just starting out," Dortmunder reminded her. "I told you that, remember?"

"You can't do it without an instructor," she said, "and it's pretty clear you don't *have* an instructor."

Dortmunder said, "Why can't we just read up on it in a book?"

"Because," she told him, "there are only two ways you can dive. Either with an accredited instructor right there beside you, or with your certification that you've taken and passed the three-day introductory course."

Kelp said, "You know, you're not supposed to drive a car without a license, too, but I bet some people do."

She gave him a severe look and shook her head. From a sunny happy healthy young woman she had segued with amazing suddenness into the world's most disapproving Sunday School teacher. "It doesn't work quite the same way," she said, sounding pleased about that. Pointing at the display of tanks, she said, "I'll sell you as many of those as you want. But they're empty. And the only place you can get them filled is an accredited dive shop. And they won't fill them unless you show your certification or agree to have an instructor go with you." Her look of satisfaction was pretty galling. "Diving *or* walking, gentlemen," she said, "you will not want to go very far underwater, or for very long, with empty tanks. If you'll excuse me?" And she turned on her heel and went off to sell a $350 Dacor Seachute BCD to a deeply tanned Frenchman with offensively thick and glossy hair.

Leaving, slinking away, clumping morosely down the wide stairs toward Paragon's street level with their tails between their legs, Dortmunder said, "Okay. We gotta getta guy."

CHAPTER SIXTEEN

It was raining. Doug Berry, owner and proprietor and sole full-time employee of South Shore Dive Shop in Islip, Long Island, sat alone in his leaky shingle shed built out on its own wooden dock over the waters of the Great South Bay, and read travel brochures about the Caribbean. Steel drum calypso music chimed from the speakers tucked away on the top shelves behind the main counter, sharing space with the Henderson cold-water hoods and the mask-and-snorkel sets. The rickety side walls of the structure were decorated with posters distributed by various manufacturers in the diving field, all showing happy people boogieing along underwater with the assistance of that manufacturer's products. From the fish net looped below the ceiling were hung shells, ship models and various pieces of diving equipment, either the real things or miniatures. In a front corner, facing the door, stood an old used store-window dummy dressed in every possible necessity and accessory the well-turned-out diver could possibly want.

Outside was more of Doug Berry's empire. The dock, old and shaky, rotting planks nailed to rotting pilings, was three feet wider than the shed, which was built flush to the right edge of the dock, leaving the three feet on the left for an aisle back to the eighteen feet of additional dock extending out into the bay beyond the rear of the shed. Piled on this dock, under gray or green tarps, were spare air tanks and gasoline tanks and other equipment, all chained against thievery. Tied up on the left side of the dock, also under a tarp, was Doug Berry's Boston Whaler, with its 235-horse Johnson outboard. The compressor from which air tanks were filled was also out there, under its own shiny blue plastic tarp.

On the landward side of Doug Berry's domain was the gravel width of customer parking area, containing at the moment only Berry's custom-packaged black (with blue and silver trim) Ford pickup, with the inevitable bumper sticker on the back: DIVERS GO DEEPER. Beyond the parking area was the potholed blacktop driveway leading out past the marine motor dealership and the wholesale fish company to Merrick Road. All of this was Doug Berry's, and there he sat, in the middle of his realm, dreaming about the Caribbean.

Yeah, that was the place to be. No goddamn April showers down there. Just warm sun, warm air, warm sand, warm turquoise water. A fella with Doug Berry's looks and training and skills could . . .

. . . rot on the beach.

There he went again, dammit. Doug Berry's worst flaw, as far as he himself was concerned, was his inability to ignore reality. He'd *like* to be able to fantasize himself into the dive king of the Caribbean, the bronze god in flippers, slicing through the emerald waters, rescuing beautiful heiresses, discovering buried treasure, either joining pirates or foiling pirates, he'd *like* to sit here in this miserable shack on this rainy no-business day and dream himself two thousand miles south and twenty degrees warmer, but the reality bone in his head just wouldn't ever give him a break.

The fact was, guys whose total assets were youth, health, good looks, and an advanced diving certificate were not in exactly short supply in the Caribbean basin. (The pestiferous phrase "dime a dozen" kept circling through Doug Berry's irritated head, above the aborted fantasies.) And when, in addition, the fellow also already had a couple of clouds over his head—charged with (but not convicted of) receiving stolen goods, for instance—and when he's already been ejected from the two largest and most prestigious licensing associations in the field, PADI (Professional Association of Diving Instructors) and NAUI (National Association of Underwater Instructors), and when in fact he was now found acceptable only by DIPS (Diving Instructors Professional Society), the newest and smallest and least picky association around, his smart move—no, his only move—was to stay right here in Islip, do a moderate summertime business with college kids and Fire Islanders, do a miserable wintertime business selling equipment to people going away on vacations (there was no way to compete more directly with the big outfits, furnished with their own indoor swimming pools), supplement his livelihood with carpentry and clamming, stock his shelves as much as possible with goods that fell off the back of the delivery truck, and sit here in the rain trying to dream about the Caribbean.

Doug Berry, twenty-seven years old. He used to have a hobby; now, the hobby has him.

Movement beyond the rain-streaked front window made him look up from Aruba—tan sand, pale blue sky, aquamarine sea, *no rain*—to see a vaguely familiar car coming to a stop out there next to his pickup. It was a Chevy Impala, the color of a diseased lime. Its windshield wipers stopped, and then three of its four doors opened and three men wearing hats and raincoats climbed out, flinching as though water were poisonous.

Squinting through the streaky window, Doug finally recognized one of the three: the driver, a bent-nose type named Mikey Donelli. Or maybe Mikey Donnelly. Doug had never been certain if the accent was on the first syllable or the second, so he couldn't be sure if Mikey were Irish or Italian. Not that it mattered, really; Doug and Mikey had a business-only relationship, and the business would be the same wherever Mikey's forebears hailed from.

Mikey was, in fact, the provider of those stolen goods Doug was alleged to have received, and of a lot of other stolen goods as well. Given the realities of the South Shore Dive Shop, Mikey was just about the company's most important supplier.

But who were the other two? Doug had never met any of Mikey's associates and was just as glad of it. This pair walked with their hands in their raincoat pockets, chins tucked in low, hat brims pulled down over their eyes as though they were extras in a Prohibition movie. Mikey led the way from the car to the door as Doug got to his feet, closed the Caribbean brochure, and tried to put a ready-for-business expression on his face. But what was Mikey *doing* here? And who were the two guys with him?

Doug spent most of his life just slightly afraid. At the moment, it was up one notch above normal.

Mikey came into the shop first, followed by his friends. "Whadaya say, Dougie?" Mikey said.

"Hi, Mikey," Doug said. No one else on Earth had ever even *thought* to call him Dougie. He hated it, but how can you tell somebody named Mikey—particularly a *tough* somebody named Mikey—that you don't like to be called Dougie? You can't.

All three of his visitors looked around at the shelves, the two strangers with the curiosity of people who'd never been in a dive shop in their lives before—which Doug could well believe—and Mikey with a kind of professional interest. "Gee, Dougie," he said, "you haven't moved much product, have you, kid?" He was probably the same age as Doug, within a year or two, but he called him Dougie and "kid."

"It's just the beginning of the season," Doug explained. "Things'll pick up."

"You know, kid," Mikey said, "it could be, what you could use is a nice burglary. You gotta be insured, huh?"

Oh, no. Doug was living on the edge of disaster as it was, and he knew it. False burglaries for the insurance were *exactly* the way to integrate a state prison, a goal Doug had never held for himself. "Not just yet, Mikey," he said, trying to produce a cool and untroubled grin. "If I ever need anything like that, you'll be the guy I call. You know that."

"Sure, kid," Mikey said and grinned, spreading his hands as though to say *naturally you'll come to me*. With that round tough face and lumpy nose and curly black hair and those penetrating dark eyes, Mikey could be just as easily Italian or Irish, Irish or Italian. Doug had no idea why it mattered to him to know what Mikey was, but it did. Maybe because the question was essentially unanswerable.

Now Mikey turned to his companions, saying, "I wanna introduce you a couple guys. This is John and this is Andy. That's Dougie. He runs this place."

"How are you," said Doug, nodding at them, not liking the flat emotionless way they both studied him.

"Fine," said the one called John. "You got the certification, huh?"

That was a surprising question. "Sure," Doug said. "I couldn't run the dive shop unless I did." And he gestured to the sticker in the bottom right of the front window: DIPS.

"Dips," said the one called Andy in a thoughtful tone of voice. "I don't think I know that one."

Surprised that somebody like Andy would know *any* of diving's professional associations, Doug said defensively, "It's a new group, very lively, very forward-looking. The best, I think. That's why I went with them."

With a raucous laugh, Mikey said, "Also, Dougie, they'd *take* you, don't forget."

Doug was offended, and for the moment forgot his fear. Looking hard at Mikey, he said, "It wasn't exactly that way, Mikey. What have you been telling these friends of yours, anyway?"

"Hey, take it easy, Dougie," Mikey said, laughing again, but putting his hands up mock defensively. *He's* afraid! Doug thought with astonishment, as Mikey went on, saying, "All I said to Andy and John, maybe you were the guy could help with a little problem they got. I'm not in it at all, okay? It's strictly between you and them."

Doug, pushing his unexpected advantage, said, "*What's* between me and them?"

"Why don't you guys talk it over?" Mikey said, backing toward the door, grinning at everybody. "I'm just John Alden here, right? Dougie, I can guarantee these guys, Andy and John'll treat you straight. Guys, Dougie here is a hundred percent." Waving generally, he said, "I gotta couple calls to make in the neighborhood. Be back in fifteen, twenty minutes, okay?"

"Sure, that's good," the one called John said. He nodded at Mikey, but his brooding eyes were on Doug.

"See you, guys," Mikey said, and reached for the doorknob. But then he pointed playfully at Andy and said, "Remember, if it works out . . ."

Andy nodded as though this reminder was unnecessary. "Don't worry, Mikey," he said. "You've got your finder's fee."

"Great," Mikey said. His grin was bigger and bigger. "I love to get friends together," he said, and pulled open the door at last and left.

They all watched out through the window as Mikey slogged through the rain to his diseased-lime Impala and climbed in. After a few seconds, the windshield wipers started, and then the Impala backed away in a semicircle and drove out toward Merrick Road. And they were alone.

Doug looked at his unexpected visitors, wondering what this was all about. More stolen goods? He had to be very careful here, dealing with strangers; there was such a thing as entrapment.

My God, yes! Suppose the cops had the goods on Mikey for something or other—Doug had no idea what Mikey's activities were beyond the finding of goods that had fallen off trucks, but he was sure those activities must be wide-ranging and far from legal—suppose Mikey had got himself caught, and the cops had offered him a deal if he'd turn somebody else in. Didn't they do that all the time? They did.

Okay, in that case, who would Mikey choose to betray? Some other tough guy like himself, who'd grown up with him and knew all about him and knew where he lived? Or would he choose Doug Berry, a guy he barely knew, who wasn't connected to anything that Mikey thought important?

These guys didn't *look* like cops. But they wouldn't, would they? Giving the pair a very critical and cautious look, Doug said, "You need some help with a diving problem?"

If he'd expected a *no* to that question—and he had—he was both disappointed and surprised, because the one called John turned and said, "That's it, okay. A diving problem."

"You *do*?"

"Yeah," John said. "Andy and me, we got to go underwater, and we never did that before, and it turns out it's not so simple like we thought."

Doug just couldn't get this straight. "You really do want to dive?"

"Walk," Andy said. "We wanna walk in from the shore to where it's fifty feet deep."

Doug looked out the side window at the rain-pocked gray waters of the Great South Bay. "Around here?"

"Somewhere else," John said.

"Where?"

But John spread his hands and said, "We got to talk first, you know? We got to know we're all on the same team, then we'll talk about where."

Andy said, "You see, Dougie, John and—"

"Doug," Doug said.

They both frowned at him. Andy said, "I thought Mikey said you were Dougie."

"That's what he calls me," Doug agreed. "Everybody else calls me Doug."

They looked at each other and came to some sort of decision. Nodding briskly, Andy said, "Got it. Okay, Doug, here's the story. John and me, we got to go into a body of water, like a lake—"

"Freshwater, you mean," Doug suggested.

"Yeah," Andy said. "Down at the bottom of this lake, there's a box we want. A big box. So we got to get to it, tie a rope on, pull it out."

John said, "We thought it should be kind of simple. But then we went to a store to buy the stuff, and it turns out there's this secret society or something, nobody gets to go underwater unless they know the password."

"We have no fatalities in the sport in the United States," Doug told him, "and that's why. Safety first."

"I believe in safety first," John said. "I don't want to go anywhere that it *isn't* safety first. So maybe this is okay after all. We can't pull the job without a pro."

"Not if it's underwater," Doug agreed.

"But," John said, "we need a very particular special pro. Not just any pro."

"Not the pro in just any dive shop you see around," Andy said, expanding on the idea.

Here comes the illegality, Doug thought. Entrapment. Temptation. They're probably both wired. Be very careful about *everything* you say. "Mm," he said.

"So we asked around," John went on, "among people we know, particular people we know . . ."

"And I happened to know Mikey," Andy said. "We've been in trade together a couple times. And he said you were exactly the guy we were looking for."

"So here we are," John said.

"Mm," Doug said.

They all looked at one another for a minute. Finally, Andy said, "Don't you wanna know what we want?"

"I thought you were going to tell me," Doug said, trying not to sound too eager to commit anything illegal.

Andy and John looked at each other again, and then John nodded and said, "Okay. Here's what we want. We want the expertise and the equipment so we can do down into this res— this lake and get this box. That's what we want."

Doug said, "Mm."

Again they all stood around gaping at one another, and this time Andy said, "You want to do it?"

Doug had to ask the question somehow, without suggesting he was open to criminal considerations. Tone flat, he said, "What's illegal about it?"

They looked surprised. "Illegal?" John said. "Unless you're gonna sell us stuff you got from Mikey, I don't know *what's* illegal about what we want here."

"You're the pro, that's all," Andy said.

Doug shook his head, bewildered, but still afraid to expose himself to risk. "Then why me?" he asked. "I mean, it's not that I'm—that I do illegal things or anything. I'm not suggesting here that I'm open to uh, um, criminal enterprises or anything, but why did you need a *special* pro and all that?"

They stared at him, as bewildered as he was. John said, "Criminal *en*terprises?"

But then Andy laughed and clapped his hands together and said, "John, he's afraid we're wired!"

John looked surprised, then offended. "Wired? You mean like FBI men? Do we look like FBI men?"

"Well, you wouldn't, would you?" Doug said. "Not that it matters, I'm not proposing any, uh . . . ."

"Criminal enterprise," John suggested.

Andy said, "Look, Doug, somebody's gotta start by trusting somebody, so I'm gonna start by trusting you. You got an honest face. See, there's a fella we know, a long time ago he went to jail, and he just got out now, and it turns out before he went inside he buried some money—"

"Criminal enterprise money," John interpolated.

"Right," Andy said. "Your basic ill-gotten gains is what we're talking about here. And now he's out and he wants these gains, and it turns out there's a reservoir there now."

Doug couldn't help himself; he laughed. He said, "A reservoir? He buried the money and now it's *underwater*?"

"That's why we're here," Andy told him. "And to tell you the truth, Doug, there *is* gonna be some criminal enterprise in all this. For instance, when we go over the fence around the reservoir, that's already breaking a law. Trespassing or something. And when we go into the reservoir, actually into the water, there's another law laying dead on the ground."

"And," John said, "when we get the box with the money in it, we won't give it back to the bank, so there we go again. Who we'll give it to is the guy that buried it, and he'll give us some for helping out, and we'll give *you* some for helping out."

"How much?" Doug couldn't help from asking.

"A thousand dollars," John said, "over your regular fees and expenses and the cost of the stuff we use."

"Doug," Andy said, sounding very sincere and confidential, "in all honesty and truth, Doug, I never in my life even *thought* about being an FBI man."

Doug wanted to believe these two—and God knows he could use a thousand dollars—but a lot of Congressmen had once wanted to believe a couple of fellas like this were Arab sheiks. He said, "If we're gonna start familiarizing ourselves with the equipment and all, you two will have to take your coats and, uh, shirts off, you know. Strip to the waist."

Andy, grinning, said to John, "He still thinks we're wired."

"No, no," Doug said, "it's just to, uh, fit everything, that's all."

John shook his head, with a faint look of disgust, and took his coat off, and Andy followed suit. With no hesitation at all, they both stripped down, revealing physiques no one in history could have been proud of. But no microphones, no tape recorders, no *wires*.

Spreading his arms, pirouetting slowly, grinning at Doug, Andy said, "Okay, Doug?"

"Okay," Doug said, and covered his confusion with a deep layer of professional manner. "Have either of you ever breathed through a mouth-piece before?"

"You could keep it warmer in here," John said.

"A mouthpiece?" Andy asked. "I've *talked* to one or two, but I've never breathed through one, no."

"Okay," Doug said, turning to his well-stocked shelves. "We'll start now."

CHAPTER SEVENTEEN

I wish you'd take that thing off, John," May said. "It makes you look like something in science fiction."

Dortmunder removed the mouthpiece from his mouth; not to accede to May's request, but to make it possible to answer her. "I'm supposed to get used to breathing through it," he said, and put it back in his mouth. Then he immediately forgot and breathed through his nose, as usual; underwater, he would have drowned half a dozen times by now.

Fortunately, he wasn't underwater. He was in the living room with May, watching the seven o'clock news (which is to say, watching the headache and laxative commercials) and waiting for Tom Jimson to come back from wherever he was when he wasn't here. He'd been waiting for Tom since he'd come back from Long Island and Doug Berry and the wonderful world of underwater late this afternoon.

May said, "John, you *aren't* breathing through it."

"Mm!" he said, startled, and grasped his nose between thumb and forefinger of his right hand, to *force* himself to do it right. Breathe through the mouth, doggone it. The mouth gets dry almost immediately, but that's all right. It's better than the lungs getting wet.

So Dortmunder went on sitting there, on the sofa, next to the silently disapproving May, breathing through his mouth and watching the news over the knuckles of the hand holding his nose. That was his position when Tom noiselessly appeared in the doorway just as the news anchorman was smiling his last. (Though what he had to smile about, considering everything he'd had to report to the world in the last half hour, was hard to figure out.) But there, all at once, was Tom Jimson in the doorway, raising an eyebrow, looking at Dortmunder and saying, "Something smell bad, Al?"

"Mm!" Dortmunder said again, and took the mouthpiece out of his mouth and sneezed. Then he said, "This is the mouthpiece for going underwater."

"Not very *far* underwater," Tom suggested, giving the mouthpiece a critical look.

"This is just one part of it," Dortmunder explained. "In fact, Tom, I've gotta talk to you about that. It's time to come up with some cash."

Tom's face, never exactly what you'd call mobile, stiffened up so much he now looked like a badly reproduced photo of himself. From somewhere deep within the photo came the hollow word, "Cash?"

"Come on, Tom," Dortmunder said. "We agreed on this. You'll dip into your other little stashes to finance this thing."

The photo crumpled a bit. "How much cash?"

"We figure seven to eight grand."

Animation of a sort returned to Tom's face. That is, his eyebrows climbed up over his forehead as though trying to escape into his hair. "*Dollars?*" he asked. "Why so much?"

"I told you how we need a pro," Dortmunder reminded him.

Coming farther into the room, glancing briefly at the television set on which the news had now been followed by a comedy series about a bunch of very healthy and extremely witty teens who all hung out at the same sweet shop, Tom said, "Yeah, I remember. For air. You can't get air without a pro. But I never hearda air costing seven, eight grand before."

Getting to her feet, May said, "Nobody's watching TV." She sounded faintly annoyed by the fact. Crossing to switch off the set, she said, "Anybody want a beer?"

"I think I'm gonna need one," Tom said, and he crossed to take May's seat as she left for the kitchen. His eyebrows still well up on his forehead, he said, "Tell me about this rich air, Al."

"To begin with," Dortmunder told him, "we had to find the pro. One we could deal with. So the guy that found the right guy, some fella that Andy knows, he wanted a finder's fee. Five hundred bucks."

"To find the pro," Tom said.

"That's very cheap, Tom," Dortmunder assured him. "You got a better way to find the exact right guy we need?"

Tom shook his head, ignoring the question more than agreeing with it. He said, "So this is the exact right guy, is it?"

"Yeah, it is. And he isn't in it for a piece, just a flat payment in front. We're getting him for a grand, and that's *very* cheap."

"If you say so, Al," Tom said. "Inflation, you know? I still can't believe the prices of things. When I went inside twenty-three years ago, you know how much a steak cost?"

"Tom, I don't even care," Dortmunder said, and May came in with two cans of beer. Looking at them, Dortmunder said, "May? Aren't you having any?"

"Mine's in the kitchen," May said. "You two talk business." And, with a blank smile at them both, she went away to the kitchen again, which was hers once more now that Dortmunder had removed all his books and papers and pencils and pens and pictures from it, stowing the whole mountain of stuff in the bottom dresser drawer in the bedroom.

Tom swallowed beer and said, "So we're up to fifteen hundred."

"The rest is equipment and stuff," Dortmunder told him. "And training."

Tom frowned at that. "Training?"

"You don't just go underwater, Tom," Dortmunder explained.

"I don't go underwater at all," Tom said. "That's up to you and your pal Andy, if that's what you wanna do."

"That's what we want to do," Dortmunder agreed, not letting a single doubt peek through. "And to do it right," he went on, "we got to train and learn how it's done. So we'll take lessons from this guy, and that's why I'm practicing with this mouthpiece here, learning to breathe through my mouth. So that costs. And then there's the air and the tanks and what we wear and the underwater flashlights and all the rope we're gonna need and lots of other stuff, and it all comes out to seven or eight grand."

"Expensive," Tom commented, and drank more beer.

"It's gotta be expensive," Dortmunder told him. "This isn't a place you just walk into, you know."

Tom said, "What about the little fella with the computer? Any thought outta him?"

"Wally?" Dortmunder made no effort to keep victor's scorn out of his voice. "He had a lot of great ideas," he said. "Spaceships. Giant magnets. Giant lasers. Even more expensive than me, Tom." Shrugging, Dortmunder said, "No matter how we do this, it isn't gonna be cheap."

"Oh, I dunno," Tom said. "Dynamite and life are cheap."

"We agreed, Tom," Dortmunder reminded him. "We do it my way first. And we finance from your stash."

Tom slowly shook his head. "Those lawyers really cleaned me out, Al. I don't have that much left."

Dortmunder spread his hands. Tom sat there, brooding, holding his beer, wrestling with the problem. There was nothing more for Dortmunder to say to him—Tom would dope it all out for himself or not—so he put the mouthpiece back in and practiced breathing through his mouth without holding his nose. Underwater, of course, he'd have goggles on that would make a tight seal all around his eyes and nose, so he wouldn't be able to hold his nostrils shut anyway. He had a practice pair of goggles, in fact, that Doug Berry had loaned him, but he would have felt foolish sitting next to May and wearing goggles to watch television, so they were on the dresser in the bedroom.

"There's one," Tom said thoughtfully, "up in the same area."

"Mlalga," Dortmunder said, and took the mouthpiece out and said, "Under the reservoir?"

"No no, Al, nearby. One of the towns they didn't drown. We can go up there tomorrow and get it. Rent another car and drive up."

"No," Dortmunder said. "I don't drive up there again. And no more rentals. I'll call Andy, he'll arrange transportation."

CHAPTER EIGHTEEN

Wally said, "Well, the truth is, Andy, I'm kind of embarrassed."

"Yeah, that makes sense," Andy Kelp agreed, nodding. Seated on the brown Naugahyde sofa in Wally's cluttered living room, he munched cheese and crackers while Wally sat facing him, frowning in agony. Andy said, "I felt kind of embarrassed, too, Wally. Talking you up to John the way I did. And then we get Zog and all this."

Wally squirmed. His big wet eyes blinked over and over in discomfort. His little pudgy hands made vague unhappy gestures. He felt very awkward in this whole situation. He said, "Gee, Andy, I think . . . well, I just think maybe I ought to tell you the truth."

Andy raised an eyebrow, gazing at him over a cheese-topped cracker. "The truth, Wally?"

Wally hesitated. He hated having to trust his own instincts, particularly when it meant disagreeing with the computer. But on the other hand, this was a computer that didn't know the difference between Zog and Earth, which was perfectly all right in some applications but kind of a problem in others. So maybe Wally was right to override the computer's decision this time. On the *other* other hand, exposing himself to these people was definitely scary. "The warlord has no pity," the computer had reminded him, more than once.

Did Andy have pity? His eyes seemed very bright, very alert, as he looked at Wally, waiting for the truth, but he didn't really look—Wally had to admit to himself, reluctantly—what you could call *sympathetic*. As Wally hesitated, Andy put the cracker and its shipment of cheese back on the plate on the coffee table and said, "What truth was that, Wally?"

So there was nothing for it but to go forward. Wally took a deep breath, swallowed once more, and said, "The treasure is seven hundred thousand dollars in cash stolen from a Securivan armored car in a daring daylight robbery on the New York State Thruway near the North Dudson exit on April twenty-sev—"

Andy, staring at him, said, *"What?"*

"Tom was one of the robbers," Wally rushed on, "and he's been in jail ever since, but not for that, because they never found the people who robbed the armored car."

Wally, blinking more and more rapidly, sank back in his chair, exhausted. He looked at the plate of cheese and crackers and suddenly desperately wanted to eat all of them; but he was afraid to. He'd have to leave his mouth clear in case he had to talk, in case he had to, for instance, plead for his life. Reluctantly, hesitantly, he looked up away from the food at Andy's face, and saw him grinning in admiration and astonishment. "Wally!" And said in unmistakable pleasure. "How'd you *do* that?"

Wally gulped and grinned in combined relief and delight. "It was easy," he said.

"No, come on, Wally," Andy said. "Don't be modest. How'd you do it?"

So Wally explained the reasoning he'd worked out with the computer, and then demonstrated his access to the *New York Times* data bank, and actually brought up the original news item about the armored car robbery, which Andy read with close attention and deep interest, commenting to himself, "Not much finesse there. Just smash and grab."

"I wanted to tell you so we'd have better communication," Wally explained, "and better input to help solve the problem. But I was afraid. And the computer advised against."

"The comput—?" Andy seemed startled, but then he grinned again and said, "How come?" Walking back over to the sofa, he said, "Computer doesn't like me?"

Wally followed, and they took their seats again, Wally saying, "It wasn't so much you, Andy. It was mostly Tom the computer was worried about."

"Smart computer," Andy said, and frowned, thinking it over. "Do we let Tom in on this?" he asked himself. Absentmindedly he picked up a cheese and cracker, pushed it into his mouth, and talked around it. "In some ways it's simpler," he said, more or less intelligibly. "We can talk up front with each other. On the other hand, I can see Tom getting a little testy."

"That's what the computer and I thought, too," Wally agreed.

Andy swallowed his cheese and cracker, thinking. "I tell you what we say," he decided.

Wally leaned forward, all ears. Well, mostly ears.

Andy reached for another cheese and cracker and pointed at himself with it. "*I* told you," he said. "I decided the only way to get good input from you was to give you the whole picture. So I explained to you how Tom had been involved in this robbery years and years ago, brought in to it by bad companions and all, and how now he's old and not wanting to be a robber anymore, and how he was let out of prison, and all he wants to do is retire, and this money's all he's got for his golden years, so we're all getting together to help him get it back. Because, by now, whose money is it, anyway? So that's what I told you. Right?"

Wally nodded. "Okay, Andy," he said. "But, Andy?"

"Yeah?"

"Is, uh," Wally said. He *craved* a cracker piled with cheese. "Is, uh," he said, "any of that the truth?"

Andy laughed, calm and innocent and obviously easy in his mind. "Why, Wally," he said. "Except for leaving out the part where Tom continues to be a homicidal maniac, it's *all* the truth."

CHAPTER NINETEEN

Myrtle Street slowly turned the crank of the old-fashioned microfilm viewer, and on its metal floor all the yesterdays of Vilburgtown County crept languidly by, recorded for posterity in the pages of the *County Post*. From the year before Myrtle's birth up till the year Mother married Mr. Street, the cake sales and high school dances and Boy Scout meetings inched inexorably past, the Town Council sessions and selectman elections and volunteer fire department fund raisers leisurely unwound, the fires and floods and severe winter storms floated through (sapped of all urgency), the automobile accidents and burglaries and the one big armored car robbery out on the Thruway all popped into view and faded like sudden puffs of smoke. But through it all there wasn't the slightest hint of the identity of Myrtle Street's father.

In the week since Edna had blurted out that astonishing sentence—"That was your *father* in that car!"—Myrtle had thought of nothing else. Suddenly she burned with the desire—no, the *need*—to know her true origins. But Edna was no help at all. After that initial sudden outburst and that quick (equally startling) string of profanity, Edna had shut up like a safe on the subject, had refused to talk about it, had refused even to let Myrtle talk about it. Clearly she regretted that flare-up, that window into the past she'd inadvertently and briefly opened, and was waiting only for that out-of-control moment to be forgotten.

Well, it wasn't going to be forgotten. Myrtle had the bit well and truly in her teeth now and was determined to learn *everything*. From knowing *nothing*, she wanted to know *all*. Her earlier complacence now astonished her. She'd always known, of course, that Gosling was her mother's maiden name, that Street was the only other name Edna had ever possessed, and that she herself had entered the world long before Edna and Mr. Street had ever met. She had known it, but she'd never actually thought about it, wondered about it, followed through the implications. And now?

Now, she had to know. The window was open, and there was no shutting it. If Edna wouldn't talk, there had to be another way. Myrtle had two elderly female cousins in the area, one a widow in a nursing home in Dudson Falls, the other an old maid still in her family's farmhouse (though without the farm acreage) outside North Dudson. Myrtle had tried talking to both of them this last week but had gotten nowhere. The frustrating thing about trying to deal with doddering oldsters was that it was impossible to know for sure whether they were lying or merely feeble-minded. Both old ladies had sworn ignorance of Myrtle's male parentage, though, so that was that.

What else was there, what other way to learn about the past? Twenty-six years ago. Who was spending time then with Edna Gosling, already thirty-six years of age and chief librarian at the Putkin's Corners municipal library? It was really too bad the Vilburgtown Reservoir had drowned Putkin's Corners a few years later; there might have been clues there. Well, they were unreachable now.

And the *County Post* seemed to contain no clues at all. No photos of the younger Edna Gosling on the arm of this gentleman or that at VFW Post clambakes or Dudson Consolidated School reunions, no "and passenger Edna Gosling" in stories of automobile accidents, no "accompanied by Miss Edna Gosling" in social-page wedding reports.

What else had Edna said about the man she claimed to be Myrtle's father back there at her first startled instant of recognition? "It couldn't happen, but it did," she'd said, meaning, presumably, that she hadn't believed the man would—no, *could*—ever return to this part of the world. Because she'd thought he was dead? Out of the country? Permanently hospitalized? But then she'd called the man, as Myrtle remembered it, a "dirty bastard son of a bitch." Was that because he'd left her, pregnant and unwed, so many years ago?

If *only* Edna would open up!

But she wouldn't, that's all. But there was nothing. And now it was nearly six o'clock, time for Myrtle to leave work and go pick up Edna at the Senior Citizens Center. Having finished going through for the third time the papers covering the year before her birth, Myrtle sighed, fast-cranked the roll of microfilm back onto its reel, put it away in its box, said good evening to Janice (the employee who would steer the library through the twilight hours), went out to the employee parking area behind the library, got behind the wheel of the black Ford Fairlane, and drove across town and down Main Street to where Edna stood irritably on the curb, waiting.

The clock on the Fairlane's dashboard assured Myrtle she wasn't late, so Edna's irritation was simply at its normal level of background static and nothing for Myrtle to worry about. Therefore, she had a welcoming smile on her face as she pulled to the curb before the dour old lady and pushed open the passenger door, calling, "Hello, Mother!"

"Hm," Edna commented. She stepped forward to climb into the car, then glanced up over its top at a passing vehicle and suddenly shouted, "God*damn*!"

Now, "god*damn*" was not something Edna said. It certainly wasn't something she ever shouted, and it absolutely positively wasn't something she would shout in the middle of the public street. Astounded, Myrtle gaped at her mother as Edna clambered into the car, slammed the door, pointed a trembling and bony finger at the windshield, and cried, "Follow that son of a bitch!"

Then she understood. Peering out, seeing a clean new tan automobile driving away from them down Main Street, Myrtle said, "My father again?"

"*Follow* him!"

Myrtle was, God knows, willing. Putting the Fairlane in gear, she pulled out onto Main Street just about a block behind that tan car, with only one other automobile in between. Weaving left and right to see past that intervening car, she could make out that the tan car was a new Cadillac Sedan de Ville, with MD plates. Myrtle, waiting impatiently for a chance to pass the extraneous car, said, "Is my father a doctor?"

"Hah!" Edna said. "He liked to *play* doctor plenty enough. Don't you lose him, now."

"I won't," Myrtle promised.

"What's he up to?" Edna muttered, beating her bony fist against the dashboard.

The car up ahead had four people in it, two in front and two in back. Maybe I'm going to get to know my father after all these years, Myrtle thought.

"Prick son of a bitch cocksucker."

And she was sure as heck getting to know her mother better, too.

CHAPTER TWENTY

Car following us," Kelp said.

Dortmunder, in the backseat with Wally, twisted around to look out the rear window. They'd just put yet another little town behind them, and three vehicles were visible back there, strung out along this country road flanked by forest and small clearings containing tiny aluminum-sided houses with dead automobiles in their front yards. "Which one?" Dortmunder asked. "The black Fairlane. The one right behind us."

The Fairlane was about three car lengths back; pretty close for a tail. Frowning at it, Dortmunder tried to make out the people inside through the sky-reflecting windshield. "You sure?" he said. "Looks to me like a couple women in there."

"Been right on our ass for miles," Kelp said.

"They don't act like pros," Dortmunder said.

Wally, excitement making his eyes and mouth wetter than usual, said, "Do you think they really are, Andy? Following us?"

Tom, up front next to Kelp, said, "One way to be sure. We'll circle once. If they're still with us, we'll take them out. Anybody carrying?"

"No," Dortmunder said.

Wally, very eager, said, "Carrying what?"

"You aren't," Dortmunder told him. "Don't worry about it."

"But what is it?" Wally asked. "Carrying what, John? What aren't I carrying?"

"A gun," Dortmunder explained, to shut him up, and Wally's eyes grew huge and even wetter with this new thrill.

Meanwhile, up front, Tom was saying, "There's a left just up ahead. You'll take it, then the next left, and it'll swing us back to this road just this side of that town we went through. If your Fairlane's still with us then, we'll have to get rid of them." Twisting around, he frowned at Dortmunder and said, "This peaceful impulse of yours, Al, you're letting it take over your life. You don't want to go around all the time without heat."

"As a matter of fact, I do," Dortmunder told him.

Tom grimaced and shook his head and faced front. They made the left, onto a smaller and narrower and curvier road. "The Fairlane made the turn," Kelp said, looking at the rearview mirror.

They drove along quietly then, the four of them in the purring Cadillac. Kelp had, as Dortmunder had known he would, come up with excellent transportation. And an extra passenger, too, since Kelp on his own had decided it would be a good idea to tell Wally the actual story here (which Tom hadn't liked one bit, but it was already done, so there you are) and bring the little butterball along so he could have a look at the actual terrain, to help him and his computer think about the problem better. So here they all were, the Unlikely Quartet, driving around the countryside.

Around and around. A few miles farther along this secondary road, just after a steep downgrade and a one-lane stonewalled bridge, they came to the second left, as Tom pointed out. Kelp took it, and looked in the mirror. "Still with us," he said.

"Heat would solve this problem," Tom commented.

"Heat brings heat," Dortmunder told the back of his head. Tom didn't bother to answer.

"I'll go around again," Kelp suggested, "and when we get to that one-lane bridge from before, I can squeeze them."

"A Caddy can beat a Fairlane," Tom pointed out. "Why not just floor this sucker?"

"I don't break speed limit laws in a borrowed car," Kelp told him.

Tom snorted but made no comments about the superior qualities of rented cars.

Dortmunder looked back, and the Fairlane was still on their tail, far too close for anybody who knew anything about surveillance. Unless somebody *wanted* them to know they were being followed. But why? And who were those two women? He said, "Tom, why would anybody follow you?"

"Me?" Tom said, looking over his shoulder. "Whadaya mean, me? How come it isn't one of you guys? Maybe they're computer salesmen, want to talk to Wally."

"The rest of us aren't known around here," Dortmunder said.

"Neither am I," Tom said. "Not after twenty-six years."

"I don't like it," Dortmunder said. "Right here in the neighborhood where we're supposed to do the main job, and we've got new players in the game."

"Here's the turn," Kelp said, and took it. Then he looked in the rearview mirror and said, "They kept going!"

Dortmunder looked back, and now there was no one behind them at all. "I don't get it," he said.

Wally, tentative about making suggestions among this crowd, said, "Maybe they were lost."

"No," Dortmunder said.

"Well, wait a second," Kelp said. "That's not entirely crazy, John."

"No?" Dortmunder studied Kelp's right ear. "How much crazy is it?" he asked.

"People get lost," Kelp said, "particularly in the country. Particularly in places like this, where everything's got the same name."

"Dudson," commented Tom.

"That's the name, all right," Kelp agreed. "How many Dudsons are there, anyway?"

"Let's see," Tom said, taking the question seriously. "North, East, Center, and Falls. Four."

"That's a lot of Dudsons," Kelp said.

"There used to be three more," Tom told him. "Dudson Park, Dudson City, and Dudson. They're all under the reservoir."

"Good," Kelp said. "Anyway, John, how about that? You go out for a nice ride in the country, all of a sudden everywhere you look another Dudson, you're lost, you don't know how to get back, you're driving in circles."

"*We* were the one driving in circles," Dortmunder said.

"I'm coming to that," Kelp promised. "So there you are, driving in circles, and you decide you'll pick another car and follow it until it *gets* somewhere. Only they picked us. So when we start going in circles, too, they figure we're *also* lost on account of all the Dudsons, so off they go."

"Sounds good to me," Tom said.

Timidly, Wally said, "It does make sense, John."

"I never seen that to matter much," Dortmunder commented. "But, okay, maybe you're all right. Nobody around here knows any of us, those two women didn't act like they knew how to tail anybody, and now they're gone."

"So there you are," Kelp said.

"There I am," Dortmunder agreed, frowning.

Tom said, "So *now* can we go pick up my stash?"

"Yes," Kelp said.

"Just the same," Dortmunder said, mostly to himself, "something tells me we got that Ford in our future."

CHAPTER TWENTY-ONE

"Mother," Myrtle said, keeping her attention straight out the windshield as they drove together through the twilight back toward Dudson Center, "you just *have* to tell me the truth."

"I don't see that at all," Edna said. "Keep your eyes on the road."

"My eyes *are* on the road. Mother, please! I have the right to know about my own father."

"The right!" Even for Edna, that word was flung out with startling fury. "Did *I* have the right to know him? I thought I did, but I was wrong. He knew *me*, God knows, and here you are."

"You've never said a word about him." Myrtle found herself awed by it, by Edna's years of silence, by her own blithe acceptance of the status quo, never questioning, never wondering. "Can he be that bad?" she asked, believing the answer would simply have to be *no*.

But the answer was, "He's worse. Take my word for it."

"But how can I?" Myrtle pleaded. "How can I take your word, when you don't *give* me any words? Mother, I've always tried to be a good daughter, I've always—"

"You have," Edna said, suddenly quieter, less agitated. Myrtle risked a quick sidelong glance, and Edna was now brooding at the dashboard, as though the words *mene mene tekel upharsin* had suddenly appeared there. Myrtle was surprised and touched to see this softening of her mother's features. Imperfectly seen though her face might be in the light of dusk, some harsh level of reserve or defense was abruptly gone.

And abruptly back: "Watch the road!"

Myrtle's eyes snapped forward. The two-lane blacktop road was now bringing them past the Mexican restaurant at the edge of Dudson Center; they were less than fifteen minutes from home.

Myrtle hadn't at all wanted to give up the pursuit. It was true the people in the backseat of the Cadillac kept turning around to look at her, it was true the Cadillac was driving in circles around the countryside, it was true these things suggested they'd realized they were being followed and therefore had no intention of going on to their original destination until she stopped following them, but what did any of that matter? She didn't care where they were going, she cared only about *who they were*. Or not even all of them, only the one: her father. To her way of thinking, if she followed them long enough, if she made her presence both obvious and inevitable, sooner or later wouldn't they have to either arrive somewhere, or at least *stop* somewhere, so that she could get out of her car and go look at them, see them, talk to them? Talk to *him*?

But Edna had said no. "They're on to us," she snarled out of the side of her mouth, displaying another previously unknown side to her personality. "Forget it, Myrtle. We'll go home."

"But we're so close! If we lose them—"

"We won't lose that son of a bitch," Edna had said grimly. "If he's back—and he's back, all right, damn his eyes—one of these black days he'll come around, you see if he doesn't. It's only a matter of time. Myrtle, if they take that goddamn left again up there, you *don't* follow them! You go straight ahead!"

And the Cadillac *had* taken the g———left, and obedient Myrtle, the good daughter, had gone straight ahead. And now they were almost home, the adventure almost finished, long before it had ever really begun. Myrtle had no faith in her mother's conviction that her father would "come around" one of these days, black or otherwise; after all these years, why should he?

And he'd been so close!

Once Mother gets out of this car, Myrtle thought, I've lost the truth forever. "Please," she said, so faintly she wasn't sure Edna would be able to hear her at all.

The answer was a sigh; another surprising example of softness. In a voice so gentle as to be almost unrecognizable, Edna said, "Don't ask me these things, Myrtle."

Her own voice as soft as her mother's, Myrtle said, "But it hurts not to know."

"It never used to," Edna said with a return of her normal tartness.

"Well, it does now," Myrtle said. "Knowing you just won't *talk* about it."

"For Christ's sake, Myrtle," Edna cried, "don't you think it hurts *me*? Don't you think that's why I don't *want* to talk about the goddamn man?"

"You must have loved him very much," Myrtle said, gently and consolingly, the way they do such scenes in the movies. She'd never imagined the day would come when she'd play such a scene herself.

"God knows," Edna answered bitterly. "I suppose, at the time, I must have thought I . . ." But then she shook her head, eyes flashing. Sharply she said, "And what did I get out of it?"

"Well, me," Myrtle reminded her, and tried a little smile, saying, "That wasn't so bad, was it?"

"At the time?" Edna's answering smile was twisted and lived only on one side of her face. "It wasn't so wonderful, either, back then. Not in North Dudson."

"I can't even imagine it."

Edna cocked an eye at her as Myrtle stopped for a red light on Main Street. Ahead, the windows of the library gleamed yellow in the gloaming. "No, I don't suppose you can imagine it," Edna said. "Did I do that to you? Well, I guess I did."

"Do what to me?"

"The light's green," Edna said.

Myrtle, feeling an impatience and an irritation that were rare in her, looked out at the green light and tromped down on the accelerator. The Ford bucked across the intersection, not quite stalling, but then Myrtle settled down to her normal way of driving.

Musingly, not even having noticed Myrtle's *jack rabbit start*—which is what she would have called it, with withering disapproval, under normal circumstances—Edna said, "I brought you up to be careful, cautious, obedient, mild. . . ."

Laughing, but awkward and self-conscious, Myrtle said, "You make me sound like a Girl Scout."

"You are a Girl Scout," her mother told her, without pleasure. "I wasn't brought up that way," she went on. "I was brought up to be independent, make up my own mind, take my own chances. And what did it get me? Tom Jimson. That's why I went the other way with you."

Excited, Myrtle said, "Tom Jimson? Is that his name?"

"I'm not even sure of that much," Edna said. "It's one of the names he told me. The one he told me most often, so maybe it's his."

"What was he like?" Myrtle asked.

"Satan," Edna said.

"Oh, Mother," Myrtle said, and smiled in condescension. She knew this story. Edna had been madly in love with . . . Tom Jimson . . . and he'd abandoned her, pregnant and unwed, and the hurt was still there. *Now* Edna thought he was Satan. *Then* she'd loved him. So how bad, really, could he be?

Myrtle made the turn onto Elm Street, and then the turn onto Albany Street. Ahead lay Spring Street, and beyond that Myrtle Street. "Myrtle Jimson," she said softly, testing the sound of it.

"Hah!" Edna snorted. "That was *never* in it, believe me!"

"I wonder where they were going," Myrtle said.

"Well, not to church," Edna told her. "I can tell you that much."

CHAPTER TWENTY-TWO

The church was beautiful in the waning light of day. A small white clapboard structure with a graceful steeple, it nestled into its rustic setting like a diamond in a fold of green felt. The hillside behind it was a rich tumble of evergreens mixed with stands of beech and birch and oak, falling away to well-manicured lawn that swept like a thick-piled carpet around the tidy white building with its oval-topped stained-glass windows well spaced along both side walls.

The road outside, Church Lane, curving up into these foothills from State Highway 112, came nowhere but here, to the Elizabeth Grace Dudson Memorial Reformed Congregational Unitarian Church of Putkin Township. (Five different churches, and five separate congregations, had been combined down to this one, absorbing the remnants of churches flooded by the reservoir or emptied by shrinking attendance.) Since Church Lane ended here, the road simply ballooned at its terminus into a large parking area, from which the asphalt path ran straight up the slight incline to the church front door. The white of the church, the rich indigos and maroons and golds and olives of the stained-glass windows, the varied greens of the surrounding lawn and hillside, the bottomless black of the asphalt, were never more beautiful than now, in the fading light at the end of another perfect day.

And even more beautiful than the church and its setting was the bride, blushing pink in her swaths of organdy white, climbing from the family station wagon with her parents and baby sister. They were the first arrivals, half an hour before the scheduled ceremony, father looking uncomfortable and thick-fingered in his awkwardly fitting dark suit and badly knotted red tie, baby sister an excited bonbon in puffy peach, mother beribboned and bowed in lavender, dabbing at her tear-filled eyes with a lavender hankie and saying, "I *told* you not to go all the way, you little tramp. Just get him off with your *hand*, for heaven's sake! Oh, I *so* wanted a June wedding!"

"*Mother!*" the bride replied, elaborately ill-tempered. "I'll be *showing* by then."

"Let's get this thing over with," said father, and led the way heavy-footed up the path and into the church.

Snickering cousins of the bride came next, some to be ushers and flower girls, some just to hang out, and two burly fellows in blocky wool jackets who'd volunteered to be parking lot attendants, to see to it that all of the cars of all of the guests would fit in this space at the end of Church Lane.

Relatives of the bride continued to predominate for the first ten minutes or so; giggling awkward large-jointed people wearing their "best" clothes, saved for weddings, funerals, Easter, and appearances in court. Soon this group began to be supplemented by members of the groom's family: skinnier, shorter, snake-hipped people with can-opener noses and no asses, dressed in Naugahyde jackets and polyester shirts and vinyl trousers and plastic shoes, as though they weren't human beings at all but were actually a chain dental service's waiting room. Intermixed with these, in warm-up jackets and pressed designer jeans, were the groom's pals, acne-flaring youths full of sidelong looks and nervous laughter, knowing this was more than likely a foretaste of their own doom: "There but for the grace of the Akron Rubber Company go I." The bride's girlfriends arrived in a too-crowded-car cluster and hovered together like magnetized iron filings, all demonstrating the latest soap opera fashion trends and each of them a sealed bubble of self-consciousness and self-absorption. The groom, a jerky marionette in a rented tux, a wide-eyed pale-faced boy with spiky hair and protuberant ears, appeared with his grim suspicious parents and entered the church with all the false macho assurance of Jimmy Cagney on his way to the electric chair. The church door shut behind him with a hollower boom than it had given anyone else.

As the hour of the service approached, the last few cars, each with its couple snarlingly blaming each other for causing them to be late, came tearing up Church Lane and was slotted into one of the remaining spaces by the volunteer attendants. And then it was TIME. The attendants grinned at each other, pleased with their accomplishment, and were about to turn and enter the church themselves when headlights alerted them to one last car load of wedding guests. "They *are* gonna be late!" one attendant told the other, and both stepped out to the road to wave frantically at the oncoming car to get a move on.

Instead of which, at first it slowed down, as though the driver were suddenly uncertain of his welcome. "Come on, come on!" shouted an attendant, and ran forward, still waving. The car was a new Caddy—a lot better than *most* of the cars here—and the driver had the narrow nose and bewildered expression that suggested to the attendants (cousins of the bride) that these people represented the groom's side.

"Park over there!" the attendant yelled, pointing at one of the few remaining slots.

The driver had lowered his window, the better to display his confusion. He said, "The church . . . ?"

"That's right! That's right! There's the church right there, it's the only thing on this *road*! Come on, will ya, you're late!"

Someone in the car said something to the driver, who nodded and said, "I guess we might as well."

So then at last the Caddy was driven to its slot, all four of its doors opened, and a bunch of extremely unlikely wedding guests emerged. The attendants, waiting for them, exchanged a knowing glance that silently said, *Groom's side, no question.* Along with the sharp-nosed driver were a short fat round troll, a gloomy slope-shouldered guy, and a mean-looking old geezer. Shepherded by the attendants, these four made their way up the walk and into the now-full church, where the ceremony hadn't yet begun after all, having been delayed by both a sudden loss of courage on the groom's part (being treated now from an uncle's flask) and a screaming cat fight between the bride and her mother.

A tuxedoed usher approached the latecomers, while the attendants went off to the seats saved for them by other cousins. Leaning toward the new arrivals, the usher murmured, "Bride or groom?"

They stared at him. The sharp-nosed one said, "Huh?"

The usher was used by now to the wedding guests being under-rehearsed. Patiently, gesturing to the pews on both sides of the central aisle, he said, "Are you with the bride's party or the groom's?"

"Oh," said the sharp-nosed one.

"Bride," said the mean-looking old man, but at the same instant, "Groom," said the pessimistic-looking guy.

This under-rehearsed was ridiculous. "Surely," the usher began, "you know whi—"

"*We're* with the groom," the pessimist explained. "*They're* with the bride."

"Oh," the usher said, and looked around for empty seats on both sides of the aisle. "Here's two for the bridal party," he said, "and two over—"

He broke off, astonished, because the group seemed to be arguing fiercely and almost silently among themselves as to which of them was to be with which. Noticing him noticing them, they cut that business short and sorted themselves out with no further trouble, except for sharp looks back and forth. The usher seated the pessimist and the little round man among the bride's family and friends, then placed the mean-looking old man and the sharp-nosed fellow in among the partisans of the groom.

As he did so, the uncle with the flask (tucked away out of sight) emerged from a side door down by the altar and made his somewhat unsteady way (he'd been medicating himself as well, since the cap was off anyway) to his seat on the aisle down near the front on the groom's side. He was still settling himself and grinning his report on the groom's condition to his neighbors when the mother of the bride, rather red of face and grim of expression, but with shoulders triumphantly squared, came from the rear of the church, escorted by an usher, and marched down the center aisle to sit in the front row.

A moment of extremely suspenseful silence ensued, during which the minister's wife, out of sight in the vestry, placed the needle on the turning record, and a scratchy but full-throated version of Mendelssohn's "Wedding March" poured forth from the speakers mounted high in the four corners of the nave.

As the music swelled and the minister came out of the vestry to stand by the chancel rail, the mean-looking old guy with the bridal party gave a disgusted look across the aisle at the pessimist among the groom's people. The pessimist gave him the disgusted look right back, then shook his head and sat back to watch the wedding.

The music stopped. The speakers in the corners of the nave said, "Tick . . . tick . . . ti—" And stopped.

The minister stepped forward, crossing the front of the church behind the chancel rail, smiling bland encouragement at the parents and immediate family in the front row. He was a round-faced round-shouldered slender amiable man with a round sparsely haired head and round highly reflecting spectacles, and he wore thick-soled black shoes like a cop and a long-sleeved black dress with a white dickey at the neck. The black dress showed off his round potbelly as he crossed to the pulpit and climbed the circular staircase.

On the bride's side of the aisle, the mean-looking old guy leaned forward and looked significantly across the aisle at the pessimist, who didn't seem to want to have his eye caught. But the old guy kept nodding, and widening his eyes, and waving his eyebrows, until finally everybody else in the immediate area was in on it, so then at last the pessimist turned and nodded—"I know, I know"—which didn't keep the old guy from pointing very significantly with his eyebrows and ears and elbows and nose and temples toward the general area of the pulpit and the climbing minister. The pessimist sighed and folded his arms and faced determinedly forward. The little dumpling beside him kept looking back and forth between the pessimist and the old guy, open-mouthed and eager. Next to the old guy, the sharp-nosed fellow ignored the whole thing, concentrating instead on the cleavage in the dress of the friend of the bride on his other side.

Meantime, the minister had attained the pulpit, from where he beamed out amiably upon his congregation. After pausing to adjust the microphone on its gooseneck stalk in front of him, at last he said, "Well, we all want to thank Felix Mendelssohn for sharing that wonderful music with us. And now, if you'll all rise."

Shckr—shckr—shckr*oop*.

"Very good, very good." The minister's face and smile were at the pulpit, but his voice came from the four upper corners of the nave. "And now," he said, "we will all turn to our neighbor, and we will greet our neighbor with a handshake and a hug."

Embarrassed laughter and throat-clearing filled the church, but everyone (except the mean-looking old guy) obeyed. The sharp-nosed fellow very enthusiastically embraced the friend of the bride next to him, while the pessimist and the dumpling hugged each other in a much more gingerly fashion.

"Very good, very good," the minister's voice boomed down at them from the four corners of the nave. "Resume your seats, resume your seats."

Schlff—schlff—*fflrp*.

"Very good." The minister's eyeglasses reflected the interior of the church, creating gothic wonders where none in fact existed. Beaming around at the congregation, giving them back this much more interesting reflection of themselves, he said, "We have come here this evening, in the sight of God and man, mindful of the laws of God and the laws of the State of New York, to join in holy wedlock Tiffany and Bob."

He paused. He beamed his sweet smile into the farthest corner of his domain. He said, "You know, the blessed state of matrimony . . . ."

His voice went on, for some extended time, but the words did not enter one brain in that church. A great glazed comatosity o'ercame the congregation, a state of slow enchantment like that in the forest in *A Midsummer Night's Dream*. Like the residents of Brigadoon, the people in the church drifted in a long and dreamless sleep, freed of struggle and expectation.

". . . . . with Bob. Bob?"

A slow sigh escaped the slumbering assembly, a faint and lingering breath. Shoulders moved, hands twitched in laps, bottoms shifted on the wooden pews. Eyes began to focus, and there was Bob, as if by magic, a bowed beanpole inaptly in a black tux at the head of the central aisle, standing with his look-alike best man—slightly heavier, grinning in nervous relief, left hand clutching jacket pocket (no doubt to feel the ring still safe within)—the two of them in profile to the crowd, Bob blinking like the terrorists' kidnap victim he was, the beaming minister descending the pulpit and striding toward the lectern set up just within the chancel rail. The speakers in the corners, said, "Tick . . . tick . . . tick . . ." and a slow, heavy-beated, orchestral version of "Here Comes the Bride" battered the people below.

Now it all began to move. Tiffany, on her father's arm, and her attendants made their uncertain way down the aisle, trying but failing to keep pace with the music, stumbling and tripping prettily along, concentrating so totally on their feet that they forgot to be self-conscious. Bob watched them as though they were an approaching truck.

Bride and groom met in front of the lectern and turned to face the minister, who beamed over their heads at the people and announced, "Bob and Tiffany have written their own wedding service," and everybody went back to sleep.

When they awoke, the deed was done. "You may kiss the bride," the minister said, and some smart-aleck pal of the groom said, "That's about the only thing he *hasn't* done to her," perhaps a little more loudly than he'd intended.

Bride and groom made their hasty grinning way up the aisle as the congregation stood and stretched and talked and cheered them on, and from the speakers high above came the Beatles' "I Want to Hold Your Hand." The mean-looking old guy turned to the sharp-nosed fellow and said, "If I had a gun, I'd shoot somebody."

"I wouldn't know where to start," the sharp-nosed fellow answered in agreement.

"How about with these two?" the mean-looking old guy said as the happy couple hurried past.

Across the aisle, the round troll dabbed his moist eyes and said, "Gee, that was nice. Better even than Princess Labia's wedding." The pessimist sighed.

Most weddings take place in daylight, but there'd been a certain urgency in the planning of this one, and all the potential daytime slots here at Elizabeth Grace Dudson Memorial Reformed Congregational Unitarian Church of Putkin Township had already been taken. The mother of the bride had been determined that her daughter would have a church wedding, and women who successfully name their infant daughters Tiffany do tend to get their own way, so an evening wedding it was. Exterior lights had been turned on at the end of the ceremony, so that when the wedding party emerged, laughing and shouting and throwing superfluous rice (it was unnecessary to wish fecundity upon Tiffany and Bob), the scene looked more like a movie than real life. Many of the revelers, becoming aware of this, started to *perform* wedding guests rather than *be* wedding guests, which merely increased the general air of unreality.

Inside, the church was nearly empty. The minister chatted up front with a small group of ladies, a few other relatives and friends drifted slowly doorward, and the four latecomers sat stolid in their pews, as though waiting for the second show. A departing aunt said to them, "Aren't you coming to the party?"

"Sure," said the pessimist.

She continued on. "Come along, now," said another exiting in-law.

"Be there in a minute," the sharp-nosed fellow assured her.

"It's over, you know," kidded a grandmother with a grandmotherly twinkle.

Twinkling right back, the butterball said, "We're looking at the pretty windows."

The minister, passing with the last of the ladies, smiled upon the quartet and said, "We'll be closing up now."

The mean-looking old guy nodded. "We wanna pray a little more," he said.

The minister seemed taken aback at that idea, but rallied. "We must all pray," he agreed, "for long life and joy for Tiffany and Bob."

"You bet," said the mean-looking old guy.

The pessimist slowly turned his head—his neck made faint cracking sounds—to watch the minister and the final few of his flock amble on to the door and out. "Jeez," he said. Which *was* a prayer.

CHAPTER TWENTY-THREE

J eez," said Dortmunder.

Across the aisle, Kelp said, "Okay, Tom? Okay? Can we get it now?"

Sullen, Tom said, "It wasn't my idea to come to a *wedding*."

"It was your idea," Kelp reminded him, "to stash your stash in a church."

"Where's a better place?" Tom wanted to know.

Dortmunder rose, all of his joints creaking and cracking and aching. "Are you two," he wanted to know, "just gonna sit there and *converse*?"

So everybody else stood up at last, their knees and hips and elbows making sounds like gunshots, and Tom said, "Won't take but two minutes now that the goddamn crowd is gone."

He stepped out to the aisle, turned toward the front of the church, and a voice back at the door said, "Gentlemen, I really must ask you to leave now. Silent prayer in one's home or automobile is just as efficacious—"

It was the minister again, coming down the aisle at them. Tom gave him a disgusted look and said, "Enough is enough. Hold that turkey."

"Right," said Kelp.

As Tom walked down the aisle and Wally gaped at everything in fascinated interest—the true spectator—Dortmunder and Kelp approached the minister, who became too belatedly alarmed, backing away, his voice rising toward treble as he said, "What are—? You can't— This is a place of worship!"

"Sssshhh," Kelp advised, soothingly, putting his hand on the minister's arm. When the minister tried to pull away, Kelp's hand tightened its grip, and Dortmunder took hold of the sky pilot's other arm, saying, "Take it easy, pal."

"Little man," Kelp said, "you've had a busy day. Just gentle down, now."

The minister stared through his round spectacles at the front of his church, saying, "What's that man doing?"

"Won't take a minute," Dortmunder explained.

Up front, Tom had approached the pulpit, which was an octagonal wooden basket or crow's nest built on several sturdy legs. The underpart of the pulpit was faced by latticed panels inset between the legs, the whole thing stained and polished to the shade generally known as "a burnished hue." Tom bent to stick his fingers through the diamond-shaped holes in the latticework panel around on the side, half hidden by the circular stairs. He poked and tugged on this, but the last time that panel had been moved was thirty-one years earlier, and Tom had been the one to move it. In the interim, heat and cold and moisture and dryness and time itself had done their work, and the panel was now well and truly stuck. Tom yanked and pushed and prodded, and nothing at all happened.

At the other end of the church, the minister continued to stare at these suddenly hostile wedding guests, trying to remember his emergency-techniques training. He knew any number of ways to calm a person in a traumatic or panic-inducing situation, but they all worked on the assumption that *he* was an outside observer—a skilled and concerned and compassionate observer, it is true, but *outside*. None of the techniques seemed to have much relevance when *he* was the one in a panic. "Um," he said.

"Hush," Kelp told him.

But he couldn't hush. "Violence is no way to solve problems," he told them.

"Oh, I don't know," Dortmunder said. "It's never let me down."

From the front of the church, underlining the point, came a crash, as Tom, exasperated beyond endurance, stood up, stepped back, and kicked the pulpit in the lattice, which smashed to kindling. The minister jumped like Bambi's mother in Dortmunder and Kelp's hands. They held him in place, quivering, while Wally, excitement making him seem taller but on the other hand wider, waddled hurriedly to the front of the church to see what was going on.

Up there, Tom was on his knees again, pulling out from inside the pulpit an old black cracked-leather doctor's bag with a rusted-out clasp. "There's the son of a bitch," he said, with satisfaction.

"Gee!" Wally said. "The treasure in the pulpit!"

Tom gave him a look. "That's right," he said, and carried the bag down the aisle toward the others, Wally bouncing along like a living beachball in his wake.

"Is that it?" Dortmunder asked. "Can we go now?"

"This is it," Tom acknowledged, "and we can go in a minute. Hold on here." He put the doctor's bag on a handy pew and fiddled for a while with the clasp. "Fucking thing's rusted shut," he said.

Shocked, the minister blurted, "Language!"

Everybody looked at him, even Wally. Tom said, "How come that's talking?"

"I really don't know," Kelp said, studying the minister with unfriendly interest. "But I don't think it's gonna happen again."

Taking a good-size clasp knife from his pocket and opening it, Tom said, "I hear from him again, I take his tongue out."

"Drastic," Kelp suggested calmly, "but probably effective."

"Very."

The minister stared round-eyed at the knife as Tom used it to slice through the old dry leather around the clasp, freeing the bag, opening it, and then putting the knife away. The minister sighed audibly when the knife disappeared, and his eyes rolled briefly in his head.

Tom reached into the bag, pulled out a wad of bills, peeled off a few, dropped the wad back into the bag, and turned to slap the bills into the minister's enfeebled hand. Since the minister couldn't seem to do it for himself, Tom closed his fingers around the money for him, saying, "Here's half a grand to fix up the pulpit. Keep your nose clean." To the others he said, "*Now* we can go."

Dortmunder and Kelp released the minister, who staggered backward against a pew. Ignoring him, the others headed for the door, Dortmunder saying to Tom, "You're a generous guy. I never knew that."

"That's me, okay," Tom said. "Ever surprising."

As they reached the door, the minister, beginning to recover from his fright, called after them, "Don't you want a receipt? For your taxes?" But they didn't answer.

CHAPTER TWENTY-FOUR

All was quiet in East Amity, a tiny bedroom community on the south shore of Long Island. Well after midnight, and the commuters were all tucked between their sheets, dreaming of traffic jams, while out on the village streets there was no traffic at all. The village police car drove by, all alone, down Bay Boulevard, idling along, Officer Pohlax yawning at the wheel, barely aware of the boutiques and tire stores he was here to protect. Ahead on the left bulked Southern Suffolk Combined High School (*yay!*), from which Officer Pohlax himself had graduated just a very few years earlier.

How old it made him feel now, still in his twenties, to look at the old school and remember that feeling of infinite possibility back then, the absolute conviction that a determined fellow, if he kept himself in shape and didn't drink too much, could eventually sleep with every girl in the world. Various girls he had and had not slept with during those halcyon days drifted through his mind, every one with the same identical smile, and he and his police car drifted on past the high school, wafted by the gusts of imperfect memory.

Doug Berry, at the wheel of his black pickup with the blue-and-silver styling package, watched that goddamn slow-moving police car inch by and tapped impatient fingers against the steering wheel. He was parked on a dark side street across from the high school, engine running but lights off, waiting for the coast to be clear. He knew that would be old Billy Pohlax at the wheel—they'd gone to high school together, that very high school across the street, way back when—and he knew Billy wouldn't pass by here again for at least an hour. Which should be plenty of time, if his students showed up when they were supposed to.

Three blocks away, brake lights gleamed like rubies on the village police car, which then made a right off Bay Boulevard, heading down to the docks and marinas along the waterfront. Doug slipped the pickup into gear, left the lights off, and scooted across Bay and onto the driveway leading up to the big parking lot wrapped halfway around the school, on its left side and rear. Doug drove around to the back, the equipment in the bed of his vehicle thumping and clanking from time to time, and pulled in close up against the rear door to which he had bought the key, just the other day, from another old classmate, now an assistant building custodian (janitor) at this same school.

Doug opened his pickup's door, the interior light went on, and he slammed the door again, scared out of his wits. The light! He'd forgotten about the light! If somebody saw him . . .

Was there a way to turn off that damn light? Trying to study the dashboard in the dark, he succeeded only in briefly switching on the dashboard lights. Finally, he decided the only thing to do was chance it, and move as fast as he could. Pop open the door (*light on!*), scramble out, close the door rapidly without slamming it (light off), sag in relief against the side of the pickup.

Okay, okay. No problem. Not a single light showed in any of the houses on Margiotta Street, out behind the high school. No one had seen him. There was nothing to worry about.

Reassuring himself like mad, Doug went over to the door, tried the key, and was relieved, faintly surprised, and also faintly disappointed, when it worked and the door swung open. Standing in the open doorway, he was about to check the time on his waterproof, shockproof, glow-in-the-dark watch/compass/calendar when motion made him look up to see a long black car—a Mercedes, he realized—traveling without lights and just coming to a stop next to his pickup. In the extreme dimness, he could just make out the MD plate on the Mercedes, which was a real surprise. Those guys weren't doctors. Standards haven't slipped *that* much.

Both front doors of the Mercedes opened, without the interior light going on. (How did they *do* that?) Andy was the driver, John the passenger. They shut the car doors quietly and approached, Andy saying, "Right on time."

"I've got the door open," Doug announced, unnecessarily, since he was standing in it. Then he gestured at the pickup, saying, "All the gear's here. It weighs a ton."

It did, too. Wearing half the stuff and carrying the rest, the three staggered into the school building, Doug closing the door behind them and then leading the way with his pencil flash along the wide empty dark corridor—that well-remembered smell of school!—to the stairs, and then down the long flight and along the next corridor—not quite so wide down here—to the double swinging doors leading to the boys' locker room, and through it to the entrance to the pool. An interior room in the basement, the pool area had no windows, and so there was no reason not to turn on lights, which Doug did: all of them, revealing great expanses of beige tile and heavily chlorinated water. Footsteps and voices echoed wetly in here, so you always had the feeling there was somebody else around, just behind you or on the other side of the pool.

The two students looked at that great ocean in the bottom of the school building, and Andy said, "Where's the shallow end?"

"It's the deep end we want," Doug told him. "Right here. Let's get our gear on."

"At the real place," Andy said, "we're just gonna walk in."

"Look, guys," Doug said. "That was your decision, that I'm not going to the real place with you. So I arranged for us to use this pool. And believe me, wherever it is you're gonna walk into, when you get fifty feet deep it's gonna be a lot farther down than the deep end of this pool."

They both took a moment to look into the pool, contemplating that truth. Then John sighed and shook his head and said, "Okay, we've come this far. Let's do it."

"Fine," Doug said. "We'll get out of our street clothes, into our swimsuits and our wetsuits and all our gear, and get *to* it."

Two less athletic or more reluctant students Doug had never had. They didn't like their wet suits, they didn't like the way the tank straps felt on their shoulders, they didn't like the weight belts around their waists (he'd given them each fourteen pounds), they didn't like their masks, they *hated* their BCDs. Finally, Doug said, "Look guys, the idea was, you wanted to do this, remember? I'm not forcing you into it."

John held up his BCD, a thing that looked like a larger and more elaborate life vest, and said, "What *is* this thing, anyway?"

"A BCD," Doug told him.

Which didn't seem to help much. "That's the alphabet," Andy pointed out. "A, B, C, D."

"No, no," Doug said. "Not *A* BCD, *a* BCD. Buoyancy Control Device. Simply, the amount of air you put in the BCD determines at what level you hover when you're underwater."

"When *I'm* underwater," John said, "I generally hover at the bottom."

"Not with the BCD," Doug assured him. "Let me demonstrate."

"Go right ahead," John said.

So Doug went into the pool, wearing all the gear and with the BCD inflated enough to keep him at the surface. Head out of the water, he said, "I'm going to raise my arm and press the button on the top of the control to release some of the air from the BCD. This pool is only eight feet deep, so I can't descend very far, but I'll hover in the water, *above* the bottom, and then I'll add air to the BCD from my tank, and I'll rise again. Now, watch."

They looked at each other. Doug said, "Watch *me*."

"We're watching," John said.

So Doug did exactly as he'd announced he would do, keeping his knees bent upward so his feet wouldn't touch the bottom when he floated downward. He hovered near the bottom for a while, then lay out flat and stroked across the pool, the BCD maintaining his depth at about five feet. Stroking back, he added air and rose to the surface. Looking at those two skeptical faces, he said, "See how easy?"

"Sure," said John.

"So let's do it," Doug said. "Jump on in."

No. They would not "jump on in"; no matter how he assured them they wouldn't sink, they insisted on going down to the shallow end and coming down the steps there. And even then, they were barely knee deep when both stopped. Looking as startled as a man whose face is encumbered with mask and mouthpiece can possibly look, Andy cried, "This suit doesn't work!"

"Sure it does," Doug told him. I'm *earning* my thousand dollars, he told himself. "Come on in, fellas."

"It's wet inside the suit!"

John said, more quietly and fatalistically, "Inside mine, too."

"It's supposed to do that," Doug explained, holding to the side of the pool at the deep end. "The wet suit is Neoprene rubber. It lets a layer of water in. Your body warms the water, the suit holds it in, and you stay warm."

"But *wet!*" Andy complained.

Doug shook his head, losing heart. "I don't know, guys," he said. "Maybe you just aren't cut out for this."

"No," John said, "it's okay. Just so we know the score. If that's the way it's supposed to work, okay, then. Come on, Andy," he said, and plowed on into the water with the expression of a man tasting his aunt's favorite eggplant recipe.

Once he actually got his students in the water, Doug's problems *really* began. These two guys simply did not want to breathe underwater. They'd descend, mouthpiece clamped in teeth, eyes wide behind the goggles, and they'd *hold their breath*. Eventually, asphyxiating, they'd surface and take in great huge gulps of air.

"Oh, come on, fellas," Doug kept saying. "That's *air* in that tank on your back. *Use* some of it." But they wouldn't.

Eventually, Doug saw that drastic measures were the *only* measures with these guys. Climbing out of the pool, but still wearing all his equipment in case of trouble, he convinced and cajoled them toward the deeper end. Their BCDs were full, of course, so they couldn't sink, and they kept holding to the edge, but at least they were in water that was theoretically over their heads.

Now to turn theory into practice. Gently but firmly disengaging their clutching fingers from the pool's rim, Doug shoved each of them away toward the middle. As buoyant as Macy's parade floats, they drifted in the middle of the pool, blinking at him through their glass masks.

"Fine," Doug told them, standing at the edge of the pool. "Mouthpiece in mouth. Are you breathing through your mouthpieces?"

They nodded. Above the water, they were happy to use scuba air.

"Fine," Doug said. "Now we'll test another part of the equipment. Don't worry, nothing's going to happen. Each of you, lift your left arm. You know the silver button on that control there? Fine. Press it."

Trustingly, they pressed it. Astounded, they sank.

Doug looked down through the water at their shifting swaying images. They were standing on the bottom of the pool, staring at each other in horror and shock. At this point, they would either panic and have to be rescued, in which case everybody could go home because the whole idea was impossible, or they would learn to *breathe*. Doug watched, and waited.

Bubbles. First from John, then from Andy. Bubbles; they were breathing.

Doug smiled, conscious of that rare swell of pride and accomplishment that teachers attain all too seldom, and a voice behind him screamed, *"AAAKKK! Spaceman! Don't move! Don't move!"*

Doug about jumped into the pool. He did jump, but in a circle, landing to face Billy Pohlax, Officer William Pohlax, the beat cop who wasn't supposed to be around this area for at least another half hour, but who was in this school, in the doorway to this very room, not twenty feet from the pool, shakily pointing a gun in Doug's general direction. Billy was so obviously terrified, so out of control, that his gun could surely go off at any second.

Doug cried, "Billy! Billy, it's me, Doug!"

"Don't move, don't move!" Fear, fortunately, was keeping Billy way back in the doorway, where he couldn't see the people inside the pool.

Doug froze. "I just want to show you my face, Billy. Remember me? Doug Berry?"

"Doug?" Billy's trembling perceptibly eased.

Doug risked lifting his hands to his head, removing the mask and mouthpiece, showing his white face to Billy's white face.

And Billy sagged with relief, saying, "Jeez, Doug, I thought you were a man from Mars or something. They had that movie *Cat People* on the box the other night, d'jever see that?"

"No," Doug said.

Looking around, Billy said, "Anybody else here?" He took a step forward into the room.

"Uhhh, no," Doug said, and moved casually but quickly to join Billy at the doorway. "What I'm doing here, Billy," he explained, "Jack Holsem let me have a key, you remember Jack?" Subtly, he moved in a half circle, turning Billy away from the pool.

"Sure," Billy said. "Dumbest kid in school. Works here now."

A three-quarter turn away from the pool was the best Doug could make Billy do. "Still in school," he said, and tried a casual grin, just to see if he could do it. "Anyway, I don't have any place to try out new equipment, test it, you know. This time of year, the bay's too cold."

"Yeah, I guess it would be," Billy agreed.

"Listen, Billy," Doug said, being very confidential, pressing hard on their old friendship, "I'm not supposed to be here, you know. Jack wasn't supposed to let me have the key. But I'm not *stealing* anything or anything, not doing—"

"Yeah, yeah, I get it," Billy said, looking down, watching himself with awkward intensity shove his gun back into its holster.

"I don't want to get Jack in trouble," Doug said, and over Billy's shoulder he saw John and Andy's heads emerge, way down at the shallow end of the pool. They were walking out! But then they turned and saw him talking to the cop, the quite obvious cop, and without even pausing they reversed direction and plodded stolidly back underwater again.

Oh, very good! Very smart! Doug, turning his relief into good fellowship, said, "Billy? You can forget about this, can't you? For Jack's sake?"

"Sure," Billy said. "You I don't have to worry about. But what about that stolen car out there?"

"Stolen car," Doug echoed, while his stomach joined John and Andy at the bottom of the pool.

"Mercedes," Billy explained. "MD plates. Reported stolen in the city about an hour ago. I came back behind the school"—and he grinned sheepishly—"to tell you the truth, Doug, I was gonna coop a little."

Doug didn't know the word. "Coop?"

"Take a little nap," Billy translated. "Back behind the school here's the perfect place. Anyway, I recognized your pickup, you know, because of the bumper sticker, and right next to it's this stolen Merc." Consciously becoming more formal, more official, Billy said, "You want to tell me about that, Doug?"

"A stolen Mercedes?" Doug's mind skittered with a million unhelpful thoughts.

"MD plates," Billy amplified. "What about it?"

"I don't know," Doug said, floundering. "What about it?"

"You don't know anything about this car?"

"Well, no," Doug said, as innocent as anything. "It wasn't there when I parked the pickup. I've been down here maybe half an hour. They must've left it there after I came down."

"Abandoned it," Billy decided, nodding in agreement. "Okay, Doug. I better go report it. You ready to get out of here?"

"Aw, gee, Billy," Doug said. "I've still got another, I don't know, ten, fifteen, maybe twenty minutes to do down here, testing, uh, equipment. Can't I, uh—"

"Well, the thing is," Billy said, "our department wrecker's gonna come here for the Merc. If they see your pickup, you know, the least I'll have to do is give you a ticket. There's no parking behind the school after ten P.M. except on game nights."

"Well, uh . . ." He couldn't leave John and Andy in the bottom of the pool for the rest of their lives! "Give me, uh, Billy, give me just five minutes, okay?"

"Well, a couple minutes," Billy agreed reluctantly. "But I can't be away from my post, away from the radio—"

"You go back to the radio," Doug told him. "I'll just finish up down here. I'll be right out."

"Now, don't take too long," Billy said.

"No no no, I promise."

Billy looked out toward the pool, as though he'd walk over there and look in after all. "Spooky down here at night. Just like *Cat People*. You gotta see that flick, Doug. The original, not the dumb remake."

"I will, I will. Don't forget your radio."

"Right." Billy pointed a stern finger at Doug, becoming official again as he said, "Five minutes."

"Thanks, Billy."

Then, at last, Billy left, and the instant he was gone, Doug ran to the pool and jumped into the water, descending to where John and Andy stood around as though waiting to be picked up by the next submarine. With pointings and other frantic gestures, he showed them yet again how to add air to the BCD to increase their buoyancy, and up all three rose together. As soon as their heads broke the surface, all three started loudly to talk, but Doug's urgency was greater and he shouted them both down, screaming, "We don't have *time!*"

"That was a cop!" Andy yelled.

"Looking for the people who stole the Mercedes!"

Andy and John became very silent. Floating in the pool, they exchanged a glance, and then John said to Doug, "You didn't happen to mention us down there in the pool."

"Don't worry, I said I was alone. But I've got to leave now, and take the pickup away before Billy calls the department wrecker to come get the Mercedes."

John said, "Billy?"

"The cop," Doug told him. "I went to high school with him. This high school."

"Those early contacts," Andy suggested, "are so all-important."

"Yeah," Doug said. "Anyway, I gotta leave, but you can't. So what I'll do is, I'll wait till they come for the Mercedes and everybody's gone, and then I'll come back and pick you guys up and all this equipment."

John said, "How long?"

"How do I know?" Doug asked him. "An hour, maybe."

John said, "And what are we supposed to do down here for an hour?"

Doug looked around the pool, then back at his students. "Well," he said, "you could practice. Tell the truth, guys, you need it."

CHAPTER TWENTY-FIVE

Tom Jimson was a criminal! That was the first thought in Myrtle Street's head every morning when she awoke, and the last thought every night as she drifted—later and later, it seemed—into sleep, and it was somewhere in her mind all day long: at the library, at home, in the car, shopping, everywhere. Tom Jimson, her father, was a major criminal.

She'd known this fact for nearly two weeks now, and it still hadn't lost its power to astonish and appall and excite. The very next morning after that evening of pointless pursuit of her father in the car that merely circled and circled, when Myrtle had gone to work at the library, she'd started to look for Tom Jimson in every reference work she could think of, and there he was right away in, of all major-league places, the index of the *New York Times*!

She had been two years old, just on the brink of entering play school, when Tom Jimson had entered Sing Sing for what the newspaper account said would be the last time: ". . . seven life sentences to run consecutively, with no possibility of parole."

Now she understood why her mother had been so unbelieving when she'd first seen Tom Jimson ride by in an automobile in the bright light of day, why Edna had been startled into such uncharacteristic language and behavior. Tom Jimson was supposed to be in prison forever!

Had he escaped? But he wouldn't boldly show himself in his old neighborhoods, would he, if he'd escaped? And wouldn't there have been something in the newspaper if he'd escaped? But that twenty-three-year-old report of his conviction and jailing was the last time Tom Jimson—born in Oklahoma, sometime resident of California and Florida and several other states—had made the newspaper.

So what else could have happened? Maybe—*this* was a thrilling thought!—maybe they'd let him go! Maybe it had all been a mistake; he hadn't committed all those crimes after all, and finally the truth had come out, and her father was a free man today, exonerated.

But wouldn't *that* have gotten into the papers? And wouldn't he, if a wrongly convicted innocent man, have returned to his family? Did he even know he *had* a family? Had Edna ever told him that Myrtle existed? (Edna herself refused to talk at all about the subject anymore and would fly into a rage if Myrtle dared start to question her.)

Myrtle spent nearly every waking moment of her life now going over and over these questions, considering the possibilities, thinking about her *father!* This morning, driving to the library, she concentrated so exclusively on the enigma of Tom Jimson that she never noticed the ancient, battered, rusty yellow Volkswagen Beetle that had been parked across the street from her house and that then followed her all the way downtown, even parking just a few slots away in the parking lot behind the library building. Nor did she feel the Beetle driver's eyes on her as she entered the building.

It was half an hour into her workday when the little fat man with the wet eyes approached her at the front desk and asked what books the library had on computers. "Oh, we have a large number," she assured him, and pointed across the room at the card catalogue, saying, "Just look in the subject heading drawers under *computer*, and you'll—"

"But," he interrupted, being timid and yet at the same time forceful, doing some pointing of his own toward the computer terminal on the counter to her right, "won't you have it all in there?"

Myrtle looked with a kind of remote distaste at the computer terminal, one of four in the building, put in a few years earlier as part of a statewide program. Money that could have been spent on *books*, as the librarians often told one another. "Oh, that," she said. "I'm sorry, the person who runs that isn't in today."

There was in fact no one who ran the computer, and hadn't been since a few months after the four were installed. At that time, a half-day orientation course had been offered up in Albany, and the only member of the staff willing to spend the time had been the most recent employee, a flighty young woman named Duane Anne, who'd just wanted the day off from regular work, and who in any case had shortly afterward enlisted in the navy.

Usually, telling someone that "the person who runs the computer" was unavailable was enough to deal with the problem, but not this time. The little round man turned his wet eyes on the machine, blinked at it, and said, "Oh, that's a very simple one, just an IBM-compatible VDT."

"VDT?" She didn't even like the *sound* of these things.

"Video display terminal." His large wet eyes—they did look unappetizingly like blue-yolked eggs—swiveled toward her and he said, "The main frame's up in Albany, isn't it?"

"Is it?"

"The entire state wide catalogue's available there," he said, as though that were something wonderful. "Everything in every branch!"

"Oh, really?" Myrtle could not have been less interested, but she did her best to sound polite.

But then the little man suddenly moved, saying, "May I?" as he ducked around the end of the desk to stand in front of the computer, rubbing his little fat hands together and absolutely *beaming* at the machine. His broad stubby nose actually *twitched*, as though he were a rabbit suddenly faced with an entire head of lettuce.

At a loss, knowing she'd somehow lost control of the situation but unsure what to be alarmed at, Myrtle said, "Excuse me, but I don't think—"

"Now, we turn it on *here*," he said, smiling, and his little hand darted out. There was a faint flat *tik*, and the TV screen of the computer went from its normal dead flat gray to a living virulent bottomless black. The little man's hands touched the typewriter keys, and green letters bounced horribly into existence on that black abyss.

"Oh, please!" Myrtle cried, half reaching out toward him. "I don't think you should—"

He turned toward her, smiling with pleasure, and she saw his face was really very sweet and harmless; beatific, almost. "It's all right," he told her. "Really it is. You don't have to be afraid of computers."

Which changed her attitude in an instant. "Well, I'm certainly not *afraid* of them," she said, insulted at the implication of primitive ignorance. If she chose to have nothing to do with computers, it wasn't out of aboriginal fear. She simply saw no reason for the things, that's all.

But the little man clearly didn't view the situation that way. Shaking his head, smiling sadly at her with his ridiculously wide mouth, he said, "It's just a wonderful help, that's all. It's a *tool*, like that pencil."

Myrtle looked at the pencil in her hand, seeing absolutely no link between it and the machine the little man was now so fondly fondling. "I really don't think you should do that," she told him. "Authorized personnel . . . insurance . . . my responsibility . . ."

He smiled at her, obviously not listening to a word. "Now, let's see," he said, studying her, but not in an offensive way. "You aren't going to care about computers, so what shall we access for you?"

"Access?" The word drew a blank in Myrtle's brain.

"You have such lovely flowers around your house," the little man went on, and before Myrtle could react to that, could ask him how he *knew* she had such lovely flowers around her house, he was saying, "So let's see what all the libraries around the state have for you on flowers."

"But—" she started, trying to catch up. "My house?"

"Look!" he cried, indicating the TV screen, gesturing to it like an affable host welcoming a favored guest to the best party of the year. "I bet you didn't know all *this* was here."

So she looked at the screen. She really had no choice but to look, even though it was difficult at first to make her eyes focus on those sharp-edged green letters. But then it did all come clear, as though some kind of mist or scrim had been swept away from in front of her eyes, and she stared in absolute astonishment. Gardening, flower arranging, picture books of flowers, histories of flowers: title after title went by, in as much profusion as any spring meadow. "But—" she stammered, "we don't have all those books *here!*"

"But you can *get* them!" the little man told her. "See? These symbols show you which libraries in the system have which books, and this code shows you how to request through the central computer in Albany, and they'll loan you the books to your library from theirs."

"Well, that's wonderful!" Myrtle was delighted at this cornucopia out of the blue, this sudden magic box. "Wait!" she cried. "They're going too fast! I want to see— How do I order?"

"I'll show you," he said. "It's really easy."

And the next forty minutes disappeared in a haze of floral technology. With the help of the little round man—he was like the elves in the fairy stories who make the shoes—Myrtle learned to master the computer, the VDT, to ask it questions and give it commands and *use* it like, like, like a pencil! How astonishing! How liberating! How unexpected!

At the end of the forty minutes, when he asked her if she thought she could run it by herself now, she said, "Oh, yes, I can! Oh, thank you! I never realized!"

"People think computers are bad," the little man said, "because whenever they want to do something somebody always says, 'You can't now, the computer's down.' But if you know what you're doing, it's easy. Gee whiz, you know, pencils break their points, too, but people don't panic and say pencils aren't any good."

"That's true," she said, warming to him, wanting to agree with him.

Suddenly shy, he smiled hesitantly, half turning away from her, and said, "We've talked all this time, and we haven't even been introduced. My name's Wally Knurr."

Why she said what she did Myrtle could never afterward understand. Maybe it was that the name had been so pervasively in her mind recently. Maybe it was because at long last she wanted there to be *someone* in the world who didn't think of her as Myrtle Street of Myrtle Street. Maybe it was simply that this was the first time she'd introduced herself to someone new since she'd learned the true identity of her father. Whatever the reason, what Myrtle said, putting her hand out to be shaken by his soft pudgy fingers, was, "Hello. I'm Myrtle Jimson."

He beamed happily at her. "Would you like to have lunch with me, Miss Jimson?" he asked.

CHAPTER TWENTY-SIX

The warlord's daughter!

The purpose of the Princess is to be rescued.

Wally pushed back from the computer, his swivel chair rolling on the scratched floor. His hands trembled as he looked at the machine's last response. Out of the program. Into real time, real consequence, real challenge. Real life.

Wally took a long slow deep breath. As much as was possible for him to do, he firmed his jaw. Real life. The greatest interactive fiction of them all.

CHAPTER TWENTY-SEVEN

At three in the morning, the only action on two-block-long Ganesvoort Street, in the middle of the wholesale meat section of Manhattan, south of Fourteenth Street in the far West Village, is Florent, a good twenty-four-hour-a-day French bistro operating in an old polished-chrome-and-long-counter former diner. The diner's short end is toward the street, so the counter and tables run straight back under the vivid lights, with hard surfaces that bounce and echo the noise of cheerful conversation. While all around this one building the meat packers and wholesale butchers are closed and silent and dark, the bone trucks all empty and hosed down for the night, and the metal gates closed over the loading docks, the cars and limousines still wait clustered in front of the warm bright lights of the bistro, which seems at all times to be filled with animated talking laughing people who are just delighted to be awake *now*. Taxis come and go, and among them this evening was one cab containing Dortmunder and Kelp.

"You want the restaurant, right?" the cabby asked, looking at them in his mirror, because what else would they want on Ganesvoort Street at three in the morning?

"Right," Dortmunder said.

The space in front of Florent was lined with stretch limos, some with their attendant drivers, some empty. The taxi stopped in the middle of the lumpy cobblestone street, and Dortmunder and Kelp paid and got out. They maneuvered between limos to the broken curb, moving toward the restaurant, as the cab jounced away to the corner. When it made its right, so did Dortmunder and Kelp, turning away from the inviting open entrance of the bistro and walking east instead, past all the dark and empty butcher businesses.

Kelp said, "Which one, do you know?"

Dortmunder shook his head. "All she said was, this block."

"I see it," Kelp said, looking forward. "Do you?"

"No," Dortmunder said, frowning, squinting at the empty nighttime view, not liking it that Kelp had gotten the answer first, if in fact he had. "What do you think you see?"

"I *think* I see," Kelp answered, "a truck over there on the other side, down a ways, with a guy sitting at the wheel."

Then Dortmunder saw it, too. "That's it, all right," he agreed.

As they started across the street, Kelp said, "Maybe after we talk to Tiny we can go back to that place, grab something to eat. Looked nice in there."

Dortmunder said, "Eat? Whadaya wanna eat at *this* hour for?"

"Ask the people in the restaurant," Kelp suggested. "*They're* eating."

"Maybe they got a different body clock."

"And maybe *I* got a different body clock," Kelp said. "Don't take things for granted, John."

Dortmunder shook his head but was spared answering because they'd reached the truck, an anonymous high-sided aluminum box with a battered cab, on the door of which some previous company name had been sloppily obliterated with black spray paint. The driver was a twitchy skinny owlish man who hadn't shaved for seventy-nine hours, which was not for him a record. He sat nervously, hunched over the wheel of his truck, its engine growling low, like something asleep deep in a cave. He stared straight forward, as though it was the law in this state to keep your eye on the road even when your vehicle was stationary.

Dortmunder approached the driver's open window and said, "Whadaya say?"

Nothing. No answer. No response. The driver watched nothing move in front of his unmoving truck.

So Dortmunder decided to cut straight to the essence of the situation. "We wanna talk to Tiny," he said.

The driver blinked, very slowly. His left hand trembled on the steering wheel, while his right hand moved out of sight.

"Wait a second," Dortmunder said. "We're friends of—"

The truck lunged forward, suddenly in gear. Dortmunder automatically flinched back as the dirty aluminum side of the truck swept past his nose, about a quarter of an inch away.

Kelp, behind Dortmunder a pace, cried out helpfully, "Hey! Dummy! Whadaya—!" But the truck was *gone*, rattling away down Ganesvoort Street, reeling past Florent, tumbling to the corner, swaying around to the right, and out of sight. "Well, now, what the hell was *that* for?" Kelp demanded.

"I think he was a little nervous," Dortmunder said, and a voice behind them growled, "Where's my truck?"

They turned and found themselves facing a bullet head on an ICBM body lumpily stuffed into a black shirt and a brown suit. It was as though King Kong were making a break for it, hoping to smuggle himself back to his island disguised as a human being. And, just to make the picture complete, this marvel carried over his shoulder half a cow; half a naked cow, without its fur or head.

"Tiny!" Dortmunder said inaccurately. "We're looking for you!"

"*I'm* looking for my truck," said Tiny, for that was indeed the name by which he was known. Tiny Bulcher, the blast furnace that walks like a man.

Dortmunder, a bit abashed, said, "Your driver, uh, Tiny, he's a very nervous guy."

Tiny frowned, which made his forehead like a children's book drawing of the ocean. "You spooked him?"

Kelp said, "Tiny, he was spooked long before we got here. *Years* before. He never said a word to us."

"That's true," Dortmunder said.

Kelp went on, "We just told him we're your friends, we're looking for you, and *zip*, he's gone."

Dortmunder said, "Tiny, I'm sorry if we made trouble."

"You're right to be," Tiny told him. "You called my place, huh? Talked to Josie?"

"That's right."

"And she just told you I was down here, huh?"

"Sure."

Tiny looked discontented with this idea. "Somebody calls that girl on the phone, says, 'Where's Tiny,' and she says, 'Oh, Tiny's downtown committing a felony right now.'"

"She knows me, Tiny," Dortmunder pointed out. "You and me met J. C. Taylor together, remember?"

Kelp added, "We been through the wars together, Tiny, us and J.C. Rescued the nun and everything."

Tiny ignored Kelp, saying to Dortmunder, "Josie knows you, does she?" He was the only one in the known universe to call J. C. Taylor "Josie." "On the phone, she knows you. Could be a cop calls, says, 'Hello, J.C., this is

John Dortmunder, your pal Tiny committing any felonies at this particular moment?' 'Oh, sure,' says Josie."

"Come on, Tiny," Dortmunder said, "J.C. recognized my voice. I didn't say my name at all, she did. And I said I wanted to get in touch with you right away, so that's when she told me you were down there. So she did the right thing, okay?"

Tiny brooded about that. He shifted the half a cow from his right shoulder to the left. "Okay," he decided. "I trust Josie's judgment. But what about the truck?"

Kelp said, "The guy ran off, Tiny. What are we supposed to do, come down here with tranquilizer darts? The guy was very spooked, that's all. We show up and that's it, he's gone."

"Well, here's the situation," Tiny said. "The situation is, I agreed I'd come down here for a guy, with the guy's truck and the guy's driver, and I'd make my way in this place and pick up six sides a beef, on accounta I can do that quick and easy."

"You sure can, Tiny," Kelp said admiringly.

"And the *further* idea is," Tiny said, glowering at the interruption, "I throw a seventh side in the truck and that one goes home with me. A side a beef for a half hour's work."

"Pretty good," Dortmunder admitted.

"So the guy's truck and the guy's driver run off," Tiny went on, "so that's it for his six sides a beef. *But*"—and he whacked his open palm against the half a cow on his shoulder: *spack!*—"I got mine."

"Well, that's good," Dortmunder said. "You wanna get yours, Tiny."

"I *always* get mine," Tiny told him. "That's just the way it is. But now what do I do about taking this side home? Sooner or later, I make my way into some more populated parts a town, I'm gonna attract attention."

"Gee, Tiny," Kelp said, "I see what you mean. That's a real problem."

"And I think of it," Tiny said, "as *your* problem."

Dortmunder and Kelp looked at each other. Kelp shrugged and spread his hands and turned to Tiny to say, "I could argue the point, Tiny, but let's just say I feel like helping you out. Everybody wait right here."

He took a step away but stopped when Tiny said, "Andy." He turned back and looked alert, and Tiny said, "None of your doctors' cars, Andy."

"But doctors have the best cars around, Tiny," Kelp explained. "They understand the transitoriness of life, doctors, and they've got the money to make things smooth and even along the way. I always put my faith in doctors."

"Not this time," Tiny said, and whacked his cow again. "Me and Elsie here don't want no cute Porsches and Jaguars. We don't like that crowded feeling."

Kelp sighed, admitting defeat. Then he looked up and down the street, thinking, his eye drawn to the light spilling from Florent. His own eyes lit up, and he grinned at Tiny. "Okay, Tiny," he said. "What would you and Elsie say to a stretch limo?"

CHAPTER TWENTY-EIGHT

On the drive north, Kelp at the wheel of the silver Cadillac stretch limo with the New Jersey vanity plate—KOKAYIN—Dortmunder and Tiny on the deeply cushioned rear seats, the half a cow draped in front of them like the mob's latest victim on top of the bar-and-TV console and the rear-facing plush seats, Dortmunder explained the job: "You remember Tom Jimson."

Tiny thought about that. "From inside?"

"That's the one," Dortmunder agreed. "That's where we both knew him. He was my cellmate awhile."

"Nasty poisonous old son of a bitch," Tiny suggested.

"You've got the right guy," Dortmunder told him.

"A snake with legs."

"Perfect."

"Charming as a weasel and gracious as a ferret."

"That's Tom, okay."

"He'd eat his own young even if he wasn't hungry."

"Well, he's always hungry," Dortmunder said.

"That's true." Tiny shook his head. "Tom Jimson. He was the worst thing about stir."

Looking in the mirror, Kelp said, "Tiny, I never heard you talk like that before. Like there was a guy out there somewhere that worried you."

"Oh, yeah?" Tiny frowned massively at this suggestion that another human being might give him pause. "You're lucky you don't know the guy," he said.

133

"But I do," Kelp corrected him. "John introduced me. And I'm with you a hundred percent."

"Introduced you?" Tiny was baffled. "How'd he do that?"

Quietly, Dortmunder said, "They let him go."

Tiny switched his frown to Dortmunder. "Let him go *where*?"

"Out."

"They wouldn't. Even the law isn't *that* stupid."

"They did, Tiny," Dortmunder told him. "On accounta the over-crowding. For a seventieth birthday present."

Tiny stared at his cow as though to say *do you believe this?* He said, "Tom Jimson? He's out right now? Walking around the streets?"

"Probably," Dortmunder said. "He usually comes home pretty late."

"Home? Where's he living?"

"Well," Dortmunder said reluctantly, "with me at the moment."

Tiny was appalled. "Dortmunder! What does May say?"

"Nothing good."

"The thing is, Tiny," Kelp said from the front seat, "John's agreed Tom can stay until after the job."

Tiny slowly shook his massive head. "This is a Tom Jimson job? Forget it. Stop the car, Andy, me and Elsie'll walk."

"It isn't like that, Tiny," Dortmunder said.

But Tiny was still being extremely negative. "Where Tom Jimson passes by," he said, "nothing ever grows again."

Kelp said, "Tiny, let John tell you the story, okay? It isn't the way you think. *None* of us would sign on a Tom Jimson job."

Tiny thought that over. "Okay," he said, "I tell you what I'll do. I won't just automatic say no."

"Thank you, Tiny," Dortmunder said.

"I'll listen," Tiny said. "You'll tell me the story. *Then* I'll say no."

Dortmunder and Kelp exchanged a glance in the rearview mirror. But there was nothing to do but plow forward, so Dortmunder said, "What this is, it's a buried stash." And he went on to explain the background, the reservoir, the circumstances and the split, which should be around a hundred twenty thousand dollars for each of the three in this car.

"Tom Jimson," Tiny interjected at that juncture, "has a way of not having any partners left to split with."

"We know that about him," Dortmunder pointed out. "We'll watch him."

"Birds watch snakes," Tiny said. "But okay, go ahead, tell me the rest of it."

So Dortmunder told him the rest of it, and Tiny didn't interrupt again

until the part about going underwater, when he reared around in astonishment and said, "Dortmunder? *You're* gonna go *diving*?"

"Not diving," Kelp insisted from up front. "We're not gonna dive. We're
gonna *walk in*."

"Into a reservoir," Tiny said.

Kelp shrugged that away. "We been taking lessons," he said. "From a very
professional guy."

"Tiny," Dortmunder said, getting the narrative back on track, "the idea is,
we'll go down in there, we'll walk in from the shore, and we'll pull a rope
along with us. And there'll be a winch at the other end of the rope."

"And you," Kelp explained, "at the other end of the winch."

Tiny grunted. Dortmunder said, "When we get to the right place, we dig
up the casket, we tie the rope around one of the handles, we give it a tug
so you know we're ready, and then you winch it out. And we walk along
with it to keep it from snagging on stuff."

Tiny shook his head. "There's gotta be about ninety things wrong with
that idea," he said, "but let's just stay with one: Tom Jimson."

"He's seventy years old, Tiny," Dortmunder said.

"He could be seven hundred years old," Tiny said, "and he'd still be God's
biggest design failure. He'd steal the teeth out of your mouth to bite you
with."

Kelp said, "I gotta admit it, Tiny, you really do know Tom."

"Tiny," Dortmunder said, "I'll be honest with you."

"Don't strain yourself, John," Tiny said.

"With me and Andy down there at the bottom of the reservoir,"
Dortmunder told him, "and Tom Jimson up on the shore with the winch
and the rope, I'd feel a lot more comfortable in my mind if you were up
there with him. And not just to turn the winch."

"I think you should have the National Guard up there before you could
feel really *comfortable* in your mind," Tiny told him, "but I agree. You don't
want to go down in there without insurance."

"That's right," Dortmunder said. "Will you do it, Tiny?"

"You can buy a lotta sides of beef with a hundred twenty thousand, Tiny,"
Kelp chipped in.

Tiny brooded, looking at his cow. The thing looked deader and nakeder
than ever. "Every time I tie up with you, Dortmunder," he said, "something
turns weird. The last time, you had me dressed like a nun."

"We had to get through the cops, Tiny. And that one did work out, didn't
it? We wound up with most of the loot that time, didn't we? And you
wound up with J.C."

"And think of it this way," Kelp said, sounding chipper and positive and gung ho, like a high school basketball coach. "It's an adventure, kinda, and getting outta the city into the healthy country—"

"Healthy," Tiny echoed.

"—and it's like a real basic enterprise," Kelp finished. "Man against the elements!"

Tiny cocked an eyebrow at the back of Kelp's head. "Tom Jimson's an element?"

"I was thinking of water," Kelp explained.

Dortmunder said, "Tiny? I could really use your help on this."

Tiny shook his head. "Something just tells me," he said, "if I sign on to this cockamamie thing, I'm gonna wind up looking like Elsie here."

Dortmunder waited, saying nothing more. It was up to Tiny now, and he shouldn't be pushed. Even Kelp kept quiet, though he looked in the mirror a lot more than he looked out the windshield.

And finally Tiny sighed. "What the hell," he said. "If I had any sense, I wouldn't know you two in the first place."

CHAPTER TWENTY-NINE

Midnight. The Dodge Motor Home with the MD plates eased off the county road onto the gravel verge and cut its lights. A moon just rising over the Showangunks gave vague amber illumination, turning into copper the metal-pipe barrier across the dirt side road, glowing softly and almost confidentially on the sign beside that road: NO ADMITTANCE—VILBURGTOWN RESERVOIR AUTHORITY.

The living room door of the motor home opened and Tiny Bulcher stepped down, carrying a large gimbaled metal cutter. He crossed to the barrier, snipped the padlocked chain holding it shut, lifted the horizontal bar out of its groove, and pivoted it out of the way. Then he waved the metal cutter at the motor home, which drove slowly through the opening onto the dirt road, rocking dangerously as it came. Once it was by and had come to a stop, its brake lights turning the scene briefly dramatic, Tiny put the barrier pipe back in place and reboarded the motor home.

Inside, Kelp sat at the large bus-type wheel, while Dortmunder and Tom Jimson sat silent, facing each other in the dark living room area. Putting the metal cutter back with a clank on the other tools, Tiny sat in the swivel chair to Kelp's right, looked out the windshield, and said, "Can you see anything?"

"From time to time," Kelp told him. "The moon helps a little."

Dortmunder, hearing this conversation, got up from the convertible sofa and moved forward as the motor home rocked like a boat in a heavy sea, inching along the rutted dirt road. Peering over Tiny's shoulder at the

137

darkness out front, Dortmunder said, "Andy? You can't see a goddamn thing out there."

"I'm doing fine," Kelp insisted. "If everybody'll stop distracting me. And you don't want me to use lights in here."

"Nothing against you, Andy," Tiny said, "but why aren't we using a driver on this job? Where's Stan Murch?"

"We don't need a driver," Dortmunder explained, "because we don't expect to make any getaways. And the more men on the job, the smaller the split for each of us."

A cackle sounded from the back. Tiny and Dortmunder exchanged a glance.

Kelp rolled his window down, letting in a lot of cool damp spring air. "There," he said. "That's better."

Tiny frowned at him. "What's better about it?"

"I can hear when we rub against the bushes," Kelp explained. "Keeps us on the road."

Tiny swiveled slowly around to face Dortmunder. "Thirty thousand is what Stan Murch would cost me," he said. "Right?"

"About that," Dortmunder agreed.

"I'll keep that in mind," Tiny said, and swiveled front.

The motor home rocked and swayed through the second-growth forest, Kelp listening to bushes, Tiny and Dortmunder squinting hard as they stared through the windshield, Tom sitting back in the dark by himself, thinking his own thoughts.

Dortmunder said, "What's that?"

"What's what?" Kelp asked.

"Just stop," Tiny told him.

"If you say so," Kelp agreed nonchalantly, and stopped with the nose of the motor home half an inch from another metal-pipe barrier.

Tiny said, "Okay? Do you see it now?"

Kelp peered out the windshield, gazing too high and too far away. "See what?"

"He can only hear it," Dortmunder suggested.

Tiny shook his head in disgust and got up out of the swivel chair to look for the metal cutter. Kelp leaned his head out the open window beside him, looked around, and at last saw the barbed-wire-topped chain-link fence sketched into the face of the forest, picking up scattered muted highlights from the moon, extending away into nothingness to left and right. "Well, look at that," he said.

"We already did," Dortmunder told him.

Tiny got out and dispatched this barrier the same way as the first, and the motor home steered slowly, majestically, with all the dignity of a great passenger liner, through the opening in the fence and onto Vilburgtown Reservoir property. Then it stopped and Tiny climbed aboard again, saying, "I could see a bit of it out there. Ahead of us."

"A bit of what?" Kelp asked him.

"The reservoir."

"Don't drive into it," Dortmunder suggested.

"He won't," Tiny said. "He'll hear the splash."

Ahead, through the trees, as Kelp continued to ease them slowly forward, tiny winks of gold and saffron showed where moonlight reflected from the restless water of the reservoir. About fifteen feet from the water's edge they came to a dirt clearing, and Kelp stopped. "There you are," he said. "Through doubt and scorn, I made my way."

Tiny said, "You couldn't of done it without the bushes."

They all emerged from the motor home and went down to the water's edge to look out across the quietly rippling surface. It *looked* deep. It didn't look man-made at all. In the orangey light of the swollen moon just above the mountaintops, the Vilburgtown Reservoir looked ancient, bottomless, black, menacing. Things must live down in there; long silent things with large eyes and sharp teeth and long bony white arms. "Hmmm," Dortmunder said.

"Well, uh," Kelp said. "We're here. I guess we should get on with it."

"No time like the present," Tom said.

"Right," Dortmunder said.

Dragging their feet a little, Dortmunder and Kelp led the way back to the motor home and off-loaded all their gear: wet suits, air tanks, underwater flashlights, the whole schmear. As they started to strip off their street clothes in the chilly night air, Tiny frowned away to the left, saying, "Dam's down there somewhere, isn't it?"

Tom, pointing, said, "You can make out the curve of it right there. See?"

Tiny said, "Nobody inside there can look down this way?"

"Naw." Tom waved both bony hands, dismissing that problem. "The windows all face down the valley. Don't worry, Tiny, we're all alone here."

Nearby, Dortmunder and Kelp, changing into their wet suits, heard that remark and looked at each other. But they didn't say a word.

• • •

"Hey, it's the husband!"

"Welcome back, honeymooner! Hey, you got *some* bags under your eyes!"

"You gotta take time out to sleep, boy! It'll still be there when you wake up! Is he thinner?"

"Thinner? He's wasted away to nothin! He's got *no* lead in his pencil!"

"He barely got a pencil anymore!"

"Siddown, Bobby, siddown, you got to start building up your strength!"

"Yeah, yeah," Bob said, nodding at his tormentors, keeping his bitter thoughts to himself. He'd known all along that when he finally came back to work here at the dam he'd be sure to take some ribbing, and the thing to do was just play along and wait for these jerks to get bored with themselves.

But it wasn't easy, under the circumstances, to keep his mouth shut. The fact is, he'd screwed Tiffany a hell of a lot more *before* the wedding than during the so-called honeymoon. The first couple days of married life, Tiffany'd been in a *really* shitty mood, just mad at everything, at the airplane ride, the hotel, the whole island of Aruba. Bob had been pretty patient and reasonable, all things considered, and at last on the third day she'd relaxed and her disposition improved, and they'd had several kind of nice hours together before the onset of morning sickness, a thing Tiffany was apparently going to be experiencing all day long for the next five months. (The worst so far, the absolute worst for everybody concerned, everybody in the *vicinity*, had been the plane ride back.)

So all this hooting and hollering was pretty well aimed at the wrong guy. But there was no point saying so, or saying anything at all to these clowns, come to that. His three coworkers on the night shift at Vilburg-town Dam were not famous for empathy or thoughtfulness. (Well, to be honest, neither was Bob.) So while they made increasingly crude remarks, in their desperate pseudo-friendly determination to get a rise out of him, Bob went glumly to his work station and settled back into the routine of things. There were forms to be filled out, computer input to be caught up on, safety checks and maintenance checks that hadn't been dealt with while he was gone, consumption reports for the New York City water people, pension and insurance and overtime and union and tax documents on the four-man detachment of New York Police Department cops assigned to the dam, electric and phone bills . . .

And they just wouldn't let up; they just had to keep making their brilliant remarks, even though he was trying to get some *work* done. These three bozos, janitor clerks like himself, handmaidens of the dam, with no Civil Service seniority, had drawn this utterly boring and unchanging night shift as their introduction to the world of grown-up work, would be here for *years* until youths even more callow than themselves were hired by the city and stuffed into this dam like worms into a hydroponic tank, so that Bob and his pals could at last move up to a life of daytime inactivity, to spend their days watching cloud formations and guarding the reservoir against fishermen, boaters, skinny dippers, malfunctions, and madmen carrying enough LSD to drive the entire Eastern Seaboard mad.

Day duty: when sometimes the phone did ring, when sometimes a passing motorist wanted to stop and chat about engineering marvels, when sometimes something *happened*. But until that happy day, the four of them were stuck together in here in utter tedium, and so any event at all, including (perhaps especially including) a coworker's return from his honeymoon, was something to be savored, to be dwelt on, to be consumed slowly and completely, to be driven right flat into the fucking ground.

"I'll be back," Bob finally announced, knowing he could stand no more of it for a while. Getting to his feet, he turned away from his data sheets and computer terminal and best friends, and muttered, "I need some air."

"What you need is oysters!"

"By now, what he needs is a splint! A little short splint about, what, Bobby, about four inches long?"

"That Tiffany's a lucky girl, you know. Bobby can do his dirty deed on her with that little wiener, and she won't know a thing about it, can go right on sleeping."

Jesus. Bob went out the door and up the concrete steps and out onto the catwalk on the reservoir side of the dam, just below the lip of the roadway. Beautiful out here; since Aruba, Bob had become something of a student of beauty, and he could tell that this scene, this northern spring scene here, with its outlined pine trees and big orange moon and scraggle-toothed mountains and the peaceful water, was *beauty*.

And he was all alone with it. Down there to his left, where the roadway atop the dam met the land on the far side, was the only structure in sight, a low square one-room building made of local stone, which housed the office of the police detachment, and which was empty right now. There were no cops on duty at night, though they were on call in their homes nearby in case of trouble, and the state police were also close by and available in case of *real* trouble.

But if you ignored that little stone building and turned your back on the dam to look straight out across the water, it was almost the way it would have been back in Indian times, before the Europeans ever came up the Hudson River and started their settlements. Squinting, you could almost imagine silent Indians out there in their canoes, skimming across the water. Of course, this particular body of water hadn't actually been here back in Indian times, that imaginary canoe of Bob's would have been fifty or sixty feet up in the air among the treetops back then, but the *idea* of it was right.

And he alone here, the only observer. That faint splash from some distance off to the right, for instance. If he wanted to pretend that was an Indian paddle, what was wrong with that? Even if he really knew it was just some fish.

• • •

While Kelp splashed his fingers in the water to see how cold it was—and winced—Dortmunder fitted his goggles on and inhaled through his nose, the way Doug Berry had showed him, to create the seal that would make the goggles watertight. Then he put the mouthpiece in his mouth and started breathing the air out of the tank, and once again he got that claustrophobic feeling. When his head was enclosed in face mask and mouthpiece, for some reason it always reminded him of prison.

"You ready?" Kelp asked, which of course meant he himself *wasn't* ready, because if he could talk his mouthpiece wasn't in. For answer, Dortmunder went plodding toward the water.

Because they weren't diving in but walking in, and because they didn't intend to do any swimming while they were in there, just walking, they didn't wear the normal flippers, but had chosen low zippered boots instead. This made their entry into the water a bit more dignified than the usual flapping flipper-wearer. A bit more dignified, but not much.

Or, that is, it would have been dignified if the water hadn't been so cold, causing first Dortmunder and then Kelp to jump right back out the instant they stepped in. Then, looking wide-eyed at each other through the masks, clutching their flashlights, each with his small folding shovel hooked to his weight belt, and with the end of the long white rope lashed loosely around Dortmunder's middle, they both tried again.

Cold. Wading in was the worst possible way to do this. Each inch of the body was given its own opportunity to start freezing, separately, serially. When Dortmunder was about thigh deep, he knew he could stand no more of this death-by-a-thousand-freezes, so he simply sat down in the water, which flooded the wet suit right up to his neck. My heart's gonna stop! he thought, but then the wet suit began to do its job, warming the water next to his skin the way it had done every time in the swimming pool out on Long Island, and his shivering lessened, and the severe ache in his teeth abated, and the hair reattached itself to his scalp.

Next to him, Kelp, seeing what he'd done, had echoed it, and was no doubt going through the same tortures. I am extremely uncomfortable,

Dortmunder told himself, but I'm gonna live. There was a kind of gloomy satisfaction in the thought.

Well, it was time to move on. With some difficulty, Dortmunder got his feet under himself once more, but he didn't stand up all the way. He remained crouched to keep his body underwater, and looked back at the shore, where Tiny and Tom were visible against the lighter mass of the motor home—Tiny leaning on the winch on its tripod, Tom just standing there to one side, like the evil spirit of the lake.

Tiny can handle him, Dortmunder told himself. Tiny can take care of himself. Sure he can. Tiny's a big guy, he's alert, he'll keep control of the situation. Telling himself this stuff, Dortmunder turned away and started duck-walking deeper into the lake.

The ground underfoot underwater was very muddy and very kind of squidgy. As Dortmunder moved deeper, the bottom began to tug at his boots, trying to pull them off, so he had to move more and more carefully, *drawing* his heel out of the muck every time, while invisible fingers down there clutched at the back of his boot.

Then cold water touched his bare chin, beneath the mouthpiece. I'm gonna go underwater! Now! I'm gonna go underwater now! He turned and stared wildly shoreward one last time, but he was too far out over the water now and could no longer make out anything clearly. Tiny and Tom and the motor home were all in the darkness under the trees.

Everything's fine. I'm gonna go underwater now. And he did.

Flashlight. How the hell do you turn on the flashlight? There's gotta be a button, there's—

A faint glow off to his right: Kelp's flashlight. So it's possible, no reason to panic, just look down in the darkness and try to figure out where the flashlight button is. Concentrating on the problem at hand, he forgot to breathe through his mouth, tried to breathe through his nose, and his nostrils pinched shut as the edges of the mask pressed painfully against his cheeks and forehead.

I'm strangling! Terrified, he gulped air through his mouth, discovered he was breathing, found the flashlight button, clicked the damn thing, and he *still* couldn't see much of anything.

This was very dirty water. A lot dirtier than the stuff that comes out of faucets down in New York City. This water was *brown*. It had millions of tiny hairy dirt atoms floating in it, bouncing the flashlight glow back in a sepia halo.

He couldn't even see the bottom. He angled the flashlight straight down, and he could just make out his own knees, but no deeper. His boot-clad feet were lost in the brown murk. Behind him, the thick white rope angled upward, buoyant enough to hover just a few inches below the surface, its braided white line disappearing no more than two feet away.

The original idea was, if they just kept moving forward, they'd come to the old road that used to go from Dudson Park to Putkin's Corners; downhill to the right would be the direction they wanted. According to Wally Knurr's computer, the old blacktop should still be there, though it might be partly covered with drifting mud. Of course, if they couldn't see the bottom at *all*, that was gonna make it a little tougher to find the road. Except that blacktop, even underwater blacktop, wouldn't try to pull his boot off at every step, so that would be a clue.

So the thing to do was stick together and move forward. Stick together. Dortmunder looked around, and couldn't see Kelp's flashlight anymore. Was it because of the glow of his own light? Finding the damn button again—why do they make it so hard to find the *button*?—he switched off his light, then turned in a slow circle, staring through the goggles at nothing at all. Pitch-black darkness. No light. Darkness. Blackness. Cold wet blackness, pressing in, pressing down, pressing against his chest and his forehead and the flimsy glass between his eyes and—

Button!

The hazy tan glow came back, re-creating the narrow round tube of dim light in which he stood, this murky closet surrounded by all that black.

Where was Kelp? Jeez, he could get lost down here. I hope he doesn't panic, Dortmunder told himself, afraid that Kelp might not have his own nerves of steel, and knowing for certain that Kelp didn't have the long white braid of rope that, no matter what else might happen, still linked Dortmunder's waist to the winch and Tiny and the shore and the whole upper world of air and light.

Move forward, that was the thing to do. Move forward. Keep the flashlight on as a guide to Kelp, keep tight hold of the rope, that absolute lifeline, and move forward, feeling one's way, waiting for that goddamn road.

Why am I *doing* this?

His foot hit something, hard. The something was hard, and his foot *hit* it hard. Damn! Now what?

Dortmunder bent low, sticking the flashlight down into the murk, and saw a tree stump there, right in front of him. Most of its bark had rotted away, the interior was rusty-looking and crumbly, and some of its roots had been exposed by the shifting mud. Roots as bent and dark as witches' fingers, they were all around his feet.

Dortmunder moved to his right, and bumped into something else. It was another stump, about a foot high, a little thicker than the first one. He remained bent over to swing the flashlight in an arc, and more and more of them appeared out of the darkness; a squat army of tree stumps, some thick, some thin, all frayed and crumbling, standing at grubby attention in uneven rows, none more than a foot high. He moved the flashlight in a wider arc, half turning, and they were behind him, too, thousands of them, crowded together, roots overlapping as though they lolled at their ease here, just waiting for him, waiting all these years, biding their time, in no hurry, knowing some black night Dortmunder would descend among them and . . .

All right, all right. They aren't alive, okay? They're tree stumps, that's all. Get hold of yourself, goddammit.

Then he remembered one of the items factored into Wally Knurr's computer model of the valley when it was flooded. Most of the trees had been cut down before the water was put in. Yes, and most of the buildings had been towed away, except for totally useless ones or some overly large stone or brick ones like a couple of churches and firehouses and the library Tom had buried his goddamn stash behind. And those had been stripped of doors and windows and floors and anything else that might be of use.

He hadn't thought before about what all that meant. He hadn't stopped to think how difficult it was going to be to walk downhill through a forest of short tree stumps. On the other hand, even if he'd thought about tree stumps, he still wouldn't have known about the murky darkness, the complete inability to see anything more than a few feet in front of a flashlight. And he hadn't known just how difficult this mud was going to be to move around in.

Bent over, the rope and the weight belt digging into his waist, Dortmunder tried to find a path through the tree stumps. Shuffling forward, bumping into roots and stones—now there's *rocks* in here, too—having to turn this way and that to make any progress at all, he soon realized he'd lost all idea which way was *forward*.

Well, forward is downhill, right? But which way was downhill? With just this narrow tiny area of light for reference, with all the crud floating around in the water, it was impossible to tell which was uphill, which was downhill, which was crosshill.

Which way is forward? More importantly, which way is back? He aimed the flashlight at the floating rope trailing him, but it weaved and drifted with tiny currents, forming half loops, coming from everywhere and nowhere.

Still gazing upward, trying to peer farther back along the line of rope, Dortmunder moved, bumped into something *else*, lost his balance briefly, compensated fast, and stepped out of his right boot.

Oh, *hell*! His bare foot was down now in cold wet slimy mud, sinking into it. He tugged upward, and felt a thick root pressed across the top of his instep. Clutching at him!

Bending quickly down, swinging the flashlight around fast to see what was going on with his foot, Dortmunder inadvertently slammed the light into yet another stump. It bounced from his hand. It went out.

Darkness. Blackness. Don't panic. The flashlight's down there somewhere, in the dark. The boot's down there somewhere, in the dark. The foot's down there somewhere, in the dark, caught by roots. Don't panic!

How long have I been down here? I've only got an hour of air! Have I been down here an hour? Does this air taste funny?

Don't panic? Don't *panic*? *Why the hell not*?

• • •

Leaning on the rail of the catwalk, gazing out over the still silent beauty of the reservoir in the increasingly pale bright light of the rising moon, Bob found himself reflecting on the changes that had come so recently into his life, and for the first time he wished he actually had a *friend*. Not the so-called friends he'd had all his life, in grade school and high school, not those gape-jawed assholes so like the three clowns down in the dam, but a *friend*, a real friend, someone he could talk to about his innermost thoughts.

For instance. He couldn't possibly talk to the jerks in the dam about *waking up* with a woman; they didn't have the maturity for the subject. And the fact is, although Bob had what he considered plenty of experience in *going to bed* with women, the whole phenomenon of then waking up with one, waking up in the morning with another person right there, a woman, an entire life-size woman, first thing in the morning, an entire experience to deal with the second you open your eyes, was something he'd thought insufficiently about before it started to happen.

And what was it like? That was the weird thing; it wasn't particularly pleasant. It sure wasn't sexy. It was like having some kind of big animal in the room with you, a deer or a sheep, maybe a goat, sometimes more like a horse. There it was, coughing and blowing its nose and scratching itself, moving around the room, opening and closing drawers, looking as pale and bloodless as a vampire victim without its makeup on. It was like—

Sea monster! Bob stared, thrilled and terrified, as the thing broke the surface way out there across the reservoir, a huge saurian head with long laid-back ears, its reptile eye reflecting white from the moon. It was scaly, almost metallic; a definite sea monster, no question.

The thing moved toward shore. Bob panted, staring at it, almost fainting. Here! Here in the Vilburgtown Reservoir! Like Loch Ness! Like, like, like Stephen King! Right here in front of his eyes!

Near shore, the sea monster—lake monster? reservoir monster?—dove again and disappeared, a widening circular ripple left in its wake. Bob stared and stared, but it never came back. And here, he thought, his awe tinged with bitterness, here's something else I'll never be able to tell anybody. Not even Tiffany.

Maybe especially not Tiffany.

Hmmm.

• • •

Kelp surfaced again, closer to shore, and saw Tiny and Tom watching him from up the bank with the interest of uninvolved spectators. Boy, he thought. Get to know who your friends are.

What a bad few minutes that had been, back down there in the lake. He'd lost contact with John, he was stuck in mud down in among all those tree stumps, and he'd lost every bit of his sense of direction. He didn't even have the rope linking him to shore; John had that. If he hadn't remembered the BCD, he might of got really worried down there.

As it happened, though, just as he was considering he might start to get really nervous, he remembered that the *B* in BCD stood for "buoyancy," and he even remembered how to operate the son of a gun; you press the button on the *side* of the control box. Not the one on top.

And what a *glorious* feeling that was, to rise up and up, out of the muck and mire, up through the crud-filled water, floating upward like a bird, like a balloon, like Superman, then *bursting* through the skin of water into the air above, to find the moon higher, brighter, whiter, the great water-filled dark bowl of the valley holding him in its comforting dark-green cupped hands, and himself floating safe and serene in the middle of it all, *master* of his fate!

Over there was the shore. And over there on the shore was the light blur of the Dodge motor home. Kelp was not really a smooth swimmer, not one of your Olympic types, knifing gracefully through the water. What he tended to do was dangle his arms and legs down in the water, agitate them in busy random motion, and gradually move forward. Now, he tried heading for shore via this usual method, but the BCD had him *so* buoyant that he just bobbed up and down in the water like an abandoned beer can.

Finally, he let some air out of the BCD, enough to drift down just a bit below the surface, and then his usual method regained its usual level of inefficiency. He progressed that way awhile, until one dangling foot hit ground, and after that he walked the rest of the way, emerging from the reservoir like the latest salesman on the staff, the one who'd been given the worst route.

Ridding himself of mouthpiece and goggles, Kelp waded ashore as Tiny came down to meet him, saying, "What's the story?"

"It's no good," Kelp told him. He moved toward the motor home, meaning to rid himself of all this gear. "Can't *see* anything. And there's tree stumps all over the place. You just can't move down there."

Tom joined them on their move toward the motor home, looking concerned, saying, "You can't get to my money?"

"I don't see how," Kelp told him. "John and me, we—" He stopped and stared around the clearing. "Where *is* John?"

Tiny said, "Where's John? He was with you!"

"Gee," Kelp said, "I figured he'd get back before me. He had the rope, he had . . ."

Kelp's voice faded away to silence. He turned and looked at the silent dark water. Deep as hell out there; he knew that now. Tiny and Tom also looked out over the reservoir, listening, watching, waiting. . . .

"Jeez," said Tiny.

The winch and its tripod fell over.

They spun around, startled by the noise, to see the winch and tripod sliding toward the water, zipping down the bank in a long shallow ground-hugging dive, determined to go for a moonlight swim.

"He's pullin the rope!" Tiny cried.

"Stop it!" Kelp yelled, and Tiny ran forward and jumped, to slam both big feet down on the snaking white rope, pinning it to the ground just in front of the suicidal winch, while Kelp flung away his goggles and flashlight and ran to the water's edge, where he gazed at the taut rope angling straight into the water.

Tiny picked up the slack part of the rope, the part between his imprisoning feet and the winch, and wrapped it around one wrist. "Should I pull it in?"

"Sure!" Kelp told him, excited and relieved. "That's gotta be John at the other end!"

So Tiny began, hand over hand, to haul in the rope. "Heavy," he commented, but kept pulling.

Tom approached the taut line of rope and looked along its length to where it disappeared in the dark water. He said, "Do you suppose he got it?"

"Jeepers," Kelp said. "Do you think so? He just kept going! We lost each other, but he just kept at it, moved right on down in there, and found the box, and now he's—" But then doubt crossed Kelp's brow and he shook his head. "I was down there," he said. "No way."

"Whatever it is," Tiny said, "it's heavy."

They stood there on the bank, water lapping just beyond their feet, Kelp and Tom tensely waiting while Tiny drew in rope, hand over hand, straining, putting his back into it. Then, all at once, Tiny fell over backward, landing with a major *thump*, his big legs flipping up into the air to catch a lot of suddenly loose-flying rope, and an instant later Dortmunder, who had let go the rope when he'd finally seen the surface of the water above him, came charging up onto dry land, flinging his remaining equipment left and right.

(If Bob had really wanted to see a sea serpent, he should have stuck around for this one. Unfortunately, though, the apotheosis of having sighted the first sea serpent had led him to realize that in fact he hated his bride, loathed his friends and coworkers, and despised his job, so Bob had left work and driven to the nearest town with an all-night newsstand to buy a copy of *Soldier of Fortune* magazine. Happiness, he now knew, would be found as a mercenary soldier on some different continent.)

Having been dragged headfirst through tree stumps and roots and mud for what had seemed like miles, Dortmunder was not at the moment at his most presentable. He'd lost both his boots by this stage, plus the weight belt, plus the collapsible shovel, and several times had come damn close to losing his grip on both the rope and his mind. The wet suit had half unzipped itself and was full of mud. So were the goggles.

This creature, looking in fact less like a sea serpent and more like one of the clay people of Mayan mythology and Flash Gordon serials, stomped up out of the reservoir and slogged straight to Tom, who actually looked kind of startled at this abrupt approach, saying, "Al? You okay?"

"I got one word to say to you, Tom," Dortmunder announced, pointing a muddy finger at Tom. "And that word is *dynamite!*"

Tom blinked. "Al?"

"Blow it up!" Dortmunder ranted wildly, waving in the general direction of the reservoir. "Do it any way you want! I'm through!"

Tiny, sitting up from his supine position, said, "Dortmunder? You're giving up?"

Dortmunder swiveled around to glare at him. In a clear and praiseworthy effort to keep himself more or less calm and under control, he pointed again at the reservoir with his mud-dripping finger and said, "I am not going in there again, Tiny. That's it."

Kelp approached his old friend, worry creasing his features. He said, "John? This isn't you. *You* don't admit defeat."

"Defeat," Dortmunder told him, and squished away to the motor home.

SECOND DOWN

CHAPTER THIRTY

May put on her mitts, opened the oven door, and took out the big white-with-tiny-blue-flowers Corning bowl containing her famous tuna casserole. It was perfect; already she knew it. The smell alone was enough to tell you. Little bubbles of the grand aroma within kept breaking through the crusty golden-brown surface—a surface composed of grated cheese and riced potatoes sprinkled liberally over elbow macaroni—and just filled the kitchen with promises of culinary pleasure to come. May hoped John could smell it from the living room.

It was only, in fact, the promise of her tuna casserole that had persuaded John to permit this meeting in the first place. "I don't want to talk about it!" he'd kept raging at the beginning. "I don't want anything more to do with it! I don't want *him* living in this house anymore! And I don't want to ever *be* underwater, or *talk* about being underwater, or even *think* about being underwater, for the rest of my life!"

This was a pretty negative attitude to overcome, but May's famous tuna casserole had worked wonders before, and so she'd promised she would make it and serve it at a nice social dinner that would also *happen* to be a discussion of the feasibility of trying for Tom's buried/drowned cache again. That's all it would be, just a discussion, just to talk about the *possibility*, just to see if it really and truly was no more than a hollow hope that Tom Jimson could ever get hold of his seven-hundred-thousand-dollar stash without blowing up the Vilburgtown Reservoir dam, or if somebody, just maybe, if somebody *might* come up with something.

"They better not," John had said, but at long last he'd agreed to this dinner. And now all May could do was present the tuna casserole and hope for the best. From here on, it was up to everybody else.

When they had six for dinner, like tonight, they moved the coffee table out of the living room into the bedroom, and the kitchen table out of the kitchen into the living room, and the four kitchen chairs into the living room, and the other armless wooden-seated chair from the bedroom into the living room, and John would sit on a telephone book on his regular living room chair, which would still have him lower than everybody else but at least high enough to see his food and enter into the conversation. The kitchen table was really quite a good size with both its leaves open, and if you put a really thick pad under the tablecloth, you wouldn't hardly hear at all the hollow *clack* of Formica every time you put down your glass or your knife.

When May walked into the living room carrying the casserole like an offering in front of her, at arm's length, in her mitted hands, they were all already seated at the table, but given the smallness of the room and the way the kitchen table filled and dominated it, there was hardly much of anything else for them to do. On the other hand, May knew full well that even if the living room were the size of a baseball field, a couple of these people present would be seated at the table anyway.

"Dinner," she announced, put the casserole bowl on the middle of the table, and began to dispatch her troops: "John, see if anyone wants a beverage. Andy and Tiny, you two—"

"Anybody ready for a beer?"

"Sure."

"Yeah."

"Naturally."

"*Andy and Tiny*, you two get the vegetables, they're on the counter beside the sink. Tom, would you bring in the bread and butter, please?"

"You know," Tom said, as he got to his feet, "I'm getting used to this living on the outside, living with other people and all. Like on the television."

John flashed May a look as he left for the beer, which May refused to acknowledge.

Little Wally Knurr looked up, smiling his wet smile and saying, "Miss May, what can I do to help?"

"You're the special guest," May told him, "because it's your first time here."

"Oh, I want to do my part," Wally said, sounding worried, his broad brow knitting.

"You can help with dessert," May promised him, and Wally smiled again, happy.

Wally was a new experience for May, unlike just about anything she'd ever met before, including John's odd friends and some of the customers at the supermarket where she worked as cashier. For one thing, his appearance; enough said. For another thing, his manner toward her, which was a sort of childish courtliness; when he'd first come in this evening and called her Mrs. Dortmunder and she'd told him she *wasn't* Mrs. Dortmunder (without giving him her actual last name) and saying he should call her May, so that he didn't know any formal name for her at all, he'd stumbled and spluttered awhile, and then had finally decided she was "Miss May," and that was that. Then there was his size, so large horizontally and yet so small vertically; in fact, this was going to be the first meal in this apartment with *two* people seated on telephone books, John on the white pages and Wally on the business-to-business yellow pages to bring him up to a normal height with all the others.

Food and drink were quickly assembled, and everyone took their places. May sat nearest the door since she'd have to be going to the kitchen from time to time, and John sat facing her at the inner end of the room. Tiny sat to May's left and Wally to her right, with Andy beyond Tiny and Tom beyond Wally. Once all were settled and served, they all tasted the famous casserole, and the usual round of sincere but hurried praise ensued. Then, the amenities out of the way, silence took hold as everyone tucked in.

Nothing had been said about Tom's buried stash before dinner, and hardly anything was said on any subject at all during dinner, so it wasn't until after May and Wally had brought in the coffee and two kinds of ice cream and pound cake and raspberries and whipped cream that anyone raised the topic of the day, and then it was left to May to do it. "I guess everybody knows," she said, into the murmur of five people working their way through a number of terrific desserts, "that John doesn't think there's any way to get down into that reservoir and get Tom's money except to blow up the dam."

Wally's big wet eyes got bigger and wetter. "Blow up the dam! But that would be terrible! People would get hurt!"

"They'd get worse than hurt," May said gently. "And that's why John won't be a party to it."

"That's right," John said around a mouthful of pound cake.

"I won't do it either," Andy announced.

Tom, who'd been putting various desserts into his mouth without opening his lips, now spoke without opening his lips: "Somebody will. Lotta money down there. Tiny?"

"Include me out," Tiny said.

"But Tom's right about that," May told the table. "He's willing to do it, and some people would be willing to help him."

"Gee," Wally said, apparently contemplating previously unguessed—neither by himself nor his computer—depths of human depravity.

"So the question is," said May, "is there any other way to get in there and get that money? Any way that John could go along with."

"If that's the question," John said, "I got the short answer."

"Wait a minute, John," Andy said, and turned to May, saying, "May, I was down there, too, and I'm sorry, but I gotta go along with John. Your basic problem down there is you can't *see* anything. It isn't like regular water."

"They must clean the hell out of it," John commented, "before it gets down into our sinks here."

"What it reminds me of," Andy said, "is a book I read once."

John gave him a dubious look. "Are we gonna hear about *Child Heist* again?"

"That isn't the only book I ever read," Andy told him. "I'm a pretty big reader, you know. It's a habit I picked up on the inside, when I had a lotta leisure time to myself."

Tom said, "I spent my time on the inside thinking about money."

"Anyway," Andy insisted, "about this book. It was a story about the *Normandie*, the ship that sank at the pier in New York in—"

"I got pictures of that," John said, "in that *Marine Salvage* book."

"Well, this is a different book," Andy told him. "It isn't a fact book, it's the other kind. A story."

"The *Normandie*'s a fact," John maintained. "I've got pictures of it."

"Still and all," Andy said, "this is a *story* about the *fact* of the *Normandie*. Okay?"

"Okay," John said. "I just wanted to be sure we understood each other." And he filled his mouth with more pound cake, stuffing a little mocha butterscotch cashew ice cream in around the edges.

"Well, the *story*," Andy said, with a little more edge than necessary, "is about the divers who went down inside the *Normandie* and tried to fix it up so they could float it again. And I was thinking when I was down in that lake, what we had there was exactly the same as what this guy described in the book."

John looked at him with flat disbelief. "Down in that lake? You were down in that lake and you were thinking about *books*?"

"Among other things."

"I was concentrating on the other things," John said.

May said, "John, let Andy tell us about this book."

"Thanks, May," Andy said. "The only point about the book is, it's all about the divers going down inside the *Normandie* and down to the bottom of the Hudson River off Forty-fourth Street, and how they had the same kind of problem we did. It's very exciting, very dramatic. Make a terrific movie, except of course you couldn't see anything."

"Maybe radio," Tiny suggested.

"Yeah, maybe so," Andy agreed. "Anyway, what they had, down at the bottom of the Hudson River, was just what we had. Everything's black and dirty, the water's full of this thick *mud*, and if you turn on a flashlight it's like turning on your car headlights in a thick fog; it just bounces the light back at you."

"That sounds terrible," May said.

John pushed food into one cheek in order to be able to say, "I've been *telling* you it was terrible, May. Do you think I give up *easy*?"

"No, I don't, John," May assured him. "That's why we're talking this over now."

"Getting our book reports," John said.

Tiny said, "Andy? Did this book say what they did about it, how they got around it?"

"I don't remember," Andy said. "I just remember they were down in there, inside the *Normandie* and around under the *Normandie*, in all this black dirty water."

"Not while I'm eating," John said while he was eating.

May said, "Well, it seems to me, one thing we could do is look at this book and see what solution *they* came up with."

"Couldn't hurt," Tiny agreed. "Andy? You still got the book?"

"I don't think so."

Wally, wriggling on the yellow pages in his eagerness to be of help, said, "I could find it! I could get us all copies of it!"

May said, "Andy? What was the title?"

"Beats me," Andy said. "It had '*Normandie*' in it."

"Do you know who wrote it?"

Andy shook his head. "I can't ever remember writers' names."

"That's okay," Wally said. "I can do it."

John said, "Not to be a wet blanket, but—"

Andy said, "Meaning, to *be* a wet blanket."

John gave him a look. "*But*," he repeated, "even if we find out there's some magic way so you can see through mud, an idea in which I personally have no belief, but even if there is such a thing, some special thing so you can see bright as day through *mud*, I'm still not goin down in there again. And I'll tell you why."

"That's okay," Tom said. "Dynamite's easy."

"The *why* is," John went doggedly on, "tree stumps. Even if you could see down there, *that's* what you'd see. Tree stumps. And you can't tell which is uphill, which is downhill—"

"That's true," Andy said. "I noticed that myself. Disorienting, that's what they call that."

"I call it a couple of things myself," John told him. "And that's why I'm not going down in there. Tree stumps, and you can't tell up from down, and you can't *walk* through that stuff. And even if you could walk through it, which you can't, you couldn't drag any heavy casket *up* through it."

Wally said, "Maybe it would work better if you took the railroad line."

Everybody stared at him. Embarrassed at all the sudden attention, Wally's face grew as red as the raspberries on his spoon which didn't make him look like a raspberry, but like a hyperactive tomato. John said to him, "Railroad? Wally, there isn't any *train* to Putkin's Corners."

"Well, no, gee, no," Wally said, bobbing his tomato head, spilling raspberries off his spoon. "But there's still the *line*."

Andy, looking suddenly very alert, said, "Are you sure about this, Wally?"

"Sure," Wally told him. "That was part of the information I input when I did the model in the computer. The old DE&W used to go through—"

"DE&W?" asked May and Andy.

"Dudson, Endicott & Western," Wally explained.

"That's great, then," Andy said. "If we could find the old rail bed, there wouldn't be any tree stumps there, and it would be like a clear path all the way."

Tiny said, "And you could walk it right down into town. Is that the story, Wally? It went to Putkin's Corners?"

Tom said, "The railroad station was across the street from the library. Tracks went behind the station, Albany Road went in front."

"So," Andy said, "we could walk the rail line right down into town."

"If," John said, "we could see, which we can't. And if I was ever gonna go underwater again, which I won't. And if we could find the old rail bed, which we can't."

"Well, uh," Wally said hesitantly, "*that* part would be easy. The tracks are still there."

Again he got the general stare, and again his reaction was to turn bright red.

This time it was Andy who picked up the ball, saying, "That doesn't make any sense."

"It's true, though," Wally insisted.

Andy said, "Wally, they took out all the buildings they could use. They cut down all the trees. You're telling me they left the railroad tracks? Hundreds of pounds—no, what am I saying? *Thousands* of pounds of reusable steel, and they left it there, under the reservoir?"

"Well, it's kind of interesting what happened," Wally said. "It was all ecology and conservation groups. I guess in the old days, if New York City needed more water, they'd just go up and pick a valley and move everybody out and put in the dam. But now there's all kinds of different groups and impact statements and all that stuff, so they always have to do compromises, and this time one of the groups was one that was trying to preserve the old railroad lines anyway, because there's people that want the railroads to come back because of all the traffic jams on the highway, and the pollution, and—"

"Close with it, Wally," Andy suggested.

Wally looked embarrassed again. His feet, which didn't reach the floor, started swinging back and forth. "Well, that was the compromise," he said. "They're trying to keep the railroad lines, not let them get torn up and housing developments put on them, so they can be used again someday."

"Underwater?" John asked.

"Well, only that one stretch of the line was underwater," Wally explained. "It was all mixed in with a great big negotiation, all kinds of problems and construction projects and other stuff, so part of the compromise was that these groups wouldn't complain about the reservoir and a couple of other things, and the government wouldn't tear up the railroad line all the way from Endicott up to the state line at Vermont. So it's all still there."

"Even the underwater part," May said faintly.

"Well, that was the way it was written," Wally told her, "in the compromise agreement, the whole line was supposed to stay. I guess they didn't think about the reservoir part of it when they wrote the compromise. Then later on nobody felt like they could go against what it said."

"And to think," John said, "my old parole officer—what was his name? Steen—he wanted me to become a productive member of society."

Tom said, "You see why I favor dynamite. Direct action startles those people."

Everyone looked uncomfortable, but nobody answered Tom directly. After a brief awkward silence, Andy said, "Well, you know, that's gotta make it easier. We go down in there—"

"Huh," John said.

"—and we just stay between the tracks," Andy went on. "And we don't get lost."

"No," John said.

Andy said, "John, I hear you. If we can't *see*, we don't go. But if this *Normandie* book—"

"I'm gonna get it," Wally piped up, all eagerness and bounce. "I really am."

"And if it shows us," Andy said, "how to solve the seeing problem, then, John, you know, just maybe we still got a chance."

John busied himself scraping the last bit of ice cream out of his bowl with the edge of his spoon. The sound of spoon against bowl was very loud in the small living room.

May said, "John, you put in so much time and effort on this already. And you learned all that scuba-diving knowledge. It seems such a waste, not to use it."

John looked at her. "May," he said. "You want me to go down in there again? When I just barely got *outta* there the last time? When if I go down in there again, what we're mostly talking about is what they call a watery grave? May? Do you really want me to do that again?"

"Of course not, John," May said. "Not if the problems can't be solved. I don't want to *lose* you, John. I don't want you to risk your *life* on this."

"Well, that's what I was risking," John told her. "More than I knew. And that's the end of it."

"All I'm asking, John," May said, "is you keep an open mind."

"And let all that muddy water run in."

"Just to see," May persisted. "Just to see if it's possible, to explore the options. And then, if it isn't, it isn't, and Tom goes and does it some other way."

"Boom," said Tom cheerfully.

"Okay," John said to her. "And if we keep this thing going, if we keep looking around for some kind of magic three-D glasses to look through mud with, then while we're doing all this, where's"—he jabbed a thumb at Tom, sitting comfortably to his left—"where's *this* gonna live?"

May was sure she looked as stricken as she felt. "Well," she said, "well, umm . . ." And she turned to Tiny, on her left, raising her eyebrows, hoping for a volunteer.

But Tiny looked embarrassed, and fumbled with his spoon, and wouldn't meet her eye. "Josie," he mumbled, "she wouldn't, uh, it wouldn't work out so good."

May's pleading gaze slid onto Andy, who flashed three or four quick panicky smiles and said, "Gee, May, I'd love to, but you know, my place's so small, I can barely fit *me* in there, I been planning to look for somewhere bigger for a long . . ."

May sighed and looked toward Wally on her right, but he was already shaking his head, saying, "Oh, I wish I could help, Miss May, I really do, but my little apartment's so filled up with electronics and computers and all, well, John and Andy can tell you, it's so cramped in there you can't barely sit down anywhere, and, uh . . ."

Sighing, May looked across the table at John, who met her gaze with grim satisfaction, saying, "Let's put it this way, May. I leave it up to you. You want me to forget this thing, and send everybody away? Or you want me to keep looking for underwater Seeing Eye dogs?"

May refused to look toward Tom, knowing he would be at his blandest and most careless, just sitting there, toying with his spoon. Tuna casserole curdling within her, she turned to Wally again. "How long will it take you to find that book, Wally?" she asked.

CHAPTER THIRTY-ONE

The book was called *Normandie Triangle*, and the writer was called Justin Scott, and according to the book the divers *didn't* solve the problem of cruddy, black, filthy water, also known as "turbidity." What they did was, they made a model on shore of the parts of the ship they wanted to work on, and they practiced on the model until they could do the work with their eyes closed, and *then* they went down into the water and did it; and it might just as well have been with their eyes closed.

So the book itself wasn't that much help. However, Wally, with his incredible unlimited computer access to what was apparently every piece of knowledge in the world, had come up with the fact that Justin Scott lived in New York and had a telephone. Wally had the number.

"We'll call from my place," Kelp decided. "I got a speakerphone."

"Of course you do," Dortmunder said grumpily. Andy was well known to have surrounded himself with all the latest in telephone technology, and Dortmunder was too proud to admit he didn't know what a speakerphone was.

At least Kelp wasn't one to put out cheese and crackers, though when Dortmunder arrived at his place—which wasn't that small, actually, a one-bedroom with a separate kitchen—Kelp had apparently anticipated some sort of party, because he looked past Dortmunder at the hall and said, "Where's everybody?"

"Who everybody?" Dortmunder asked, walking into the living room.

"Well, Tiny," Kelp said, standing there with the door still open. "Maybe Tom or Wally. Or could be May."

Dortmunder stood in the middle of the living room and looked at him. "Why don't you close your door, Andy?"

"Oh. Sure." And he did.

Dortmunder said, "Everybody's gonna be guided by my judgment, so they don't need to come along. If I decide I'm crazy enough to go down in that lake again, everybody's gonna let me do it."

"Let *us* do it," Kelp pointed out.

Dortmunder shook his head at him. "I don't know why you're so eager," he said.

"I'm not exactly *eager*," Kelp said. "But the thing is, I remembered about the BCD when I was down there—"

"When you weren't thinking about books."

"The BCD," Kelp said. "That's the difference right there, John. I was getting nervous, the same way you were getting, but then I remembered that good old BCD. One push on the button and up you go. When you know you can always get outta there if you need to, it makes things easier."

"Yeah, yeah," Dortmunder said. It rankled with him that he *hadn't* thought of the BCD in his moment of direst need, and it rankled double that Kelp *had* thought of it. "BCD or no BCD," he said, "if I can't walk and I can't see, I ain't going."

"So let's have a beer," Kelp suggested, "and call this guy, and see what's the story."

So they did. Dialing the number, Kelp said, "I'll switch to the speaker-phone after we start talking."

"Sure," Dortmunder said.

A little pause, and then Kelp made a face. "It's the answering machine."

"You're the *last* to complain," Dortmunder told him.

Kelp ignored that. "I'll leave my number," he decided, and sat there waiting for the answering machine message to finish itself. Then he said, "Hi, I'm a fan, my name's— What? Oh, hello! You're there!"

Little pause, Kelp nodding and grinning. "Yeah, I do that sometimes, too," he said. "Screening your calls, that's very— Oops, hold on a second."

He reached down, hit a switch on the side of the phone, and suddenly the room was filled with a voice saying, "—never get any work done."

"I agree a hundred percent," Kelp told the phone while Dortmunder stared around in shock for the source of the voice.

Which now said, "What can I do for you?"

The phone. Dortmunder got it at last; the phone had a loudspeaker in it, that's why it was called a speakerphone. So this was the writer talking.

But now it was Kelp talking, saying, "My name's Andy . . . Kelly, and

I want to tell you, I just read *Normandie Triangle* again, so that's I think the third time, and it's really terrific."

"Well, thanks," said the speakerphone. "Thanks a lot."

"Now, the reason I happened to read it again," Kelp went on, "is I have a friend with a summer house upstate on Parmalee Pond. You know Parmalee Pond?"

"As a matter of fact, I do," said the speakerphone. "A friend of *mine* has—"

"My friend," Kelp said hastily, "just bought his place. He's new there. And what he did, his first time up there, he went out in his rowboat and he was gonna take a picture of his house from the lake with this very expensive Nikon camera—"

"Don't tell me," said the speakerphone. "It fell overboard."

"It sure did."

"Reason I know is, my novel *The Shipkiller* is always falling overboard. It's about boats, and sailors drop it in the water accidentally. I know it's accidental because they call me up for another copy. They can't find it in the stores. Well, *I* can't find it in the stores either, and—"

"A truly excellent novel," Kelp silenced the writer. "My friend on Parmalee Pond admired it greatly, my friend who dropped his camera. Overboard."

Dortmunder watched Kelp with grudging admiration; this crock of horse elbows just flowed out of the guy with no effort at all.

"And he tried to get it back," Kelp was going on, spinning his story, "by putting on his scuba gear and walking into where he dropped it. But he ran into all this turbidity."

"Oh, sure," said the speakerphone. "He would. Walking in? He just roils up the bottom that way."

"That's what he did, all right," Kelp agreed. "And I remembered your book, and I read it again to see how those divers of yours got around the problem."

"They didn't," the speakerphone said. "Those who didn't wash out worked entirely by feel."

"Wash out?" Kelp echoed. "You mean, you can wash out the turbidity? With clean water, you mean?"

"No, no," the speakerphone said. "Washed out on the test they had to take before they were hired, to find out how they'd handle themselves in total darkness underwater. Eighty percent failed the test."

"Oh, yeah?" Kelp said while Dortmunder raised an eyebrow at him. "Why'd they fail, mostly?"

"They went insane from claustrophobia."

"Insane?" Kelp said, and chuckled, trying to sound light and carefree. "Really?"

"Why wouldn't they go insane?" asked the speakerphone. (A reasonable question, as far as Dortmunder was concerned.) "Consider the terror underwater in total darkness," the writer offered. "Cold and silent, you can't see your own air bubbles. You can't tell up from down." (Dortmunder nodded vigorously.) "The loudest sound is your own heart pumping. Then you start imagining things."

At that point, Dortmunder went out for two more beers, and when he came back Kelp was saying, "But the water *might* help."

"It's a funny idea," Justin Scott said. "Use water to clean the water. It might make things better, it might make them worse. But you'd have to be really braced before you turned that nozzle on."

"Yeah, I can see that. Well, thanks a lot, Mr. Scott."

When Kelp hung up, Dortmunder said, "So it isn't gonna work. I'm sorry to unleash Tom Jimson on that valley, but there's nothing we can do about it."

"Well, there's this idea of using water against the water," Kelp said.

"What idea was that? I was getting beer."

"You take a fire hose down in there with you," Kelp explained, "and turn it on to blast fresh water out in front of you, push the dirty water out of the way."

"That's a hell of a long fire hose," Dortmunder said.

"We get lengths and put them together."

"And where do we attach it?"

Kelp said, "There's a hydrant at the end of the dam. Didn't you notice it?"

"No," Dortmunder told him. "But I *did* notice your writer friend said the water idea might make it worse instead of better."

"Could make it easier to dig up Tom's stash, though," Kelp suggested. "Do it with high-pressure water instead of shovels."

"But we don't get that far," Dortmunder said, "because we go off our heads first from claustrophobia like all those other divers. Forget it. It can't be done."

"Only eighty percent of the other divers," Kelp reminded him. "Maybe we're in the other twenty percent."

"I know me better than that," Dortmunder said.

CHAPTER THIRTY-TWO

So the agreement was Tom could stay one more night, but the next day he'd have to make other arrangements. "I want you to know, Al," Tom said, when Dortmunder came back from his telephone conversation at Kelp's place, "I got to give you an A for effort."

"I think it's an E for effort," Dortmunder said.

"Whatever it is, Al," Tom told him, "you got it from me. I tell ya, I kinda wish it'd worked out. A nice quiet little heist would've been better in a lotta ways."

"Yeah, it would," Dortmunder agreed.

"Well," Tom said, with a little shrug, "you win some, you lose some."

Everybody was depressed that evening and didn't feel like talking. Dortmunder went to bed early and lay awake awhile, thinking about water: dirty dark water all around his own personal head, or billions of gallons of water crashing in a tidal wave into Dudson Falls and Dudson Center and East Dudson. After a while, he fell asleep, and then he dreamed about water in a whole lot of different uncomfortable ways.

And then, middle of the night, all of a sudden he woke up wide awake, staring at the ceiling. "Well, hell," he said out loud.

"Mrm?" said May, beside him.

Dortmunder sat up in the dark bedroom, glaring at the opposite wall. "Goddamn son of a bitch bastard all to hell and *shit*," he announced.

May, waking up, propped herself on an elbow to say, "John? What's wrong?"

"I know how to do it, that's what's wrong," Dortmunder told her. "Tom stays. And I go down in that goddamn reservoir again. Hell!"

CHAPTER THIRTY-THREE

Real life. Wally sat in the *front seat* of the baby-blue Lincoln Continental, the road maps on his round knees, and directed everything. Andy was at the steering wheel beside him, while John slumped on the backseat and frowned to himself like a person doing multiplication problems in his head. Directly in front of Wally was the windshield, like technology's largest and most true-fidelity monitor screen, displaying endlessly . . . *the real world*.

A cellular telephone was mounted on the floor hump between Wally's knees and Andy's knees, and for some time as they drove north out of the city it intermittently rang; fifteen or twenty rings, and then silence for a while, and then another six rings, and silence, and so on. When it first happened, Wally said, "Andy? What's that? Should I answer it?"

"In my experience," Andy answered, "it's usually the doctor, wanting his car back. So I tend to leave it alone."

Wally digested that, while the phone stopped ringing, and then started again. But no Greek was ever as obsessed by the cry of the Sirens as the average American is by the ringing of a telephone; any telephone, anywhere. In this respect, at least, Wally was a true American. There was no way this phone call could be for him, since it was neither his phone nor his car, and yet his left hand twitched with the need to reach out and pick the thing up. After a while, a bit plaintively, he said, "Andy? Are you sure? Maybe it's something important."

"Important to who?"

"I guess so," Wally said, still pensive.

Andy shrugged. "It's up to you, Wally," he said. "If you want to hear an angry doctor make a lot of empty threats, go ahead, pick it up."

Wally kind of visualized that doctor. He was in a long white lab coat, holding the phone in one hand and a scalpel in the other, and boy, was he mad! Wally thought it over and decided he probably didn't need to hear what the man had to say, and shortly after that the phone stopped ringing for good. Either the doctor had given up, or they'd moved out of range.

They were quite far north now. Big green signs announced North Dudson as the next exit from the Thruway. Wally, suddenly nervous, began to rattle his maps, self-conscious and shy. He had maps for the area as it was now, and maps for the area from before the reservoir was put in, and the reservoir was only one of the changes that had taken place in the intervening years. Wally felt the awful weight of his responsibility, to guide these people and this car through the modern map to one specific spot on the old map. And to do so without revealing his own extra knowledge of the terrain.

None of the others knew about that private trip of his up here; not telling them about it had been another part of the computer's advice. In fact, the whole trip had been at the advice of the computer. After Wally had input the story of the unknown women following them around in circles, the computer had said he should definitely find out who those people were.

The hero must identify his helpers.

The hero must know his enemies.

All players in the game must be aware of one another.

So he had gotten out his little old yellow VW Beetle that he only drove four or five times a year and that he kept otherwise in a Department of Transportation garage on Twelfth Avenue rent-free (arranged through his computer access), and he'd putt-putted all the way up to North Dudson—the farthest he'd *ever* gone in that car—and he'd driven around and around looking for a black Ford Fairlane, knowing that even in a town like this there couldn't be more than one such vehicle, and when he saw it at last—just got a glimpse of it, really—at the end of a driveway, in front of an old-fashioned two-door garage, being washed by an angry-looking old lady, the rest had been easy.

Wally, who was almost always tongue-tied and shy with other people—especially girls—had partly by luck and partly out of a sense of self-preservation begun his conversation with Myrtle Jimson on the one topic that would permit him to be fluent, even eloquent: computers. By the time they were through with that, some level of rapport had been established, and he was even confident and relaxed enough to ask her to join him for lunch.

All through lunch at Kitty's Kountry Kitchen on Main Street they'd just talked. Wally told her about growing up in Florida, and she told him about growing up in North Dudson, and there was just nothing in any of what she told him to explain the car-following incident.

Was she even related to Tom Jimson? But the name *couldn't* be a coincidence, it just couldn't. In the first place, coincidence does not exist in the world of the computer. [Randomness (a.k.a. chance) has been factored into some of the more sophisticated games, but coincidence (a.k.a. meaningless correspondence other than junk mail) violates the human craving for order. Which is why puns are the pornography of mathematicians.] But knowing the computer would be just as confused as he when he reported back to it (and it was) didn't help Wally's mood much.

Myrtle had insisted on paying for her own lunch, and then he'd walked her back to the library, where she'd promised to keep using her computer terminal from now on, and where he'd gotten back into his yellow VW and putt-putted away to the city. And this was the first time he'd been back among the Dudsons since. "It's our next exit, Andy," he said, rattling his maps.

"I know that, Wally," Andy said, amiably enough. "The State of New York spent three hundred thousand dollars to put up a sign there to tell me so."

"Oh," Wally said. "I wasn't sure you saw it."

"Thanks, anyway, Wally," Andy said.

So Wally subsided again, as Andy steered the Lincoln Continental expertly off the Thruway and around the ramp and down the narrow road into North Dudson.

As usual, the town was full of people who'd forgotten why they were driving. In a pleasant voice, Andy made speculative remarks about such people's ancestry, education, brain power, and sexual bent, while Wally, scandalized, his ears burning (his earlobes actually felt hot, so suffused with blood from his blushing were they), blinked obsessively at his maps, double-checking and triple-checking his projected route, and from the backseat John gave an occasional long sigh. His sighs didn't seem to comment on Andy's language or the quality of North Dudson's drivers so much as on life itself.

"Pilot to navigator," Andy said, as pleasant as ever.

Wally jumped, rattled, the maps sliding from his knees to the floor. "What? Me?"

"We're out of that charming village," Andy pointed out. "It's time to give me directions, Wally."

"Right! Right!"

"Turn right?"

"Not yet!" Wally was scrabbling about for his maps. "Stay on this road until, uh, uh . . ."

"Take your time," Andy said, and John sighed.

Wally found his maps and his place. "We turn right," he said, "at, uh, where the road says to Dudson Falls."

"Check," Andy said, and a few miles later made the turn, and all the subsequent turns Wally told him about, as they maneuvered their way through the spider web of back roads; these roads, already a planless catch-as-catch-can hodgepodge by the middle of the twentieth century, had only been made more complicated when the reservoir was dumped in their midst.

"It should be around here somewhere, shouldn't it?" Andy asked as they bumped over an old railroad track.

Wally stared at him to be sure he wasn't joking. "Andy? That was it!"

Andy frowned at the rearview mirror. "What was it?"

"We're looking for the railroad," Wally reminded him. "We just drove over it, Andy."

"By God, you're right," Andy said, and swung the Lincoln off the road to wait for an oncoming bulk milk truck to pass. "I think what it is, Wally," he said, "I never went looking for anything so *short* before."

"I guess," Wally said.

Andy swung around behind the milk truck, reapproached the railroad line, and again pulled off onto the verge, where a million spring weeds were in flower. They all climbed out, stretched, shook their legs as though looking for a quarter that had fallen through a hole in their pocket, and went over to look at the railroad line.

It was a singleton, one pair of rusty tracks stretching off both ways into the woods, here and there partly covered by encroaching weeds and brush. The section across the blacktop road was less rusty than the rest, which had aged to a dull dark blackish red. Set back on both sides of the road were barriers across the rail line, these consisting of two broad bands of horizontal metal attached to metal stakes set in concrete footings. The barriers had once been painted white, but most of the color had rusted away. Signs reading NO ENTRY were screwed to them.

Andy beamed at the railroad line. "You know what this reminds me of?"

"Yes," John said. "It reminds you of Tom Thumb." He didn't sound particularly cheerful about it.

But Andy *was* cheerful. "You're right!" he said.

John looked back and forth, then said to Wally, "Which way's the reservoir?"

Wally pointed to the right. "Two miles that way."

"Two miles," John repeated, and sighed.

"That isn't so far," Andy told him. "Two miles, just a good healthy walk."

"Four miles," John said. "Unless you figure to live there."

"Well, let's get started," Andy said, walking around one side of the barrier.

John said, "I don't suppose there's any way to get that car onto the tracks."

"Even if it was the same gauge, John," Andy said, leaning on the barrier on its other side, "we'd have to chop down these three or four trees here to get the car in."

John glared at him. "Gauge? What do you mean, gauge?"

Andy pointed at the tracks. "If the width between the rails is the same as the width between the tires on the car, then we can let some of the air out of the tires and put the car up on the tracks and drive on in. But it probably isn't the same, and we can't get the car in here anyway, so why are we talking about it? Why don't we just walk?"

"I wore the wrong shoes," John said, but then he shook his head and walked around the barrier, and the three of them set off along the old line toward the reservoir.

As they walked, trying to adjust their pace to the distance between the old half-rotted ties, Wally said, "Andy? What did you mean, Tom Thumb?"

"It was a locomotive," Andy explained. "One time, John and me and some other people, we had to get into a place with an electrified fence, and there was an old track like this, and we got a locomotive from a circus—pretty locomotive, painted all different colors, called Tom Thumb—and we drove right through the fence." To John, he said, "Things worked out that time, too."

"Later on they did," John admitted grudgingly. "Kind of."

Wally wanted to know *what* place they had to get into that had an electrified fence and *why* they had to get into that place, but he didn't exactly know how to ask, and he suspected anyway that Andy wouldn't tell him. Andy was very cheerful and open and everything, but then later on you realized he told you as much as he wanted to tell you and then he stopped. Wally imagined the bright-painted locomotive crashing through the electrified fence. "Were there sparks?"

"You bet!" Andy said, and laughed. "The crazy people were running everywhere!"

"I guess they must have been," Wally agreed, hoping for more.

But John interrupted, saying, "Isn't this two miles?"

"John," Andy said, "we can still see the *barrier* back there."

"I don't know why I wore these shoes," John said.

Then they walked in silence for a while, Wally contemplating the fact that an accent had been wrong in that last thing Andy had said about the train and the electrified fence. He should have said, "The crazy *people* were running everywhere," but what he'd said was, "The *crazy* people . . ." Why?

"Fence ahead," Andy said.

It was a chain-link fence, eight feet high, with three strands of barbed wire at the top, and it crossed the railroad line from left to right. When they neared it, they saw the expected sign.

NO ADMITTANCE
VILBURGTOWN RESERVOIR AUTHORITY

"Gosh," Wally said. "What do we do now?"

"*I'm* gonna sit down," John said, and went over to a nearby log and sat on it.

Meantime, Andy approached the fence, took a pair of wire cutters out of his inner jacket pocket, went down on one knee, and started snipping the fence from the bottom. Wally goggled: "You're cutting the fence!"

"Well, we're not going over it," Andy said, snipping away, "and I didn't bring a shovel to dig under it, so this is pretty much what's left."

Wally looked at the official sign: NO ADMITTANCE. In games, sometimes, it was necessary to do shortcuts across the regular routes; so this must be the real-life equivalent. And when Wally stopped to think about it, what startled him mostly was not what Andy was doing, but his *calm* while doing it. Whenever Wally set out on an adventure in the computer, the *excitement* was what it was all about; but Andy and John did adventures as though they were *jobs*.

"There," Andy said, straightening, putting the wire clippers away. "John? You wanna go first?"

John sighed, got up from the log, and came across to study the fence. Andy had snipped a vertical line up about four feet; it barely showed at all. John said, "That isn't enough."

"Sure it is," Andy told him. "Wally, you pull that side in. I'll push this side out. Plenty of room to get through."

There was barely room enough, as it turned out. With Wally pulling and Andy pushing, it was like opening an envelope. John slithered through, complaining, and then he took over Wally's role while Wally grunted and squeezed past, not quite ripping any of his clothing, and then Wally and John held the fence for Andy, and there they were on the other side.

But still some distance from the reservoir. They walked and walked, with John complaining from time to time and Andy pointing out pretty flowers or oddly shaped tree limbs, and at last they saw the bright glint of sunlight reflecting from water out ahead.

That was very strange. The railroad tracks ran straight into the reservoir, under the water and gone. On both sides, tangled brush and small trees made an impassable obstruction right down to the water's edge, with no path or cleared shoreline in either direction.

Andy pointed to the left along the overgrown bank, saying, "That's where we went in last time, way over there. So we're farther from the dam now."

"Don't remind me of the last time," John answered. Turning to Wally, he said, "You're sure this goes all the way down in there to the town."

"Oh, sure. And out the other side," Wally promised him, pointing to the far shore. "But over there, it's a lot farther from Putkin's Corners."

Andy, looking dubious, said, "I dunno, John, I guess we *could* go look at the tracks on the other side, if you think we ought to."

"No," John said. "What matters is what happens underwater, and we can't know that until we . . ." another long sigh, accompanied by a headshake ". . . go down there."

"Well," Andy said, "the point of the trip was to see are the tracks here, and do they go into the water. They are, and they do."

"And they go all the way across underneath," Wally assured them.

"Well," John said, "I look, and I look, and I just can't find any reason not to do it. So I guess that's it."

Excitement leaped in Wally's breast. They were going to try again. Maybe this time, he thought, they'd let him come along. Not to go down into the reservoir, he had no desire at *all* to do anything like *that*, but just to be one of the people up here on the bank, helping out, waiting, doing whatever the people up here did while John and Andy were down there in the cold and the dark and the wet. Trying not to sound too eager, he said, "Well, John? What do you do now?"

"Now," John said, "I talk to Tom about more money."

CHAPTER THIRTY-FOUR

Dortmunder kept squinting. He couldn't help it. It wasn't the light in *here*, which was ordinary enough, it was knowing about all that space out *there*, sensing it, just the other side of these blank walls. In *here*, in an airport terminal building in the unnecessarily large, flat, *tan* state of Oklahoma, Dortmunder stood against one of the walls with two small suitcases at his feet, hurrying travelers eddying around him as Tom, at one of the chest-high counters across the way, rented a car (again!) from a robot shaped like a short smiling girl. Dortmunder had shown his driver's license to this automaton, since he would be driving the car when rented, but then he had retreated to this distant vantage while Tom handled the repellent commercial aspects of the transaction.

Finally finished, Tom stepped across the stream of travelers as though they weren't there, causing several people to bump into one another but none to bump into him, and picked up his bag from beside Dortmunder's left foot. "Okay," he said. "We go out and wait for the bus."

"No cars?" Dortmunder asked.

Tom lowered his eyebrows at him. "The bus to the car," he said. "Don't start with me, Al."

"I don't know about these things," Dortmunder reminded him, picking up his own bag, and they went out of the terminal building, watched by every cop, Federal agent, and private security guard in the place, all of whom were certain in their hearts those two birds were up to *something*.

When a lawman looked at Dortmunder and Tom Jimson, particularly together, he said to himself, "*Probable Cause* is their middle name."

Outside, it was still just airport, normal airport, with horizontal concrete between the slabs of vertical concrete, but Dortmunder *knew* Oklahoma was just out there, just a step away, just around a concrete corner. "Sunny," he complained.

Every car rental company had its own buses, and they were *all* weird-looking, with oddball color patterns and hatlike outgrowths and strangely placed fins, as though they were designed by the same people who draw spaceships in comic books. Tom rejected several of these, for no reason Dortmunder could see, and then accepted one, and they got aboard with a lot of white men in suits carrying garment bags. Among these solid citizens, Dortmunder and Tom looked like exactly what they were: ex-cons, up to no good. The driver was the only person who noticed them, and he kept an eye on them in his rearview mirror all the way out of the airport and down the wide sunstruck road to the rental company's parking lot.

The driver had collected a stuffed envelope from each of his passengers, including Tom, and now he dropped off each renter right at the car he'd been assigned in the great lottery, giving Tom and Dortmunder a small white vehicle like a washing machine with four tiny doors. "I like Andy's cars better," Dortmunder said as they jammed their small bags into the no-leg-room backseat.

"I like a car the state cops aren't looking for," Tom told him.

They got into the front, Dortmunder at the wheel, and as he steered the little machine along, following one exit sign after another, Tom checked out the radio, to discover that his choices included thirty-seven stations playing rock music, four religious broadcasters, and one all-news station operating under the theory that "all news" meant "sports." Tom finally settled on one of the religious programs and sat back, content.

"The bad man *is* among us, my friends, he is in our hearts and our minds, and our Lord and Creator *sees* him, my friends, *sees* us *shelter* him. . . ."

"Hee-hee," said Tom.

• • •

Soon enough they had left the airport and come out to nothing. *Nothing.* As far as the eye could see. "You wouldn't believe how empty this all was before the white man came," Tom said, looking around at the nothing.

"Uh-huh," Dortmunder said.

For somebody who had lived his entire life in cities or the tumbled landscapes of hills and mountains, this nothing was extremely scary. If somebody a thousand miles over *that* way accidentally shot a gun, he could blow your head off. Dortmunder drove the little white washing machine down the broad white road in the scanty-to-moderate traffic, and tried to pretend something had gone wrong with his peripheral vision so that there really *was* something to left and right; a building, a hill, a few trees, *something*. He was glad, at least, to be sitting down; if he stood up he'd run a real risk of losing his balance.

"Head toward Norman," Tom said as they approached a cloverleaf interchange with another highway. The overpasses stood out like croquet hoops on a lawn.

"I'll be able to see it, won't I?" Dortmunder asked.

"What, Norman? No, we'll turn off before we get there and head west toward Chickasaw."

"No, I meant as soon as I turn toward it," Dortmunder explained.

Tom frowned, working that one out, while on the radio the preacher described in loving detail various activities taking place even now in Hell. "You mean," Tom said seriously, "that it's kinda flat around here."

"Something like that."

"I grew up in this territory," Tom said. "When the dust came."

"The Okies, you mean," Dortmunder suggested.

"I guess I was an Okie," Tom said. "Not like in that movie, though."

"No."

"Sit around the campfire, sing a song. Go into a gas station with your big old dead truck fulla mattresses, women, dying old men, whadda you do?"

"Run," said Dortmunder.

"In the movie," Tom said, "they *bought gas*. Paid for it."

"You rent cars," Dortmunder pointed out.

"Not the same thing," Tom said. "I do what I gotta do to make life smooth. I rent cars because I *can*."

"Wha'd you do, back in the Okie days, in that gas station?"

"Shot parts off the kid until he remembered the combination to the safe," Tom said. "There's your turn up there."

CHAPTER THIRTY-FIVE

The way it turned out, the stash in the church had been the only one of Tom's unofficial banks situated in the northeast. Tom did grudgingly admit there were other stashes still out of the lawyers' hands, but they were all far away, in different parts of the country. He didn't feel like traveling, didn't like the idea of giving up all his last stashes, didn't want to be helpful at all, so finally Dortmunder had suggested the two of them go together to wherever the hell it was, bringing along overnight bags for if they had to stay a little while, but planning to do it all as quickly as possible. Go there, make the withdrawal, come back.

"But an easy one, okay, Tom?" Dortmunder had said. "No more weddings, okay? Not crowds of people all around."

"Well," Tom had said, "how about a place with *nobody* around? How do you feel about a ghost town?"

So that's where they were headed, and along the way Tom explained what had happened to Cronley, Oklahoma, to turn it from a bustling cow town and transportation hub at the turn of the century into the dry, crumbling, empty shell it was today. "It was the railroad done it, mostly," Tom said.

"Railroads," Dortmunder echoed, steering along an empty two-lane road in the middle of Oklahoma but thinking about the steel tracks running down into the water back up in the green mountains of upstate New York. "All of a sudden there's railroads all over this."

"It was the other way around in Cronley," Tom told him. "All of a sudden, no railroads at all."

"Well, that happened everywhere."

"Not like this," Tom said. "See, Cronley was a farm town to start with, on a little stream between the Canadian and Cimarron Rivers, the place where people went to buy their salt and sell their milk. Then, when the railroad come through, after the Civil War, Cronley got bigger, got to be county seat, a whole lot of warehouses got built, offices for businessmen, a big five-story hotel down by the railroad station for traveling salesmen, tallest building in town."

"Five stories?" Dortmunder asked.

Tom ignored that, saying, "So, the drought in the thirties hit Cronley pretty hard, because all the farmers around there went away, cut down the population. But the town kept going until the fifties, when Oklahoma made its big mistake."

"The whole state?"

"That's it," Tom said. "See, Oklahoma stayed dry after Prohibition. What it is, you take people, you give them a lot of trouble and misery, what they *always* do, every single time, Al, you can set your watch by this, what they do is, they decide *God* gave them all this trouble and misery because they done something wrong, so if they give *themselves* even *more* trouble and misery maybe God'll let up on them. You see it everywhere. In the Middle Ages—a guy inside told me this—back then, the big way to keep from getting the plague was to beat yourself with whips. So Oklahoma, poor and miserable and dry as dust, decided to make itself even drier so then maybe God would leave them alone. So, no booze."

"That was the mistake?" Dortmunder asked. "That's what killed Cronley? No booze?"

"It set the situation up," Tom answered. "See, what happens is, you put a law on the books, no matter how dumb it is, sooner or later somebody's gonna come along dumb enough to enforce it. That's what happened back in the fifties. Oklahoma cops boarded a through passenger train and arrested the bartender in the bar car for serving drinks in a dry state."

"Wait a minute," Dortmunder said. "On the *train?*"

"The through train, comin in this side of the state, goin out that side. Took the barman off, put him in jail overnight, the railroad people come around the next day and got him out." Tom did that thing of grinning without moving his lips. "Fun night for the barman, huh? Al, you're gonna take that county road up there."

Up ahead, a small sign indicated a side road on the left. Since Tom had steered them off the interstate a while back, each road he'd put them on had been smaller and less populated, and now he was directing Dortmunder from an empty two-lane blacktop road onto a *narrow* two-lane oiled gravel road wandering off across scrub land as though it had been laid out by a thirsty snake.

At least the countryside wasn't so flat in this middle part of the state; low, bare, brown hills now rose up around them, with taller and craggier (though just as barren) hills out ahead. This new road angled upward slightly, becoming rutted and rocky, as though rain sometimes fell here. Using both hands on the wheel to steer around the bumps and holes, Dortmunder said, "The last we heard, the bartender spent the night in jail."

"Right," Tom said. "So what the railroads did, the next couple years, they kept shifting routes around, and when they were done there *wasn't* any trains in Oklahoma anymore."

Surprised, but also pleased at the thought of such extensive revenge, Dortmunder said, "Is that right?"

"That's right, all right," Tom told him. "Even today, you take a look at the Amtrak map, the railroad lines go all around Oklahoma, but they never go *in*. And that's what killed Cronley. No trains, no reason for the damn place. Now, there's gonna be a turnoff along here somewhere, Al, but they probably don't keep it up a hell of a lot, so we gotta watch for it."

"Left or right?"

"Right."

Dortmunder slowed the little white washing machine to a walk and hugged the right edge of the narrow roadway, but still they almost missed it. "Damn, Al!" Tom suddenly cried. "That was it! My fault this time, I shoulda seen it."

Dortmunder braked to a stop and considered Tom. "Your fault *this* time?"

"That's what I said," Tom agreed, looking over his right shoulder at the ground behind them. "Come on, Al, back up, will ya?"

Dortmunder took a deep breath and held it. Then he nodded to himself, released the deep breath, shifted into reverse, and squirted the washing machine backward, gravel spraying hither and yon.

"Take it easy, Al," Tom said calmly, looking out his window. He stuck his arm out the open window into the air and pointed, saying, "See it? See it there?"

Then Dortmunder did; crumbled blacktop, covered with dirt and weeds. "That's it?"

"This was the back road in the old days," Tom said. "This thing we're on used to be paved, too."

"Well, why don't we take the front road?" Dortmunder asked him.

"It's gone," Tom said. "They ripped up part of it when they put in one a the interstates, and another part got sold off to some agribusiness. So now this is it."

"How far from here?"

"Maybe six miles."

"I don't know," Dortmunder said. "Maybe we want a Jeep for this. Or a tank, maybe."

"We'll be fine," Tom assured him. "Just drive, Al."

So Dortmunder drove, steering his little white appliance out onto a surface it had never been intended to know. Much of the roadway was crumbled away or undercut and gullied by rain, and a lot of the rest had weeds growing up right through the blacktop. The road had originally been a fairly wide two lanes, but the worst damage had worked inward from the outer edges, so now in parts it was barely as wide as the car, and *never* was it within the range of the civilized or the acceptable.

Which Tom didn't seem to mind. While the vehicle made about four miles an hour—an hour and a half to Cronley, at this rate—and Dortmunder hunched over the steering wheel, forehead pressed to the windshield as he looked for axle-breaking holes out there, Tom chatted casually on, saying, "This is one of my oldest stashes, you know. Just after the war, it was. GI Joe comin home from everywhere, the streets lined with sharpers with decks a cards in their hands, just waiting. There was a fella in Cronley, stayed at the hotel there, had a girl named Myra. Lotta soldier boys got off the train there, headed back to the farm, or transfer to another train. Those days, you could take the train from Cronley down to Wichita Falls or up to Wichita or over to Amarillo, or all kinds of places. This fella—what was his name?—doesn't matter. Him and Myra, they worked those soldiers pretty good, the fella play some poker with them up in the hotel room, Myra stand around looking sexy. So I got in good with Myra for a while, had her give me the high sign when there was a lotta money in the room, leave the door unlocked, and me and two other guys walked in and took it." Tom nodded. Without moving his lips, he said, "Hee-hee." Then he said, "Those other two guys, they didn't know about me and Myra. So they run into the elevator and I shut the door on them and yanked the power and carried the cash to the room Myra'd rented for me."

Dortmunder said, "Yanked the power? You mean you shut off the electricity in the hotel?"

"To confuse things," Tom explained.

"With your partners in the elevator?"

"Ex-partners," Tom corrected, and did his chuckle again, and said, "The soldiers got kinda rough on them two until the law got there."

"Didn't they search the hotel?" Dortmunder asked.

"Oh, sure," Tom said. "But Myra fixed me up so I was her sister, and—"

"Sister!"

"Myra was the one with the looks," Tom said. "But I was the one with the brains, so when the deck-a-cards guy found out Myra'd been in with the hijackers—"

"How'd he find out about that?"

"Well, how do *you* think, Al?" Tom asked.

"That's how," Dortmunder said, steering around the dangers in the road.

"So by then," Tom said, "I was outta there. But I couldn't take much of that cash with me, so I left it right there in the hotel, where it was safe."

"How much?"

"We got sixteen thousand in the heist, so I took along two with me, left fourteen."

"And now," Dortmunder said, as the little tires of the machine plunged into the holes and clawed up the other sides, "you think this fourteen grand is gonna still be there, forty years later."

"Absolutely," Tom said. "I'm not comin all the way out here, Al, for the fresh *air*. And not to look up Myra either."

"How old would she be now?" Dortmunder asked.

"She wouldn't," Tom told him. "Broads like Myra don't live long."

Not for the first time, Dortmunder found himself wondering just what in *hell* he was doing in association with Tom Jimson in any way at all. Back in prison there hadn't been any choice in the matter—cell assignments hadn't become negotiable until he'd been in there considerably longer—but in any case, back there he always had the comfort of knowing there was armed assistance constantly within shouting range.

What do I care about the people in that valley? Dortmunder asked himself, as the little white LEM progressed toward the dead Cronley. If I *went* there, walked around one of those Dudsons, people look out their windows, they see me, they'd call the cops. Saving that valley from Tom Jimson isn't *my* obligation, dammit. I got into this thing because he startled me, that's all, and it didn't seem like it was gonna be that hard, take that long, have so many problems. So now I'm in it, and here I am in *Oklahoma*, like some kind of pioneer or something, driving this beer keg with wheels. Makes no sense at all.

"There it is," Tom said, breaking a long and uncharacteristic silence.

Dortmunder slowed the vehicle almost to a dead stop so he could risk looking up and out. They'd just come over a low humpback ridge, and out ahead of them now was more greenery than Dortmunder had seen since the salad on the plane. This greenery, though, was mostly trees, short squat trees, deeply green, a thin platoon of them stretching to left and right. Since they'd spent most of the afternoon crossing this miserable imitation road, the trees' shadows spread long pointing fingers out to the right, as though suggesting visitors would be advised to take a detour. Sticking up above this linear forest were a couple of buildings and a church steeple.

Dortmunder said, "Trees on account of a river there, huh?"

"Al, you're a regular woodsman," Tom said.

"And that's your town, huh?"

"That's my *stash*," Tom said. "The tall building there, that's the hotel."

"Tall building," said Dortmunder.

"You can laugh, Al," Tom said, though Dortmunder had done no such thing. "But from Myra's room up there on the top floor, you could see for miles."

"See *what* for miles?"

Tom did his chuckle. "Well, us, for instance," he said.

CHAPTER THIRTY-SIX

Guffey watched the little white car roll slowly toward town. The binoculars made it seem closer than it was, but flattened everything out. The scope on the 30-03 was better; more definition. He could just about put a round through the windshield into either one of those bobbing heads from here, at this range. If he wanted to. Not that there was any particular reason to shoot those two strangers down like dirty dogs; not yet, anyway. Not until they got close enough, not until he could see who they were.

And what if it was—Guffey's leathery old hands trembled on the stock of the rifle—what if one of them was *him*?

Tim Jepson. At long long last.

"The fella that ruint my life," Guffey whispered through dry cracked lips. He lowered the rifle and his rheumy old eyes watched unaided as the small white car rocked and bobbed slowly this way. Tim Jepson.

Except it wouldn't be, of course. It never had been yet, no matter how long he waited, no matter how much he cultivated his patience. In twenty-six years, it had never once been Tim Jepson coming back to Cronley, coming back to pick up his fourteen thousand dollars.

But it *would* be! Someday! Someday it would be! But never today.

At first, in the early sixties, the occasional visitor—trespasser? invader? transient?—to the recently dead town of Cronley had been mostly just another looter hoping to find plumbing fixtures or brass doorknobs the previous looters had missed. Those had been tough, gritty, nasty city people

184

in greasy green work clothes, driving slat-sided trucks and smoking cigars. They reminded Guffey of the toughest element back in prison, and so he kept out of their way, moving his few possessions with him, and not one of them had ever even known Cronley still possessed one last resident.

In the latter sixties, a different kind of visitor started to arrive: young dropouts in bright-colored clothing and headbands, like goofy Indians. They came in beat-up Volkswagen buses, they lit a lot of campfires, they played mopey music on portable phonographs, and they planted corn and tomatoes and marijuana. Only the marijuana came up, and soon each hopeful band decided to drop back in; Guffey would watch their buses jounce away over the ridge.

Very few of the dropouts became aware of the old hermit of Cronley, though a few of the girls did catch him peeping at them while they skinny-dipped in the river. Most of the girls got scared and mad, and told their boys, and Guffey would have to go off again and hide in the woods for a few days until they stopped looking for him; but one girl had beckoned with a crooked little finger and a crooked little grin, and my *goodness*! That was Guffey's only sexual experience since before he'd gone to prison—over forty years now, it must be—but it was a humdinger. Well worth remembering. Kept a fella going when the nights got cold.

The hippies and yippies and trippies and flippies thinned out in the early seventies, and for a few years Guffey had Cronley absolutely to himself. Then, starting in the late seventies, the professors began to show up: archaeologists, anthropologists, ethnologists, social historians. Men and women alike, they wore khaki trousers and heavy boots and lots of clothing with labels that read L. L. BEAN. (Guffey stole some of their gear to replenish his own worn-out stuff.)

Eventually, though, grant money must have veered off in some other direction. It had been almost ten years now since Guffey had seen a safari-hatted, heavy-booted professor out around these parts. More recently there'd been a little spate of carpenters and architects and interior decorators looking for wood; barn wood, staircase newels, old and interesting panels. They encouraged the further deterioration of Cronley pretty well, but that was a short-lived fad, over and done with while the town was still moderately full of good wood. Guffey guessed it must be three, maybe even four years since another human being had ventured out this way.

And now this little white car. With his natural sense of caution, as the car approached the outskirts of town Guffey gathered up his few belongings, left his room on the top floor of the Cronley Hotel, and made his way down the peeling, scabrous hall to the stairs. The elevator hadn't worked for years, of course, and in any event Guffey would never ride that elevator again.

That or any other elevator, but especially *that* one. *That* elevator was where his troubles had begun.

It was him and Eddie Hobbs and Tim Jepson when it started. Jepson was older than him and Eddie. They knew he was a hardcase, and they wanted to be hardcases just like him, and when he invited them to throw in with him on the hijacking, it had just seemed like a lark, kind of. They weren't going to rob anybody *good*, after all, but were going to hit up a card shark, a fella that had been taking advantage of the returning GIs. That's the way Jepson had presented it, and him and Eddie, nineteen and dumb and fresh off the farm, had gone right along with it.

And Jepson had betrayed them. Stuck them in an elevator without any power and took off with the loot. Him and Eddie were frantic in that elevator, in the dark, and things didn't improve any once the lights came back and the elevator started again to move. When it reached bottom, they knew, when it reached bottom and the door slid open, all hell would break loose.

And it did. The trouble was, nobody *else* bought the idea that him and Eddie were stealing from a card shark. The way everybody else saw it—including the soldiers who'd been in that room with playing cards in their hands when him and Eddie and Tim busted in with guns in their hands—who him and Eddie were stealing from was *soldiers*.

Brave soldiers, just barely home, the war just barely over. People who would steal from soldiers didn't get much benefit of the doubt in those days.

In the next few years, Guffey got beat up a *lot*. It started the instant that elevator door opened, and there were all the soldiers who'd been playing poker in that room upstairs. The cops were there by then, too, but they were in no hurry to break up a good solid thrashing, so it was quite awhile before him and Eddie were carried from the hotel to the hospital.

That was the last Guffey ever saw of Eddie, who had some sort of aunt who knew a state legislator or something, and so got his case separated from Guffey's. Eventually, Guffey went on trial, where he drew the maximum, twenty-five to forty, because it was soldiers and because he'd been carrying a gun and because he already had a little record from some wildness in his youth (which was why he wasn't in the army), but mostly because Tim Jepson had got away with all the money.

Guffey's reputation had preceded him to the state pen, where first the guards beat him up and then the other prisoners beat him up and then the guards took a turn again. That slackened off after a while, but just around then some ex-soldiers began to show up in the prisoner population. Most of them felt they'd faced injustice in one way or another while they were in uniform, and Guffey was a handy way to gain redress.

Somewhere in through there, a fellow named Mitch Lynch came in, doing a heavy term for a long-con frammis against an oilman in Tulsa. Guffey didn't recognize Lynch as the sharper him and Eddie and Tim Jepson had hijacked, but Lynch recognized Guffey as one of the assholes who'd come storming into his private suite with a gun in his hand, so Lynch set himself the task of beating the hell out of Guffey, only to discover it was already gone. The hell had *been* beat out of Guffey; having a go at that little fella was like punching out a mop. Lynch ran him around the track a couple times, but got no real satisfaction out of it, and gradually, in some weird way, Guffey and Lynch became friends. Acquaintances, anyway.

It was from Lynch that Guffey learned how Lynch's girl Myra had betrayed Lynch for Tim Jepson, and then how Tim had betrayed Myra to Lynch before taking off with the dough. Or, not with the dough; that was the interesting part.

Myra had sworn to Lynch that Tim was stashing most of the sixteen thousand he'd taken in the robbery—fourteen, she was pretty sure—somewhere right in town, that he didn't want to have to travel with a suspicious amount of cash on him, and that he figured he'd just leave the money there until he needed it someday.

Lynch had questioned Myra pretty rigorously on the subject of *where* Tim had hidden the fourteen thousand, and so he was damn certain in his mind that Myra didn't know the answer, or she would have told him. "Someday I'm gettin out of here," Lynch said, more than once. "And when I do, I'm goin back to Cronley, and I'm gonna wait. Get a job, do whatever, I don't care. Because someday that son of a bitch is gonna show up."

Well, so far, Lynch had been wrong on just about everything. He *hadn't* gotten out of prison, not standing straight up; an exercise yard argument in 1952 had ended with a sharpened spoon handle stuck through Lynch's ribs and into his heart. And even if he'd lived to get back to Cronley, it would have been empty by then, so there wouldn't have been any job for him. And up till now, Tim Jepson had not come back for his fourteen thousand.

When Guffey had been released from prison, after doing eighteen years of his time, the man who'd come blinking out onto the street was a lot older than his chronological thirty-seven. He no longer had any of his own teeth. So many of his bones had been broken so often that he moved like an arthritis sufferer of eighty. And he'd pretty well lost all capacity to live as a social animal. He was a solitary, who either cowered or snarled. He couldn't hold a job, couldn't keep a room to live in, couldn't get on a *bus* without making some kind of trouble. His parole officer hated him, and his parole officer was well known to be a living saint.

It was when Guffey found himself seriously considering what sort of crime he could commit that would guarantee his old cell back that he knew he had to take corrective action real quick, and that's when he remembered Tim Jepson, the man who had ruined his life, and Mitch Lynch, the man who had planned to be patient and alone and await his revenge. The memory of those two men, and the thought that Cronley had *no people* in it, was enough. By bus, by stolen bicycle, and at last on foot, Guffey made his move.

For twenty-six years, Guffey had been Cronley's only resident, waiting, nursing his resentments, rebuilding his shattered ego, creeping around the occasional visitor, waiting for the *one* visitor.

Over the years, too, Guffey had searched for that fourteen-thousand-dollar stash. He'd never found it, but he knew it was here. Tim Jepson would've been clever in how he hid it; that cleverness *proved* the money was here, somewhere in this town. And some day, Tim Jepson would come back for it.

Today?

The front marquee of the Cronley Hotel had long since fallen in. The sidewalk, where in the forties and fifties doormen had pocketed quarters from the drummers to hail them cabs to take them out to the illegal roadhouses outside town, was now a mess of ancient rubble, across which Guffey snaked and squirmed, toting his rifle and burlap bag, his knapsack (stolen from a professor) across his bony shoulders. The last rays of sunlight gleamed along the length of California Street. Down at the end there, the little white car jounced into view, turning this way, yellow sunlight glaring back from its windshield.

Not professors, these people, and not hippies. No, and not scavengers, either, in search of twentieth-century plumbing or nineteenth-century moldings.

Tim Jepson? Come for his stash at last? Guffey gripped his rifle tight and slithered away down the alley beside the hotel.

CHAPTER THIRTY-SEVEN

Dortmunder was annoyed, disgusted, irritated, irked, and pissed off. "And now," he said, "I'm gonna have to drive *back* over that goddamn road in the *dark*."

"Well, they'd have a room for us at the hotel," Tom said. "No problem about that."

"No? There are *some* problems."

They were in the town now, on the main drag, and on both sides of the street were two- and three-story wooden or brick buildings with storefronts on the ground floor. All the glass had been broken out of all the windows years ago, and here and there structures had been partly consumed by ancient fires. The concrete of the main street and its sidewalks was all broken into great chunks, like ice floes, heaved and buckling, covered with dirt and debris, around all of which Dortmunder had to steer. A few business names painted over storefronts were still faintly visible.

ZOMONSKI'S LADIES WEAR

PHILCO * GROSSER'S APPLIANCES * ADMIRAL

OLEKSIUK RADIO & TV

VICTORY TAXI

NEW ATOMIC DINER

"For one thing," Dortmunder said, "there's nothing to eat. That diner's closed."

"It wasn't much good when it was open," Tom commented. "Well, looka that," he said. "The marquee fell off the hotel."

"Oh, yeah?"

"Used to be a big marquee stuck out over the revolving doors," Tom explained. "Said 'Cronley Hotel' on both sides, had a big fancy *C* on the front."

"That pile of rubble up there? Is that where I'm headed?"

"That's it, all right," Tom said, and then he shook his head and said, "I dunno, Al. I traveled with people had better dispositions than you got, I can tell you that."

"Not on that road you didn't," Dortmunder told him, and came to a stop at the pile of rubble in front of a five-story brick structure polka-dotted with glassless windows. "Are you sure?"

"Tallest building in town, Al," Tom told him. "Marquee or no marquee, this is the Cronley Hotel."

"Tom," Dortmunder said patiently, "are you sure your *stash* is still in there? After all this time?"

"Absolutely," Tom said, opening his door. "And let's go get it."

It felt good to get out of the car, even here in Cronley. Dortmunder stood, pressed knuckles into his waist at the back, and stretched as he said, "Looks to me like this place, this whole town's had a lotta breakage, probably looting. Forty years, Tom, a long time. You sure nobody found it by now, nothing happened to it?"

"Absolutely not." Tom had opened the back door on his side, was prying his bag out. He paused to look over the top of the little white lemon at Dortmunder and say, "We're gonna need our flashlights in there, Al. These people ain't paid their electric bill in a long time."

"Okay, okay." Dortmunder opened his back door and yanked his own bag out. "If this isn't some wild-goose chase."

They opened their bags more or less companionably together on the hood while Tom explained, "Ya see, I hadda hide the money, in cash, in the hotel. I couldn't leave the place for a few days, while I was being Myra's sister Melissa. And I hadda figure they'd *know*, sooner or later they'd know I hid it, and they'd know it had to be in the hotel. So it had to be someplace they weren't going to look. Not behind a picture that could be taken down, not inside a window frame that could be opened up, not down inside the tubes of a brass bed that could be moved out. It had to be somewhere nobody would look, and that wouldn't be moved, and what I come up with is a place that's gonna be there forever, unless they turn *this* into a reservoir, and from the look of the area, Al, I don't find that much of a worry. Let's see, I need my wrench and my hammer, too, and that's it."

As they put their bags away on the tiny backseat, Dortmunder said, "So where's this magical place you found?"

"You'll see it, Al, soon enough," Tom said, and shut his door. "I don't think we gotta lock," he said.

Slowly and carefully they made their way over the rubble to the gaping entrance to the building. Years and years ago the entire revolving door, with its roofplate *and* its floorplate, had left Cronley lashed to the back of a pickup truck, so the entrance was now considerably less grand than when Cronley's Chamber of Commerce had wanted the town known as "Gateway to the Great Washita-Kiowa-Jackson Super-Region." Stepping through this portal, Dortmunder and Tom switched on their flashlights and shone them over dust, dirt, rubble, and decay. Carpets and wall sconces and the facings on brick pillars and even the entire front desk were all long gone, leaving a stripped and grubby shell.

"Lobby looks like hell," Tom commented. "We go back this way, behind the manager's office. We want the stairs to the basement."

As they made their way through the debris, around slopes of plaster dust, porcupines of lumber piles with nails sticking out, tangles of wiring with frizzy ends, Tom said, "What I did, I had Myra get me a few empty wine bottles from the kitchen. *With* their corks."

Dortmunder said, "Wine bottles? I thought this was a dry state. I thought that was the trouble."

"You don't understand, Al," Tom said. "It's hypocrisy makes the world go round. Oklahoma was a dry state, but you could drink in a private club if you were a member. So all the hotels and restaurants were private clubs."

"Jesus," prayed Dortmunder.

"Well, yeah," Tom agreed. "How you became a member of the club in a restaurant was to order something to eat, and how you became a member of the club in a hotel was by checking in."

"I don't get it," Dortmunder said. "Why go through all that?"

"Well, I figure they had their reason," Tom said. "The stairs oughta be— Cripes, somebody even took all the *doors*. I hope they left the stairs."

"I hope they left your stash."

"They didn't touch it, Al. Trust me on this. Now, one of these doorways should lead to the— Here it is."

Their flashlight beams shone on rusted metal steps leading down into pitch-black total darkness. Looking down there, Dortmunder said, "No matter where I go with you, Tom, sooner or later it's the descent into the depths."

"This is a very solid structure, Al," Tom assured him. "There's no way it's gonna collapse on us."

Dortmunder hadn't even been thinking of that, but *now* he was. "Thanks, Tom," he said.

"Sure," Tom said, and started down the stairs, carrying his wrench and hammer in one hand, flashlight in the other, Dortmunder reluctantly following, Tom saying over his shoulder, "Anyway, the wine bottles. I rolled the dough into wads and stuffed them into the bottles, and it took three bottles. Then I brought them down here under my skirt one night."

"Under your skirt. You were still being the sister."

"I went on being the sister, Al," Tom said, "until Nogales, New Mexico. Let's see now, which way?"

They'd reached the bottom of the steps and stood in a smallish open area with doorways leading off in all directions. Anonymous mounds of stuff; crumbly-looking brick walls; pockmarked concrete floor. As Tom turned in a slow circle, pointing the light here and there, trying to reorient himself after all these years, he said, "Did you ever think, Al, in a hotel room, when you flush the toilet, where all that water goes? All those toilets, all those sinks, hundreds of them all in one building, hundreds of people pissing and crapping and brushing their teeth and flushing foreign objects down the commode even when they've been told not to do that, you ever wonder where all that water and stuff goes next?"

"Never," Dortmunder said.

"We go this way," Tom decided, and set off down a wide low-ceilinged filthy hallway, Dortmunder following. "Well, the water comes down here," Tom said, continuing the conversation as they walked. "The pipes get bigger, and there's traps to keep certain stuff from clogging the whole arrangement, and then there's one big last pipe that goes out under the street to the city sewers. And just in front of that last pipe is the last trap and sump. There's access to it so a plumber can get in there if anything really horrible happens, but mostly it's left alone."

"*I'd* leave it alone," Dortmunder said.

"Believe it or not, Al," Tom told him, "people looking for fourteen thousand dollars will *also* leave it alone. Guaranteed."

"That's where you put the three wine bottles?"

"I can still smell it," Tom said, shaking his head at the memory.

They went through another doorless doorway into a larger area. Dortmunder's flashlight picked up the scattered skeletons of a couple of small animals on the floor. The air down here smelled dry but rancid, like having your nose rubbed in rotted wood. "I think I can smell it, too," he said.

Tom did his chuckle sound. "Been a long time since anybody's flushed a toilet in this town, Al," he said. "It shouldn't be bad by now. Just up ahead there."

Just up ahead was another brick wall. On the floor in front of it Tom's flashlight picked out a metal plate about three feet by two, held in place with bolts at the corners. Kneeling at one of these corners, bending down to blow dust and trash away from the bolt, Tom said, "Gonna get loud in here for a while."

And it did. Tom hooked the wrench onto the head of the bolt, then began to whale away at the metal handle of the wrench with his hammer. WANG! WANG! WANG! And in the pauses *angang, angang, angang,* as the sound echoed and rang and reverberated all around the enclosed space.

After about five minutes of this craziness, Tom stood up and mopped his brow and said, "Spell me awhile, Al," so Dortmunder got to make the horrible noise himself, and it was on his watch that the bolt finally reluctantly started to turn, adding its SKRAWK-SKRAWK to all the WANG*angang*ings.

The bolt never did get easy. The wrench had to be hit for every fraction of every turn. But at last the thick, rusty, *long* bolt came all the way out and fell over, clattering with the wrench still attached onto the metal plate, making another charming sound.

Tom said, "Terrific, Al. Only three to go. I'll take a turn now."

All in all, Dortmunder later figured, they were down in there nearly an hour before the last bolt grudgingly released its grip on the floor and fell over, and then the damn plate itself didn't want to move, until Tom and Dortmunder had both hit it a hundred million times around its edges. And then at last, slow, heavy, rusty, difficult, it lifted up and out of the way.

Oh, boy. Forty years hadn't done a thing to lessen *that* aroma. "Aaaaa!" cried Dortmunder, releasing the plate as it fell over onto its back. While Tom watched him with interest, Dortmunder staggered backward, hands to his nose. It was as though somebody'd just hit him in the face with a used shroud.

"This isn't even it, Al," Tom told him calmly. "The bottles are down inside that trap, fastened with wires. See the trap?"

But Dortmunder didn't want to look down into that place. "I believe you," he managed to gasp through a throat uninterested in breathing, not if *this* was what air had become. "It's okay, I believe you."

Pointing his flashlight into the hole beneath the metal plate, Tom said, "This is just the access to the pit with the equipment. Hmmm; a lot drier than it used to be."

"Tom," Dortmunder said through his hands, "I'm sorry, but I can't hang around in here anymore." He looked wildly around on the floor for his flashlight, staring over his protective knuckles, trying to breathe without inhaling. And there it was, the flashlight, on the floor, gleaming toward that awful place. Moving to retrieve it, Dortmunder said, "I'll just wait for you upstairs. You don't need me anymore, right?"

"You're gonna miss something, Al," Tom said. "Those wine bottles, full of cash. Over forty years down in there."

"If that's what I'm gonna miss," Dortmunder said, shakily pointing the flashlight toward the doorway on the far side of the room, "then I'm just gonna have to miss it. See you upstairs."

"Can you find your way?"

"Yes."

With a feeling that he understood the phrase "asshole of the world" better than he ever had before, Dortmunder went out of that room and headed for an environment more compatible with man. His sense of direction, sometimes shaky, had him doubtful at one turning or another, but as long as he stayed ahead of that smell he knew he'd be all right. Though it would be nice to have that rope around his waist right now, with Tiny pulling at the other end.

Another corridor, but smelling only of the usual dry brick dust and decayed wood. Dortmunder traversed it, went through the doorway at the far end, and *there* was the staircase up. And amazing was its transformation: what on the way down had been rust-diseased and battered and filthy was now, in Dortmunder's eyes, marble and gold, strewn with rose petals and glisten'd o'er with dew, leading upward to Paradise. Or at least to normal air.

At the head of the stairs, as he'd remembered, were the offices behind the main desk. These were interior rooms, without windows, and Dortmunder wanted windows, so he set off toward the lobby, rounded a corner into a hall, and his flashlight shone on a scrawny old ragamuffin of a guy holding a rifle pointed straight at him. "Sssh," said the guy.

Dortmunder nodded. When a person pointing a rifle at you says, "Sssh," you don't speak out loud in response, but you do nod.

"Point that light at the floor!"

Dortmunder pointed the light at the floor.

"Come on around me and walk out to the lobby."

Dortmunder did that, too. What the hell, that's where he'd been going, anyway.

The sudden western twilight had come and been and gone, leaving a faint but clear silvery greenish-gray illumination at every exterior rectangle, returning to these former windows and former doors a bit of their one-time dignity.

"Shine the light over to the left."

Dortmunder did so and saw another doorway, leading into what had once been the hotel bar (members only). "You want me to go over there?"

"Sssh!"

Dortmunder nodded.

Something—probably not the old guy's finger—prodded Dortmunder's back, and the old guy's hoarse harsh voice, nearly a whisper, said, "Where's your partner?" He pronounced it "pardner."

"Downstairs," Dortmunder answered in the same near whisper. "In the basement. Looking at the, uh, plumbing."

"Plumbing?" That seemed to bewilder the old guy but only for a second because, with another prod in Dortmunder's back, he said, "Go on in over there."

So Dortmunder did that, too, entering one of the most completely stripped rooms in the hotel. Tables, chairs, banquettes, barstools, bar, back bar, mirrors, cabinets, sinks, refrigerators, carpets, light fixtures, light *switches,* imitation Remington prints, window shades and curtains, cash register, glasses, ash trays, tap levers, duckboard floor behind the bar, both clocks, and the sawed-off baseball bat; all were gone.

Dortmunder's flashlight picked out the peeling rotting plywood floor, the brick walls, and in the middle of the floor a black box, three feet tall and about one foot square. Pointing the light beam directly at it, Dortmunder saw it was a speaker cabinet from some old sound system, not looted because somebody at one time had kicked it in the mouth, ripping the black-and-silver front cloth and puncturing the speaker's diaphragm. Maybe somebody who'd heard "Rock Around the Clock" once too often.

"Sit down," said the raspy rusty voice.

"On that?"

For answer, he got another poke from the non-finger. So he went over to the speaker and turned around and sat on it, being careful to point the flashlight beam downward and not directly toward his captor. "Here I am," he said.

"Shine the light on your face."

He did, which made him squint. Resting the butt of the flashlight on his knee, he pointed the business end at his nose and said, "This kinda makes it tough."

"Point it to the *side* a little," the voice said out of the darkness, sounding petulant all at once. "This ain't the third degree."

"It isn't?" Dortmunder pointed the light beam over his right shoulder, which was better.

"I just gotta see your face," the old guy explained, "so I can see if you're telling the truth."

"I always tell the truth," Dortmunder lied, and gave the old guy a good clear view of his face while doing so to see how things could be expected to go.

Pretty well. "You better be sure you do," the old guy said, having just failed the test. "What do you know about . . ." Portentous pause, that. ". . . Tim Jepson?"

Ah-*hah*. With the lightning speed of a main-frame computer, in nano-fractions of a nanosecond, Dortmunder got the picture. "Tim Jepson" = "Tom Jimson." Old guy with rifle = ex-partner left in elevator. Long-term revenge from a loony. A loony with a rifle. A loony with a rifle and a legitimate grievance against the guy he'd already referred to as "your pardner." Face held unflinchingly into the light, "Never heard of him," Dortmunder said.

"He didn't send you two here for . . . anything?"

"Not us," Dortmunder said, knowing it was the fourteen thousand dollars the old guy was hinting around about, knowing—old computer brain still clicking along at top speed—this old guy would have searched high and low for that money, but not low enough. Tom had been right about that; fourteen grand wasn't enough to get most people to go down into that trap in the large intestine of the Cronley Hotel.

Just how long was it going to take Tom to finish down there? And when he came up, what would happen then? This old guy hadn't recognized Tom yet, but wouldn't he sooner or later?

"If Jepson didn't send you," the querulous voice said out of the darkness, "what are you doing here?"

Oh, good question. "Inspection," Dortmunder said, floundering a bit, the old computer brain beginning to hiccup. What *was* he doing here? "We were told there wasn't anybody living in, uh, Cronley," he said, filling time, being innocent, waiting for the computer to come through.

"*Who* told you?"

"Well, the state," Dortmunder said, as though it were the most obvious thing in the world. "The State, uh, Department of Recovery."

"Department of Recovery?"

"You never heard of the D.O.R.?" Dortmunder shook his head, aston-ished at such unworldliness. "You gotta know about the housing shortage, right?"

"You mean . . ." The old guy's voice quavered. "*Here?*"

He's buying it! Dortmunder kept his face innocently blank and earnest as he said, "Well, that's what we're here to check out. To see if the, uh, you know, the, uh, infra, infra, infra . . ."

What *was* that word? Knowing he was losing his audience, knowing his right hand and therefore the flashlight beam was beginning to tremble, knowing his look of simple honesty was falling apart only because he couldn't remember one single *word,* realizing that hotshot computer inside his head was *down,* Dortmunder gaped in the light, struggled—infra, infra, infra*something*—and gave it up. "Well," he said pleasantly, "bye now," and switched off the flashlight as he dove for the floor.

"Infrastructure!" he shouted, the goddamn word blazing across his brain too late, his voice drowned out by the roar of the rifle.

CHAPTER THIRTY-EIGHT

Infrastructure!" shouted the interloper in the dark.

So Guffey'd missed him, dang it. Aiming at where he thought the voice had come from—hard to tell in this enclosed space, though, with the *brang* of his first shot still echoing in his ears—Guffey fired again.

"Infrastructure! Infrastructure!"

What was that, some new word for *I surrender*? Lowing his rifle, Guffey peered angrily into the darkness. He was getting confused, and he *hated* that. What was going on? Why had this state inspector—if that's what he was—suddenly switched off his flashlight and started running around the darkness shouting out foreign words?

And if he and his partner *weren't* state inspectors from the Department of Recovery, then who were they? Would Tim Jepson send other people to get his fourteen thousand dollars, or would he come himself? If Guffey knew Tim Jepson, and he thought he did by now, Tim Jepson wasn't a man who trusted other people a whole lot. Not enough to tell some other people where he'd hidden a stash of money. And certainly not enough to send those other people out here by *themselves* to get it.

Could one of these two interlopers be Tim Jepson in disguise? The features of the man who had ruined his life were seared permanently into Guffey's brain, undimmed by the more than forty years that had passed since he'd last laid eyes on that devil in human shape. Slick black hair parted in the middle and pasted flat to his skull with Vitalis. Piercing dark eyes under thin eyebrows of midnight black. A cruel hard smile showing big white teeth. A kind of loping walk, shoulders loose. A big-framed but skinny body. There was no way Tim Jepson could disguise himself that Guffey wouldn't recognize him.

So these were just looters, weren't they? Not officials from state government, looking to move people back into this old town. And not people connected with Tim Jepson. Simple looters, looking for *plumbing fixtures* at this late date! Dumb as they looked, in other words.

"Infrastructure!"

"Oh, shut up," Guffey said, trying to think.

Surprisingly, the idiot shut up. He also stopped running back and forth and stood still. Guffey knew that because the fellow had stopped in front of a window, not realizing he was outlined against the starlight outside. And therefore he had no idea Guffey could now drop him with one shot, simple as pie.

But Guffey no longer wanted to shoot him. The way he saw it, he was already in so much trouble just having shot *at* this idiot that he'd probably have to hide out in the woods for a *year* before the state cops stopped looking for him. If he actually killed himself a couple plumbing-fixture thieves, the state cops wouldn't give up looking until they found him.

And if they ever did find him, he knew what they'd do next. They'd put him back inside. Back inside *there*. The thought made Guffey's hands tremble so hard he almost dropped the rifle. "Turn the flashlight back on, will you?" he asked, hating the quaver he couldn't keep out of his voice.

"What, and get shot?"

"You're standing in front of a *window*," Guffey told him, forgetting his fear in his exasperation. "If I wanted to shoot you, you'd be shot by now."

He saw the shadowy figure spin around to stare at the window, heard the shadowy figure gasp, and then the flashlight came on again, pointing at the window, illuminating the street out front and their little car parked there.

Little car. Hmmmm . . .

"Wait a minute," Guffey said, and the flashlight swung around to point in his direction. Ignoring the light, Guffey said, "People who come here to steal toilets and sinks, they don't drive little cars like that."

"I told you," the interloper said, "we're from the State Department of Recovery, checking on the *infrastructure* so we can report—"

"Cow doody," Guffey told him. "People from the government come around here sometimes. They're in big Ford LTDs with air, with a big state seal on the side. Or Chrysler LeBarons. People from the government don't drive dinky little Jap cars like that."

"We're, uh, outside consultants," the interloper said.

Dealing with other human beings was so aggravating. They constantly made Guffey angry, or scared, or confused, or sad. "Goddammit," Guffey said to this one, "you just stop lying to me right now, or I don't care what happens, I'll shoot you anyway."

"Why would I lie to you?" the interloper demanded, foolishly, and pointed the flashlight up at his own face again. A dumb and completely untrustworthy smile was crookedly attached to it now, like a sign half knocked down by a hurricane.

"That's what I wanna know," Guffey told him, and brought the rifle butt up to his shoulder as he pointed the business end at that insulting smile. Aiming dead at that face down the length of the rifle barrel, Guffey said, "You ain't looters, and you ain't from the government. I know you're nothing to do with Tim Jepson, I know I still got longer to wait till he shows up, but he *will,* and I'm gonna be here, and you and your partner ain't gonna make trouble for me. By God, I will shoot you, shoot the both of you, and bury you where they'll never find you, and drive that little car of yours into the river, and won't nobody ever know a thing about it. So you better tell me the truth."

There was a little silence then, while the half-attached smile fell off the interloper's face and he blinked a lot; but his wavering hand kept the flashlight pointed toward his own face, accepting Guffey's dominance. And there was a bad smell in the air all of a sudden. Was the fellow that scared? Good; he'd tell the truth sooner.

"Come on, you," Guffey snapped, trying to sound as gruff as some of the really bad fellas back in prison. "Talk!"

The interloper stared over Guffey's shoulder. "Hit him, Tom," he said.

"You're trying my patience," Guffey told him.

"Hit him with the *bottle*."

"That's the oldest trick in the

CHAPTER THIRTY-NINE

W onder which one he was," Tom said.

"That money stinks," Dortmunder said.

"No money *stinks*, Al," Tom said.

The little white car crept through the night, twin beams of light across the barren land, bouncing and bucking away from Cronley and its lone aching-headed domiciliary.

CHAPTER FORTY

When Andy Kelp walked into the OJ Bar & Grill on Amsterdam Avenue at six in the evening, the regulars were discussing the proposition that the new big buildings that had been stuck up over on Broadway, one block to the west, were actually spaceships designed and owned by aliens. "It's for a zoo," one regular was suggesting.

"No no no," a second regular said, "that isn't what I meant." So he was apparently the one who'd raised the suggestion in the first place. "What I meant is for the aliens to come *here*."

A third regular frowned at that. "Aliens come here? When?"

"Now," the second regular told him. "They're here already."

The third regular looked around the joint and saw Kelp trying to attract the attention of Rollo the bartender, who was methodically rinsing seven hundred million glasses and was off in a world of his own. The regular frowned at Kelp, who frowned back. The regular returned to his friends. "I don't see no aliens," he said.

"Yuppies," the second regular told him. "Where'd you think they came from? Earth?"

"*Yuppies?*" The third regular was a massive frowner. "How do you figure *that?*"

"I still say," said the first regular, "it's for a zoo."

"You *need* a zoo," the second regular told him. "Turn yourself in." To the third regular he said, "It's the yuppies, all right. Here they are all of a sudden all over the place, every one of them the same. Can actual adult

202

human beings live indefinitely on ice cream and cookies? No. And did you ever see what they *drink*?"

"Foamy stuff," the third regular said thoughtfully. "And green stuff. And green foamy stuff."

"Exactly," the second regular said. "And you notice their shoes?"

The first regular said, dangerously, "Whadaya mean, turn myself in?"

"Not in here," Rollo said absently. He seemed to look at Kelp, who waved at him, but apparently Rollo's eyes were not at the moment linked up with his brain; he went on with his glass-rinsing.

Meanwhile, the second regular had ignored the first regular's interruption, and was saying, "*All* yuppies, male and female, they all wear those same weird shoes. You know why?"

"Fashion," the third regular said.

"To a *zoo*, you mean?" demanded the first regular. "Turn myself in at a zoo? Is that what you mean?"

"Fashion?" echoed the second regular. "How can it be fashion to wear a *suit* and at the same time these big clunky weird canvas *sneakers*? How does it work out to be fashion for a woman to put on all kindsa makeup, and fix her hair, and put on a *dress* and earrings and stuff around her neck, and then put on those *sneakers*?"

"So what's your reading on this?" the third regular asked, as the first regular, zoo partisan, stepped slowly and purposefully off his stool and removed his coat.

"Their feet are different," the second regular explained. "On accounta they're aliens. Human feet won't fit into those shoes."

The first regular took a nineteenth-century pugilistic stance and said, "Put up your dukes."

"Not in here," Rollo said calmly, still washing.

"Rollo?" Kelp said, wagging his fingers, but Rollo still wasn't switched to ordinary reception.

Meantime, the other regulars were gazing upon the pugilist with surprised interest. "And what," the second regular asked, "is *this* all about?"

"You say it isn't a zoo," the pugilist told him, "you got *me* to answer to. You make cracks about *me* and zoos, we'll see what happens next."

"Well, wait a minute," the third regular said. "You got a zoo theory?"

"I have," the pugilist told him while maintaining his fists-up, wrists-bent, elbows-cocked stance, one foot in front of the other.

"Well, let it fly," the third regular invited him. "Everybody gets to say their theory."

"Naturally," the second regular said. He'd been gazing at those upraised fists with interest but no particular concern.

The pugilist lowered his fists minimally. "Naturally?"

"Rollo," said Kelp.

"You got an idea that's better than yuppies," the second regular told the pugilist, "let's have it."

The ex-pugilist lowered his arms. "It is yuppies," he said. "Only it's different."

The other regulars gave him all their attention.

"Okay," the zoo man said, looking a little self-conscious at being given the respectful hearing he'd been demanding, "the thing is this: you're right about those new buildings being spaceships."

"Thank you," the second regular said with dignity.

"But they're like roach motels," the ex-pugilist said. "They *attract* yuppies. Little tiny rooms, loft beds, no moldings; it's what they like. See, the aliens, they got these zoos all over the universe, all kindsa creatures, but they never had human beings before, because there weren't any human beings that could live under zoo conditions. But yuppies do it naturally!"

"Rollo!" insisted Kelp.

"So, what," asked the third regular, "is *your* reading of the situation?"

"Once all the buildings are completely rented out," the ex-pugilist told them, "they take off, like ant farms, they deliver yuppies all over the universe to all the different zoos."

"I don't buy it," the second regular said. "I still buy mine. The yuppies *are* the aliens. You can tell by their feet."

"You know, but wait a minute now," the third regular said. "Botha these theories end at the same place. And I like the place. At the end, the new buildings and all the yuppies are both *gone*."

With a surprised look, the second regular said, "That's true, isn't it?"

"Spaceship buildings," agreed the ex-pugilist, "fulla yuppies, *gone*."

This idea was so pleasing to everyone that conversation stopped briefly so they could all contemplate this future world—soon, Lord—when the yuppies and their warrens would all be away in some other corner of the universe.

Kelp took the opportunity of this silence to say, very loudly, "Well, Rollo, looka this! You got a customer here!"

Rollo lifted his head at that, at last, but then he looked past Kelp toward the door, saying, "Well, if it isn't the beer and salt."

"No, I'm the—" Kelp started, but was interrupted by a voice saying, "Hey, there, Andy, whadaya say?"

Kelp turned to see Stan Murch, a stocky open-faced guy with carrot-colored hair who'd just come in. Approaching the bar, waving amiably at Rollo, Stan said, "Don't tell *me* the Williamsburg Bridge is open."

"I wasn't," Kelp said.

Rollo brought a freshly rinsed glass full of beer to Stan, took a saltshaker from the back bar, and plunked it down beside the beer, saying, "The rent is paid now, all right. The beer and salt is here."

Stan didn't seem to mind this badinage, if that's what it was. "A little salt in the beer," he explained, "gives you the head right back, when it goes flat."

"Most people," Rollo told him, "finish their beer *before* it goes flat. Then they have another."

"I'm a driver," Stan said. "I gotta watch my intake."

"Uh-huh," said Rollo. At long last, he looked at Kelp and said, "The other bourbon's in back already. I gave him your glass."

"A nice clean glass, I bet," Kelp said.

"Uh-huh," said Rollo.

Stan picked up his beer and his salt, and he and Kelp walked together down the bar, past the regulars, who were now discussing whether the alien yuppies had come to earth *for* tofu or had they brought it with them. Along the way, Stan said, "The Williamsburg Bridge is a *menace*. The reason I'm late, I hadda come to Manhattan *twice*."

As they went back past the end of the bar and down the hall past the two doors marked with dog silhouettes labeled POINTERS and SETTERS and past the phone booth with the string dangling from the quarter slot, Kelp said, "Twice? You forget something?"

"I forgot the Williamsburg Bridge," Stan told him. "I came over the Manhattan Bridge—sensible, right?"

"Sure."

"Could *not* get north in Manhattan," Stan said, "not with the mess around the Williamsburg. So I went *south,* over the Brooklyn Bridge back to Brooklyn, took the BQE to the Midtown Tunnel, and that's how come I'm here at all."

"Quick thinking," Kelp said, and opened the green door at the end of the hall.

"It's what I do," Stan said. "Drive."

They went through the doorway together into a small square room with a concrete floor. Beer and liquor cases stacked to the ceiling all around hid the walls, leaving only a small open space in the middle. In that space stood a battered old round table with a stained green felt top. Half a dozen chairs were placed around this table, and the only light came from one bare bulb with a round tin reflector hanging low over the table on a long black wire.

Seated at this table were Dortmunder and Tom and Tiny, who was just saying, "Turns out he was right. His head *was* too wide to fit through the bars. Not all the way through."

"Hee-hee," said Tom.

"I wasn't talking to you," Tiny said.

Tiny and Tom considered each other. Dortmunder looked over at the doorway with the expression of a man hoping for an urgent phone call to take him away from here. "*There* you guys are," he said. "You're late."

"Don't ask," Kelp told him.

"Williamsburg Bridge," said Stan.

"Well, come on in," Dortmunder said, "and let's get to it. Stan Murch, you know Tiny."

"Sure," Stan said. "How you doin, Tiny?"

"Keepin fit."

"And this," Dortmunder said reluctantly, "is Tom Jimson. He's the source of the job."

"Hiya," Stan said.

"The thirty-thousand-dollar driver," Tom said, and did his chuckle noise.

Stan looked pleasantly at Dortmunder. "Am I supposed to get that?"

"No."

"Good."

Kelp and Stan took chairs at the table, Kelp sitting next to Dortmunder, who had in front of him two glasses—one of them sparkly clean—and a muddy bottle with a label reading AMSTERDAM LIQUOR STORE BOURBON—"OUR OWN BRAND." Kelp took the bottle and the clean glass and poured himself a restorative.

Meantime, Stan was saying, "So you've got something, huh, John? And you need a driver."

"This time," Dortmunder said, "we're gonna do it right."

Stan looked alert. "This time?"

"It's kind of an ongoing story we've got here," Dortmunder told him.

Kelp put his glass down, smacked his lips, and said to Stan, "It's trains again."

"Let's do it from the beginning, okay, Andy?" Dortmunder said.

"Sure," Kelp said.

Stan sprinkled a little salt into his beer and looked around, expectant.

CHAPTER FORTY-ONE

Stan Murch and his Mom rode around Brooklyn all morning in Mom's cab, with the off-duty light on. Having to drive this vehicle during her leisure hours, when she was already behind the wheel of the damn thing eight to ten hours a day, put Mom in a crusty mood. "I don't see it," she kept saying as they drove through the sunny spring day. "I don't see the why so picky. A car is a car."

"Not this time," Stan told her. "This time it's a *gift*. A gift has to be something special, Mom, you know that. Hondas and Acuras he's got. Max has an entire used-car lot of Toyotas and Datsuns. Whenever I bring him an Isuzu or a Hyundai, he nods and he looks bored and he says, 'Put it over there.'"

"He *pays* you, Stanley," his Mom pointed out. "It's a business relationship. You bring him cars in off the street, and he pays you for them. Bored and excited aren't what it's about."

"But *this* time," Stan told her, "I don't want to be paid. This time I want a favor. So this time I can't show up with a Chevy Celebrity Eurosport or a Saab. This time I gotta attract Max's attention."

His Mom looked all around to be sure there weren't any cops in the vicinity and made an illegal right turn on red into Flatbush Avenue. "On the other hand," she said.

"You don't have to run lights, Mom," Stan told her. "We're not in any hurry."

"*I* am," Mom corrected him. "I'm in a hurry to get out of this car and into a tub. And you interrupted me when I was speaking."

207

"Sorry."

"What I was about to say," Mom went on, "was on the other hand, you don't want to give your friend Maximilian a car that's *so* special and customized and different that the owner can recognize it so well that Max gets put in jail. That's a gift he doesn't need."

"Don't worry, Mom," Stan said, "I'll know it when I see it."

"Then look at it," Mom said, applying the brakes and pointing.

They had just passed through Grand Army Plaza and were running along Prospect Park West, with the park on their left and the fine old stone apartment buildings on their right. Some well-to-do people live in this neighborhood, and one of them—or, more likely, a visitor to one of them—had left his dove-gray Aston Martin parked at the curb in the sunlight.

"Well, well," Stan said as his Mom brought the cab to a stop beside this gift. "Right you are, Mom."

"Make sure, Stanley."

So Stan got out of the cab, and the first thing he saw was that the Aston Martin was parked next to a fire hydrant. And the second thing he saw was the red, white, and blue diplomat license plate; diplomatic immunity, as the frustrated cops well know, extends also to fire hydrants.

Stan grinned at the plate and turned back to the cab to lean in the passenger window and say, "It's okay, Mom, it's a diplomat. The cops won't even write this one down."

"See you at Maximilian's," Mom said, and took off as Stan brought out his bunch of keys from his pocket and turned back to the Aston Martin.

The fifth key did the trick, and the same key worked in the ignition. Stan swung the Aston Martin out away from the fire hydrant, made his U-turn, went back up through Grand Army Plaza, and headed east northeast across Brooklyn and Queens to Maximilian's Used Cars, near the Nassau County line. When he got there, he took the side street beside the gaudily flagged car lot and turned in at the anonymous driveway behind it. He stopped in an area of tall scraggly weeds, flanked by the white clapboard backs of garages. Climbing out of the Aston Martin, patting it affectionately on the hood, he stepped through an unlocked gate in a chain-link fence and followed a path through more weeds and shrubbery to the rear of Maximilian's office, a small pink stucco structure with a shabbily California look. Going through the rear door into a gray-paneled office, Stan nodded to a skinny severe hatchet-faced woman typing at one of the two nondescript desks and said, "Hi, Harriet. Where's Max?"

The woman went on typing, as though her hands were separate creatures with an independent existence of their own, while her head turned and she smiled and said, "Hi, Stan. Your Mom's waiting out front. And Max is out there selling."

"Not to my Mom," Stan said.

Harriet laughed. "He wouldn't even try," she said, and went back to observing her hands type.

Stan opened the connecting door to the outer office, stepped through, and looked out the window at the lot, filled with Colts and Golfs. Beyond them, Mom's yellow cab sat at the curb in the sunlight. To the right was Max, over where the poorest, cheapest, most hopeless cars were kept, the cars with !!!ULTRASPECIAL!!! and !!!CREAMPUFF!!! and STEAL THIS CAR!!! written on their windshields in whitewash. Max was a big old man with heavy jowls and thin white hair who looked as though he'd been put out there in the sunlight by mistake; a windowless room with damp industrial carpet on the floor seemed more appropriate. But there he stood, glaring in the sunshine, hands on hips, dressed in his usual dark vest, hanging open over a white shirt smudged from leaning against used cars, plus shapeless shaggy black trousers and shoes like loaves of black bread.

Max was, as Harriet had said, selling, or trying to sell, something out of his tin collection to two customers. Leaning on the windowsill, Stan observed these customers, who looked as out of place in the healthy brightness of day as Max. They were short and young, barely twenty, with thick black hair and bushy drooping mustaches and swarthy black-eyed faces. They were dressed in bulky dark sweaters and corduroy pants and rope shoes, and while one talked with Max the other kept looking out at the street. Then they'd switch, and the second would listen to Max's line of crap for a while.

Stan watched them dismiss a Honda hatchback without a pause, then as quickly refuse a Renault Le Car and an American Motors Hornet. They paused briefly over a Subaru station wagon, but then one of them pointed at the rear window and the other one nodded, agreeing this wasn't their car. Max, misunderstanding, showed them a couple times how well the tailgate worked, but they weren't interested, so at last Max shrugged and they moved on to a puke-green Chevy Impala, which sparkled both customers right up; they almost danced at the sight of it.

Which wasn't rational. The Impala was at least eighteen years old, probably the most ancient vehicle on the lot. The side panels were half rusted out, deep rust pits circled the headlights, and the antenna was a wire coat hanger. It was also one of the biggest cars still in existence, a mastodon, a huge heavy gas guzzler, one third hood, one third trunk, and one third passenger space.

But the two young mustachios loved it. They stopped looking out at the street so both could examine this beauty at the same time. While one went around to the front, poking and prodding at the bumper to be sure it was solid, the other had Max open the trunk so he could bring a tape measure out of his pocket and confirm the vastness of the interior.

When Max started the engine and let them take turns behind the wheel—they cared about the steering, that's all, doing little runs forward and back in the lot, whipping the wheel left and right—Stan decided it was time to interfere. Obviously, Max was prepared to sell these clowns a car, which it would be better if he didn't do.

First, Stan went back over to the connecting door, opened it, leaned his head in, and said, "Harriet, would you call the precinct and ask them to run a car by here? Not to stop, just drift by."

"Right," Harriet said, without asking questions, and reached for the phone.

Stan shut the door, recrossed the room, went out into the sunlight, and gave his Mom a little stick-tight wave as he walked over toward Max and his customers, who were out of the Impala now, standing on the blacktop, nodding impatiently as Max went through the rest of his spiel, the double talk about guarantees and stuff he always rushed through once the sale was secure. Approaching him, Stan said, "Max, I want to—"

"In a minute," Max said, glowering in surprise at Stan, who after all should know the etiquette of never interrupting a sale.

But Stan went blithely on, as though he'd never heard of etiquette. "The precinct just called," he said.

Max glowered even more at that news, while the customers gave each other a quick startled look. Max said, "The law? *Now* what do they want from my life's blood?"

"I dunno," Stan said. "Something about being on the lookout for terrorists or some damn thing."

"Terrorists?" Max demanded. "In a *car lot*?"

The customers were getting less swarthy. Ignoring them, being open and innocent, Stan said, "I think it's something about car bombs. You know?"

"No, I don't know," Max said, trying to turn away.

But Stan wouldn't let him get back to his spiel. "I mean those suicide car bomb things," he said, "where one of them just drives into a place and blows everything up. Usually, you know, they use some old clunker, a big car, something with a lot of power under the hood, something tough that can crash a barricade, good steering to go around the obstacles, lots of room in the trunk for the dynamite." As though just noticing the Impala, Stan gave it a careless wave and said, "This kinda car, like."

Max didn't say a word. The customers again looked at each other, and then turned to watch a police car prowl slowly past, both cops gazing toward the lot. The customers spoke to each other in a language.

Max licked his lips. He said, "Stan, you'll be so good, you'll wait in my office." Turning, he said, "Gentlemen, excuse the inter—"

But the gentlemen were leaving, walking away between the rows of hopeless wrecks in the Ultraspecial department of Maximilian's Used Cars, moving unhurriedly but steadily until Max raised his voice, calling, "Gentlemen, don't you want this car?" Then they walked faster, not looking back.

Stan said, "They were gonna pay cash, right?"

"You're goddamn right they were," Max said. "Until *you* come along."

"Max," Stan said, "don't you still get it? Don't you know what those guys were?"

"Customers," Max said. Then, before Stan could speak, Max raised a grimy-knuckled and nail-bitten hand, showed Stan its callused palm, and said, "But even if you're right, so what? If you're right, you know what I got? The *perfect* customer. Not only do they give me cash, so there's no problem with the paper, the credit line, discounting with the bank, having to eat the damn car when they repossess, none of that, but these are customers who will *never* bring the car back to argue the way they always do. The transmission, the brakes, all this *stuff* they bitch about. These customers weren't like that. Even saying you're right, Stan, and I *don't* say you're right, these customers were the best kind of customers you could get. They're like the army. They buy the product, they blow it up, everybody's happy."

"Except you," Stan said.

Max glowered at him. "The sun is baking your brains," he decided. "Come into the office, explain me this favor you did."

"Be right there," Stan told him, and walked over to Mom's cab, where Mom looked up at him out her open window and said, "This is taking long."

"There was a little complication," Stan told her. "I'll tell you on the way home."

"You're done? He said yes?"

"A few minutes," Stan promised, and went back over to the office, where Max was seated behind his desk, chewing an imaginary cigar, the only kind the doctor would let him have.

"Good," Max said, looking at him as though he'd believed Stan might run away rather than face him. "The expressman with the downside. Deliver."

"The FBI," Stan said.

Max shifted the imaginary cigar from one corner of his mouth to the other. "The FBI? Whadda they gotta do with me?"

"Your customers," Stan explained, "your perfect customers out there, they go away with that heap, and a week or two from now some embassy blows up, maybe some airline office, maybe even a police station, the UN Building."

"Good," Max said. "The car is out of my inventory and *out* of my inventory."

"But there's enough of it left," Stan said, "for identification, registration, history of the car. The FBI likes to say it checks out every lead, and that car's a lead, and it leads *here*."

"So what?" Max demanded, taking the imaginary cigar from his mouth and waving it in his hand. "This happens to be a time I'm innocent! I don't know those people! I sold them a car! That's what I *do*!"

"Max, Max," Stan said, "don't use the word *innocent*, okay? I look out the window here, I see half a dozen cars *I* sold you, and I know where I got them. You want police attention, Max? For any reason at all?"

Max didn't answer. He gazed at Stan wide-eyed. The imaginary cigar had gone out.

Stan said, "The FBI comes in here looking for evidence on crime number one, checking you out, going through the records, studying the paper. But there isn't any evidence on crime number one, because you're innocent, you aren't involved. So do they go away? Do they just ignore all the evidence they pick up on crimes number two through twenty-eight? Or do they turn over this big thick report to the local cops?"

"You're right," Max said. He sounded stunned. Shaking his head, dropping the imaginary cigar in an imaginary ashtray, he said, "I'm not used to innocence, it clouded my judgment. You saved me, Stan," he went on, his agitation pushing him up onto his feet. "I owe you on that. I owe you a big one."

Stan looked interested. "You do?"

Max spread his hands. "Name it. I know you come here to sell me a vehicle, but that—"

"Well, kinda, yeah," Stan said, shifting gears, moving straight into plan B. "A beauty, actually, better than—"

"But that can wait," Max said firmly. "I can see you got something in mind. What is it?"

"Well, as a matter of fact, Max," Stan said, "I was gonna ask your advice."

"Ask."

"You see, I need a car, and—"

"*You* need a car?"

"This is a special car," Stan explained, "with special kinds of modifications on it. I was thinking, the guys in your body shop—"

"Can do anything," Max finished. "So long as you don't need a vehicle more than, say, two, three weeks, my boys can give you whatever you want."

"This is short-term," Stan promised.

"Everything I do here is short-term," Max said. "That's what the customers refuse to accept. Whadda they want for fifteen ninety-five? Would they buy a TV set as old as these cars?"

"A good point," Stan said. "Maybe you should put it in the advertising."

"There are fine points of business, Stanley," Max told him, "you'll never understand. Tell me about this car you need. Fix up the engine? High speed?"

"Well, no," Stan said. "The fact is, one thing we need is the engine taken out."

Max looked at him. "Is this humor?" he asked. "Harriet keeps telling me about this stuff, humor; is that what this is?"

"Absolutely not," Stan told him, and took the specifications out of his pocket. "Now, the most important thing is, the dimension side-to-side between the tires has got to be four feet, eight and a half inches, from the middle of the tread to the middle of the tread. The front tires got to be that wide apart, and the back tires."

"Sure," Max said.

"Then," Stan said, "no engine. And either a convertible, or we cut the top off the car."

"Cut the top off the car," Max said.

"Well, here's the list," Stan said, and gave it to him. "You want to see the creampuff I brought?"

"In a minute." Max studied the list, nodding slowly. "My boys are gonna laugh and laugh," he said.

"But can they do it?"

"They can do anything," Max repeated. "When do you need it?"

"In a hurry," Stan said.

"How did I know?" Max put the list in his pocket. "So let's see this creampuff you brought me."

"And in appreciation for what you and your boys are doing," Stan said as they went through Harriet's office and out the back to go look at the Aston Martin, "I'm gonna let you call your own price on this one. Max, I'm almost *giving* it away!"

CHAPTER FORTY-TWO

hat time is it?" Judy murmured in his ear.

Doug Berry reared up on his elbows, rested his wrist on Judy's nose, and looked at his waterproof, shockproof, glow-in-the-dark watch/compass/calendar. "Five to three," he said.

"Oh!" she cried, suddenly moving beneath him on the life jackets spread on the bottom of his Boston Whaler much more enthusiastically than at any point before this. "Damn! The lesson's over! Let's go!"

"Judy Judy Judy," Doug said, holding on to her bare shoulders. "I didn't know I was finished."

"It doesn't matter when *you're* finished," she told him. "I pay for the lessons. And I have a waxing appointment this afternoon. Off, big boy."

"Wait a second!" Doug stared around; all he needed was half a minute, less, he was sure of it. "Your hair's stuck!" he announced, leaning his weight back down on her, lowering his face beside hers as though to help. "Stuck in this buckle here, be careful, you'll h-h-h-*hurt* yourself, I'll just get it-it-it-it *loose*, and you're all-l-l-l-l-l-l, oh, buhbuhbuhbuh, AH!"

When the shivering stopped, he raised himself onto his elbows again, grinned down into her skeptical eyes, and said, "There. It's loose now."

He rolled off her, and they both sat up in the sunlight, Doug looking off toward the distant shore of Long Island, out across the Great South Bay, as Judy said caustically, "Are you satisfied now?"

"If you are, Judy," he told her, grinning, not giving a shit anymore. "You're paying for the lessons."

She was. Judy was the wife of an ophthalmologist in Syosset, and this was the third year she'd come to Doug for diving lessons. All *kinds* of diving lessons. Each May first she'd appear, regular as clockwork, and would help pay his rent and divert his hours three days a week until the fifteenth of July, when she and her husband would go off for their month on St. Croix.

She was a good-looking woman in her late thirties, Judy, whose hard body was severely kept in trim with aerobics, jogging, Nautilus machines, and pitiless diets. The ruthlessness showed in her face, though, in the sharpness of her nose and the coldness of her dark eyes and the thinness of her lips, so it was unlikely anyone other than the ophthalmologist—who had no choice—would have willingly hung out with her over an extended period *without* something more than her companionship to be gotten out of it. Who salted her restless tail the rest of the year Doug had no idea, but his annual two-and-a-half months of the pleasure of her company was just about all he'd be able to stand.

May was still a little early for most water traffic on the bay, especially in midweek, except for the ubiquitous clammers and the occasional ferries over to Fire Island. It was easy at this time of year to find an anchorage in the shallow water of the bay away from other boaters, dive a bit, screw a bit, and thus while away the two hours of each lesson. Doug would have been happy to give her extra time today for free, since he had nothing else at all on his plate this afternoon, but, as usual, Judy's self-maintenance program came first. Leg waxing. Right.

Doug started the motor and steered the small boat toward Islip, soon making out his own shack and dock straight ahead. Judy wasn't much given to small talk, particularly over the roar of a 235 horse Johnson outboard, so they rode in silence—not particularly companionable—all the way to shore, and were almost there when Doug spotted, beyond the shack, a silver Jaguar V12 in his parking area, next to Judy's black Porsche.

A customer! And a rich one, at that, judging from the car. So Judy's wax job was a blessing in disguise, after all, and Doug was feeling almost kindly toward the bitch as he tied up at his dock and offered his hand to help her ashore. "See you Wednesday," he said, smiling his professional smile.

"Mm," she said, already thinking of other things. Off she marched while Doug finished tying up and removed the spent tanks from the boat.

She was already gone, in a cloud of dust, when Doug walked around to the front of the shack and looked at the two customers he'd least expected ever to see again. And particularly driving a car like that Jag.

Oh; MD plates.

"*There* you are," said Andy.

John pointed accusingly at the door. "Your note says back by three."

"And here I am," Doug said as he unlocked his shop door. Leading the way inside, he said, "You two decided not to make the dive?"

"Oh, we *made* it," John said, sounding disgusted, while Andy shut the door.

Doug was astonished. "You did?" He'd taken it for granted these two, no matter how much expert professional training he'd given them, would never survive a real dive in the actual world under uncontrolled conditions. But they'd done it, by golly, and they'd lived through it.

And now what? Hoping they weren't here to try to sell the equipment back, Doug said, "Everything worked out real good, huh?"

"Not entirely," Andy said, with a grin and a shrug. "Unexpected little problems."

"Turbidity," John said, as though it were the filthiest word he knew. And maybe it was.

"Oh, turbidity," Doug said, nodding, seeing the problem now, saying, "I'm a saltwater man, deep-water man, so I don't run into that too much. But in a reservoir, sure, I suppose you would. Screwed things up, huh?"

"You sum up good," John told him.

"If you came to me for advice," Doug said, "I'm sorry, but I'm the wrong guy. Like I say, turbidi—"

"We already got advice," Andy told him. "From a famous writer that's an expert on these things. You know the big ship called the *Normandie*?"

"That's not the point," John interrupted. "The point is, we think we know how to do it right this time—"

"Go in from above," Doug suggested. "I know that much. Take a boat out—"

"Can't," John said. "But we still got an idea. What we don't got is air."

"Ah," Doug said. "I get it."

"We figure," Andy said, "you could fill our tanks just like you did last time."

"Well, I don't know," Doug said, wondering how much extra he could charge.

Andy told him, "We'll pay double, for two tanks."

"You know," Doug said slowly, thinking vaguely there might be something extra in this for him somewhere, "what you probably need is a pro along, somebody to deal with the problems right there, when they happen."

"No, we don't," John said.

"Thanks a lot, Doug," Andy said, grinning at him and shaking his head. "I appreciate the thought behind the offer. But we think we got it pretty well doped out this time."

"We hope," John said.

"We're pretty confident," Andy reminded his partner, and turned back to Doug to say, "So all we need is air."

"Then that's what you'll get," Doug said, but as he led the way out of the shop and around to the compressor under its shiny blue tarp on the dock behind the shack, he kept thinking, There's got to be something in this for me. Something. For me.

CHAPTER FORTY-THREE

The thing is, the railroad doesn't have handcars anymore. Those terrific old handcars with the seesaw type of double handle so one guy would push down while the other guy facing him pulled up, and then vice versa, and the handcar would go zipping along the track, that old kind of handcar that guys like Buster Keaton used to travel on, they don't have them anymore. All the good things are gone: wood Monopoly houses, Red Ryder, handcars.

Which is why the big sixteen-wheeler that Stan Murch airbraked to a coughing stop at the railway crossing on the old road west of Vilburgtown Reservoir at one A.M. on that cloudless but moonless night did not contain a handcar. What it contained instead, in addition to diving gear and a winch and other equipment, was a weird hybrid vehicle that had mostly been, before the surgical procedures began, a 1976 American Motors Hornet. A green Hornet, in fact; so not everything is gone.

Still a two-door small car with a minimal backseat and small separate trunk (not a hatchback), this Hornet was now without engine, transmission, radiator, radio, hood, hubcaps, bumpers, head- and taillights, spare tire, windshield wipers, dashboard and roof. It still contained its steering mechanism (not power steering), brakes (ditto), seats, windshield, windows and 1981 New York State inspection sticker. It also had new axles front and back, and new wheels, the very old tires of which had been reduced to half pressure, which made it slump lower than normally to the ground, as though its transfiguration had reduced it to gloom.

Also looking reduced to gloom was Dortmunder, who had ridden along in the truck cab with Stan, allegedly to give him directions, since this was Stan's first trip up here to the north country, but actually just to rest and be by himself and brood about the fact that he was *going underwater* again; Stan, in any case, followed the beige Cadillac driven by Kelp and containing Tom and Tiny.

"*Ppphhhrr*-AHG!" said the airbrakes, and, "We're here," said Stan.

"Yeah, I guess so," Dortmunder said.

"Which side do I want?"

Dortmunder looked around. Everything was different at night. "The left," he decided.

"Good," Stan said, "that'll be easier. I'll just back it up short of that guard rail, right?"

"That's it," Dortmunder said, and sighed, and climbed down out of the cab. This was one time when planning the job was a lot better than actually going out and doing it. A lot better. What haven't I thought of? Dortmunder asked himself. Sssshhhhh, he answered.

Kelp had pulled into the side of the road beyond the crossing, and now he and the other two walked back to join Dortmunder, Kelp saying, "Nice and smooth, huh?"

"If traffic came along right now, it could really screw us up," Dortmunder said hopefully.

"Nah," Kelp told him. "Don't worry, John. There's no traffic along here this late."

"That's good," Dortmunder said hopelessly.

"This hour of night, all these people around here are in bed," Kelp said.

"Uh-huh," Dortmunder said, thinking about his own bed.

Stan, backing and filling, had turned the big semi now, putting it crossways on the empty road, its rear bumper two feet from the rusty white metal lower crosspiece of the barrier. Leaning out his window, Stan called, "Let's hurry it up, guys. Somebody comes along here, he could broadside me."

"Nobody will come along," Dortmunder said bitterly.

"The bars up here even close at midnight," Kelp explained.

Everybody but Stan went to the back of the semi, where Tiny opened the big rear doors, and then he and Kelp climbed up inside while Dortmunder and Tom went around to the other side of the barrier, Tom shining his flashlight here and there, Dortmunder waiting for the planks to come out.

This part was going to be kind of tricky, and yet simple. The upper crosspiece of the barrier was about ten inches higher than a standard loading dock, and so the same height above the floor of the semi. They had a vehicle to pull out of the truck and over that barrier, and so a normal ramp wouldn't do the job. They'd had to invent.

Tiny and Kelp pushed out the first plank, a long and heavy two-by-six. When it thunked into the barrier, Dortmunder called, "Hold it," and he and Tom lifted it up to the top of the barrier and helped slide it on out. It was very heavy.

"Here comes the tricky part," Kelp called from inside the truck.

"Right, right," Dortmunder said. "Just let it come down."

"It isn't *let*," came Tiny's voice from inside the truck. "It's *coming* down."

And it did. Overbalanced, the plank abruptly seesawed on the fulcrum of the metal barrier and, as Dortmunder and Tom scampered out of its way, the end of the thing crashed down to the ground in the general vicinity of the railway tracks. The other end of it, still just within the truck opening and angled up to about the height of Kelp's head in there, was now shown to be hinged to another two-by-six plank slanted down into the dark interior.

"You guys ready?" Kelp called.

"Sure, sure, just a minute," Dortmunder told him, and said to Tom, "Shine the light around, will ya? Where's the end of the board?"

"Here it is," Tom said, standing over it, pointing the light down.

Dortmunder joined him, and the two of them moved the end of the heavy plank farther along the trackbed, lifting it, swinging it, dropping it, repeating the cycle until Dortmunder noticed he was doing most of the work, since he was using two hands and Tom only one. "Use both hands, Tom," he said.

"I gotta hold the flashlight."

"Hold it in your mouth."

"No way, Al."

Tiny called from the truck, "What's the holdup?"

"Give me the flashlight," Dortmunder said.

Reluctantly, Tom handed it over, and Dortmunder stuck the other end of it in his mouth, clamping it with his teeth, aiming it by moving his head. "Rurr," he explained. "Gar rurr gar-gar."

"Whatever you say, Al," Tom said.

It went a little easier with four hands at the task, and finally Kelp called, "That's it!" and they lifted the plank one last time, putting it on one of the rails, before going back to the barrier.

The hinge holding the two planks together now straddled the barrier, the second shorter plank angling back and down into the truck. Kelp and Tiny were already pushing out the plank for the other side, and this one seemed to go easier, now that they'd all had some practice.

Next came the car. Kelp was heard puffing and grunting (no sounds from Tiny), and then the eyeless noseless face of the green Hornet came into view, its half-flat tires waddling up the slope of the planks, Kelp and Tiny pushing from behind.

Up and over the hinged plank the abused little vehicle went, tires squlging along, its human servitors patting and prodding it along its way like circus roustabouts unlading a baby elephant. When the front tires hit the rails, the soft treads sagged around the shape of the metal, making a loose grip, keeping the tires firmly in place as the rest of the car continued on down the planks. When all four wheels were on the rails, momentum pushed the Hornet another dozen feet, before it drooped to a stop.

The planks wouldn't be needed again. They were pushed sideways and dumped onto the ground behind the barrier, parallel to the road. Then the rest of the gear was unloaded from the semi and stowed into the roofless Hornet: diving suits, tanks, trash bags of Ping-Pong balls, winch, rope, shovels, poles (for pushing), wire cutters, and all the rest.

When that was done, Kelp and Stan got back into the vehicles that had brought them here and drove away to abandon the truck, which was too big to hide and in any event was no longer needed. Then Kelp would drive Stan back, and they'd stash the Cadillac in a nearby dirt road they'd noted earlier.

Meantime, Dortmunder and Tiny and Tom started pushing the Hornet along the track. They'd thought they might need somebody at the wheel, but the softness of the tires made that unnecessary; the car rolled right along, the overhanging bulge of tires keeping them from veering off the rail. On the other hand, the soft tires also increased friction and made the car harder to push; the best they could do was a slow walking pace.

If the work hadn't been so hard, it would have been a pretty trip, strolling along the cleared railway roadbed through the forest, with the starry sky far above the trees in the pollution-free deep-black up-country sky. Their flashlights beamed this way and that through the tree trunks and shrubbery, making aisles of light in the dark forest, the green of spring's young leaves standing out like wet paint. Now, at nearly two in the morning, the forest was silent and peaceful, the only sounds the scuffling of their feet on the gravel and their occasional grunted remarks: "Son of a bitch bastard," and the like.

By the time Kelp and Stan caught up, the trio with the car had reached the chain-link fence marking the boundary of reservoir property, in which Tiny was in the process of wire-cutting a *huge* opening. "No problem," Kelp announced.

"Please don't say that," Dortmunder told him.

"It's your plan, John," Kelp pointed out. "What could go wrong?"
Dortmunder groaned.

• • •

Bob shone the flashlight beam on the padlock securing the bar across the dirt road leading to the reservoir. As usual, it had not been tampered with. Of course it hadn't. The event had happened once, that's all, and would never happen again. Making Bob come down here every night and doublecheck every padlock on every entry road around the reservoir was just a sneaky punishment for his failure to understand what was actually going on the night it happened.

The night *it* happened. Not a sea monster, after all, but some weird form of breaking and entering. Who would break and enter a reservoir, and for what possible reason? It didn't make any sense, but that's what somebody did, all right; the clipped-through padlocks found next morning, and the tracks of some large heavy vehicle leading right down to the bank of the reservoir, proved that much.

Unfortunately, these mysterious midnight prowlers had chosen to strike at a particular moment when Bob himself was overwrought, what with his just having returned from his honeymoon and starting back to work and all, and so he'd had this excessively emotional response when he'd looked out at the lake and seen what it turned out must have been a person swimming, but which, to his overwrought and excessively emotional eyes had, uh, seemed to be, um . . .

. . . a sea serpent.

Bob and the counselor had worked all this out pretty extensively the last month. In fact, Bob was beginning to believe that his terrible experiences of that moonlit night in April were a blessing in disguise, since they'd led him to Manfred, the counselor who was having an absolutely *significant* effect on Bob's life.

But what a mess he'd made of things along the way, starting with his inability to find *Soldier of Fortune* magazine later that night when he'd driven away from the dam and home and Tiffany forever. Without *Soldier of Fortune*, his plans to become a hard-bitten mercenary soldier on some different and more interesting continent had been stymied, and so he'd bought a couple sixpacks instead and parked all night alone up on Ten Eyck Hill, overlooking the reservoir, waiting for the sea serpent to return.

It had not, of course, and at some point in his vigil Bob had finally passed out from exhaustion and beer (and, as he and Manfred now understood, overwroughtness and excessive emotion), and when he'd returned, bleary and messy, to his normal life the next day, he'd learned that nobody wanted him anymore. Tiffany, furious, had moved back with her parents. Down at the dam, they were talking about dereliction of duty. It wasn't until Bob had agreed to accept counseling that his boss had decided not to fire him.

Once Tiffany had learned he was so serious about solving his problems that he'd started counseling, she'd come back as well—which had its pluses and minuses, to tell the truth—and over the course of the last month Bob felt that he and Manfred had made great strides together. Bob felt himself really coming together these days, both intellectually and emotionally. Right now, he was feeling very good about himself, very comfortable in his space.

It was going to take a little longer, though, for the crowd at work to settle down and forget the past and accept the new Bob. In the meantime, the other guys mostly didn't talk to him—which was okay, too, considering the kind of talk they talked when they *did* talk—and he had this ridiculous extra duty every night, checking all the padlocks and all the roads to be sure those mysterious unknown swimmers had not returned.

But who were they? What made them do it? Cutting through pad-locks, destroying official property like that, was serious business. Nobody would do such a thing just so they could go skinny-dipping with their girlfriend. Not when there were so many actual lakes and ponds all around this whole area. And not at *all* in April; way too cold. Some sort of Polar Bear Club branch of the ancient Druids was the only possibility Bob had come up with so far, which just didn't sound all that probable, not even to him.

Well, again tonight, this padlock on the barrier next to the state highway was unharmed. Nevertheless, he was required to unlock it, open the bar, get into his car, drive to the property-line fence and the second padlocked barrier, check *that* lock, open it, and drive on to the reservoir, to the spot where *it* had happened.

Criminals do not return to the scene of their crime. Manfred said that was just superstition. But on the other hand, Manfred also said he should go along with everybody else for now, with all their myths and rituals, until the general community feeling was that he had atoned for his abandonment of them and their values. So that's what he'd do.

Once he had the barrier unlocked and open, Bob sighed and got back into his car, shifted into drive, and headed down the dirt road, among the trees, in the dark, toward the water.

• • •

The water looked darker tonight, with no moon. Darker, and colder, and even more unfriendly. Changing into his wetsuit, boots, gloves, airtank, weight belt, and BCD, Dortmunder muttered, "Last chance to get outta this."

"What?" Kelp asked chirpily, nearby.

"Nothing," Dortmunder said grumpily.

Because, of course, it *wasn't* the last chance to change his mind, he'd missed that moment a long time ago. He was here now, with Kelp and Tiny and Tom and Stan Murch and this vivisected Hornet and this winch and all this rope, and there was no choice. Into the drink. "I could use one," he muttered.

"What?"

"Nothing!"

"All set over here," Stan said, standing beside the car.

All set. Tiny had broken off a couple of pine tree branches to chock the wheels of the Hornet, though it didn't give much impression of any lively desire to race down the gradual slope into the water. One end of the long rope from the winch was tied to a frame piece where the bumper used to be attached; not because they had any hope of winching the entire car back up to the surface, but only because that was the simplest and safest way to be sure they had the rope with them. The two big trash bags of Ping-Pong balls were in the trunk, which was closed only with a simple hook arrangement to make it easy to open underwater in the dark. The underwater flashlights waited on the front seat, the shovels and a four-foot-long fireplace poker in back. A second long coil of rope also lay on the backseat, one end extended forward between the front seats and tied firmly to the steering column. The two long poles, to push them along as necessary, were placed behind the front seats, sticking up and back over the rear seat.

The idea was, the Hornet would roll on down the track underwater, downhill almost all the way into Putkin's Corners. Now and again, if they came to a stop, they'd stand up in the car like gondoliers and pole themselves along. Since only the points of the poles would ever touch bottom, they could minimize turbidity.

Once they reached Putkin's Corners, they'd have to get out of the car and walk, which would roil up the bottom some, but that couldn't be helped. They would use the second rope then to keep in contact with each other and with the car as they made their way around the library—directly across the street from the railroad station, *that's* a help—and into Tom's goddamn field. The four-foot-long poker would be poked into the soft bottom in the area where Tom had buried his casket, and when they hit it they'd dig it up and drag it—this would be a tough part, full of hard work and turbidity—

back to the Hornet. There, they'd attach the long rope to a casket handle, then open the car's trunk—carefully! don't want the trash bags of Ping-Pong balls to escape and float up to the surface—tie the bags of Ping-Pong balls to the casket on both sides to lighten it, then give the prearranged three-tug signal to Tiny and walk back up the track with the casket as Tiny cranked the winch.

Not exactly a piece of cake, but not absolutely impossible either. And this time, if anything went wrong, Dortmunder would definitely remember his BCD and rise up *out* of there. Count on it.

"*I'm* ready," Kelp said. "You coming, John?"

"Naturally," Dortmunder said, and plodded over to get into the Hornet, sitting behind the wheel, the underwater flashlight in his lap, Kelp on the seat beside him, grinning around his mouthpiece. At *what?*

Dortmunder put his own mouthpiece in and nodded to Tiny, who pulled away the tree branch chocks, and nothing happened. Dortmunder made pushing gestures, and Tiny said, "I know, I know," and went around to the back of the car.

While Tom stayed with the winch, Tiny and Stan pushed on the car, which rolled sluggishly, and then less sluggishly, down the incline toward the reservoir. "Mmmmmm!" said Kelp, in delight, as the Hornet's front end plowed into the black water.

The front wheels hit with a little splash. Dortmunder expected the water's drag to stop the damn car again, but it didn't, at least not right away. Rolling slowly, but rolling, the Hornet moved easily down into the reservoir, water bubbling up into the passenger compartment around their feet through the holes where the accelerator and clutch pedal used to be, then pouring in through the larger space where the dashboard once spread, as the hoodless front went beneath the surface. The windshield and side windows caused a little wake to boil past them as they rolled on, water bubbling on the outside of the glass. There was no rear window anymore, it having gone with the top, so all at once the interior was *full*, water halfway up their chests, a few seconds of freezing icy numbness, as Dortmunder had expected, and then it was okay.

Breathe through the mouth.
Breathe through the mouth.
Breathe through the mouth.
Breathe through the mouth.

Kelp pulled his mouthpiece out long enough to cry, "It's working!" and then popped it back in as the water closed over their heads. Water tumbled around their face masks. Trapped bubbles of air in the car's doors and trunk and frame began to work their way clear for the straight run up through the black water to the eddying, then quieting, surface.

• • •

Second padlock untampered with. Nobody at the clearing down by the reservoir at the end of the road. Naturally not.

Bob switched off his headlights, got out of his car, and stood leaning his skinny butt against a front fender, arms folded, gazing out over the water. Nobody could say for sure how long it would take him to do this pointless inspection every night, since nobody had ever had to go through this nonsense before him, so there was no reason why he shouldn't take a little time out for himself along the way.

Darker tonight, without the moon, but lots of high tiny white pinpoints of stars in clusters and lines and patterns all across the black sky, looking as though they really ought to mean something. If only the thousands of white dots were numbered, you could connect them, and then you'd know it all. The secret of the universe. But nobody even knows which dot is number one.

Maybe the sun? Our own star? Maybe we can't see the pattern because we're *in* the pattern. Have to talk to Manfred about that.

Ever since he'd started the counseling, Bob had learned there were depths and complexities within himself that his schooling and his family—and *certainly* his retarded boyhood friends—had never evoked. Ways of seeing things. Ways of relating himself to the world and the universe and time itself.

What did it all matter, really, in the vastness of space, the fullness of time? Maybe Tiffany wasn't exactly the ideal person to spend the rest of one's life with, but what the heck, maybe *he* wasn't anybody's lifelong ideal either.

Look up at all those pinpricks of light up there, all those stars, billions and billions, so many with planets around them, so many of the planets bearing *some* form of life. Not human beings, of course, and not the kinds of aliens and monsters and ETs you saw in science fiction, either. Maybe life based on methane instead of oxygen; maybe life closer to our plants than our animals, but intelligent; maybe life in the form of radio waves. And all going on for billions of years, from the unimaginable beginning of the universe to its unthinkable end. What were Bob and Tiffany in all that? Not very important, huh?

So take it easy, that was the answer, don't get so *excited* about things. Don't get so excited about sex—that's what got you where you are today—or your future or your job or sea serpents or the simple-ass stupid asinine meatheaded *dumbness* of one's pals and coworkers. Accept the life you've got. One little life in the great heaving ocean of space and time, the *hugeness* of the universe.

Think about all those lives up there in space, unguessable lives, millions and millions of miles away. Each life its own, each life unique, unrepeatable, soon ended, a brief shining of the light.

"And this is mine," Bob whispered, accepting it, accepting all of it: himself, Tiffany, Manfred, his shit-for-brains buddies, his small destiny in this unimportant spot on this minor planet circling this mediocre sun in this lower-middle-class suburb of the universe. "I accept," Bob whispered to the universe.

Bubbles. Little air bubbles breaking the surface of the water, out a ways and off to the right. Hard to see, in this thin starlight barely brushing the black surface of the reservoir. Just a few little bubbles, rippling the water. Bob smiled, calm, accepting it. Some fish down there, moving around.

• • •

Dortmunder moved around as the Hornet came to a stop. Their progress had been very slow from the time they'd been completely submerged, just drifting down along the railroad track, but that hadn't been at all bad. Actually, the gradualness of their descent helped control the turbidity, so whenever Dortmunder aimed his flashlight back up the track there was very little extra roiling of the water.

Which didn't mean the damn stuff was clean. Far from it. Their flashlight beams still glowed dimly on murky brown water full of drifting hairy tendrils and clumps of stuff that Dortmunder could only hope were not what they looked like. But visibility was a lot better than last time; by which is meant, *some* visibility existed. It was possible for a light beam to cut at least partially through the sludge and drifting guck and pervasive brownness of the water to show the slimy gravel and rusty track over which they were passing, the furry tree stumps on both sides.

At one point, Kelp had poked Dortmunder's arm to direct his attention to a low stone wall they were traveling by on their right, with more stone walls going away at right angles into the murk at both ends. A building foundation. That was spooky; people used to live there. Way down here, in the dark.

The Hornet had still been moving at that time, the old stone foundation gradually receding away behind them. But now it was stopped, with no town at all in sight within the short uncertain range of their lights. As with the last time they'd been down in here, spatial disorientation had taken place, so it was impossible to tell if they were still on a hillside or had reached flat ground. So who knew how much farther it was to Putkin's Corners?

Oh, well. Time to go to work. Dortmunder got to his feet, putting one foot on the soggy seat as he turned, holding the flashlight with his left hand as he picked up the pole from the back with his right. Beside him, Kelp, moving more easily without this useless steering wheel in his way, was doing the same thing.

Kelp elaborately mimed, with his entire body, a counting cadence: One, two, *three*; ready, set, *go*. On the first two, they positioned their poles, more or less even with the rear tires, pressing down into the gravel roadbed. On *three*, they pushed, and the Hornet moved forward, but only as long as they kept pushing.

One, two, *three*; forward.

One, two, *three*; forward.

One, two, *three*; forward.

One, two, *three*; up.

One— *Up?*

Dortmunder and Kelp stared at each other in wild surmise, goggle-eyed inside their goggles. Shakily, Dortmunder aimed the flashlight over the Hornet's side, down at the ground, which was farther away.

Jesus *Christ*! *Now* what?

Only the front tires still touched the tracks. As the rear of the Hornet swayed gently back and forth, still lifting slowly, tilting them forward, Dortmunder and Kelp turned this way and that, bewildered, losing the poles, bumping into each other. The Hornet, off balance, tilted ever more forward and now leftward as well, the right front tire lifting off the rail as delicately as a mastodon's foot.

The Ping-Pong balls! They'd misunderstood the buoying capacity of two large trash bags full of Ping-Pong balls, that's what had happened. Trapped in the trunk of the Hornet, now that they'd reached the increased pressure of this depth, they were lifting the rear of the car.

And if Dortmunder and Kelp tried to keep poling them deeper, closer to Putkin's Corners, despite the Ping-Pong balls? No way. But what could they do instead? Gotta think. Gotta think! Gotta have a minute to think!

Dortmunder made frantic pushing gestures at Kelp: Sit down! Sit down, you're rocking the car! Kelp, not sure what Dortmunder wanted of him, moved this way and that, stumbled forward, blundered into Dortmunder, and grabbed the steering wheel beside Dortmunder's elbow to regain his balance.

Now all the weight was on the Hornet's left side, and suddenly the car flipped right over, catching the two of them within itself like a clam rake snagging a couple of clams. Both their flashlights went tumbling away into the murk.

BCD! That's all Dortmunder could think when he found himself in the dark again, underwater and lost again, enclosed inside the Hornet. Scrabbling all over himself, he found the right button, managed to lift his left arm up into the area around the steering column, jammed the button down *hard*, and the BCD filled right up with air, just as it was supposed to, increasing his buoyancy wondrously, pressing him ever more firmly against the Hornet's upside-down front seat, increasing the Hornet's buoyancy as well, moving the whole mass slowly and ponderously upward, through the black water.

• • •

So many stars. If you looked very closely, you could see them reflected in the calm black surface of the reservoir, as though this small man-made bowl of water on the planet Earth contained within itself the entire universe.

Gee! Bob thought, I'm coming up with *so many* insights! I'll have to write all of this down on paper when I get back to my desk in the dam so I'll be able to talk about it all with Manfred, next time we—

Something broke the still surface. Out a ways, off to the right, near where the bubbles had been. Something . . . something hard to make out.

Bob stood up straighter, taking a step away from his car, squinting toward that unknown object emerging out of the reservoir. *Not* a sea serpent, he told himself jokingly; he knew all about that sort of thing now, knew the deep wellsprings of self-discontent that had led him to that particular error. This would simply be some sort of fish, that's all, surfacing briefly; probably the same one that had caused the bubbles a little while ago.

But, no. Not a fish. Still not a sea serpent, but not a fish either. Starlight glinted mutedly on metal. A machine of some sort. Round constructions on top, a wider metal surface below, angling away, downward into the water. Hard to see details in the dark, but certainly metal, certainly a machine.

A submarine? In the *reservoir*? Ridiculous. It couldn't possibly—

And then, with a sudden leap of the heart, Bob *knew*. A spaceship! A flying saucer! A spaceship from the stars, *from the stars!* Visiting Earth secretly, by night, hiding here in the reservoir, taking its measurements or doing whatever it was doing, now rising up out of the water, going back, back to the stars. To the stars!

Bob ran forward, arms upraised in supplication. "Take me with you!" he screamed, and tripped over a root, and crashed flat onto the ground at the edge of the water, knocking himself cold.

• • •

"Now, if you want to get to South Jersey in the *afternoon*," Stan said, "the Verrazano and the Outerbridge Crossing are still your best bet. It's just it's a little tricky getting across Staten Island. What you do, when you—"

"I had to bury a soldier on Staten Island once," Tiny reminisced, leaning on the winch.

Tom, hunkered down on his heels beside the tracks like a refugee taking five, said, "Because he was dead, I suppose."

"Not when we started," Tiny said. "See, what we—"

Stan, looking out at the reservoir, said, "What's that?"

They all looked. Tom slowly rose, with a great creaking and cracking of joints, and said, "Tires."

"The Hornet," Tiny said. "Upside-down."

"Floating," said Stan.

Tiny said, "I don't think it's supposed to do that."

Stan said, "Where do you figure John and Andy are?"

"In the reservoir," Tom said.

Tiny said, "I think I oughta winch it in."

Stan said, "Did you hear somebody shout?"

They all listened. Absolute silence. The rear wheels and axle and a bit of the trunk and rear fenders of the Hornet bobbed in the gloom.

Tiny said, "I still think I oughta winch it in."

"I'll help," Stan volunteered.

Tiny turned the winch handle rapidly at first, taking up a lot of slack, while the car sat out there like a newly discovered island; then the rope tautened, the winching got harder, and the Hornet wallowed reluctantly shoreward.

The car was still several yards offshore, but in water only perhaps five feet deep, when a sudden thrashing and spouting took place on its left side, and Dortmunder and Kelp appeared, apparently fighting each other to the death, struggling, clawing, swinging great haymaker lefts and rights. But, no; what they were really trying to do was untangle from each other, separate all the hoses and equipment and feet.

Kelp at last went flying ass over teakettle, and Dortmunder turned in a great swooping circle, found the shore, and came wading balefully forward, flinging things in his wake: face mask, mouthpiece, tank, BCD. Emerging from the water too wild-eyed for anybody to dare speak to, he unzipped the wetsuit, sat on a rail to remove the boots and peel off the legs of the wetsuit, stood in nothing but his underpants to heave the boots and wetsuit into the reservoir (just missing Kelp, who was still struggling and floundering and falling and scrambling shoreward), and turned to march away, between the tracks.

"Oo! Oo! Oo!"

He stopped, growling in his throat, grinding his teeth, and turned about to march back to the reservoir. "Oo! Oo! Oo!" Wading into the cold water, he felt around in it for the boots, found them, carried them back to shore—"Oo! Oo!"—sat down again on the rail, pulled the boots on, stood in nothing but his underpants and boots, and this time *did* go marching away down the railroad line.

Mildly, Tom said, "If I'd blown it up to start with, we would've all saved ourselves a lot of time and trouble. Well, live and learn." And he followed Dortmunder away toward the highway.

THIRD DOWN

CHAPTER FORTY-FOUR

May stepped off the curb and hailed a cab. Though its off-duty light was lit, this particular cab immediately cut off a bakery van and a black TransAm from New Jersey to swerve across the lanes and yank to a stop at May's feet. Since the backseat already contained three people, May opened the front door and slid in beside the driver, who was Murch's Mom. "Right on time," she said, slamming the door.

"Naturally," Mom said, and slashed the cab back into the flow of traffic, causing a great tide of imprecation to rise up into the air behind her.

"We would've been late," Stan said from the backseat, "if I hadn't told Mom to come down *Lex* and forget *Park*."

"Know-it-all," muttered Mom darkly.

May shifted around in the seat so she could see Mom and Stan and Andy and Tiny all at once. "I want to thank you all for coming," she said.

"Sure, May," Tiny said, his voice like a far-off earthquake. "All you gotta do is ask."

May smiled at him. "Thank you, Tiny." To Mom, she said, "And thanks for letting me use your cab."

"My pleasure," Mom snarled, blatting her horn at a tourist from Maryland, sightseeing out the window of his Acura Silly.

"The problem is," May said, "John still won't even talk about it. Not even talk. So we couldn't meet at my place. If he knew I was—"

Andy said, "May, believe me, I understand John's position on this. I was trapped inside that car, too. Now, I'm not one of your broody kind of

235

pessimistic guys, you know me, but I got to tell you, May, I had a minute or two there, down in there, when I was seriously rethinking the various choices of my life. 'What could I have done instead,' I was saying to myself. 'What could I have done different, maybe in third grade, maybe last year, that would have me now at the VCR store putting *To Catch a Thief* in my armpit instead of where I am?' A situation like that can give you those kinds of thoughts."

"I know that," May said. "I know you and John went through a terrible experience. But it's been two weeks, Andy, and *you've* gotten over it."

"Well, not entirely, May," Andy said. "The fact is, I still have to carry a flashlight when I open my closet door. But at least I'm washing my face again, so there's been some improvement."

"John washes his face, all right," May said, "but he *will not* talk about the reservoir, or the money, or Tom's plan to blow up the dam."

"I think," Andy said carefully, "I think he's trying to restrict his involvement with the situation."

"When Tom moved out," May told them, "I made him promise to let me know where to get in touch with him, just in case John came up with a new idea. Tom was going away to East St. Louis, Illinois, to pick up another of those money caches of his, and he told me when he'd be back, and he promised he'd call me as soon as he was in New York again, and that's *tomorrow*. If I don't have anything to tell him tomorrow, he's going to find a couple of people to help him, which won't take long—"

"Not for that money," Tiny agreed. "Take him an hour, maybe, unless he's picky. Then it'll take two hours."

"By the end of this week," May said, "he could have that dam blown up and that entire valley destroyed and everybody in it dead."

"You know," Stan said thoughtfully, "I looked over that terrain while we were up there, and I'm not sure Tom could get outta there if he goes the dynamite method. The way the roads are, the way the hills are, he might not have an escape. I mean, he'd get the money, drive down in there in a tractor or an ATV or something, maybe a backhoe, yank the casket up outta the ground, drive back up out of the mud, but when he gets to the road I *think* he's screwed. I could study the terrain some more, but that's my first impression."

"Tom won't listen to that," May said. "He'll go ahead and do it anyway, and he'll get caught, and they'll put him back in prison where they should *never* have let him out in the first place, but all those people in the valley will be *dead*. It won't matter then if Tom says, 'Gee, Stan, I guess you were right.'"

"That's true," Stan admitted.

"We need another plan," May told them. "We need some other way to get to that money that isn't dynamite and that Tom Jimson will go along with. But John won't even talk about it, and he absolutely won't *think* about it. So what I was hoping from this meeting, I was hoping one of *us* would come up with something I could tell Tom, something that would at least slow him down, some kind of plan, or even an idea for a plan. *Something*."

There was a little uncomfortable silence in the cab, punctuated by Mom's maledictions against the world of drivers and pedestrians and New York City traffic conditions generally. At last Tiny spread his catcher's-mitt hands and said, "May, that ain't my field. I pick up heavy things, I move them, I put them down, that's what *I* do. Sometimes I persuade people to change their minds about certain things. I'm a specialist, May, and that's my specialty."

Stan said, "I'm a driver. I'm the best in the business—"

"He is," his Mom said, as she swerved around a wallowing stretch limo driven by a Middle Eastern refugee who'd cleared Customs & Immigration earlier that morning. "I'm his mother, but I've got to admit it, my boy Stan is a good driver."

"The best," Stan corrected. "But, May, I don't do plans. *Getaways* I can do. *Vehicles* I can drive; there isn't a thing in the world with wheels and a motor I can't drive. I could give Tom Jimson *very* professional advice on how he'll never get away from that county if he blows the dam, but that's about it from me."

May said, "Andy? What about you? You have millions of ideas."

"I sure do," Andy agreed. "But one at a time. And not connected with each other. A plan, now, a plan is a bunch of ideas in a row, and, May, I'm sorry, I've never been good at that."

"God *damn* the State of New York!" Mom cried, sideslipping past a pipe-smoking psychiatrist in a Mercury Macabre. "They give *anybody* a license to drive a car!"

"They also released Tom Jimson," May pointed out.

Tiny cleared his throat. "Usually," he said, "what I'd do at this point is go to the guy that's the problem and give him a little vacation in the hospital for maybe three months. But the truth is, Tom Jimson—I don't care if he's seventy *hundred* years old—he's the nastiest guy I ever met. I wouldn't say this about almost anybody else, but I'm not absolutely one hundred percent sure he's the one would wind up in the hospital. And then you'd *never* change his mind. He'd go ahead out of spite."

May frowned, saying, "Tiny, how can he be that dangerous?"

"He doesn't care," Tiny said. "That's what it comes down to. He knows everything there is to know about doing the other guy and not getting done yourself. He's the only guy I knew, when we were in stir, that could sleep with a twenty-dollar bill stickin out of his hand. See, me," he went on earnestly, "if I gotta do a little pressure somewhere, I do what I do and that's it. I mean, unless you really annoy me, I don't break bones I don't haveta break. But Tom, he *likes* to go too far. It's tough for a normal human being to gear up to that kind of viciousness right away."

May sighed. "What are we going to do?"

"Well," Stan said, "I think maybe we shouldn't watch the TV news much the next few weeks."

They were all abruptly flung forward when Mom had to slam both feet onto the brake to keep from creaming *two* bicycle messengers snaking through the traffic with big flat square packages strapped to their backs. One of them looked around over his shoulder through his goggles and surgical mask and rode one-handed long enough to give Mom the finger. Mom stuck her head out the window to give him the verbal finger back, and then turned to glare at May and say, "You want a vacation?"

May blinked at her. "A vacation? No, I want—"

"It's the same thing," Mom snapped. "You want to take care of this problem with the dam. *I* want a vacation. If you've got a brain in your head, May, you want a vacation, too."

Spreading her hands, wondering if traffic conditions had finally driven Murch's Mom over the brink, May said, "I don't know what you mean. What's the connection?"

"I'll tell you the connection," Mom snarled. "I've got the idea. I know how to stop Tom Jimson."

CHAPTER FORTY-FIVE

When Dortmunder opened the apartment door and stepped inside to call, "May! I'm home!" and a voice from the living room called back, "In here, John," that would have been perfectly all right except for two problems: 1) It wasn't May's voice. 2) It wasn't even a woman.

Warily, Dortmunder moved forward to the living room doorway, where he looked in at Stan Murch, seated on the sofa, holding a beer can, his expression troubled. "I don't want to talk about it," Dortmunder said.

"I understand that," Stan told him, "but things have changed."

"*I* haven't changed."

"Maybe you ought to get yourself a beer," Stan suggested.

Dortmunder studied him. Stan the driver's personality usually matched his carrot-colored hair; optimistic, straightforward, a little aggressive. At this moment, though, he was subdued, troubled, almost gloomy; a new Stan, but not an improved one. "I'll get myself a beer," Dortmunder decided, and did so, and came back from the kitchen to sit in his normal chair, take a drink from his beer can, wipe his chin, and say, "Okay. You might as well tell me."

"May moved out," Stan said.

This was the *last* thing Dortmunder had expected. He'd been braced for more pressure about that goddamn reservoir, for Stan having been set up to talk to Dortmunder about it by May, but—

May? Moved *out*? Impossible. "Impossible," Dortmunder said.

"Well, she did," Stan insisted without satisfaction. "The cab left about twenty minutes ago. Take a look in the closet, if you want. Look in the dresser."

"But—" Dortmunder couldn't bend his mind around this idea. "She *left* me? May *left* me?"

"Nah," Stan said. "She says you can come live with her all you want. Her and Mom both."

No matter how closely Dortmunder listened, none of this made the slightest, tiniest, least bit of sense. "Your Mom?" he demanded. "What's your Mom got to do with it?"

"They're living together," Stan said. "That was the cab May went in; Mom's last fare." Sounding bitter, he said, "It was even Mom's idea. She got a leave of absence from the cab company on account of traffic burnout, and May said she was due a sabbatical from the supermarket, so they did it. They say we can both go live with them any time we want."

Dortmunder was on his feet, slopping beer. *"Where?"* He was ready to go, wherever it was. Go there now, get an explanation he could understand, bring May home again. "Where, Stan?"

"Dudson Center," Stan told him. With a long sigh, he shook his head and said, "In front of the dam. That's where they're living now."

CHAPTER FORTY-SIX

It's amazing how many reservoirs there are in upstate New York, all piping their water south. New York City doesn't look particularly clean, so they must be drinking all that water down there. Or mixing it with something. Or maybe they just leave the faucets on.

Anyway, in addition to the number of reservoirs, there was also the complication of Doug Berry's regular job and life. It had been tough to get enough time free and clear so he could take several days off from the normal routine, close the dive shop, get into his customized pickup every morning, and barrel north to check out the reservoirs of the Berkshires and the Catskills and the Shawangunks and the Adirondacks and the Helderbergs. So it wasn't until now, almost two weeks after refilling John and Andy's air tanks, that Doug at last arrived at North Dudson to check out the Vilburgtown Reservoir.

Was he already too late? Had John and Andy and their unknown friend already reclaimed the drowned and buried loot? They'd had a long time since he'd refilled their tanks. But even so, even if they were ahead of him, if he could just find the right reservoir, find the right trail, he firmly believed he could somehow or other manage to deal himself into whatever was going on. But first he had to figure out which of New York's myriad reservoirs the loot was or had been under.

This is how his thinking went on that: if you steal a lot of money (something he'd fantasized himself doing more than once in his life), you will either hide it or carry it, but not both; therefore the robbery would probably have taken place somewhere in the general vicinity of the reservoir, but must have happened *before* the reservoir existed.

So, in each case, he first found out how old the reservoir was, and if it was older than fifty years he immediately crossed it off, because how long ago could the original robbery have been? Then, he would look in the local paper for some big robbery to have occurred in that area not too many years before the reservoir was born. Major robberies are not that common in the kinds of rural areas that succumb to reservoirs, which meant that so far he had only two faint possibilities, both of them extremely unlikely, though he'd go back to both if nothing better showed up.

In the meantime, here he was in North Dudson, pulling to a stop in the parking lot behind the library, ready to do his Vilburgtown Reservoir research. Climbing out of the shiny black pickup in the warm June sunlight, he made a handsome picture, a fine complement to the day. With his tall and well-built frame, in his casual khaki slacks, soft blue polo shirt, and aviator-style sunglasses, with his weathered tan and carelessly wavy dark blond hair, the only thing wrong with the picture was that he didn't look at all like somebody who would be going to the *library*, not on such a beautiful day. Nevertheless, that's where he headed, bounding up the steps with athletic grace, pushing the sunglasses up into the hair on top of his head as he entered the cool dim interior.

The girl at the counter was pretty enough, though not as pretty as he, which he knew without gloating about it; his good looks were simply a fact of nature, a part of who he was. (Pretty men feel differently about their beauty from pretty women, are less proud of it and protective toward it and prepared to display it. Their attitude toward their looks is rather like the attitude of the old rich toward their money: they're pleased to have it but consider mentioning it vulgar, even in their thoughts.)

Doug approached the pretty-enough girl, smiling a winning smile, and said, "Hi."

"Hi," she answered. As women tended to do, she perked up in his presence. "What can I do for you?"

"I'm interested in two things," he told her, then grinned at himself and shook his head and said, "Let me rephrase that. Right *now*, there's two things I'm interested in."

"Two library things," she amplified, flirting with him just slightly.

"That's the key," he agreed. "I'm interested in your local reservoir—"

"Vilburgtown."

"Right. And I'm interested in your local paper. Do you have microfilm?"

"Well, that depends how far back you want to go," she told him. "Before about 1920, we really don't have much at all."

"No, that's fine." He grinned, showing his white teeth. "I want to read about the building of the dam to begin with, so I need to find out from you how long ago that was."

"Eighteen years," she said promptly. "I know because I was in second grade. It was a big deal around here."

"Eighteen years ago?" He pantomimed thinking hard. "I would have been in fourth grade," he decided. "So I've got two years seniority on you."

"Yes, *sir*," she said, and gave him a mock salute.

"At ease," he told her, and said, "I'll want the local paper for the year the dam was built, and for about ten years before that."

She gave him a suddenly watchful look, saying, "That's a funny thing to ask for."

The curiosity of small-town librarians knew no limits. Doug had long since had to come up with a cover story for his interest in local histories prior to the construction of dams. "I'm with the Environment Protection Alliance," he explained. "You probably heard of us?"

"Nnnooooo." She looked doubtful.

"We're small, but we're growing," Doug assured her with his broadest grin. "A volunteer group, concerned with the environment."

"Uh-huh."

"What we're trying to do," Doug went on, embroidering the bushwah with a little eye sparkle and tooth gleam, "is help communities avoid getting taken over for things like reservoirs. So *I* look for local factors that might be a common denominator before the town was lost. Employment, local elections, all of that."

Doug's story, if considered with a cold clear eye, made no sense at all, but where is there a cold clear eye in this old world? The present girl, like the victims before her, distracted by his good looks and winning manner and open honest smile, simply heard the buzzwords—environment, volunteer, common denominator, communities, employment—and nodded, returning his smile, saying, "Well, I wish you luck. It was a real trauma around here when all those towns got taken over."

"I'm sure it was," Doug agreed. "That's what we're trying to help prevent in the future."

"My mom worked in the library in Putkin's Corners," she went on. "That's the biggest town that got evacuated. And my grandfather ran the funeral parlor there."

This was more information than Doug absolutely had to possess for his purposes. "Then you know what I mean," he said, turning down the voltage a bit on his smile.

"I sure do."

"So, I guess I better get started. Then."

"Oh!" Seeming to come awake, the girl said, "Of course." Pointing across the room, she said, "That's the microfilm viewer over there. I'm sorry it isn't a very modern one, not like our VDT here."

He drew a blank: "VDT?"

"Video display terminal," she explained, and gestured at a small neat computer terminal on her side of the counter. Its dull black screen was blank. "It's really a wonderful help to us all," she said. "But I'm afraid we don't have a modern microfilm viewer yet. You'll have to crank that one."

"I took my vitamins today," he assured her, and grinned as he made a muscle.

She pretended not to look at his arm. "I'll bring you the microfilm," she said, and turned away.

Doug walked across the airy quiet room to the old table bearing the old microfilm viewer. He was almost the only customer in here this morning; two or three old people read old magazines, and at one reading table sat a lone state trooper bent in agonized intense study over some thick book dense with print.

Doug faltered a second when he saw the uniform, then moved on, realizing the trooper was too deeply involved in his book to care about other patrons of the library. Besides, what did Doug have to fear from state troopers? At this stage of the game, nothing.

He sat in front of the viewer, and a couple of minutes later the girl brought him four rolls of microfilm, saying, "This is the year they built the dam, and these are the three years before. When you finish those, bring them to the desk and I'll get you some more."

"Thanks a lot." Doug leaned toward her, lowering his voice to say, "Listen. Can I ask a question?"

"About the library?"

"Kind of. What's the cop doing?"

She turned her head, as though not having noticed the state trooper before, then gave an indulgent laugh as she said, "Oh, Jimmy. He's studying for his civil-service exam." Bending toward Doug—a nice fresh faint aroma came from her—she lowered her own voice to say, "He's not very good at studying. It drives him crazy."

"That's the way he looks, all right." Then Doug grinned broadly and stuck out his hand and said, "I'm Doug, by the way. Doug Berry."

Her hand in his was small and gentle, but disconcertingly bony. "Myrtle," she told him, and then seemed to hesitate or stumble or something for just a second before she said, "Myrtle Street."

"Myrtle's a nice name," he told her, holding on to her hand, getting used to it. "You don't run into too many Myrtles anymore."

"I think it's old-fashioned," she said, gently disengaging her hand from his. "But I guess I'm stuck with it. Well, I shouldn't keep you from your research." She gestured to the microfilm viewer, smiled, and went away to her counter.

Doug watched her go, pleased by her, then did get to his research. Like most small-town papers, this one didn't have a useful master index, so it was simply the tedious job of going back through the first pages, week after week; the kind of robbery he had in mind would definitely have made the front page, probably more than once.

Nothing in the first four rolls. Nothing in the first of the second batch of rolls. But then, five years before the dam was built, there it was: a major armored car robbery out on the Thruway near town. Seven hundred thousand dollars stolen! Two guards killed. Police had leads. In later weeks, gang members were found dead. The mastermind and the money had both disappeared. Police had leads. Then the story faded away. Police had no more leads. The mastermind had the money.

This was it. There wasn't the slightest doubt in Doug's mind. Seven hundred thousand dollars! That was certainly enough to make a couple of nonathletic types like Andy and John put on scuba gear and walk into a reservoir. And there was possibly a way to find out if they'd actually got their hands on that money as yet.

So let's check. Taking all the rolls of microfilm back to Myrtle—a pretty-enough name for a pretty-enough girl, he thought unkindly, but then was sorry to have had such a thought because basically he liked girls, and in any event he found Myrtle pleasant and easy to talk to—he said, "Myrtle, I've got almost everything I need now, except I've got to take a look at the papers for the last month."

"You mean, this year?" she asked, obviously bewildered by his abrupt leap in time.

"This year, right," he agreed. "I'm done with the ancient past, I'm ready to get up to date, like that VCR of yours there."

"VDT."

"Whatever."

"The most recent papers," she told him, "the last six months, aren't on microfilm yet. They're on shelves on that aisle over there. See?"

"By golly, Myrtle," he said, looking over there, "the technology just keeps jumping around in here. Now I'm gonna read actual *newspapers*?"

Laughing, she said, "You'll just have to rough it, I'm afraid."

"I can stand up to it," he decided.

"Good." She picked up the microfilm rolls he'd just returned, saying, "I hope this all helped."

"You and your library have been very good to me, Myrtle," Doug told her truthfully.

She frowned down at the microfilm rolls, saying, "You didn't look at these two?"

"Didn't need to," he said airily.

"This is the year you finished with?"

"That's right."

She kept frowning at the little boxes containing the microfilm. Was she suspicious for some reason? Should he have gone through the motions of looking at the rest of the rolls? But then she shook her head, smiled rather vaguely at him, and turned away, carrying the microfilm back to where it was stored.

Doug crossed to the most recent newspapers and found some old geezer hogging half of them, reading through endless local announcements, keeping other papers firmly under the one he was studying, spread out on the table. Doug made do with the papers the old coot hadn't commandeered, but found nothing in any of them about any trouble at the reservoir—his idea was that a break-in there might leave traces that would rate a report in the local paper—so at last he turned to the old fart, who hadn't finished *one* paper in the last half hour.

"Excuse me," Doug said, reaching for the papers under the one the old bastard was memorizing.

But the old son of a bitch hunched over his papers, folding his arms around them protectively, saying, "I'm reading these!"

"Not all of them," Doug insisted, grabbing nether papers and tugging. "You're just reading the one on top."

"Wait your turn!" the old monopolist snarled, and pressed his bony elbows down onto the papers.

Doug leaned in close and looked into his ancient opponent's beady eyes. "When old bones break," he pointed out quietly, "they take *forever* to heal."

The old creep blinked, licked his lips, stared around the room. "I know that cop," he announced.

"Who, Jimmy?" Doug said, and grinned, not in a friendly way. "Everybody knows Jimmy. He's one of my best friends. Maybe I'll tell him about you."

The old snothead blinked furiously for a second, then abruptly pushed the stack of papers away, crying, "*Take* them, if it means so much to you!"

"It does," Doug told him, and slid the papers down the table to a quieter location, while the old hoarder went stumping away to some other part of the library.

It was in the fifth of this batch of papers:

SECOND BREAK-IN
AT RESERVOIR:
Junk Car
Abandoned

Almost two weeks ago. They sure hadn't wasted any time after he'd replenished their air.

Doug settled down to read the story, which was bizarre enough from the newspaper's point of view, since they didn't know what had really been going on. Someone, according to the report, or more probably several someones, had cut a great hole in the fence surrounding the reservoir at the site of an old inactive railroad line, which they had apparently used in order to get an old junk car without an engine to the reservoir, where they pushed it into the water and abandoned it.

Why anybody would go to such trouble to throw away a useless car no one could figure out, but police did speculate that the perpetrators were probably the same individuals who, a month earlier, had broken padlocks in order to enter another part of the reservoir property. In that first incident, the perpetrators had apparently done nothing but gone for a midnight swim in the extremely cold water.

Abandoning an old car in the reservoir was considered a much more serious act, though officials reassured the public that the purity of the reservoir's water would not be adversely affected in any way. This being just about the end of the school year of most colleges in the region, the possibility of a schoolboy prank, possibly a fraternity hazing or some such thing, was not being discounted.

Oh, no? Doug sat back, grinning to himself. He'd found it, all right. The Vilburgtown Reservoir was the place, and the seven hundred thousand dollars was the loot.

And now to figure out how to follow the trail from here. Rising, Doug left the papers on the table—let the doddering news buff put them away, if he loved them so much—and headed for the door, to be intercepted midway by Myrtle Street, her old smiling self again, saying, "Find what you wanted?"

"I'll have a terrific report to turn in at the office," he assured her.

"You're probably looking for somewhere to have lunch now," she suggested. "Do you want a recommendation?"

She's picking me up! Doug thought, both surprised and pleased. Seeing by the large digital clock on the wall that it was shortly after one, and aware of no reason why he shouldn't be picked up by a pretty-enough girl, he flashed her his smile and said, "Only if you'll join me. When's your lunch break?"

"Right now." She matched him smile for smile. "If we can make it dutch treat, I'll be happy to come along."

"Lead on," he said.

Leading on, smiling over her shoulder, she said, "And you can tell me all about your researches."

Like fun. "I'll bore you silly with it," Doug promised.

"I'll drive and you follow."

"Anywhere."

They went out together into the bright sunlight. Trotting down the steps, squinting until he remembered to pull his sunglasses down from his head to cover his eyes, Doug suddenly saw John ride by in a car. He stopped, stumbling, almost falling down the library steps, and when he'd recovered his balance he just stared.

It was John, all right, definitely John, in the passenger seat of a Buick Century Regal, fortunately looking straight ahead and not to the side out his window. Doug stooped to stare past that grim profile, and it seemed to him the driver was *not* Andy. And when the car went on by, it didn't have MD plates. But that had been John, all right. That gloomy pan was nobody in this world but John.

At the foot of the steps, shielding her eyes with her hand as she looked back up at him, Myrtle said, "Doug? Are you coming?"

"Oh, sure. Sure." Grinning again, careless and handsome in the brightness, Doug trotted down the steps.

They didn't get it. They're still hanging around. They missed again.

CHAPTER FORTY-SEVEN

O ak Street," Stan said as he made the left. "Forty-six, forty-six . . ."

"There it is," Dortmunder said, pointing. "Pretty goddamn place," he grumbled.

It was, too. Behind a neat green lawn stood a one-story-high white clapboard bungalow with yellow trim and shutters. Climbing roses, red and pink and cream and white, grew up across the front, enlaced with the railing of the cosy-looking broad front porch, on which the seating consisted of two rocking chairs and an actual glider, a kind of sofa without legs suspended by chains from the porch ceiling. White lace curtains made proscenium arches of every window, and the number *forty-six* was spelled out in iron script across the top riser of the stoop. Impatiens had just recently been planted on both sides of the cement walk; small now, they would soon spread and prosper, so that visitors would enter through a field of flowers. "How could anybody live in a place like that?" Dortmunder muttered, squinting at the brightness of it.

"Let's find out," Stan said.

A freshly graveled driveway ran beside the house, stopping at a chain-link fence at the rear. So there was no garage—rough in winter, huh?—but the back yard was enclosed. For puppies, no doubt. As Stan steered onto this driveway and came to a stop beside the porch, Dortmunder's face had begun to look like the first day of a nor'easter.

They climbed out of the Buick, took the secondary slate path across the lawn in front of the roses to the stoop, and went up onto the porch. The mailbox beside the door was an open wicker basket, without even a top on it, much less a lock. Stan pushed the white button beside the front door—doors: wood and screen, the wood with a large curtained window in it—and from inside *chimes* sounded. Dortmunder growled, deep in his throat.

It was May who opened both doors, smiling at them, saying, "Here you are! Come in, come in. You're early."

"Did the GW Bridge and the Palisades," Stan told her as they entered the bungalow. "Avoided all that stuff with the Tappan Zee."

May was wearing an apron. Kissing John on the cheek, she said, "Hello, John. I'm really glad you came."

"Had to," Dortmunder told her, and did his best to soften his face with a smile. If he was going to talk reason with this woman, if he was going to get her to move *out* of this crazy place and come back to the apartment where she belonged, he knew he was going to have to be pleasant, reasonable, calm, patient, understanding, and benign. He was going to have to be, in other words, everything he wasn't. "Had to talk to you," he said, and tried the smile again. It felt like it was made of wood.

Stan said, "Where's Mom?"

"Out driving her cab," May said. "She'll be back soon. Come on in the living room."

They were in a kind of entrance hall with a rug on the floor and pictures of flowers on the walls and some kind of complicated chandelier hanging from the ceiling. As they followed May through the archway on the left into the living room—sofa, chair, chair, lamp, lamp, table lamp, coffee table, end table, end table, TV console, area rug, fake marble plant stand, fern, pictures of nymphs-fauns-architecture on the walls—Stan said, "Mom's back driving her cab? She commutes to New York?"

"No, she's driving for the cab company here," May said. "Sit down, sit down."

Dortmunder looked around, but everything looked too comfortable. He sat in the middle of the sofa, but even that was cozy and soft.

Meanwhile, May was telling Stan, "She loves it, driving here. She says nobody fights back."

Dortmunder opened his mouth to say something nice about the roses, as a kind of icebreaker. "May," he said, "what the hell are you *doing* in this place?"

May smiled at him. "Living here, John," she said.

"Why?" he demanded, even though he knew the answer.

May's smile was serene but steadfast. Dortmunder knew that smile, he'd seen her use it on delivery boys, policemen, bus drivers, drunks, sales clerks, and customs inspectors, and he knew it was unbeatable. "It's good to make a change sometimes, John," she said, utterly calm. "Move to a different place, get a different slant on life."

"And when Tom blows up the dam?"

"We can only hope he won't," she said.

"He's going to, May."

Stan, sounding a little awed, said, "You can see it from here, out the window."

The sofa on which Dortmunder sat stood in front of the window but faced the other way, at the television set, the paradigm of America. Twisting around, he looked through the draped-back curtains out the clean window and across the clean street and above the clean cottages on the other side to the broad gray wall, far away, curving among the green hills. At this distance it looked small and unimportant, just a low gray wall surrounded by hills taller than itself. But it was definitely aimed this way.

The sight gave Dortmunder a headache. Twisting back to look at May again, he said, "Tom's back in New York. He's putting together a string. He gave me what he said was a courtesy call, one last chance to join in with him when he dynamites the dam."

"What did you tell him?"

"I told him no."

May, still smiling, raised an eyebrow and said, "Did you tell him I was here?"

"No."

"Why not?"

"I didn't want to hear him laugh." Leaning forward on the too-comfortable sofa, Dortmunder said, "May, Tom isn't going to care. His entire family, if he ever had a family, could move to this town, and he still wouldn't care. He's gonna blow that dam. You can't change his mind."

"I'm not trying to change Tom's mind," May said.

So that was it. Dortmunder nodded, knowing that was it. "May," he said, "I can't help. I gave that thing two tries, and that's it, I'm played out. I'm not going down in there again."

"You don't give up, John," she said.

"Sometimes I do. And I won't go down in that water again because I *can't* go down in that water again, and that's that."

"Then there's some other way."

"Well, I don't know what it is."

"You're not even trying to think about it, John," she said.

"That's right," he said, agreeing with her. "What I'm doing, I'm trying *not* to think about it. I mean, what are we supposed to do? Have Stan's friend fix up another car for us, get a lot more scuba stuff from the guy on Long Island, break through the fence all over again that they've probably got people watching now, go down in there *without* Ping-Pong balls? There'll be something else, May. It'll try to kill us some brand-new way we haven't even thought about yet. And if we even get to that goddamn town, we're gonna have to walk around on the bottom, kick up all this *muck*, and then try to find one little casket buried in a great big field, where, even if the landmarks are still there we won't be able to see them. Or anything else."

"If it was an *easy* problem, John," May said reasonably, "we wouldn't need you to solve it."

Dortmunder sat back and spread his hands. "I'll move in here with you, May, if you want. We can go together when Tom blows the dam. But that's it. I don't have anything else. Tom and me are quits."

"I know you can do it," May insisted. "If you'll just let yourself start thinking about it."

Stan said, "Here comes Mom."

Dortmunder turned to look out the window again and saw the green and white Plymouth Frenzy parked at the curb out there, with the legend TOWN TAXI on its door. Murch's Mom was getting out from behind the wheel, wearing her usual workaday garb of checked leather cap, zippered jacket over flannel shirt, chinos, and boots. She moved with an unusual and uncharacteristic languor, closing the cab door rather than slamming it, walking toward the house at a normal pace with elbows barely sawing at all, chin hardly even a little bit thrust out.

"Gee," Stan said, sounding worried. "What's wrong with Mom?"

"She's relaxed," May said.

She sure was. When she came into the house, she didn't slam the door, didn't stomp her feet on the floor, didn't even scream and holler. All she did was *hang up* her zipper jacket and cloth cap in the hall, *amble* into the living room, and mildly say, "Oh, hi, Stanley, I'm glad you could come. How you doing, John?"

"Drowning," Dortmunder said.

"That's nice." Murch's Mom crossed the living room to present a cheek for her son to kiss. He did so, looking astonished at the idea, and she studied him critically but kindly, saying, "Have you been eating?"

"Well, sure," Stan said, and shrugged. "Like always. You know."

"Can you stay over?"

Dortmunder cleared his throat. "Uhhh," he said. "The idea was, we come up here to bring you back."

Murch's Mom turned around to frown at Dortmunder. With a touch of her old pugnacity, she said, "Back to the *city?* Down there with those wahoos and yo-yos?"

"That's right," Dortmunder said.

Murch's Mom pointed a stubby finger at Dortmunder's nose. "Do you know," she demanded with a tremor in her voice, "what people do up here when you put on your turn signal?"

"No," Dortmunder admitted.

"They let you make the turn!"

"That's nice," Dortmunder said.

Murch's Mom planted her feet on the floor, her fists on her hips, her elbows to east and west, and her jaw toward Dortmunder. "Whadaya got to match *that* in New York?"

"The water isn't over your head."

Murch's Mom nodded once, slowly, meaningfully. "That's up to you, John," she said.

Dortmunder sighed.

May, apparently taking pity on him, got to her feet at that point and said, "You're probably both thirsty after that long drive up."

"*I* sure am," Stan agreed.

"I have tea made," May told him, and started for the door.

Simultaneously, Dortmunder and Stan both said, *"Tea?"*

May paused in the doorway, looking back, raising an eyebrow.

Stan, hesitant, said, "I was kinda looking forward, you know, May, to a beer."

May and Murch's Mom both shook their heads. It was his Mom who said, "You shouldn't drink beer, Stanley, if you're going to drive all the way back today."

Dortmunder said, *"I'm* not driving."

While Stan gave him a dirty look, May said, "John, that wouldn't be fair. I'll be right back with the tea. It's all made." And she left.

While May was gone, Stan tried to talk his Mom into giving up this ridiculous idea and coming home. His arguments were many and, to Dortmunder's ear, persuasive:

1) This little vacation would soon pall, and Mom would begin to miss the rough-and-tumble of city life.

2) The longer she stayed up here in the sticks, the more she would lose that competitive edge without which you can't hope to make it in Big Town.

3) The *style* of this house would soon begin to grate on her nerves something fierce, being so unlike the nice apartment over the garage in Brooklyn where they'd both been so happy for so long.

4) You can't make the same kind of money pushing a hick hack as driving a metered yellow cab in New York City.

5) Tom Jimson *will* blow up the dam.

"That's up to John," Murch's Mom kept repeating at every iteration of No. 5; the other four she just shrugged off, not even arguing back. It was a very depressing performance all the way around.

Then May came back with mugs of tea on a round Rheingold beer tray. (At least, Dortmunder thought, she hadn't gone all the way to a tea set and little cups and tiny sandwiches with all the good chewy crust cut off. So maybe there was hope.)

Or maybe not. They all sat around the living room with their mugs of tea, like a Poverty Row production for "Masterpiece Theater," and May said, "If you really want to move up here, John, there's plenty of room. You, too, Stan."

"Breathe the good air," Murch's Mom ordered her son.

"I've never *had* so much space, John," May went on, sounding infuriatingly enthusiastic about the idea. "Room after room, upstairs and down. And it all came furnished with *very nice* things."

"And you won't believe the rent," Murch's Mom added. "Not after rents in the city."

"Mom," Stan said, a plaintive twang creeping into his voice, "I don't *want* to live in Dudson Center. What would I *do* around here?"

"Work with John," his Mom suggested, "getting that Jimson bastard his money."

Dortmunder sighed.

May said, "John, I hope you don't think I'm being mean about this. I'm doing it as much for you as for me."

"That's nice," Dortmunder said.

"If Tom blows up the dam—"

"He will."

"You'll feel terrible about it the rest of your life," May assured him. "Knowing you could have prevented it."

"I'm not going down in there anymore," Dortmunder said. "Not even for you, May. I'd rather feel terrible the rest of my life than spend *one minute* down in there."

"Then there has to be some other way," May said.

"You mean some other person," Dortmunder told her. "*I* won't go. *Andy* won't go." Turning to Stan, he said, "How about it? Want to take a turn?"

"Pass," Stan said.

His Mom frowned at him. "That's not like you, Stanley."

"It *is* like me," her son told her. "It's *exactly* like me. I recognized me in it the minute I opened my mouth. Mom, they *told* me what it's like down there. And I saw them come out last time."

May said, "Isn't there some way without having to actually *walk into* the reservoir?"

"Sure," Dortmunder told her. "Wally's got a million ways. Giant magnets. Evaporate the water with lasers. Of course, the best is the spaceship from Zog."

"Not Wally's ideas," May said patiently, "and not his computer's ideas either. *Your* ideas."

"My idea," Dortmunder told her, "is to stay out of that reservoir. May, come *away* from here." Twisting around again, he glared out the window at that far-off gray wall in the hills. "He'll do it in a week," he said. "Less. You can't change it."

The wall seemed to shiver and bulge in the distance. Dortmunder could feel the water pressing on him, all around, black, heavy, holding him pinned like a straitjacket. A mad thought crossed his brain like heat lightning: steal two thousand BCDs, distribute them to everybody in the valley; people, buoyant, floating through the flood.

He turned back to the room. "May, I can't go in that water."

"And I can't leave here," she said.

Dortmunder sighed, one last time. "I'll talk to Tom," he said. "I don't know what I'll say, but I'll talk to him."

CHAPTER FORTY-EIGHT

Tom Jimson was not an easy guy to get hold of. The phone number he'd given May as a contact was a saloon in Brooklyn with a bartender who at first had no desire to be cooperative. "Never heard of the guy," he said.

"You're very lucky," Dortmunder told him. "Look around under the tables there, see if you find somebody rolling a corpse. That'll be Tom."

The bartender thought that over for a second or two, then said, "You a friend of his?"

Dortmunder responded with a hollow laugh.

"Okay," the bartender said. "I guess you're all right. Gimme your name and number. If anybody called Tom Jimson comes in, I'll pass along the message."

"Tell him it's urgent," Dortmunder said.

This time it was the bartender who gave the hollow laugh, saying, "I thought you knew this Jimson guy."

"Yeah, you're right," Dortmunder agreed gloomily.

For the next day and a half, Dortmunder hung around the apartment, not wanting to miss the call, trying to convince himself Tom hadn't had time *already* to put together his string and collect his dynamite and his all-terrain vehicle and head north. Not enough time. He couldn't have done it yet.

Stan Murch and Tiny Bulcher and Andy Kelp phoned from time to time, or dropped by, to see how things were going. "I can't talk," Dortmunder explained to Kelp over the phone at one point. "I don't want Tom to get a busy signal when he calls."

"I been telling you, John," Kelp said. "You need call-waiting."

"No, Andy."

"*And* a cellular phone you can carry with you, so you can leave the house."

"No, I don't, Andy."

"*And* a kitchen extension. I could—"

"Leave me alone, Andy," Dortmunder said, and hung up.

Finally, late on the second day, Tom called, sounding very far away. "Where are you?" Dortmunder asked, imagining Tom in North Dudson, just off the Thruway exit.

"On the phone," Tom answered. "It's up to you, Al, to tell me *why* I'm on the phone."

"Well, uhhhh, Tom," Dortmunder said, and listened to hear what he would have to say next, and didn't hear anything at all.

"Hello? Is this line dead?"

"No, Tom," Dortmunder said. "I'm here."

"You're gonna be all alone there in a second, Al," Tom warned him. "I got a lot of— Goddamn it!" he suddenly shouted, apparently turning away from the phone to yell at somebody else at wherever he was. Raucous voices were heard in the background, and then Tom's voice, still aimed away from the phone, snarling, "Because I say so, snowbird! Just sit there till I'm off the phone!" Then, louder again in Dortmunder's ear, "Al? You still there?"

"Oh, sure," Dortmunder said. "Tom, uh, is that your, uh, have you got your guys to help on the—"

"Well, naturally, Al," Tom said, sounding jaunty. "And we're all kinda anxious to get going, you know. In fact, I'm having a tiny discipline problem at the moment with this one nose jockey here. So if you could just go ahead and spit it out, you know, we could get on the road."

"Well, the thing is, Tom," Dortmunder said, gripping the phone hard, willing himself to keep talking whether he had anything to say or not, "the thing is, I've been sort of regretting how I gave up on that, uh, reservoir job. I mean, you know me, Tom, I'm not a quitter."

"Lotta water there, Al," Tom said, sounding almost sympathetic; for him, that is. "Too much water to get through, you were right about that. No sweat, no problem, nothing for you to feel bad about. Cost me a couple months, but that's okay, it was kinda interesting watching you and your pals at work."

"Well, the thing is, Tom—"

"But *now*, Al, *now* I gotta do it right. Mexico's calling, Al."

"Tom, I want to—"

But Tom was off again, yelling at his companion or companions. Dortmunder waited it out, licking his lips, grasping the phone, and when Tom finally finished with his discipline problem, Dortmunder said, very quickly, "Tom, you know May. She moved up there, to Dudson Center. She's gonna stay there."

Was that a mistake? Maybe I shouldn't have let him know I had a personal stake in the situation. Well, it's too late now, isn't it?

Tom, after the briefest of pauses, said, "Well, well. Putting the pressure on you, eh, is she, Al?"

"Kind of," Dortmunder admitted. It was a mistake.

"You know, Al," Tom said, "I got a philosophy that maybe might help you at this time."

"You do?"

"That's right. There's more than one woman in this world, Al, but there's only one *you*."

A *bad* mistake. "Tom," Dortmunder said, "I really want to make one more try. Just bear with me once more, don't blow the dam—"

"On accounta May." Tom's voice was always icy cold, but somehow right now it sounded even colder.

"On account of," Dortmunder told him, "my professional, uh, pride is at stake here. I don't want to be defeated by the problem. Also, you said yourself, you'd be happier without the massive manhunt."

"That's true, Al," Tom said, still with that absolute-zero voice. "But let us say, just for argument, Al, just let us say I'm gonna go ahead and get this over with. And let us say you can't, no matter what you do, you just can't yank that woman of yours out from in front of the dam. Now, Al, just for the sake of argument here, would you find yourself tempted to make a little anonymous phone call to the law?"

Dortmunder's hand, slippery with sweat, trembled on the phone. "I'd hate to have to face that problem, Tom," he said. "And I just think there's still a way we can do the job without the, uh, fuss."

"Uh-huh. Hold it, Al."

Dortmunder waited, listening. *Thunk* of phone onto a hard surface. Voices off, raised in anger. Sudden crashing of furniture, heavy objects—bodies?—thudding and bumping. Silence, just as sudden.

"Al? You there?"

"I'm here, Tom."

"I think I must be slowing down," Tom said. "Okay, I see your problem, Al."

"That's why I want to—"

"And I see *my* problem."

Dortmunder waited, breathing through his mouth. *I'm* his problem, he thought. In the background, at Tom's end of the line, whining voices complained.

His own voice now like thin sharp wires, Tom said, "Maybe we ought to have a talk, Al, you and me. Maybe you ought to come here."

I have to talk him out of it, Dortmunder thought. Somehow. Knowing exactly what Tom had in mind, he said, "Sure, Tom, that's a good idea."

"I'm on Thirteenth Street," Tom said.

Well, that was appropriate. "Uh-huh," Dortmunder said.

"Off Avenue C."

"Rough neighborhood, that," Dortmunder suggested.

"Oh, yeah?" Tom said, as though he hadn't noticed. "Anyway, between C and D. Four-ninety-nine East Thirteenth Street."

"Which bell do I ring?"

Tom chuckled, like ice cubes rattling. "There's no *locks* around here anymore, Al," he said. "You just come in, come up to the top floor. We'll have a good long talk, just you and me."

"Right, Tom," Dortmunder said, through dry lips. "See you—koff, kah—see you soon."

CHAPTER FORTY-NINE

Dortmunder plodded up black slate stairs, his left hand on the rough iron railing, right hand clutching a two-foot-long chunk of two-by-three he'd picked up from a dumpster on the street a couple blocks from here. Not for Tom, but for whomever he might meet along the way.

Which was, so far, nobody. Scurrying sounds preceded him up the stairwell, scuffling noises followed, but no one actually appeared as Dortmunder slogged steadily upward through a building that any World-War-II-in-Europe movie could have been shot in, if nobody stole the camera. Great bites had been taken out of the plaster walls, leaving dirty crumbly white wounds in the gray-green skin. At every level the corridor windows, fore and aft, were mostly broken out, some leaving jagged glass teeth, others patched with six-pack cardboard and masking tape. The white hexagonal tile floors had apparently been systematically beaten with sledge hammers over a period of many months, then smeared with body fluids and sprinkled with medical waste. That the bare light bulbs dangling from the corridor ceilings had once been enclosed in white glass globes was indicated by the amount of white ground glass mixed with the rest of the trash on the floors.

The apartment doors were dented metal, some painted brown, some gray, many without knobs or locks. From the cooking smells emerging through these sprung doorways, most of the tenants planned to have rat for lunch. Rounding the turn at the third floor, Dortmunder heard a baby wailing from some apartment nearby and nodded, muttering, "You're right about that, kid." Then he thumped on up.

The building was six stories high, the maximum height when it was thrown up for a building without an elevator. The stairwell, a square shaft cored from its gangrenous center, consisted of two half-flights per story; up to a landing, double back to the next floor. Dortmunder was just rounding the turn at floor five and a half when a sudden fusillade of gunfire roared out above him. "Yi!" he cried, and dropped to the filthy steps, shielding his head with the two-by-three. Wasn't Tom even going to give him a *minute* to talk?

The gunfire went on for a few more seconds, then faltered; then there was a scream; then a sudden new rattle of shots. Dortmunder peeked up past the two-by-three but could see nothing except steps and the stairwell wall.

The silence stretched, covering the entire neighborhood; nobody's home when the guns start banging. Then there was the clear sound of a metal door slammed open against a plaster wall, and an irritated voice that was recognizably Tom's said, "Assholes. *Now* see what you made me do."

Footsteps clattered down the stairs. Dortmunder got his feet under himself, rose quickly upward, and blinked at Tom as the older man reached the landing, right in front of him, concentrating on the fresh clip he was sliding into the butt of the blue-steel .45 automatic held loosely in his right hand.

Dortmunder stared at the automatic, and Tom looked up, saw him, and stopped, his eyes alight with the adrenaline of battle. They stood facing each other on the landing, Dortmunder squeezing the two-by-three in his hand, Tom lifting one eyebrow, silence all around them.

Then Tom relaxed and moved, tension gone as he tucked the automatic away inside his clothing. Casually, he said, "Whadaya say, Al? Glad you could make it."

"I come right over," Dortmunder said. His hands and throat were still clenched.

Tom glanced down at the two-by-three. Conversationally, he said, "What's that for, Al?"

Dortmunder gestured vaguely with it, indicating the building. "People."

"Hm." Tom nodded. "You better hope nobody needs a piece a wood," he said. "Come on, let's get outta here."

Dortmunder couldn't resist looking up the stairs. "Your new partners?"

"I had to let them go. Come on, Al." Tom started down the stairs and Dortmunder followed, not looking back anymore.

As they descended, Tom said, "The quality of help these days, Al, it's a real scandal."

"I guess it is," Dortmunder agreed.

"You and your pals," Tom went on, "seem to have a little trouble closing with the problem, but at least you're steady and reliable."

"That's right," Dortmunder said.

"You don't put anything in your nose except your finger."

"Uh-huh," Dortmunder said.

"And nothing at all in your veins."

"My blood and me," Dortmunder said as they reached the ground floor and headed toward the smashed defense of the front door, "have an agreement. It does its job, and I don't pester it."

"You got it in a nutshell, Al," Tom said as they stepped out to sunlight that, in this neighborhood, looked like an error. "Don't second-guess your body, that's what it comes down to. Those former associates of mine, upstairs, they didn't understand that. They messed themselves around so much they got it into their heads, since they knew where the reservoir was, they didn't need *me* anymore." Tom's laugh had an edge to it, like a church bell during the plague. "Lost touch with reality, that's what they did."

"I guess so." Dortmunder looked up toward the top-floor windows of this moldering pile. "Was it their apartment?"

"It is now," Tom said, and shrugged away all previous associations, turning to Dortmunder on the sidewalk to say, "So you've got a new plan, huh?"

"Well, no," Dortmunder said.

Tom lowered an eyebrow in Dortmunder's direction. Away from him, it was easy to forget how tall he was, and how bony. "You *don't* have a plan?"

"Not yet," Dortmunder explained. "I wanted to be sure you'd go along with me before I got into any—"

"Al, I'll tell you the truth," Tom said. "I'm disappointed."

"I'm sorry, Tom."

"You're right to be. Here I thought your love for a good woman had inspired you to come up with a really first-class notion, and everything was gonna be fine."

"Everything is, Tom," Dortmunder assured him. "Now that—"

"I might not have been quite so dismissive of those three fellas upstairs," Tom went on, "if I'd known you were just blowing smoke."

"I'm not blowing— *Three* fellas?" And one old seventy-year-old made of iron bars and antifreeze.

"That's how many I figured I needed," Tom said. "Two to carry the dynamite and get blown up with it, one to drive the backhoe and do the work down in Putkin's Corners."

"And be left there," Dortmunder suggested.

Tom's lips seemed actually to stretch, as though he might be smiling somewhere deep inside. "You know me so well, Al," he said. But then the ghost smile disappeared, and he said, "And that's why I'm so surprised you'd come to me empty-handed this way."

"Not empty-handed," Dortmunder said. "I'm going to—"

"Yeah, come to think of it," Tom said, "maybe you should throw that stick away. Those sirens I hear are getting closer."

Dortmunder had been too distracted by Tom to pay attention to the outer world, but now he did hear that, yes, there *were* sirens approaching. Fast. From not very far away. "Right," he said, and tossed the two-by-three into the gutter.

"Let's take a walk," Tom said, "since I'm carrying a gun those cops would take a great interest in, and while we walk you can tell me your ideas, and we can discuss where I'm gonna live now."

They started walking toward Avenue C. Dortmunder said, "Where you're gonna live?"

Ahead, the first police car came screaming around the corner. "My previous place," Tom explained, "isn't gonna be available for a while."

Dortmunder looked around to watch the police car brake to a stop at Tom's former address. Cops piled out of it while two more police cars joined the party, one of them coming the wrong way down this one-way street. "Yeah, I see what you mean."

"This place where May is," Tom said, "up in Dudson Center. Lotta room there?"

"She says the most she ever had," Dortmunder said, knowing what was coming but seeing no way out.

"Probably reassure her to have me there where she could see me," Tom suggested. "Keep an eye on me. Know I'm not blowing the dam when I'm in front of it myself."

"Probably so," Dortmunder said.

"Yeah," Tom said, nodding to himself as they turned the corner away from the scene of excitement. "She'll probably be glad to see me, in fact, May. Happy to have me around."

"Probably so," Dortmunder said.

CHAPTER FIFTY

I *do* like you to touch me," Myrtle told Doug Berry, pushing him away. "And that's exactly why I shouldn't let you."

"That makes no sense at all," Doug said, continuing to crowd her.

"It makes sense to me," Myrtle told him, scrinching as far over on the pickup's seat as possible, keeping her arms folded over her chest as she determinedly gazed out through the windshield at the big outdoor movie screen where Dumbo teetered on a tree branch. "Watch the movie," she said. "You said you'd never been to a drive-in before, so here we are, so watch the movie."

"At a drive-in? Myrtle," Doug said, keeping his hands to himself at last, "you're driving me crazy."

Well, if that was true, Myrtle thought, then they were even, because Doug Berry was certainly driving *her* crazy. Not in the same way, of course; not sexually, or romantically. Though Doug was certainly sexy, and he kept doing his best to be romantic, and if everything else had been okay who knew what might happen?

But everything else was *not* okay. Everything else wasn't okay because Doug Berry was a fake, and up to something, and it more than likely had something to do with her father, and she couldn't for the *life* of her figure out what it was.

But that he was a fake went without question. When he'd first come to the library, she'd accepted his story about his researches without question,

264

but when he'd suddenly stopped looking at the old microfilm three years before his alleged range of interest was finished, and when he'd suddenly switched to the present day with no explanation, she'd begun to suspect something was wrong. But what?

Lunch with him, at her instigation, had revealed nothing more than that he was fun and flirty and that he wanted to see her again, which was nice, but not enough. That first evening, on her own time, she'd gone through the microfilm of the year when Doug had stopped, the year he'd obviously found whatever he was *really* looking for, and when she'd come to the armored car robbery out on the Thruway all the pieces had come together. That robbery was almost certainly another of the "jobs" her criminal father had "pulled" before he'd been sent to prison for a different "job" several years later, and Doug Berry was almost certainly on the elder Jimson's "trail" for some reason. It was a good thing she'd resisted the urge to use the Jimson "moniker" with Doug, as she had—frightening and thrilling herself—with nice little Wally Knurr. (It was television, of course, that had given Myrtle this easy familiarity with criminal argot.)

Suspicions aroused, and fearing at first that Doug might actually be an undercover policeman of some sort, hounding her father like Javert (which would be why he'd asked about the state trooper, Jimmy), Myrtle had looked up the Environment Protection Alliance, the so-called organization Doug was supposedly doing research for, and of course there was no such thing. (The VDT at the library, now that Wally Knurr had made its mysteries plain to her, had been a great help in this study of the Doug Berry problem.)

So he was a fake; some sort of fake, specifics not yet known. His real name was Doug Berry, however, because it said so on the credit card he'd used the first time he'd taken her out to dinner, which was the second time they'd met, now being the third time, at this drive-in movie south of North Dudson, one of the few such enterprises still extant in America. Doug Berry was his name, and this ridiculously childish pickup truck with the offensively childish bumper sticker about divers on the back had a license plate from Suffolk County down on Long Island. The Suffolk County phone book in the library not only listed a **Berry Doug** but even gave a second business phone number for him which, when she'd dialed it, had produced an answering machine speaking identifiably with Doug's voice:

"South Shore Dive Shop. Sorry we're not open now. Our usual hours are Thursday through Sunday, ten to five. Licensed professional instruction, basic and advanced courses. Dive equipment for sale or rent, air refills, tank tests, all your diving needs under one roof. Hope to see you!"

What did a diving instructor from Long Island have to do with retired (presumably) criminal and former "jailbird" Tom Jimson? That Doug's initial request for information at the library had been connected to the local reservoir had to have some significance—reservoir, water, diving—but Myrtle couldn't begin to guess what it might be. One thing seemed sure, though; she should keep this connection to Doug Berry alive, without letting it get out of hand.

Or into hand, rather.

And so tonight's visit to the drive-in; their third meeting, without either of them getting anywhere. Myrtle knew Doug was feeling frustrated, but doggone it, so was she. Her natural tendency would be to find this handsome and easygoing fellow irresistible, but how could she fall into his arms unless she knew whose side he was on? What if he were, in one way or another, her father's enemy? (On the other hand, he could conceivably be on her father's side, in which case falling into his arms would be a double pleasure. He might even—remote hope—be the means by which she could actually get to *meet* her father at last.)

Her researches had done no more than show that Doug Berry was not who he'd claimed; they couldn't go farther, couldn't describe who or what he really was. It kept seeming to Myrtle that some sort of subtle indirect questioning during these dates should give her the clues she needed to find out what was going on, but she just couldn't seem to think what those subtle and indirect questions might be. People in the movies and on television always come up with the appropriate delicate probe, but—

Whoops. Speaking of delicate probes. "Come *on*, Doug," Myrtle said, putting his hand back in his own lap.

Doug sighed, elaborately long-suffering.

I wish I knew how to get in touch with Wally Knurr, Myrtle thought. I bet *he* could help me figure out what's going on. But except for that one day at the library when he'd opened the cornucopia of the VDT to her wondering eyes, she'd never seen Wally again. Probably a salesman of some kind, she thought, traveling around, maybe even selling computers or something like that. Will his sales route ever bring him back through North Dudson? And would he have any reason to return to the library?

"Doug, *please*."

"*Myrtle*, please."

"Watch the movie, Doug," Myrtle urged him. "It's a nice movie, isn't it?"

"I never miss it," Doug said bitterly.

CHAPTER FIFTY-ONE

Tom Jimson boarded the Amtrak train in Penn Station carrying the same small black leather bag he'd carried both to and from prison, the same bag that would be all he'd need to carry when at last he got his money and unloaded his latest partners and took that plane to Mexico. Sweet Mexico.

For now, though, he was going the other way. The criminal returns to the scene of his crime, he thought, and touched the tip of his tongue to his upper teeth behind his upper lip, a gesture he made whenever he amused himself with his interior monologue. (A man no one can trust is a man who can trust no one, and therefore is a man liable to take to the diversion of interior monologue.) He found a comfortable corner of four seats—two facing pairs—and settled in, ass in one seat, bag on a second, feet on a third, hand on a fourth. The train would have to get a lot more full than this midweek offpeak run was likely to before anybody would attempt to enter the principality Tom had carved out for himself.

Before the train started moving, a big lummoxy kid came along to take the seats across the aisle. About nine feet tall, with a big square head covered by wavy blond hair, he was probably twenty years old, and was dressed in huge clunky hiking boots, white tube socks, khaki shorts—his knees were enormous and knobby and covered with fuzz, like the rest of him—a T-shirt with some kind of stupid philosophical statement on it, a red headband, and a *monster* backpack looming higher than his head.

Tom watched with contemptuous interest as the kid undid all the straps that released the backpack, which then took up two seats all by itself. Glancing at Tom with the self-assurance of somebody who doesn't know anything yet, the kid said, "Watch my bag?"

"Sure," Tom said.

The kid went thumping away down the aisle, knees working like hand puppets, and Tom watched him go, then rose to give the backpack a quick efficient frisk. He transferred the two hundred dollars cash and the six hundred dollars in traveler's checks and the illustrated *Kama Sutra* to his own black leather bag (which he *never* asked anyone to watch), but left the kid his dirty socks and the rest of his shit. Settled in his own four seats again, he got out his paperback of W. R. Burnett's *Dark Hazard* and settled down.

A few minutes later the idiot came back, carrying a sandwich and a can of beer, and said, "Thanks."

"No problem," Tom told him, and went back to his book, and a few minutes later the train jerked forward.

Tom read while the train worked its way through the tunnels beneath midtown Manhattan, and he kept on reading when the train emerged into uptown and became an elevated and stopped at 125th Street, where *nobody* got on or off. Slum scenery became industrial scenery became, very gradually, countryside scenery, and Tom kept reading. He'd never been really big for nature.

It was nearly two hours, and Tom had almost finished the book—it wasn't going to be a happy ending, he could see it coming—when at last the conductor's voice came over the sound system, crying out, "Rhinecliff! Rhinecliff!"

Good. Tom put his book away, shut his bag—two straps and buckles, no zippers—and got to his feet. The schmuck across the aisle gave him a half salute and said, "Have a nice day."

"Yeah, I will."

Tom started away, but a devilish urge made him turn back and say, "You, too." The kid's fatuous grin was still all over his face as the train stopped and Tom found his exit.

"My Mom knows what you look like," Stan Murch had assured him back in New York. "Besides, she's probably the only lady cabdriver there, and the *only* one all the way from Dudson Center."

"I'm not worried," Tom had said, and there she was, no doubt about it, short and chunky, in a cloth cap and zipper jacket and corduroy pants, leaning with arms folded against a green and white car with its name on the door: TOWN TAXI.

She was shaking her head when Tom saw her, apparently arguing with another detrainer who'd wanted to hire her cab. As Tom approached, the frustrated customer raised his voice to say, "For Christ's sake, aren't you a taxi?"

"No," Murch's Mom told him. "I'm a Duane Hansen statue."

Tom interposed himself between the statue and the detrainer, saying quietly, "Here I am."

Murch's Mom, as promised, did recognize him. "Fine," she said. "Get in." And she turned to open the driver's door.

"Hey!" cried the non-customer as Tom opened the rear door. "I was here first!"

"Pay no attention to him," Murch's Mom said.

Of course not. Tom shrugged and started to get into the cab, but the non-customer crowded forward, pushing an attaché case ahead of himself into the space of the open door, blocking Tom's way, continuing to yell and carry on. So Tom looked at him.

He wasn't sure what it was exactly about this face of his, but usually when there was some sort of unnecessary trouble, if he just looked at the person making the disturbance, that was almost always enough to take care of the problem. What might be in his eyes or the set of his features to make it work that way Tom didn't really know, nor did he really care; it did the job, that's all.

And it did the job this time, too. Tom looked at the non-customer and the man stopped yelling. Then he blinked. Then he looked worried. Then he kind of pulled his jaw back in, trying to hide it behind his Adam's apple. Then he got the attaché case out of Tom's way. Then Tom got into the cab.

They were on the wrong side of the Hudson River here, the train tracks running up along its eastern bank, giving occasional beautiful views and vistas that could just as well be from before the European incursion into this continent, not that Tom had noticed, or cared. The Thruway, and the Vilburgtown Reservoir, and drowned Putkin's Corners, and all the Dudsons living and dead, were over across the river in the main part of New York State.

It happens there's a bridge across the Hudson right there at Rhinecliff. Steering across it, Murch's Mom glanced in the rearview mirror at Tom, who had removed his book from his bag and was reading it. "Have a good ride up?" she asked.

Tom looked up from his book, catching Mom's eye in the mirror. Marking his place in the book with his finger, he said, "Yeah, I did. And the weather's nice this time of year. And I'm not hungry yet, thanks. And I haven't been keeping up with the sports teams much lately. And I have no political opinions at all." Lowering his eyes, he opened his book and went back to reading.

Murch's Mom took a deep breath, but then held it awhile. With little white spots on her cheeks, she concentrated on the road ahead, looking for somebody to try to cut her off.

Nobody did, though, and Mom fumed in frustration for several minutes until, across the river and onto the Thruway, she saw out ahead of herself a car from Brooklyn, and all her rage transferred itself to that innocent vehicle. Why would anybody come here from Brooklyn, from *home*, if they didn't have to?

The reason Mom knew that maroon 1975 Ford LTD was from Brooklyn was the license plate: 271 KVQ. The first letter in New York plates gives the county: Kings, in this case, which is Brooklyn. (Queens is Queens, and there's no Jacks.)

The driver of the offending vehicle, a curly-haired young guy, was going along minding his own business when all of a sudden this Town Taxi came swooping out of nowhere, cut him off with micromillimeters to spare, and fishtailed away as though giving him the finger with its tailpipe. Apart from slamming on his brakes, clutching the wheel hard with both hands, and staring wide-eyed, he made no satisfactory reply to this opening remark, so Mom dawdled in the left lane until the other car had nearly caught up, then shot across the lanes again, shaving the distance from the Ford's front bumper even closer than before. *There! That's for nothing! Now do something!*

That was when the cold unemotional voice came from the cab's backseat: "If that guy's bothering you, I could take him out."

Which brought Mom to her senses. "What guy?" she demanded, and floored the accelerator, taking everybody out of danger. Half an hour later, with no further incidents, she steered the cab up onto the driveway beside her new home and braked to a stop just shy of the chain-link fence. "This is it," she announced.

Tom had finished *Dark Hazard* about eight miles back, and had spent the time since just sitting there, looking at the back of Mom's head. (He knew this area, knew what it looked like, wasn't curious about any changes that might have taken place around here of late, and sure wasn't likely to be keeping an eye out for old friends.) Now he looked out at the house and said, "Fine. Looks pretty big."

"It is."

The cuteness that had bothered Dortmunder didn't bother Tom because he didn't notice it. Picking up his leather bag, he climbed out onto the gravel and shut the cab door.

Mom, giving him a sour look out the window (which he also didn't notice), said, without joy, "See you at dinner." And she backed out of the driveway, spraying gravel, and drove off to become a profit-making industry again.

Tom crossed to the porch, went up the stoop, and May opened the front door for him, saying, "Have a nice trip?" (She was determined to be pleasant, to behave as though Tom were a normal human being.)

"Yes," Tom said. Then he grinned at May and said, "You got Al on the hop, all right."

May's face closed right up. "John doesn't think of it that way," she said.

"Good," Tom told her, and looked around this little hallway. "Where do I bunk?"

"Top of the stairs, second door on your left. Your bathroom is right across the hall."

"Okay."

Tom went up and found a small neat sunny room with a view through two windows of the fenced-in back yard and the rears of the houses on Myrtle Street. The bed had been made (May, downstairs, regretted now having done that), with a set of fluffy pale blue towels folded atop it. The drawers in the tall old dresser were all empty, and were still nearly empty when Tom was done unpacking. Once his few clothes were put away, he placed his shaving and toilet gear atop the dresser and hung his old suit jacket in lonely splendor in the closet.

Finally, he salted the place. While certain other armaments remained in the false bottom of the leather bag, the others were distributed in his usual manner: .45 automatic duct-taped to the underside of the box spring, handy when lying in bed; spring knife rolled into a windowshade, so it would drop into his hand when he pulled the shade all the way down; tiny snub-barreled .22 duct-taped to the underside of the water closet lid in the neat old-fashioned bathroom.

There. Home sweet home.

CHAPTER FIFTY-TWO

When the doorbell rang, Wally reassured himself it was indeed John down at the street entrance before pushing the button to let him into the building, and then he hurried off to the kitchen to get the plate of cheese and crackers he'd had in readiness ever since thirty seconds after John's phone call:

"You free this afternoon?"

"Oh, sure."

"I thought I'd come over, uh, we could talk, uh, about things."

"Oh, sure!"

"See you in a while."

"Oh, sure!"

What could it be? Turning off the random-scream alarm, Wally wondered again for the thousandth time what John might want to come here to discuss. It had been so long since he'd heard from John, or from Andy, or from *anybody*, that he'd begun to wonder if maybe they'd gone ahead and finished their adventure without him.

Was that possible? What about the princess, the warlord's daughter? He had only met the princess once; Myrtle Jimson, Wally could see her now in his mind's eye, clear as anything, though in his imagination she did seem to be wearing a high lacy headdress and some sort of long gown out of King Arthur's court. But he had rescued her from no one and nothing, in fact, and there'd been no follow-through at all. His relationships with the warlord and the soldier and the rest were barely into chapter one. Could it all have ended, just like that? Could the entire caravan have moved on, leaving him alone in this oasis?

His doubts had increased with the passage of time, even though the computer had constantly reassured him:

The story cannot end until the hero is satisfied.

Which was all well and good, assuming their postulates were correct.

What if I'm wrong? What if I'm not the hero?

Then there is no story.

Wally had begun to think that perhaps the computer didn't entirely understand the way reality works, and seismic disturbances of disbelief had just begun to shake his compact little universe, when lo and behold, John *phoned!* Fortunately, computers don't say, "I told you so."

The upstairs bell rang, and Wally hurried to open it, surprised to see John by himself out there. Looking around the landing, Wally said, "Isn't Andy with you?"

"Well, no," John said. He seemed ill at ease, less sure of himself than usual. "It's just me," he said. "Andy doesn't know about it. I come over to, uh, talk it over with you."

"Come in, come in," Wally urged him. "I've got cheese and crackers."

"That's nice," John said neutrally, nodding at the plate on the coffee table.

Wally shut the door, gestured John to the comfortable chair, and said, "Would you like a beer?"

"As a matter of fact," John said, "yes."

"Gee, you know, I think I would, too," Wally told him, and hurried to the kitchen to get two cans of beer. When he returned, John was seated in the chair Wally had indicated, gloomily eating cheese and crackers. Wally gave him his beer and sat alertly on the sofa, waiting.

John squinted through his eyebrows in Wally's direction. For some reason, he seemed to be having trouble looking straight at him. "Well," he said, "we're still trying to get that box up out of the reservoir."

"The treasure," Wally said.

"Tom really wants that money," John said.

"Well, sure, I guess he would," Wally agreed.

"He wants to blow up the dam," John said.

Wally nodded, considering that. "I guess that would work," he said. "Only, how does he plan to channel the water?"

"He doesn't," John said.

Wally's wet eyes widened: "But doesn't he know about the towns? A lot of people live down there! John, we have to tell him about—"

"He knows," John said.

Wally looked at John's grim face. The warlord has no pity. Wally whispered, "Would Tom really do that?"

"He'd've done it already," John said, "only I talked him into letting me have one more crack at it."

Suddenly John did look straight at Wally, and in that instant Wally understood just how difficult it had been for John to come here to ask for help. That's why he's here, Wally thought, with a sudden thrill. He's here to ask for help! To ask *me* for help! Wally blinked, his mouth sagging open at his sense of the importance of this moment.

John said, "May moved up there. Dudson Center. See, I quit, I couldn't do it anymore, so that's what she did."

Horrified, Wally said, "Tom wouldn't blow up the dam with Miss *May* there!"

"Tom would blow up the dam with the Virgin Mary there," John said.

"Then we have to *get* that treasure!" Wally cried, bouncing around on the sofa in his agitation. "Before he does it!"

"That's the situation," John agreed. "And here's the rest of the situation. Andy and I went down in that reservoir twice, and that's twice too much. I can't do it again. Just take my word for it, I can't. So it has to be something else. There's gotta be a way to get the money up *out* of there without *me* going down *in* there."

Wally nodded, trying to think but still overcome by the wonder of it. John came to *me*! "But what?" he asked, caught up in the story.

"I don't *know*," John told him, putting his beer can down so he could actually wring his hands. "I thought and I thought and I thought, and I just don't come up with a thing. I shot my bolt on this one, Wally, there's nothing left. I'm not finding anything because I can't get myself even to *think* about that place. And Tom won't wait much longer."

"No, I guess not." Wally felt very solemn at this moment.

John leaned toward him. "So here's the idea."

"Yes? Yes?" Wally's damp face gleamed with excitement.

"Our half of the caper," John explained, "the profit for everybody except Tom, is three hundred fifty grand."

"That's a *lot*!"

"Not when you start cutting it up," John told him. "But it's still *some*, and those of us in it split it even, all the way down. If we manage, that is, to keep Tom from double-crossing us and getting it all."

Wally nodded. "He'd do that, wouldn't he?"

"Nothing else would even occur to him," John said. "Okay. The way it stands now, there's four of us in it: Me, Andy Kelp, Tiny Bulcher, and a driver named Stan Murch that you don't know." John cleared his throat, hesitated, seemed on the point of flight, then blurted forward, saying, "You come up with the way, Wally, you're a partner."

"A partner? Me?"

"You," John agreed. "That makes it seventy grand for each of us, including you."

"Wow!"

"But you gotta come up with something," John told him. "*One* of us has gotta come up with something, and I just don't think it's gonna be me. Not anymore."

Wally, excitement bubbling in him like chocolate fudge just on the boil, jumped to his feet, saying, "Let's see what the computer has to say!"

John looked displeased. "Do we have to?"

"The computer is very smart, John," Wally said. "Let's just see."

So John shrugged, and they both went over to have a chat with the computer, Wally in his usual swivel chair, John standing beside him.

"First," Wally said, "let's bring up the model we did of the valley, with the reservoir in, and ask the computer to show us different ways to blow up the dam. Maybe in one of them, the water could be channeled down the valley away from all the towns and things."

"I don't see it," John said.

"Let's just find out." Wally sent his little fat fingers flying over the keys, and up on the screen came a side view of the valley, heavy with rich blue, trailing away to green dotted with brown and black; the brown and black dots were towns.

John touched the screen over one of the brown dots. "That's where May is."

"Now we'll see," Wally said, and proceeded to drown Miss May and a lot of other people seven times in a row. Every single time, the blue area would at first tremble, and then it would spread and suddenly swell, obliterating every last one of the black and brown dots.

After the seventh time, John said, "No more, Wally, no more. I can't take it."

"You're right," Wally agreed. "There just isn't any safe way to send all that water downstream. Not all at once."

"That's the way dynamite works, though," John pointed out. "All at once."

"Let me explain the situation to the computer once more," Wally said, "and see if it comes up with anything new."

"Just so we don't have any more of that killer blue."

So Wally asked his question, and after a brief pause the computer responded with its green-lettered series of suggestions, crawling slowly up the screen. Wally and John watched, neither saying a word until it was finished, and then John said, quietly, "This computer really has a thing for Zog, doesn't it?"

Wally cleared his throat. "I don't have the heart to tell it Zog isn't real," he admitted.

"Wally," John said, "I don't know that I'm getting anywhere here. I thought I'd come over and talk to a person, but I'm here talking to a machine that thinks a planet called Zog is a real place."

"You're right," Wally said, abruptly ashamed of himself. He felt now as though he'd been using the computer for a crutch, that he was hiding behind it. John had come here for help, and Wally had run straight to his computer. That's not the way to treat people, Wally told himself, and he reached out to hit the power button, shutting the computer down. Then, standing, turning, he said, "I'm sorry, John, that's just a bad habit. I *always* talk things over with the computer. I don't know why."

"Yeah, I always talk things over with May," John told him, "but there comes a time when you got to make your own decision."

"I'm going to," Wally said. The excitement he felt now was different from before, more tremulous and frightening. He was going to be on his own! In the *real world*! "Let's talk it over some more, John," he said, "just the two of us. Not the computer at all."

"Good."

So they sat around the cheese and crackers, ignoring them, and John told him about the way he and Andy had learned how to do underwater things from a fellow on Long Island, and how they'd tried once to walk into the reservoir and once to drive in, and how the reservoir almost drowned them both times, and all about the turbidity and the flotation power of Ping-Pong balls, and after about twenty minutes Wally said, "Gee, John, why don't you ask that guy on Long Island?"

John blinked. "Ask him what?"

"He's a professional diver, John," Wally said. "And you told me you went to him because he already does some things that aren't absolutely legal."

John shrugged. "So?"

"So I realize," Wally said, "that would mean there were six of us to share the money now, instead of five, but that would still be about sixty thousand dollars each, and—"

"Wait a minute wait a minute," John said, rearing back. "Bring *Doug* aboard, you mean."

"Is that his name? Yes, sure, bring Doug aboard. Wouldn't *he* know how to go down into the reservoir and get the box?"

John looked at Wally without speaking for quite a long time. Then he sat back, shook his head, and said, "You know why *I* didn't think of that?"

"Well, no," Wally admitted.

"Because," John said, "whatever it is I'm doing, I'm used to it *I'm* the one does it. I figure out how and I do it. I get people to help, but that's *help*, that isn't to do it *instead* of me."

Wally wasn't sure he understood. "Do you mean," he asked carefully, "it would be like against your principles or something to have somebody else do things instead of you?"

"No, I don't mean that," John said. "I'm simply trying to explain to you why I'm as stupid as I am."

"Oh," Wally said.

"Why I could never think about anybody going down into that goddamn water except *me*," John went on, "and I knew damn well it wasn't *about* to be me, not again, so that's why I was stymied."

"I see," Wally said.

"But you took one look," John told him, "once you got out from behind that machine of yours, you took one look at what *I* couldn't see at all, and you said it's obvious. And it is."

Wally wasn't sure exactly how far he was supposed to go in agreement with John's self-insults, so he made a quick defensive move, shoving cheese and cracker in his mouth so he wouldn't be able to do anything but nod and say, "Mm. Mm."

Which was apparently enough. John sat back, his whole body a study in looseness and relief. Pointing over at the computer, he said, "Sell that thing, Wally. You don't need it."

CHAPTER FIFTY-THREE

Stanch Shore Dive Shop. Sorry we're not open now. Our usual hours are Thursday through Sunday, ten to five. Licensed professional instruction, basic and advanced courses. Dive equipment for sale or rent, air refills, tank tests, all your diving needs under one roof. Hope to see you!"

Everybody in May's new living room watched Dortmunder's face as he listened yet again to that goddamn irrelevant infuriating *long* announcement. At the end, he snarled savagely into the phone, "Don't you ever listen to your messages? You're worse than Andy."

"Aw, come on," Kelp said from his perch on the sofa arm, beside May.

Ignoring him, Dortmunder told the phone, "This is John *again*. Call me, dammit. I've been out to your place, you're never there. Time's running out."

"And that's no lie," Tom said happily, seated primly on the wooden chair in the corner that had become his favorite waiting place. Murch's Mom gave him a dirty look, which he seemed not to notice.

Laboriously, Dortmunder stated May's new phone number into Doug Berry's machine, area code and all, then said, "Call *collect*, if you want, dammit. Just *call*. We've been trying to reach you for three days now." And he slammed down the phone.

In the ensuing silence, Dortmunder, Kelp, May, Stan Murch, and Murch's Mom—everybody but Tom—all sat or stood in the living room, thinking the same furious thought: Where *is* that waterlogged jerk?

CHAPTER FIFTY-FOUR

How the old glider groaned under their weight! Or was that Doug, moaning as he nuzzled his nose down into the softness at the side of her throat, his lips caressing the pulse that beat so wildly there? Or was it—good heavens!—*herself*, losing control, giving in to the sensations, the warmth flooding her body from his lips, his tongue, his hands, his body pressed to hers as they half reclined here?

The glider swayed on the front porch in bright daylight, moving rhythmically and suggestively with their movements, and when Myrtle opened her eyes, looking past his ear, past his wavy blond hair, her vision blurred and she could barely see Myrtle Street and the houses across the way and the glimpses beyond them of the houses fronting on Oak Street far away. The glider swayed in the somnolent day, no traffic at all moved on the street, and Myrtle felt again the flutter of a faint moan rise up through her throat, past his warm mouth, out her own trembling lips.

But this was supposed to be *safe*! Broad daylight! She had nothing to fear, she'd been sure of that, just sitting with him on this front porch in the middle of the day, in front of the world, with the sun beaming down. That's why she'd agreed.

Suggested. Ohhhhhhhh . . .

Edna isn't home.

The house loomed empty behind them. "Myrtle," he murmured, lips moving against her throat, "Myrtle, Myrtle, Myrtle . . ."

She closed her eyes. The heat rose from them, rose around them, surrounded them like a sauna, an invisible ball with them inside, steaming. The strength flowed away, out of her shoulders and arms, out of her knees and legs, concentrating in her belly. Her head lolled against the silkiness of his hair, unable to sustain its own weight. Her breath flowed like jasmine through her parted mouth, her lips were swollen and red, her eyelids heavy.

"Doug . . ."

No. That was supposed to have been a warning, a protest, a command to them both to stop, but she could hear herself how it had come out wrong, how the syllable had stretched, had become languorous and welcoming, had beckoned him on instead of pushing him away. She was afraid to speak again, to say anything else, afraid her voice would betray her once more. But if she said nothing, did nothing, he'd just continue, his mouth, his hands . . .

"Myrtle, say yes."

"Doug . . ."

"Say yes."

"Doug . . ."

"Say yes."

"Ououououououououghhh . . ."

"Say yessssssssssss . . ."

"Yessssssssssss . . ."

He was up on his feet, holding her hand in his, drawing her up beside him. His smile was gentle and loving, his body so strong. "Yes," he said, and turned them both toward the front door.

"*There* you are, Doug, goddammit!"

They spun around, and Myrtle's heart leaped with fear. An extremely angry man, a *stranger*, stood at the top of the stoop, *glaring* at Doug.

Who knew him. "John!" he cried in absolute stunned astonishment.

"I hate your answering machine, Doug," the angry man said. "I just want you to know that. I have a deep personal dislike for that answering machine of yours, and if I'm ever near it with a baseball bat in my hands, that's *it*."

"John, I, I, I . . ."

What is going *on*? But Myrtle couldn't even ask the question, could only stand there, romance forgotten, her body forgotten, and stare from Doug's ashen amazed face to the other man's darker angrier unloving face.

"Never mind, 'I, I, I,'" said this unloving face, and the man made a quick impatient sweeping gesture like a traffic cop. "Come on. We gotta talk."

"John, I— *Now*? John, I can't, I—"

"Yes, now! What's so goddamn important that you can't—"

"John, *will* ya?"

Oh! Face burning, Myrtle pulled her hand free from Doug's, turned blindly, groped for the door, pulled it open, and flung herself into the house as behind her Doug said to the angry man, "John, I'll never forgive you for this in my entire—"

Slam. Tottering, weaving, Myrtle staggered to the living room and dropped into the nearest chair. Through the front windows she could see them out there, both gesturing, the angry man not letting up, Doug finally assenting, shrugging, shaking his head, turning for one last lost look at the front door—Oh, Doug, how *could* you? How could you let us be interrupted, let *that moment* be broken?—before, with obvious reluctance, he followed the angry man off the stoop and across Myrtle Street and up the Fleischbacker's driveway over there and on out of sight.

It wasn't until twenty minutes later, when she was calmer, when she'd already had one cup of tea and was sipping a second, when she was already remembering that her involvement with Doug in the first place was because he was a mystery she was trying to solve, that the thought suddenly came to her:

I've seen that man somewhere before.

CHAPTER FIFTY-FIVE

Doug basically felt like a person with the bends. He'd never himself had the bends, having always been a careful and professional diver, but the condition had been described to him, and the description fit his current condition to a tee: nausea, anxiety, disorientation, physical pain. That was him, all right.

And to think how happy he'd been just instants before, in the arms of Myrtle Street, rounding the far turn and galloping for home at long, long last. What a wonderful distraction Myrtle had been from his search for John and Andy, from his watch on the Vilburgtown Reservoir; as an excuse to keep visiting Dudson Center she couldn't be improved on.

In some ways, the pursuit of Myrtle Street had become as important to Doug as his pursuit of John and Andy and the seven hundred thousand dollars from the armored car robbery. And then, just as the one pursuit seemed to be coming to its warm and beautiful and successful close, the other pursuit had made a totally unexpected about-face, the pursued had become the pursuer, and at the worst possible moment in the history of the world, *there was John!*

• • •

Looking back on it all afterward, Doug recalled that traumatic day only in quick bytes, short periods of lucidity floating in a dark menacing swirl of queasiness and panic. And beginning with a living room full of people, men and women, all of them strangers to him except John and Andy, and all of them for some reason very angry with him.

Particularly one mean-looking old guy in a chair in a corner. While everybody else was still shouting, this guy kept saying, quietly and dispassionately, "Kill him."

Kill him? Kill *me*? Doug stared around at all these cold faces, swallowing compulsively, afraid that if he threw up it would only give them *more* reason to kill him.

It was Andy who responded to the mean old guy first, saying, "I almost agree with you this time, Tom."

Oh, Andy! Doug cried in his mind, but he was too frightened and sick to say anything out loud, not even to save his life. Andy, Andy, Andy, he cried inside himself, I taught you to dive!

But John was saying, "We need him, Tom," and thank God for that. Even though John didn't sound at all happy to have to say it; no, nor did he sound entirely convinced that what he was saying was true.

And the mean old guy—Tom—said, "What's he doing up in this neck of the woods? Long Island boy. He followed you, John, you and Andy. He's on to the caper. He wants the dough for himself."

Teeth chattering, Doug found voice at last, saying, "I, I, I, I got a girlfriend, she's M-M-Myrtle St-St-Street."

"That's the next block over," said a short blunt angry woman in a flannel shirt.

"No-no-no," Doug stammered, "that's her, that's her—"

"His girlfriend can put flowers on his grave," Tom said. Then he smiled very unpleasantly at Doug and said to the others, "He's a diver, right? Let's take him to the reservoir, see how he dives with weights around his neck."

"We need him to get the money," John said.

"*I* don't," Tom said.

The other woman in the room, taller, calmer, said, "Tom, you're letting John do it his way, remember?"

Tom shrugged. "You like this diver?" he asked John. "You want this diver in our lives?"

The other fellow present, a red-haired jaunty guy who looked as though he'd be an excellent street fighter, said, "Let's see if he likes the deal. Make him the offer, John."

Offer? "I accept!" Doug cried.

They all stared at him, too surprised to be mad; even Tom looked nearly human for a second. Andy, nodding, said, "That's what I call low sales resistance."

John, sounding almost sympathetic, said, "Listen to the offer first, Doug."

"Okay," Doug said. He still had to keep swallowing, and pinwheels had started to dance in his peripheral vision. But he would listen to the offer first, if that's what he was supposed to do. Listen to the offer first.

"You know what we're going for in the reservoir," John said.

Panic again! "Oh! Well, uh—"

"We *know* you know," John told him, sounding more irritable. "Don't waste our time."

"Okay," Doug said. "Okay."

"Okay. So here's the story."

Then John made the offer, something about this and that, and percentages, and diving, and Doug nodded all the way through the whole thing, and when John finally stopped talking and looked at him for a reaction, he smiled big at everybody in the room, smiling through his nausea, and he said, "Okay. Fine. I agree. It's a deal. Where do I sign? Sounds fair to me. Hey, no problem. I'm with you. By all means. Sure! With pleasure. What's to argue? Shake on it! You got a—"

"Oh, shut up," said the short woman in the flannel shirt.

• • •

Then there was the drive to the city. The red-haired guy, whose name turned out to be Stan, drove Doug's pickup, with Doug as his passenger, following Andy and John down the Thruway in a Cadillac Sedan da Fe with MD plates. ("Listen, *I* can drive," Doug had said, but, "No, you can't," John had told him, so that was that.) Before leaving the house on Oak Street, a phone call had been made to somebody called Wally, and now they were all going to the city for this Wally to show Doug something. Sure; whatever you guys say.

Along the way, Doug tried to befriend this guy Stan, but it didn't work out too well. His opening gambit was, "You know John and Andy a long time?"

"Uh-huh," said Stan. He drove with both hands on the wheel, both eyes on the road.

"I just met them," Doug said. "Recently. I taught them how to dive."

"Uh-huh."

"I could, uh, teach you to dive, too, Stan, if you want. You know, a pal of John and Andy, I wouldn't charge you any—"

"Did you ever," Stan interrupted, "see a three-sixty?"

Doug looked at Stan's expressionless profile. "A what?"

"A three-sixty."

"I don't know what that is," Doug admitted, little flutters of panic starting up again in his stomach.

"No?" Stan nodded. "I'll show you," he said, and suddenly floored the accelerator, and the pickup flashed past the MD Cadillac into an empty bit of highway, traffic ahead and behind but none right *here*, and then Stan flicked the steering wheel left, *yanked* it right, simultaneously did something fast and tricky with brake and clutch and accelerator, and the pickup spun all the way around in a circle in the middle of the road—*still going sixty miles an hour toward New York*—wound up facing south again, shivered once, and drove on.

Doug wasn't breathing. His mouth was open, but he just wasn't breathing. He'd seen an entire sweep of the outside world flash past the windshield—the grassy center strip, the road behind them with the Cadillac in it, the forest beside the road, and then the proper road again—in just about a second; too fast to panic *during* it, so Doug was going all to pieces after it.

Stan the driver, without speaking, slowed the pickup and let the Cadillac pass. Andy, driving that other car, grinned and waved at Stan, who nodded with dignity back. And Doug hadn't breathed yet.

Finally he did, a long raspy vocal intake of breath that hurt all the way down. And then at last Stan spoke. "That was a three-sixty," he said. "You talk to me some more, I'll show you some other stuff I know."

Doug kept very quiet the rest of the way to the city.

• • •

Wally turned out to be some sort of freak of nature, short and fat and moist. The only good thing you could say for him was that he didn't seem to be mad at Doug for any reason. He even welcomed Doug to his weird apartment—it looked like an appliance repair shop—with an eager smile and a damp handshake, as he said, "You want some cheese and crackers?"

"Uh," Doug answered, not sure the others would permit.

No, they wouldn't. "No time, Wally," John said. "Show him the model, okay?"

"Sure," Wally said.

The "model" turned out not to be an actual toy train set kind of model at all, but a series of pictures on a television screen connected to a computer. Part of it was an animated movie, and much of that was pretty.

Doug stood there behind Wally, unaware of anything except the necessity to do what he was told: look at the model. After this, he'd be told something else to do, and he'd do it. He gazed at the screen, totally unaware of John, beside him, frowning at his profile. He was unaware of John finally shaking his head in irritation, raising one hand, and making a fist, with the knuckle of the middle finger extended. But he was *very* aware when John suddenly rapped him on the side of the skull with that knuckle.

Ow! That hurt! Doug flinched away, wide-eyed, staring at John, betrayed. He was doing what they wanted!

But John was dissatisfied. "You're daydreaming," he said. "You're asleep here. Your eyes aren't even in focus."

"Sure they are! Sure they are!" In his renewed panic, Doug was only grateful that mean old Tom hadn't come along. Surely, if he were present, he would right now renew his baying after Doug's blood.

Not that the others were being pleasant. Andy, crowding in on Doug's other side, said, "What's Wally showed you so far?"

Doug gasped at him. "What?"

"What did you see on the computer?"

Doug groped for an answer. "The model!"

"Of what?"

Doug stared from cold face to cold face to wet face. Desperate, he blurted, "I didn't know there was gonna be a *test*!"

John and Andy looked at each other as though trying to decide how best to dispose of the body. Between them, seated at his computer but twisted around to look up at Doug, Wally suddenly said, "Well, you know what it is; he's in shock."

John frowned at Wally. "He's what?"

"In shock," Wally repeated. "Look at his eyes. Feel his forehead, I bet it's cold and wet."

Andy pressed his palm to Doug's forehead, made a *yuk!* face, and pulled his hand back. "Right you are," he said, wiping his palm on his trouser leg.

Getting to his feet, taking Doug by the unresisting arm, Andy said, "Come on over here and sit down."

Doug crossed obediently to the sofa and, at Wally's urging, sat down. But then Wally said, "Bend down. Put your head between your knees."

"Why?" Doug asked, febrile again. "What are you gonna do to me?"

"Nothing," Wally assured him, gently pushing Doug's head forward and down as he turned to say to the others, "What *did* you do to him?"

"Nothing," Andy said, but he sounded defensive.

"Offered him sixty thousand dollars," John said sulkily.

"Hardly anything," Stan said.

Bent way over with his head between his knees, looking at the bolts, batteries, floppy disks, Allen wrenches, F-connectors, and other electric and electronic debris under the sofa, Doug felt oddly safe, as though he were in a cave, hidden and protected. He even felt brave enough to squeal on Stan. "Three-sixty," he muttered.

Wally leaned down close; being Wally, he didn't have to lean down very far to be close. He said, "What was that, Doug?"

"Three-sixty."

"Oh, for Pete's sake," Stan said, "that wasn't anything at all. That was just to amuse him."

Sounding scientifically interested, Andy said, "Do you think that's what put him in shock? When Stan popped the wheelie?"

"Tom," muttered Doug.

Stan said, "What did he say?"

Wally was the translator: "He said, 'Tom.'"

"Well, yeah," Andy said. "There are times when Tom's put *me* in shock, actually."

"Myrtle," Doug muttered.

"'Myrtle,'" Wally translated.

"That's the street where his girlfriend lives," John explained.

"It's her *name*," Doug muttered, but Wally wasn't listening this time, he was saying, "This poor fella's had a whole *lot* of things happen. No wonder he's in shock."

John said, "How long till he starts tracking again?"

"Gee, I don't know, John," Wally said. "Till he gets over it, I guess."

Doug rolled onto his side on the sofa, drew his knees up in fetal position, and closed his eyes. Not noticing him, the others kept talking. Soothing sounds. Very soothing. Surprising how soothing a soothing sound can be in its being soothing. Totally soothing.

• • •

Doug's eyes opened. Time had passed. The room was darker. The room was *empty*.

Doug sat up, memory exploding in his mind like a fragmentation grenade. Myrtle. John. Angry living room. Spinning car. Television model. Soothing. And now: alone.

Alone. Even the cheese and crackers were gone. The door was over there. The apartment was silent.

Doug, pay attention. The *door* is over *there*.

Cautiously, he got to his feet, then to his toes. On tiptoe, silent as a moth in a sweater, he crossed the messy living room to the door, silently reached out to the knob, silently turned it, silently pulled the door open.

"Look out!" screamed a voice. *"She's got a knife!"*

Doug shrieked and dropped to the floor.

"Goddamn mothuhfuckuh, Ah'm gone cut your mothuhfuckin BALLS off!"

Wally, startled from his dinner in the kitchen by the sudden sound of his scream alarm—haven't heard the crazed woman with the knife for quite some time, he reflected—hurried into the living room to find the hall door wide open and Doug flat on his face on the floor. Wally crossed to Doug, tapped him on the shoulder, and Doug screamed and fainted.

• • •

Light. Voices. Doug, eyes squeezed shut, reoriented himself gradually into space and time, and on this try memory entered like a gamboling lamb, easy and sweet. He remembered everything, and even understood why he was lying on the floor. The only thing he was confused about was why he hadn't been sliced into tiny ribbons by that crazed woman with the knife.

Don't argue, Doug; just accept.

He rolled over onto his back, opened his eyes, squinted against the light, and sat up. And Andy's voice said, "Here he is now. Sleeping Beauty."

"Slipping Beauty," said John.

Doug looked over toward the sofa and chair, and the usual four were there, gathered around the cheese and crackers: Wally, John, Andy, and Stan. The maniac woman was nowhere to be seen. "All right," he said. "Okay. Enough."

"I'll go along with that," John said. "You sane now?"

"I think so," Doug told him. "And I'll make a deal with you. I don't know who that woman was, or what her problem is, or where she is now, but I'll do whatever you want if you keep her *away* from me. I never want to see her again. Okay?"

They all looked at one another, as though baffled. Then they all shrugged at one another. Then John said, "It's a deal."

"Good," Doug said, feeling vast relief. "Now I can do it. I'll pay attention to the model, I'll think about the salvage job—"

John said, "The what?"

"Salvage job," Doug said. "That's what you want, isn't it? Bring up something from the bottom of the reservoir. That's a salvage job."

Andy, with a happy smile, said, "There, you see? A professional. As soon as you get the right guy, you got a vocabulary and everything."

"I remember about salvage jobs," John said, sounding irritated again. "From that book I got. *Marine Salvage.*"

"Great book," Doug commented.

"You just mumbled when you said it, that's all," John told him. "So, okay, it's a salvage job. So let's get to it."

So they got to it, and this time Doug could absorb the computer model, see how clever it was, and also see what some of the problems were going to be. At one point, he said, "How did you guys figure to find one little box buried somewhere in a field? What were you gonna do, dig up the whole field? Underwater?"

John, a little huffy, said, "We got a fix on the place from Tom. And we had a poker with us, to help find it."

"Great," Doug said ironically. Now that they were dealing with *his* area of expertise, he was losing the last remnants of panic and insecurity, was unconsciously becoming a little arrogant and dismissive. Shaking his head at John, he said to Wally, "How close a fix *is* this?"

Wally explained about the three streetlights that Tom had used to mark the location of the buried casket, and Doug said, "Can you give me an accurate reading on distance to the box from the back wall of the library?"

"Sure."

John, a bit nastily, said, "What are you gonna do, pace it off when you get down there?"

"I'll bring a line with me," Doug told him, "the same length as the distance from the wall to the box. Okay?"

"Mrp," John said, and stopped interrupting after that, so finally Doug could close with the problem.

At last, when Wally had shown him everything he had, Doug stepped back from the computer screen and said, "Okay. I got the picture now."

Andy said, "And it can be done?"

"Yes."

"Good," Andy said.

"But," Doug said, "it can't be done without a boat."

"Gee, Doug," Andy said. "That's a reservoir, you know? No boating."

Doug frowned at him. "I didn't think you guys worried about laws that much."

John said, "What Andy means is, we can't be *seen* with a boat."

Doug shrugged. "So we do it on a cloudy night. All we need is a small rubber boat with a little ten-hp motor."

John said, "A motor? We shouldn't be *heard* with a boat either."

"You won't hear it," Doug promised him. "But the main thing is, we have to go in from above, and that means a boat."

"Expensive," John suggested.

Doug waved that away. "A couple thou. For the boat and the motor, I mean. Then there'll be other stuff. Maybe four or five thou altogether."

John nodded. "Well," he said, "time to go tell Tom the good news. We need more money."

CHAPTER FIFTY-SIX

Goddammit, Tom," Dortmunder said, strapping on the safety harness, "why didn't you ever stash your goddamn money anywhere *easy?*"

"Easy places other people find," Tom pointed out. He sat on the ground beside the coil of rope.

"What the hell were you doing in South Dakota anyway?" Dortmunder demanded. This whole thing made him mad.

"Robbing a bank," Tom said. "You ready?"

"No," Dortmunder said. "I'm *never* gonna be ready to step out into thin air from on top of a mountain." Taking one cautious step out onto Lincoln's forehead, he looked down, *way* down, at the tops of pine trees. The whole world was out there. "Somebody's gonna see me," he said.

"They'll think you're a ranger."

"I don't have the hat."

"So they'll think you're a ranger that his hat blew off," Tom said. "Come *on*, Al, let's do it and get it over with. We gotta drive all the way back to Pierre, turn in the car, catch the plane."

"Pierre," Dortmunder said in disgust, studying Lincoln's eyebrows. Would they provide handholds? "Who calls a city Pierre?"

"It's their city, Al. Come on, will ya?"

So Dortmunder dropped to his haunches and slid forward out of Lincoln's hair, his feet reaching for those bushy thick eyebrows. Behind him, Tom paid out the rope. "How the hell," Dortmunder complained, "did you ever stash the stuff here in the first place?"

"I was a lot younger then, Al," Tom told him. "A lot spryer."

Dortmunder stopped to look back and say, "Young people aren't spry. *Old* people are spry."

"You're stalling, Al."

He was. Oh, well. His waggling feet found the eyebrows, he slid down farther, his legs straddled the bumpy nose.

He was now out of sight of Tom, in safety up there on top, calling down, "You there yet?"

"No!"

"It's the left nostril."

"Yeah, yeah."

Dortmunder slid off the nose, dangled briefly in space—the pitons they'd pounded into the ground up there damn well better hold—clutched a naris, and hauled himself in to Lincoln's upper lip.

Left nostril. Jeez, it was like a cave in there, it was so big. Dortmunder inched up into the thing, standing on Lincoln's lip, and saw the oilcloth-wrapped package tucked behind an irregularity of rock. Reaching for it, he dislodged a few pebbles, raised some dust. Inside Lincoln's nostril, Dortmunder sneezed.

"God bless," called Tom.

"Oh, shut up," Dortmunder muttered inside the nostril. He grabbed the package and got out of that nose.

CHAPTER FIFTY-SEVEN

One Monday in June, the reservoir gang converged on 46 Oak Street in the peaceful upstate rural community of Dudson Center. Already in residence at the house were May Bellamy, Tom Jimson, and Murch's Mom. Coming from Islip, Long Island (home of the lobotomy; known in psychiatric circles as Icepick, Long Island), was Doug Berry, his custom-packaged pickup laden with gear for the job ahead: diving equipment, a 10hp outboard motor, uninflated inflatable boat, lots of other stuff. In a borrowed bakery van, driving up from New York City, were Stan Murch and Wally Knurr, with Wally's computer components strapped down on the bread shelves in back. Also coming from the city, in a silver Cadillac with California MD plates, equipped with cruise control, a/c, cassette player, reading lights and extremely woodlike dashboard trim, traveled Andy Kelp (driver), John Dortmunder (front-seat passenger), and Tiny Bulcher (all over the rear seat). Of these vehicles, only the Cadillac was being followed, by a large roughhewn shambling fellow named Ken Warren, wedged with his tow bar into a small red two-door Toyota Chemistra.

The travelers in the Cadillac remained unaware of the intense interest seven car-lengths behind them and chatted mostly about their upcoming task. "I've been wrong before," Dortmunder conceded, "but I just have a feeling. *This* time, we're gonna get that box."

"The reason you're feeling good," Kelp told him, ignoring the red Toyota in all three rearview mirrors, "is the same reason I'm feeling good. We are not going into that reservoir. Not you, and not me."

293

"Let *Doug* go in the reservoir."

"Right."

"He likes that kind of thing."

"He does."

"We don't."

"We don't."

In the backseat, Tiny wriggled around, uncomfortable, and finally reached underneath himself to pull out a tambourine, which he stared at in irritated astonishment. "Hey," he said. "There's a tambourine in this car."

"A what? You sure?" Kelp looked in the interior rearview mirror as Tiny held up the tambourine, blocking the view of the red Toyota. "It *looks* like a tambourine," he admitted.

"It is a tambourine," Tiny said, and shook it. Tambourine music filled the air.

"I remember that sound," Dortmunder said. "They used to have those in the movies."

"Wait a second," Tiny said, and from the crevice between seat and back he brought out a small cardboard box. "Now we got a deck of tarot cards." Putting down the tambourine (*jing!*), he took the cards out of their box and riffled them. "Looks like a marked deck," he said.

Dortmunder said, "Andy, what kinda doctor did you get this car from?"

"I dunno," Kelp said. "He was making a house call, I think. It was in front of a Reader and Advisor on Bleecker Street."

"I don't want this doctor doing any operations on *me*," Tiny said. He shuffled the cards. "John, you want me to tell your fortune?"

"Maybe not," Dortmunder said.

• • •

The red Toyota, still unnoticed, was a block behind the Cadillac when it made the turn onto Oak Street and pulled up onto the gravel driveway beside the house. Stopping just shy of the chain-link fence, Kelp said, "Looks like we're first."

"Yeah?" Dortmunder looked interested. "What do we win?"

"Just the glory," Kelp told him.

Ken Warren steered the red Toyota past 46 Oak Street, watching the trio from the Cadillac unload luggage from the trunk. He drove on by, made the next right, took the next left onto Myrtle Street and parked near the far corner there. Leaving the tow bar behind—it would be easier to tow the Toyota with the Cadillac than the other way around—he locked up and retraced his route on foot, shambling along round-shouldered and thrust-jawed like a bad-tempered bear.

The Cadillac had been left unlocked, and he was seated behind its wheel, door open, looking through his keys for the one to fit this ignition, when a bread company van pulled in behind him, filling the rearview mirrors and blocking his exit.

Now, Ken was the big silent type, not because he had nothing to say but because of his deep nasal twang and severe glottal stop. He preferred to be thought of as a silent tough guy rather than a geek who couldn't talk right. But there were moments when speech was necessary, and this looked like one of them. "Hey," Ken said, and leaned out to look back at the van's driver, who he assumed was just making a delivery. "Moo fit!" he called.

Stan Murch, who was not exactly making a delivery, and who knew from the MD plates that (1) Andy Kelp had driven this car here, and (2) that ugly mug at the wheel wasn't Andy Kelp, switched off the van's engine, pulled on the emergency brake, and stepped out to the driveway, calling toward the house, "Andy! Mayday!"

Wally, climbing over the driver's seat to get out on the same side as Stan, said, "Who is he, Stan?"

"No idea."

"What's going to happen?"

"No idea."

There is one rule in Ken Warren's profession: If you're in the car, it's yours. Therefore, he slammed the driver's door of the Cadillac, hit the button that locked all four doors, and went back to his methodical run-through of his keys. Once he got this vehicle started, he'd use it to push the van out of his way.

People erupted from the house; first Andy Kelp, then Dortmunder, May, Tiny, and Tom. While May and Tom stayed on the porch, observing, Kelp and Dortmunder and Tiny went over to join Stan and Wally in looking at the beefy man inside the Cadillac.

"What's going on?" Kelp asked.

"No idea," Stan said.

"That man was in the car," Wally said in great excitement, "when we got here."

"He's still in the car," Kelp pointed out, and rapped on the glass in the driver's door. "Hey! What's the story?"

Got it! The Cadillac engine caught, and Ken looked over at the right-door mirror just in time to see a heavy-laden pickup pull into the driveway behind the van, filling the driveway and blocking the sidewalk as

well. A handsome blond guy in cut-off jeans and a T-shirt that said WORK IS
FOR PEOPLE WHO DON'T SURF got out and strolled curiously forward.

"What's the story here?" Doug asked.

"No idea," Stan said.

Hell! Could he push both the van *and* the pickup? Deciding he had no
choice, he could but try, Ken shifted into reverse and watched a green-
and-white taxi pull up to the curb, parking crossways just behind the
pickup.

Murch's Mom got out of her cab and joined the crowd beside the
Cadillac, saying, "What's happening?"

"No idea," said her son.

Ken considered the chain-link fence. Drive through it? Unlikely; the
metal pipe supports were embedded in concrete. It wouldn't be any good
to make the Cadillac inoperable.

Murch's Mom went into the house for a potato. Kelp leaned close to the
glass separating him from the stranger. "We're gonna put a potato in the
exhaust!" he yelled. "We're gonna monoxide you!"

Ken was feeling very put-upon. And also, come to think of it, a little
confused. This mob around the Cadillac just didn't look right. Could he
have made a mistake?

No. The car was right: make, model, and color. The license plate was
right. There was a tambourine on the backseat.

Still, *something* was wrong. As the woman cabdriver came out of the
house carrying a big baking potato in her hand, Ken cracked the window
beside him just far enough to make conversation possible, and announced
through the crack, "Ngyou're gno gnipthy!"

Kelp reared back: "*What?*"

"*Gnone* of ngyou are gnipthyth!"

"He's a foreigner," Stan decided. "He doesn't talk English."

Ken glared at him. "Ngyou makin funna me?"

"What is that he talks?" Murch's Mom asked, holding the potato.
"Polish?"

"Could be Lithuanian," Tiny said doubtfully.

Dortmunder turned to stare at him. "Lithu*a*nian!"

"I had a Lithuanian cellmate once," Tiny explained. "He talked like—"

Ken had had enough. Pounding the steering wheel, "Ah'm sthpeakin
Englisth!" he cried, through the open slit in the window.

Which did no good. Dortmunder said to Tiny, "Tell him it's our car,
then. Talk to him in Lithuanian."

Tiny said, "*I* don't speak Lith—"

"Ikn's *gnot* your car!" Ken yelled. "Ikth's the *bankth's* car!"

"Wait a minute, wait a minute," Kelp said. "I understood that."

Dortmunder turned his frown toward Kelp: "You did?"

"He said, 'It's the bank's car.'"

"He did?"

"Fuckin right!" Ken yelled.

Murch's Mom pointed the potato at him. "*That* was English," she said.

"He's a repo," Stan said.

"Ah'm a *hawk!*" Ken boasted.

"Yeah, a car hawk," Stan said.

Wally said, "Stan? What's going on?"

Stan explained, "He's a guy repossesses your car if you don't keep up the payments." Turning to Kelp, he said, "Andy, you stole a stolen car. This guy wants it for the bank."

Ken nodded fiercely enough to whack his forehead against the window. "Yeah! The bank!"

"Oh!" Kelp spread his hands, grinning at the repo man. "Why didn't you say so?"

Ken peered mistrustfully at him.

"No, really, fella," Kelp said, leaning close to the window, "no problem. Take it. We're done with it anyway."

Handing Doug the potato, Murch's Mom said, "I'll move my cab."

Handing Stan the potato, Doug said, "I'll move my pickup."

Handing Wally the potato, Stan said, "I'll move the van."

Wally pocketed the potato and smiled at the man in the Cadillac. He'd never seen a repo man before.

Ken, with deep suspicion, watched all the other vehicles get moved out of his way. Everybody smiled and nodded at him. The other woman and the mean-looking old guy came down off the porch to hang out with everybody else. The woman seemed okay, but the old guy suddenly said, "Kill him." His voice was thin and reedy, and his lips barely moved, but everybody heard him, all right. Including Ken.

The others all turned toward the old guy, and several of them said, "Huh?"

"Drag him out through the crack in the window," the old guy suggested. "Bury him in the back yard in a manila envelope. *He knows about us.*"

Everybody blinked at that, but then Dortmunder said, "He knows *what* about us?"

The mean-looking old guy kind of shifted position and looked at various pieces of gravel, but he didn't have anything else to say. So the others all turned back to Ken with their big smiles on again.

Smiles that Ken mistrusted; none of this behavior was traditional.

Lowering his window another fraction of an inch, he said, "Ngyou dough wanna argnue?"

Kelp grinned amiably at him. "Argue with a fluent guy like you? I wouldn't dare. Have a happy. Drive it in good health." Then he leaned closer, more confidentially, to say, "Listen; the brake's a little soft."

The other vehicles were all out of the way now, but people kept milling around back there. The van driver returned from moving his van to lean down by Ken's window and say, "You heading back to the city? What you do, take the Palisades. Forget the Tappan Zee."

Ken couldn't stand it. Trying hopelessly to regain some sense of control over his own destiny, he stared around, grabbed the tambourine, shoved it into the van driver's hand: "Here. This ain't the bank's," he said, the clearest sentence of his life.

The blond guy stood down by the sidewalk and gestured for Ken to back it up; he was going to guide him out to the street. Ken put the Cadillac in reverse again, and the woman from the porch came over to say, "You want a glass of water before you go?"

"Gno!" Ken screamed. "Gno! Just lemme outta here!"

They did, too. Three or four of them gave him useful hand signals while he backed out to the street, and then all nine of them stood in the street to wave good-bye; a thing that has never happened to a car hawk before.

Ken Warren had his Cadillac but, as he drove away, he just didn't look very happy about it. Much of the fun seemed to have gone out of the transaction for him.

CHAPTER FIFTY-EIGHT

Two solid weeks of beautiful weather. Clear sunny days, low humidity, temperature in the seventies, air so brisk and clean you could read E PLURIBUS UNUM on a dime across the street. Clear cloudless nights, temperature in the fifties, the sky a great soft raven's breast, an immense bowl of octopus ink salted with a million hard white crystalline stars and garnished with a huge moon *pulsing* with white light. It was disgusting.

The problem was, to take the boat out on the reservoir, they needed darkness, clouds, *no moon*. They didn't need nights so bright you could read a newspaper in the back yard (Kelp did, which Dortmunder hated). They didn't need nights so bright that the local drive-in movie shut down because people couldn't see the screen. "In darkness deep the darkest deeds are done,/And villains all retreat before the sun," as the poet put it. Dortmunder didn't know that particular verse, but he would have agreed with it.

It was a big house, 46 Oak Street, but it had never expected to house nine people and a computer. Dortmunder and May occupied the master bedroom, upstairs front over the living room. Stan and Tiny shared the other front bedroom, Stan sleeping on the box spring and Tiny tossing uncomfortably on the mattress on the floor. Kelp and Wally and the computer filled the large bedroom at the rear, Wally being the one on this mattress on the floor (he didn't seem to mind), while Doug had been shoehorned into the last bedroom, with Tom. Since Tom would not divide his bed, Doug had brought up a sleeping bag; when it was open and occupied, the room was so full the door couldn't be opened. And, finally, the small utility room off the kitchen downstairs contained a cot which was Murch's Mom's portion. The three bathrooms—two up, one down—were fought over constantly.

Idle days in Dudson Center aren't exactly the same as idle days in Metropolis. Wally still had his computer, still could spend his days and nights battling unambiguous enemies in far-flung galaxies, but for the rest of them certain adjustments had to be made. Doug had a local girlfriend, whom he kept scrupulously away from the others (not even telling her he had a place to stay here in town), and with whom he spent as much of his free time as he could, and other than that he commuted four days a week to his Dive Shop, three hours each way, driving doggedly back to Dudson Center every night just in case the weather should break. Tiny traveled with him as far as New York about half the time, not liking to be for very long away from his own lady friend, J. C. Taylor.

Other than that, though, time hung heavy.

* * *

The regulars in the Shamrock Family Tavern on South Main Street were talking about the *railroad*. "I worked for the railroad," one unshaved retiree announced, "when it was the *railroad*. You know what I mean?"

"I know exactly what you mean," said the guy to his right. "New York Central. D&H. Delaware, Lackawanna, and *Western*. Those were railroads."

Down at the end of the bar, Dortmunder and Kelp drank beer.

"Union Station up in Albany," the first regular said, with a little catch in his voice, holding up his bourbon and Diet Pepsi. "Now, that was a beautiful station. That station was like a church."

"Grand Central Station," intoned his pal. "Crossroads of a million private lives."

"You know," said a third regular, joining the conversation, "some people confuse that line with the *Naked City* motto."

A fourth chimed in: "There are eight million stories in the naked city."

"Exactly," said the third.

"Let's get outta here," Dortmunder said.

* * *

Stan had brought home a dark blue Lincoln Atlantis, a huge old steamboat of a car, which he was "fixing up" in the driveway beside the house. Along about the third day, May came out onto the porch with her hands in a dish towel—she'd never done that before, was doing it unconsciously now—and looked with disapproval at what Stan, with help from Tiny, was wroughting. On newspapers spread on the lawn squatted any number of automobile parts, all of them caked with black oily grime. The Lincoln's huge hood had been removed from the car and now leaned against the chain-link fence like a Titan's shield. The moth-eaten old backseat was out and lying on the gravel between the car and the street in plain sight of the entire neighborhood.

"Stan," May said, "I've got two phone calls already today."

Stan and Tiny lifted their heads out of the hoodless engine compartment. They were as grimy and oil-streaked as the auto parts. Stan asked, "Yeah?"

"About this car," May told him.

"Not for sale," Stan said.

"One, there's no papers," Tiny added.

Stan was about to dive back into his disassembled engine when May said, "*Complaints* about the car."

They looked at her in surprise. Stan said, "Complaints?"

"It's an eyesore. The neighbors think it detracts from the tone."

Tiny scratched his oily head with an oily hand. "Tone? Whadaya mean, tone?"

"The quality of the neighborhood," May told him.

"That's some quality," Stan said, getting a little miffed. "Down where I live in Brooklyn, I got two, three cars I'm working on at a time, I *never* get a complaint. All over the neighborhood, guys are working on their cars. And it's a terrific neighborhood. So what's the big deal?"

"Well, look around this neighborhood," May advised him, taking one hand out from under the dish towel to wave it generally about. "These people are neat, Stan, they're clean. That's the way they like it."

Gazing up and down the street, Stan said, "How do they fix their cars?"

"I think," May said carefully, "they take them to the garage for the mechanic to fix, when something goes wrong."

Appalled, Stan said, "They don't fix their own *cars*? And they complain about me?"

Tiny said, "May, I tell you what we'll do. On accounta the fence, we can't move the car around in the back, but we'll put everything in front of it, so you won't see all this mess and stuff from the street. Okay?"

"That would be wonderful, Tiny," May said.

Stan still couldn't get over it. "Hand your car to some stranger," he said, "then take it out, drive it sixty, sixty-five miles an hour. They got no more brains than that hood over there, and they're complaining about *me*."

"Come on, Stan," Tiny said, picking up auto parts from the lawn. "Help out."

Stan did so, muttering and griping all the time. Before going back into the house, May leaned out from the porch and looked up. Not a cloud in the sky.

• • •

Murch's Mom came stomping in to dinner late and bugged. "They don't fight *back*, dammit," she said, flinging herself into her chair.

They were seven tonight, crowded around the dining room table, all but Doug and Tiny, who'd be back up from the city later. Kelp looked over at Murch's Mom and said, "I thought that's what you liked about driving the cab up here."

"I'm losing my *edge*," she snarled. "I'm getting soft, I can feel it."

"I told you so," her son said.

She gave him a look. "Don't start with me, Stanley. And pass the white stuff. What is it?"

"Mashed potatoes," Dortmunder said, passing it to her.

"Oh, yeah?" She looked at the creamy white mound in the oval bowl, then shrugged and spooned a couple plops of it onto her plate.

The cooking was being done by an ad hoc committee chaired by May, with Wally, Stan, and Tiny as primary committee members, and noncommittee members responsible for clean-up. The opening of packages was the principal culinary method. The result was acceptable, but no one was anxious to prolong the experience.

Tom broke a silence composed of munching and swallowing to say, "Anybody hear the weather report?"

"I did, in the cab," Murch's Mom told him. "It's gonna be fair forever."

"Aw, come on, Mom," Stan said.

"Extended forecast," his Mom said, implacable, "sun, moon, sun, moon, sun, moon, sun *and* moon. Pass the round green things."

"Peas," Dortmunder said, passing her the bowl.

Murch's Mom rolled a bunch of peas onto her plate, then held them down with bits of mashed potato. "I met an old lady in the cab today," she said, "lives the next block over. I'm gonna go play canasta with her tonight. Not for money, just for fun."

She ate a pea—she couldn't get more than one of the little devils onto her fork at a time—then looked up at the silence and the surprised eyes. "Well?" she demanded.

Dortmunder cleared his throat. "Maybe the weather forecast's wrong," he said.

• • •

The worst of it for Doug was, he didn't have anyplace to take her. Myrtle, that is. He couldn't take her to the house on Oak Street, of course, not with it full of people all the time, and not with his own bed being merely a sleeping bag on the floor of Tom's room. And that incident of the horrible interruption from John was the only time he'd been at Myrtle's house when her mother was away.

Movie theaters and the interior of the pickup both allowed for a certain amount of personal interaction, but by no means enough. Nor could he convince Myrtle to grab a blanket one day and come with him for a nice picnic in the woods. It was extremely frustrating.

Well, at least he didn't have to lie to her anymore; or anyway not so much. Her curiosity about the environmental protection group he'd claimed to be a volunteer researcher for had been so intense and so unrelenting that first he'd told her it was merely a minor part of his life, not as important as she'd at first thought, that he was mostly a diving instructor out on Long Island. And then he'd told her he'd quit his volunteer work with that group because he didn't like their attitude. (John, in this scenario, became a demanding regional head of the environmental group, an autocratic ideologue who Doug had simply been unable to stand anymore, the last straw having been that unfortunate scene on Myrtle's front porch.)

So now, as far as Myrtle was concerned, Doug was in fact who he really was, and his trips up to Dudson Center from Long Island three or four days a week were simply because he was *crazy* about her. Since Myrtle seemed to be more or less crazy about him as well, the situation should progress swimmingly from here, and it would, too, if there were only someplace they could be alone together.

Now, after another evening of sweet hot frustration at the movies—the one local movie house was never more than half full, mostly old people and kids, people who didn't have VCRs—they were walking home, hand in hand, and Doug was trying yet again to figure out some way to get Myrtle alone.

If only the weather would break so he and the others could make the descent into the reservoir and salvage Tom's money, life would surely become easier. Doug would no longer have anything active to conceal from Myrtle, and with time and leisure and full attention to devote to this project, *surely* he could make it all happen. After all, summer was fast approaching; high season in his line of work. From Fourth of July weekend through Labor Day, he was going to be *busy*, far too busy to make six-hour round trips in pursuit of some girl.

It was a beautiful night in Dudson Center, clear and crisp, a velvety sky with a great milk-glass moon, temperature in the low sixties, humidity nonexistent. A playful breeze rustled and breathed in the dark green branches of trees, and below the mysterious upper reaches of those trees the old-fashioned streetlamps spread a yellow glow on sidewalks flanked by green lawns. Gentle music sounded from open windows here and there, late sprinklers could be heard whispering their rhythmic secrets, and the romantic in Doug just swelled with sensual delight.

But when he approached Myrtle's front porch, expecting at least to spend a little time with her on the glider, the porch light was on and someone was already out there. In fact, two people. With a table in front of them, doing something there, playing some kind of game.

Doug hadn't been present at dinner the other night when Murch's Mom had announced the news of her new local pal, so it was with a real sense of dislocation that he recognized who that was on the glider with Myrtle's mother. Oh, my God, he thought, am I supposed to know her? What's she doing here? What does Myrtle know?

"There you are," her mother said. "How was the movie?"

"Okay," Myrtle said, a bit listlessly. She'd been rather quiet and withdrawn all the way home, come to think of it.

"Gladys," the old bitch said to Murch's Mom (*Gladys?*), "this is my daughter, Myrtle."

"How do you do."

"Hello."

"And a beau of hers." Smiling like a shark at Doug, she added, "I'm sorry, I'm afraid I don't know your name."

She never did. Doug had met Myrtle's mother half a dozen times in brief passages at the beginning or ending of dates, and Myrtle always introduced him, and her mother always immediately cast his name out of her memory bank.

This time, before Myrtle could say anything, Doug smiled hugely at the nasty old witch and said, "That's okay, Mrs. Street." To Murch's Mom, he said, "It's Jack Cousteau. Nice to meet you."

All three women gave him funny looks, which he affected not to notice, turning his smile on Myrtle, saying, "See you in a couple days?"

"Sure," she said, but still looked confused.

"I'll call you at the library," he promised, shook her hand as though they'd just finished a really productive Kiwanis meeting together, and turned to say, "Nice to see you again, Mrs. Street. Nice to meet you, Gladys." And he went whistling away in the dark.

• • •

"One word!"

"Okay, okay!"

"One word to *anybody* about 'Gladys,' and I run you down with the cab!"

"Okay, okay!"

Murch's Mom released the bunch of Doug's shirt she'd held clutched in her fist and stepped back, aiming her glare out the kitchen window instead. "If it doesn't cloud up soon," she said, "I may run you down anyway."

CHAPTER FIFTY-NINE

Driving herself home from work and her mother home from the Dudson Combined Senior Citizens Center, Myrtle brooded about Doug Berry and, as usual, came to no conclusion. *Was* there really an Environment Protection Alliance, even though she could find it in absolutely no reference books or directories? Or was Doug completely and totally false, some sort of con man engaged in some secret nefarious pursuit (other than the nefarious pursuit of her body, that is)?

His having called himself Jacques Cousteau with Edna and Edna's new friend the other night had really brought the whole problem into focus. Myrtle had been feeling more and more depressed, not even noticing the change in herself, just sliding away into gloom; and all, of course, because she couldn't make up her mind about Doug Berry. And he'd used that false name, she understood, because her mother refused to remember his real name, which she did because *she* didn't trust him, either. And Edna was very often right about such things.

If Myrtle could be sure Doug wasn't a fake—or at least not a fake about anything except his extravagant claims of desire for and obsession with her own self—they would have progressed beyond the get-acquainted stage long ago. The weather was perfect, for instance, for a nice picnic up on Hochawallaputtie Hill, overlooking the reservoir. But how could she go up there with him when her heart was so full of mistrust?

"Go down Oak Street," Edna suddenly said, breaking their long silence.

306

Surprised, Myrtle glanced at her mother and then out the windshield toward Oak Street, still two blocks ahead. "But that's out of our way," she said.

"Some gypsies moved in there," Edna told her. "They've got a wrecked old car out front and everything. We're *all* calling and complaining. We're going to get up a petition next. Can't have gypsies here running down the neighborhood."

"Gypsies," Myrtle repeated with a laugh. "Oh, Mother, what makes you think they're gypsies?"

"Mrs. Kresthaven found a tambourine in their garbage," Edna said. "Go on, Myrtle, turn. I want to see if that awful car is still there. It's in the second block."

As they made the turn onto Oak Street, the world ahead suddenly grayed, losing color and tone. Myrtle leaned forward over the steering wheel to look up at the sky. "Cloud," she reported.

"*Never* trust the weather report," Edna commented. "Slow down, now, it's up there on the right. See that blue car?"

"It looks perfectly ordinary to me," Myrtle said, slowing as per instructions, looking at an ordinarily neat house with an ordinarily plain automobile parked beside it.

"They moved some of the junk," Edna said with mixed satisfaction and regret. Clearly, she was both glad the small-town peer pressure had done its job and sorry she couldn't keep exerting it. "But you can still see some by the fence," she added hopefully.

"It's hidden by the car," Myrtle said, slowing more and more so she could look at the place as they went by.

As they came abreast of the house, its front door opened and people abruptly started to emerge. Lots of people. They came pouring out of the house as though it were on fire, except that their expressions were happy, delighted, surprised. Running down the stoop and onto the lawn, they pointed skyward, laughing and capering and patting one another on the back.

Astounded, Myrtle watched the people cavort in her rearview mirror. Beside her, Edna said in doubtful surprise, "Was that Gladys?" but Myrtle paid no attention. She had recognized others among that group of people.

Doug? And *Wally Knurr*? Together? Holding hands and dancing in a circle, like something in a Breughel painting? What's going on?

"Couldn't be Gladys," Edna decided, and craned around to look back. "What are they doing out there?"

"Looking at the cloud," Myrtle told her, distracted.

Back there, too far away for identification, an older man, who had probably been napping upstairs, came hurrying out of the house, looked up, and nodded in agreement with the sky.

"Maybe they're farmers," Edna said, but she sounded doubtful.

CHAPTER SIXTY

With mixed feelings of relief and guilt, Dortmunder watched Kelp, in the living room of the house on Oak Street, work himself yet again into a wetsuit. "I couldn't do that, Andy," he said.

"I know you couldn't," Kelp said, zipping zippers. "It's okay, John, don't worry about it."

"I just couldn't do it."

"It's gonna be fine," Kelp said. "Doug's a real pro. We'll be perfectly fine down there. And he's right about one thing: even a total professional like he is shouldn't make a dive like this by himself."

"A dive," Dortmunder echoed. Then he was sorry he'd said it, because maybe Kelp hadn't thought about that part of it yet.

The fact is, this time into the reservoir was going to be different, unlike anything either Dortmunder or Kelp had ever done. On both previous attempts, they'd *walked* in. This time, Doug and Kelp were going to plop out of a boat in the middle of the reservoir and *sink* in. Only of course when a professional does it, the word for *sink* is *dive*.

Sure.

Tiny came back in from the porch, having just finished shlepping out all the equipment. "The truck's here," he said.

"All set," Kelp told him. Carrying his flippers under his arm, he followed Tiny out of the living room, Dortmunder trailing, and all three went out to the porch, where May, Murch's Mom, Wally, Tom, and Doug (he had also suited up for the dive) were watching Stan maneuver a large slat-sided open-topped truck backward up on to the driveway in the dark.

The *very* dark. Today's single cloud had by now become a cloud cover stretching from horizon to horizon like an extra-thick icing on the birthday cake of the Earth. Not a glimmer of light reached the surface of the planet from the heavens. Stan's only visual aid, in fact, beyond the truck's own back-up lights, was a streetlight some little distance away; it was by that faint gleam he was doing his best to bring the rear of the truck reasonably close to the porch without either driving on the lawn (his Mom had warned him about that) or ramming the Lincoln he still hadn't quite finished fixing up (she hadn't bothered to warn him about that). The porch light would have helped, but it would also have attracted unwelcome attention if it were on with all this activity around it at one-thirty in the morning. Small-town people are so *nosy*.

With confusing and at times contradictory advice from Tiny, Stan managed at last to place the truck where he wanted it, and then he climbed down from the cab to help load the equipment. Once all the gear was aboard, Stan got back into the cab, this time with Tom, while Dortmunder and Kelp and Doug and Tiny all clambered up into the back, which smelled faintly of several things: pine trees, possibly sheep, maybe one or two less pleasant things.

May and Murch's Mom and Wally stood on the dark porch and watched the slat-sided truck bounce and jounce back to the street and drive away toward the reservoir. None of them waved, but all of them thought of it.

Once the truck was out of sight, May sighed and said, "I hope we know what we're doing."

"No, you don't," Murch's Mom told her, and nodded after the truck. "You hope *they* know what they're doing."

Wally said, "The trouble with real life is, there's no reset button."

• • •

Why did they care about the *weather*? What in the world did Doug Berry and Wally Knurr have in common, and how did they even happen to know each other? And *had* Edna's new friend Gladys been among those capering on the lawn beneath the cloud?

Myrtle couldn't sleep. Her digital clock's luminous numbers told her it was 01:34 in the morning, which would be later than she had ever been awake in her life. But the questions were so many, and so insistent, that they just wouldn't let her go.

What did it all mean? First, a couple of months ago, Edna had seen a man she was sure was Tom Jimson ride by in a car. Then Wally Knurr had made himself known to Myrtle, in a way she now realized must have been planned and deliberate. Then Doug Berry had done the same thing and had made himself suspect to her as well by seeming to have some sort of hidden link to her father. And then Gladys had just happened to strike up an acquaintance with Edna.

Could all four of these be coincidence? Four people, apparently separate and having nothing to do with one another, but then three of them are suddenly together among a weird group dancing on a lawn, pointing at a cloud.

New Age cultists? The dawning of the age of . . . What comes after Aquarius? Pisces. Fish. A water sign, that's why they were pointing at the cloud, waiting for rain.

No, her night thoughts were getting outlandish. She'd be seeing those people as aliens from another planet next, scheming against the human race. Hmmmmm . . .

No. More realistically, they could all be part of some giant conspiracy. James Bond, or Robert Ludlum? Neither seemed quite right. That big blubbery blue Lincoln in their driveway was no Aston Martin, nor could she imagine anyone in that crowd on the lawn playing baccarat or using a cigarette holder. On the other hand, Doug and Wally both lacked that manic manliness, that completely daft take-charge self-assurance of Ludlum characters. (The ultimate Robert Ludlum character, of course, being Al "I'm in charge here" Haig.)

The old man. The old man who'd come out of the house just before Myrtle and her mother had turned the corner, the old man just barely glimpsed in the rearview mirror . . . would that have been *her father?*

This last thought agitated Myrtle right out of bed, but when she found herself standing on the floor in her white cotton knee-length nightgown, she was at a loss what to do next. Floundering, disoriented, she turned and looked out the window at the darkness of Dudson Center.

And saw lights in it. Over there, the next block over, seen past the shoulder of the Fleischbacker's house, were lit rectangles of light. Upstairs windows, in rooms with lights on. Over on Oak Street. *That* house?

Quick, the bird-watching binoculars; where were they? It had been years since . . . moving swiftly, but silent as possible so as not to wake Edna in the next room, Myrtle felt in the dark through dresser drawers until her fingers closed on the remembered blunt weaponlike heaviness of the binoculars.

Now! Hurrying to the window, she put the binoculars to her eyes, adjusted the focus, and there, swimming into view, with its flat light and muted colors and foreshortening like a Hopper painting, astonishingly close, all of a sudden there was Wally!

What was he doing? He sat in that room very intently, bent forward, hands moving at . . . at a computer terminal. Look at the tension in that pudgy face! Look at the hobnails of perspiration on that broad low forehead!

Conspiracy. Was Wally the mastermind? Or was he even now in contact with the mastermind, either in an experimental laboratory concealed within Mount Shasta (Bond) or in an unknown cavern deep beneath the Pentagon (Ludlum)? Absorbed by Wally's absorption, feeling that secret pleasure known to peeping Toms everywhere, Myrtle rested the front edge of the binoculars against the window and watched that round, gleaming, wet-eyed, passionate face. Aliens? SPECTRE? A conspiracy at the very highest levels of government?

Or could it, could it somehow be . . . the Mafia? Good God! Was she going to have to read *Jackie Collins*?

• • •

It seemed a good idea to approach the reservoir this time at a different spot, far from the sites of the first two attempts and also far from the dam itself, with its nighttime staff of employees. A minor county road crossed Gulkill Creek over a one-lane bridge not far from the upper end of the reservoir, and Gulkill Creek was one of the four small waterways that had in the old days meandered through the now-drowned valley, the four eventually combining into Cold Brook, which was still the name of the runoff stream below the dam. Where it passed under the narrow bridge on the county road, Gulkill Creek was about six feet wide, perhaps three feet deep, lined with bagel-sized rocks, and *icy*, all year. About forty yards downstream, having widened a foot or two, the creek passed beneath the fence encircling the reservoir, continued to widen and deepen as it sprinted down a gradual slope through scrub forest, and after another thirty yards entered the reservoir at a point just about opposite the dam, which even on a sunny day was barely visible from way over here. On a cloudy night, forget it.

All the way out from town, sitting in the back of the truck, Kelp and Doug went over the plans for the night, including their signal system. This time, their primary light sources would be underwater miner's lamps worn on their foreheads, though they'd have regular flashlights hooked to their utility belts as well. The signals they'd use to communicate with each other underwater involved switching the forehead lamp off and on while facing the other guy: One off-and-on meant, "Come help me," while two off-and-ons meant, "Ascend to the surface." That was it; there wouldn't be much by way of small talk at the bottom of the reservoir.

There was no traffic along this road at this hour. Stan stopped the slat-sided truck right on the one-lane bridge, and everything was off-loaded onto the weedy roadside. At this point, their boat was merely a bulky package looking something like extra blankets folded on a shelf in the closet, plus a bottle of compressed air. Guiding themselves by light spill from the truck's head- and taillights, Doug and Tiny carried these components down beside the creek. Doug untied the boat package, inserted the bottle onto the nipple, and a low windy rushing sound started, soon joined by muffled *thaps* and *boops* as the boat uncreased itself, stretching and twisting like an Arabian Nights genie waking up.

Meantime, Stan took the empty truck away. Once it was gone, the overcast night was as dark as the inside jacket pocket of a suit that's worn only at funerals. Doug put on his headlamp and lit it so they'd be able to see what they were doing.

The whoosh of wind inside the boat grew stronger, the *pops* and *whaps* louder, and before their eyes appeared the kind of rubber raft in which people survive miraculously for eighty-three days in the open sea. Or not.

The boat was pushed into the shallow rapid water and held in place by Tom while a number of long pieces of rope, the winch, the scuba tanks, the 10hp motor, and a lot of other stuff were piled inside. Then they headed toward the reservoir, Doug holding the boat by its rope like a large frisky dog on a leash, finding his way through the underbrush at the edge of the stream by aiming his forehead light almost straight down at his feet. The others, following, were a little less lucky in their illumination, and therefore frequently in their footing. Splashes, curses, stumblings, and anonymous thumps and *oofs* punctuated their way.

At the chain-link fence, Tiny went to work with the wire cutters, announcing, "I'm having déjà vu again."

It took almost twenty minutes to cut away enough fence so that the boat could go through on the stream and the people could go through more or less on dry land. Once they were all past that obstacle, Dortmunder called softly, "Doug. Hold on a second."

Doug turned his head, the forehead light flashing around the dark forest. "Yeah?"

"From here on," Dortmunder told him, "we better go without light. We're getting too close to the reservoir."

Tom said, "Al? How do we *find* the reservoir, if we don't have any light?"

"The boat knows the way," Dortmunder explained. "Doug follows the boat, the rest of us follow Doug. We each hold on to the shirt of the guy in front of us."

"Sounds good," Kelp said.

It turned out to sound considerably better than it was. The level of splashing, thumping, cursing, and stumbling to one's knees increased dramatically behind the boat as it bobbed along, happily in its element, followed by Doug, trying to hold on to the boat's rope while not getting decapitated by tree branches he couldn't see, followed by Kelp clutching the back of Doug's wetsuit, followed by Tiny clutching both of Kelp's shoulders, followed by Tom with a bony finger hooked into one of Tiny's belt loops, followed by Dortmunder holding gingerly to the back of Tom's collar.

Finally, in exasperation, Tiny called out, "Are we going the right way? Doug, where the hell's the reservoir?"

"Uh," Doug said, and splashed around a bit. "I think I'm in it."

He was. For a minute or two, they all were, but then they got themselves sorted out once more and refound the land.

The shore here, where stream met reservoir, was very wet and soft and mucky. They had to range a ways off to the left before they found solid enough ground for Tiny to set up the winch and other equipment. The boat was emptied there, the motor attached at the stern, and at last the three seafarers—Doug, Kelp, and Dortmunder—prepared to set off. It was necessary for somebody to be in the boat while the other two were on their dive, and Dortmunder was the only one available for that job, unfortunately. Also, with Kelp volunteering to join Doug in the descent, there hadn't been much Dortmunder could do to complain.

They got into the boat, which rocked and wriggled as though they were tickling it. But the thing was completely dry inside, to Dortmunder's astonishment. The bottom was rubberized canvas that moved sluggishly with you, like a waterbed, but the bulbous sides, taut with air, gave a sense of real solidity.

Dortmunder sat on the bottom in the middle, feeling the water's coldness seep upward, while Kelp sat in the front and Doug knelt beside the steering rod of the motor in back. Tiny gave them a little push away from shore, instantly disappearing back there, and Doug started the motor, which went *pock*-thrummmmm. Very quiet sound, really, after that explosive onset. You wouldn't be able to hear it very far at all.

"Everybody set?" Doug asked.

It was so dark you couldn't tell the difference between water and land. Dortmunder said, "I hope you can see where we're going."

"As a matter of fact," Doug said, "I can't see a damn thing." And he accelerated the little thrumming motor, steering them somewhere.

• • •

Look at him, Myrtle thought, watching Wally Knurr through the binoculars. The little man's eyes gleamed with green highlights as he stared at the computer screen.

Myrtle's own eyes were getting heavier and heavier. She knew she'd have to go to sleep soon. But, watching him, even though his stance and manner and expression never changed, was still repellently fascinating.

Look at him, she thought. What nefarious scheme is he planning over there?

• • •

```
But I've already met the princess.
```

Disguised as a commoner.

```
Well, not really.
```

You did not meet her in your true guise.

Wally sat back to digest that thought. Was it accurate? When he'd met Myrtle Jimson he'd told her his true name, and he'd told her the truth about his interest in computers and about where he lived and all of that. He had not, of course, volunteered the information that he knew her father, nor that he was involved with her father in a major . . .

Robbery? Well, no, actually, this wasn't a robbery, the robbery had taken place almost twenty-five years ago. There were still illegal elements in the affair, to be sure, such as breaking and entering the reservoir and the fact that the money did still technically belong to some bank or some armored car outfit or some insurance company or *somebody* other than Tom Jimson, but these seemed to Wally technical crimes at the level that caused toaster companies to pay fines in Federal court but no executives to go to prison.

His fingers padded once more over the keys.

```
I still don't see why I can't just go over to the
library and just happen to see her again and just say
hello.
```

The princess does not at this time require rescue.

```
Not to rescue her. Just to say hello. I only saw her
once. I want to see her again.
```

If the princess meets the hero in his true guise before it is time for the rescue, she will reject him, misunderstanding his role.

I don't think this princess is going to need to be rescued from anything. She works in the library, she lives with her mother, she's in a small town where everybody knows her and likes her. What is there to rescue her from?

The hero awaits his moment.

But I want to see Myrtle Jimson again.

She must not see you at this time.

(A block away, sleepy eyes closed behind drooping binoculars. Weary feet moved toward bed.)

Why mustn't she see me?

She will misunderstand, and the story will end in the hero's defeat.

I'll risk it.

Remember the specific rule of the game of Real Life.

Of course I remember it. I entered it into you myself.

Nevertheless. It is:
The tape of Real Life plays only once.
There are no corrections or adjustments.
Defeat is irreversible.

I know. I know. I know.

Why any hero would wish to play such a game is incomprehensible.

"It sure is," Wally muttered aloud, and looked sadly out the window at the sleeping village.

• • •

Thrummmmmmmmmmmmmmmmmmmmmmmmmmmmmmmmmmmmmmmmmmmmmmmmmmmmmmmmmmmmmm . . .

There were dim lights visible way down at the dam. Those were the only landmarks at all worth mentioning. Once the three men in a boat were out a ways from shore, it became roughly possible to distinguish between the grayer flatter surface of the reservoir and the darker and more tangled landscape all around them, but that was it for orientation.

Their first goal was the scene of the second disaster, over by the railroad tracks, which turned out to be extremely difficult to find when no moonlight gleamed off them. "I think it's here," Kelp or Dortmunder said, four or five times each, before one of them happened to be right.

When they'd definitely found the railroad line, Doug steered them in close to shore, then reduced the motor to idle while he went smoothly and gracefully over the side, standing in knee-deep water as he felt around with his feet for one of the tracks. Finding it, he stooped to tie to it one end of a long reel of monofilament, a high test fishing line, thin and colorless and strong.

Then they reversed positions, Doug getting into the front of the boat, Kelp moving back to the middle, and Dortmunder going all the way back to the motor, since Doug wanted him to get some practice driving and steering before he was left alone with the boat.

"I'm not sure about this," Dortmunder said, touching the motor's handle with gingerly doubt.

"It's easy," Doug assured him, and repeated the simple operating instructions one more time, at the end saying, "You just want to be sure to keep it slow, that's all. So Andy can unreel the monofilament, and so you don't run into a root or a drifting log or the other shore."

"I won't speed," Dortmunder promised.

Thrummmmmmmmmmmmmmmmmmmmmmmmmmmmmmmmmmmmmmmmmmmmmmmmmmm . . .

Dortmunder kept the dam's lights to his left, moving them forward very slowly indeed, while Kelp dangled his arms out over the water and let the monofilament unreel.

Finding the railroad line on the other side was even harder, since they'd never been over there before and so were operating with neither memory nor light, but after several useless passes back and forth Doug said, "That looks like a cleared spot. Let's try it." And he was right.

According to the old maps, the railroad had run along pretty straight through the valley, and so, once Doug had tied the other end of the monofilament to the rail on this side, they had a thin surface line that more or less paralleled the tracks crossing down below.

Now Dortmunder thrummed them even more slowly than earlier back out from shore, Doug guiding them with one hand on the monofilament. "Here, I think," he said at last, when they were well out in the middle of the reservoir and presumably directly above Putkin's Corners.

"Right," Dortmunder said, and turned the handle to *idle*. He was beginning to feel pretty good about his relationship with this motor, in fact. It was small, it was quiet, and it did what he asked it to do. What could be bad?

Doug used a short piece of white rope to tie them to the monofilament, then reached out to drop over the side a small iron weight with a ring in it through which one end of a long thin nylon cord had been tied. He kept feeding out the cord until it was no longer being pulled, meaning the weight had hit bottom. Inspecting the amount of cord that was left as he tied it to the rope lashed around the upper edge of the boat, he said, "Hmmm. Closer to sixty feet, I think. You ready, Andy?"

"I don't think I've ever been that deep," Kelp said. It was hard to see what he looked like in the dark, but he sure *sounded* nervous.

"Nothing to it," Doug assured him, lifting himself up to sit on the rounded doughnut of the boat's side, facing inward, feet on the bottom of the boat. "Now, Andy, you remember the best way to leave the boat, right?"

"Backward." Yep; nervous, all right.

"That's right," Doug told him, lowered his goggles, put his mouthpiece in place, and toppled backward out of the boat. *Plash.* Gone, without a trace.

Dortmunder and Kelp looked at each other, as best they could in the dark. "You can do it, Andy," Dortmunder said.

"Oh, sure," Kelp said. "No problem." Scrambling a bit, hampered by the scuba tank on his back, he pulled himself up to a seated position on the boat's round rim. "See you, John," he said, and, forgetting to put the goggles and mouthpiece in place, backward he went over the side.

• • •

All the fellas were so nice to Bob now. "Great to have you back, Bob," they said, grinning at him (a trifle uneasily) and patting him on the back.

"It's really nice to be here," Bob told them all with his new sweet smile. Looking around the big office inside the dam, he said, "Gee, I remember this place. I really do."

"Well, sure you do, Bob," Kenny the boss said, grinning harder than ever, patting him softer than ever. "You were only gone a few weeks."

Bob nodded, a slow drifting motion very akin to his new smile. "I forgot a lot, you know," he told them. "A lot of stuff from before. Dr. Panchick says that's okay, though."

"Whatever the doctor says," Kenny said, nodding emphatically.

The other guys all nodded and smiled, too, though not as sweetly as Bob. They all said they agreed with Dr. Panchick, too, that it didn't matter about all that old stuff Bob had forgotten.

Gee, it was nice to be back with these nice fellas. Bob almost thought about telling them how he'd even forgotten that girl, whatsername, the one he was married to, but how Dr. Panchick had told him he'd definitely start to remember her again pretty soon. That and a lot of other stuff, too. Not the bad stuff, though. Just the good stuff.

Like the girl; whatsername. After all, there she was around the house all the time, looking red-eyed and smiling so hard it seemed sometimes as though the edges of her mouth must have been tied back to her ears. Having her around all the time like that, calling him *Bob* and so on, pretty soon he'd remember her just fine. And then she wouldn't have to keep going off into other rooms and crying and then coming back with that smile on. Which was anyway a nice smile, even if kind of painful-looking.

Anyway, he was almost about to kind of *mention* that, the lapse of memory that included whatsername, but as he was taking one of his slow deep breaths, the slow deep breaths he took these days before he made any kind of statement at all, just as he was taking that breath, he remembered he wasn't supposed to talk a lot to other people about his *symptoms*.

That's right. "They needn't know you've forgotten XXXX," whatever her name was, Dr. Panchick had said just today. Or yesterday. Or sometime. So he didn't say any of that about whatsername after all, but just smiled and breathed out again, and nobody noticed.

"Well, uh, Bob," Kenny said, still grinning fitfully, washing his hands, looking around the big open office, "uh, we thought maybe you could, uh, get back into the swing of things by maybe doing some of the filing, getting caught up on some of this paperwork here. Do you think you could do that?"

"All right," Bob said, and smiled again. He was very happy.

Kenny continued to grin but looked doubtful. Peering at Bob as though this new sweet smile made him hard to see, he said, "You, uh, remember the alphabet, huh?"

"Oh, sure," Bob said, very relaxed and easy, very happy to be here in this nice place with all these nice fellas. "Everybody knows the alphabet," he said.

"Sure," Kenny said. "That's right."

Then Bob's watch went BEEP, and everybody jumped and looked scared. Everybody but Bob, that is. He raised his left arm to show everybody his watch, and smiled from watch to people to watch, saying, "Dr. Panchick gave me this. It reminds me when to take my pill. I have to take my pill now."

"Then you better, I guess," Kenny said.

"Oh, sure," Bob said, and smiled around at all the nice fellas, and went away to the men's room for water to wash down his nice pill.

("Doped to the *eyes!*" a fella named Steve said, and a fella named Chuck said, "You could sell those pills on the street down in New York City and *retire*," and Kenny the boss said, "Now, leave him alone, guys. Remember, it's up to us to help Bob get his head out of his ass," and all the fellas said, "Oh, yeah, sure, naturally, of course, you got it.")

• • •

Mouthpiece *in*; breathe normally: well, breathe, anyway. Sinking like a stone. Goggles *on*. Goggles *off*; full of water.

Oh, boy. Feeling the water rush upward into his nose as his body rushed downward toward the bottom of the reservoir, Kelp stuck his left arm straight up, pressed the button, and filled the BCD. Immediately he stopped sinking, started soaring instead, and suddenly broke through into air.

But where? Anonymous reservoir in the dark. Dortmunder and the boat were nowhere to be seen. I am not going to get lost, Kelp told himself sternly. Ignoring the tiny voice telling him he was already lost, he emptied the water from the goggles, put them on, reassured himself the headlamp was in the right place, released *some* of the air from the BCD, and floated down through the black water like a discarded love letter.

During the descent, he switched on the headlamp and kept turning his face this way and that, hoping either to see Doug's light or show Doug his own. But when his flippered feet finally found the bottom, he still had seen nothing, and in fact he couldn't even see what he was standing on until he bent almost double. Then, through the brown water, he saw he was on a flat pebbly surface covered with hairy slime. Yuck.

Still, when he straightened again and stomped both feet around, flippers flapping, he could tell he was on something solid, and not even very muddy. A road? Wouldn't that be good luck!

Kelp walked back and forth, noticing the evenness of this surface, noticing how little he was increasing the turbidity by his movements, and wondering if he were actually on a street in the town. And if so, where was the curb? Where was the side of the road so he could get some sense of where he was and where he should go?

Treading slowly, having to lift each knee unnaturally high because of the drag of the flippers on his feet, Kelp walked in ever-widening circles, looking for the side of the road or whatever this was. A parking lot? It could take him an *hour* to find the edge of a parking lot.

Wall. Low brick wall, about knee height. Kelp bent down, resting his hands on its slimy surface, and tried to see what the bottom was like on the other side before stepping over.

At first, he just couldn't see a thing. Brown water drifting and floating, but then also the bricks. Row after row of brick, on down out of sight.

What the heck? Kelp leaned lower, one arm still clutching the wall, most of his body over its edge now as he aimed the headlamp down, trying to see, following the lines of brick wall down, down . . . to some sort of dark rectangular opening, several feet below.

So hard to see through this murk, everything so distorted and deceptive, if Kelp didn't know better he'd think this brick wall went right on down and down, and that black rectangle there was . . .

. . . a window.

AAA!! Flailing back across the wall, flinging himself to the safety of the roof—*the roof!*—Kelp overshot and drifted upward, turning slowly, absolutely helpless for just an instant, but then floating back down to the roof again and standing there, *gasping* through the mouthpiece, staring around, trying to think what he could possibly do next.

I'm on a *roof!* What miserable luck. I don't even know how tall this building is. How am I going to get down off—

Wait a second. I *floated* down here. The roof was *under* me. What do I care how tall this building is?

Moving now with long penguinlike hops, like astronauts on the moon, Kelp made his way back to the edge of the roof, added just a teeny bit more air to his BCD, and floated off into space, actually putting his arms out to the sides like a kid playing airplane.

Superman! The feeling of exhilaration was suddenly so intense that Kelp laughed out loud into his mouthpiece. Kicking his legs, waving his arms, ducking his head downward, he made a complete forward roll in the middle of the water, beside the roof, heels over head. Leveling out afterward, he looked around, the headlamp beam flashing this way and that, and stared out through his goggles like a kid in a playground looking for somebody to ride the seesaw with.

This was so much *fun*! All the practice sessions, both times descending into the reservoir with Dortmunder, and neither of them had ever known how much fun this was. Oh, if only John knew it was like this, Kelp thought, he'd change his mind completely. Even John would. Even John.

Kelp cavorted beside the brick building for maybe five minutes before remembering Doug and the buried money and the job he was down here to perform. Okay; time to quit playing hookey and get to work.

With more control over his movements every second, Kelp swam back to the brick wall of the building, and made his way down its face, learning it was three stories high and that he was probably on the side of it, since there was nothing here but windows; no doors.

Choosing arbitrarily to go to the right, he kicked steadily and easily, the fins doing all the work of moving him along as he made his way to the corner, then turned left and discovered he'd guessed right: this was the front of the building, with gunk-covered slate steps leading up to a big blank opening where an elaborate doorway must once have stood. And above that opening was a broad stone lintel with words carved into it. Moving very close, putting the headlamp directly on the scum-filled letters, Kelp read:

PUTKIN'S CORNERS MUNICIPAL LIBRARY

This was it! He'd jumped out of the boat any old way, and he'd landed exactly precisely on top of the very building they were looking for. Tom's stash was buried in the field right behind here. So all he had to do now was find Doug, and they could go collect the money.

Well, that should be easy. Their first goal had been the railroad track, and then they'd intended to follow that down to the railroad station in Putkin's Corners, because the library—this library right here—was directly across the street from that station. So if he went over there, sooner or later Doug would show up.

Fine. Kelp turned away from the library and sailed across a street he couldn't see to the front wall of the railroad station, which he could see, once he was right on top of it. Or it was on top of him. A big old stone building, from back when people hadn't yet known that the railroads were a transitional technology. Again, the window and door frames and other useful parts were gone, but the stone pile was still there, easily identifiable as railroad architecture.

Unwilling to swim—sail, fly—through the building, Kelp made his way around it instead, and there was the concrete platform, much the worse for wear; and beyond it the tracks. Kelp floated over there and descended almost to the ground to study the tracks and then to look all around. No Doug, not yet. But gee, it would have been fun to pole in here in that car! Kelp could just *see* it.

Oh, well, it wasn't going to happen, that's all. Still, Kelp thought, we're here. One way or another, we're here. At least I am. Here, and raring to go.

Come on, Doug.

• • •

This, Dortmunder thought, is what I don't like about fishing. One of the things. Sitting here in a boat, pitch-black darkness all around. Getting cold. All alone. Not a sound.

SPLASH!

Dortmunder about jumped out of the boat, staring around in frenzy, and when he first saw Doug's head in the water below his right elbow he had no idea what it could be. A bomb? A coconut?

The coconut removed its mouthpiece and goggles and spoke: "Where's Andy?"

"Oh, my God, it's Doug!"

"Of course it's Doug," Doug said. "Andy isn't here?"

"No," Dortmunder told him, "he went in right after you."

"Shit," Doug commented.

Dortmunder said, "You don't think something's wrong, do you?"

"He didn't hold on to the guideline, that's all," Doug answered, wriggling for demonstration the white nylon cord that was tied to the boat and that then angled straight down into the water, its other end tied to the weight at the bottom.

Dortmunder nodded, saying, "Oh. He was supposed to hold on to that, was he?"

"That's how we keep together," Doug pointed out. "That's how I found you, coming back up."

Dortmunder said, "Probably he was thinking mostly about his mouthpiece."

"His mouthpiece?"

"And his goggles," Dortmunder added. "He forgot to put them on before he went over."

"Oh, for Christ's sake," Doug said. "Listen, if he comes up or anything, give two tugs on this line here, okay?"

"Right," Dortmunder said. "But you don't think anything happened, do you?"

But Doug was gone, shooting back down into the depths. Dortmunder looked over the side, seeing nothing. Not even his own reflection. Poor Andy, he thought.

That could be *me*, he thought.

• • •

Kelp sat on the stone bench on the westbound platform like the last-ever passenger waiting for a train that will never come. Legs crossed, arms folded, body pushed slightly forward by the bulk of the scuba tank, he sat mostly at his ease; vaguely visible in the diffuse glow from his headlamp, water lazily ebbing and flowing around him, and if he could have seen himself there, in the drowned town, in the brown water, waiting on the ruined platform for the nonexistent train, he would definitely have *scared* himself.

But he couldn't see himself, nor was there anyone else to observe him seated there. Minute after minute there was nobody else, and after a while Kelp began to fidget, began to feel a little cold and uncomfortable on this stone bench, began, in fact, to feel quite *alone* here in Putkin's Corners.

Where was Doug? Wouldn't he have to follow the tracks to the station? Wasn't that the most logical, the only thing, he could do? And then—

Light. Vague, dim, barely discernible inside the muck, made harder to see by the diffusion of his own light. Hard even to be sure it truly existed, wasn't merely some refracted ray of his own headlamp's gleam, but wasn't that, over there, not along the track but over on the far side, on the east bound platform, where he hadn't expected to see anything at all, *some* sort of light?

I should reach up, Kelp thought, and switch off my lamp to make it easier to see that light over there; if there's really a light over there to be seen. The problem was, he'd had plenty of time by now to get himself good and spooked, which he hadn't realized until that other light—if it existed—had come swimming more or less into view from a completely unexpected direction. What if it was a— Well, there aren't any ghosts, really, but— Underwater, somehow, the regular rules didn't seem to apply. Maybe anything that wanted to exist could exist, down here, at the bottom, away from people. Maybe that light was . . . anything at all.

Kelp managed to lift his right hand and touch the switch on his headlamp, but he never did summon the strength to turn it off. He just sat there, hand to head, while the light across the way floated and swayed, moved into nonexistence, flowed back again, disappeared once more, and then suddenly came straight at him! Oh, boy. Oh, boy.

It was Doug. Kelp felt vast relief and didn't even mind when Doug hauled him to his feet and shook a stern finger at him, which he then pointed at the white nylon cord wrapped around his other wrist. This cord drifted away upward into the dark, and the second Kelp saw it he remembered what he was supposed to have done first thing out of the boat.

Of course! Dummy! Elaborately, he demonstrated to Doug his under-standing, embarrassment, apology, by throwing both hands up in the air, then smacking himself on the ear, shaking his head, punching himself on the jaw, pounding his right fist into his left palm . . .

Doug grabbed both his wrists. When Kelp looked enquiringly at him, Doug released the wrists and made down-patting gestures: take it easy.

Oh. Sure. Kelp nodded, flashing his headlamp up and down Doug's person.

Next, Doug selected one of several more nylon cords hooked to his weight belt and tied the other end to Kelp's belt. Now they could be up to eight feet apart but wouldn't lose each other.

Great. Kelp expressed his pleasure in this move by firmly shaking Doug's hand with both of his. Doug nodded, a bit impatiently, pulled his hand free, and made walking movements with his fingers.

Right. Kelp nodded emphatically again, and would have turned and walked from here to the library but that Doug suddenly lifted up into the air—into the *water*—and started swimming away. Hastily, before the rope linking them could get taut, Kelp launched himself off the platform and followed.

• • •

The thing about needing a cloudy night to do whatever it is you want to do, that means you have to be prepared to accept clouds with all their implications.

Dortmunder sat in the rubber boat, bored, sleepy, a little chilly, also apprehensive about Andy Kelp. Was he okay down there? Would Doug find him? If there was some sort of trouble, wouldn't Doug have come back to say so by now?

Plip, on the back of his hand. Thinking it was some kind of splash from the water all around him, he brushed it off.

Plip. Forehead this time. *Plip-plip-plip*.

No. Dortmunder lifted his head toward the completely beclouded sky. *Plipliplipliplplplpppppppp* . . .

"Of course," Dortmunder said, and hunched his shoulders against the rain.

• • •

They kept off the bottom as much as possible to limit turbidity, but they were *near* the bottom all the time. First, the end of the measuring cord with the red ribbon tied around it was placed by Doug at the right rear corner of the library, while Kelp ranged as far as the connecting rope would permit, found a rock, brought it back, and used it to hold the red-ribboned cord in place. Then they moved along the rear wall like wasps under a house eave, setting the cord against the base of the building, till they came to the knot.

This time it was Kelp who held the cord in position, while Doug swam this way and that, exactly like a fish in a too-small aquarium, and eventually came back with a rock of his own, which was placed atop the knot.

The next part would be tricky. They wanted to mark a distance out across the field at right angles to the library wall. They'd rehearsed this in daylight, on dry land, in the back yard at 46 Oak Street, but doing it under present conditions was still kind of strange. For instance, they hadn't spent all their time flying *over* the back yard.

First, Kelp stood straddling the knot, his back—or the scuba tank, actually—against the library wall, his face turned outward so the beam from his headlamp marked the right angle. Then Doug, paying out the cord as he went, swam eight feet away along that light beam and paused there with the new line of cord resting on the bottom. Kelp now lifted into the water, kick-swam forward about four feet, and put his second flashlight on the ground beside the cord, switched on, the beam running out along the rest of the cord. Then he came forward to where Doug waited, straddled the cord again, and Doug backed away slowly, paying out more cord, keeping his alignment with the two lights until he'd gone another eight feet. Then they repeated the procedure all over again.

According to Wally's calculations, the center of the buried casket would be thirty-seven feet out from the library wall, which meant they had to go through their slow underwater gavotte five times before they reached the second knot in the measuring cord, the one that said, *Dig here*.

At last. Floating over the spot, heads close, haloed in sepia illumination, Kelp and Doug grinned around their mouthpieces at each other. Victory was in their grasp.

• • •

What happens when the boat fills with rainwater? It can't sink, can it? These doughnut sides are filled with air.

But the damn thing can sure wallow, all right. In fact, with Dortmunder's weight in it, the boat's attitude seemed to be that if it filled with water it would be perfectly happy to loll around just a few inches below the surface, soaking Dortmunder to the bone and ruining the little 10hp motor.

Number one, he wasn't dressed for this crap. He'd known he was going to be outdoors, on the reservoir, in a boat, in the dark, in June, with the temperature fairly cool, so he'd worn solid thick-soled shoes and wool socks and black chinos and a zipper-front weatherproof jacket. But none of that was enough. Not in this rain. Not *underwater*.

And that was number two. NO UNDERWATER. That was the deal this time, that's why Dortmunder wasn't suited up like Kelp and Doug. He would go along with everybody else, he would even go *on* the water if it would help, but *in* the water, no.

Also, number three, the gas tank. A small red metal five-gallon tank attached to the motor by a black flexible hose, up till now it had been content to nestle in under the doughnut curve of the side of the boat, back near the rear, where the doughnut was replaced by a solid square piece of fabric-covered wood to which the motor was clamped.

But gasoline is lighter than water, and as the interior of the boat turned itself inexorably into a wading pool the gas tank wanted to come out and play. Dortmunder had no bailing can, nothing to bail with except his cupped hands, and it was both annoying and painful to have those cupped hands constantly banging into a passing gas tank. He kept pushing it back into its corner, muttering at it as though it were a playful puppy being playful at the wrong time, but the damn thing just kept bobbing back out again.

The boat was shipping water, *that's* why it was sinking so fast. It was happening around the motor. The top of the flat piece the motor was clamped to was a little lower than the top of the doughnut anyway, and with the weight of the motor pulling that end down it was lower yet, so now, with the boat wallowing half submerged, water lapped in around the motor every time Dortmunder moved, and still did when Dortmunder didn't move because the *boat* moved. The *reservoir* moved. The *air* moved. And the water chuckled in.

He had to shift the weight somehow, get that goddamn flat rear of the boat higher than the rest. But how? There wasn't much time left; the water inside the boat kept rising, and of course the higher it rose the lower the boat sank and the more rapidly more water came in at the back.

He had shifted his own weight forward; it wasn't enough. The gas tank moved all over the place, but didn't seem to matter much. The only really heavy thing left, the thing that was causing all the trouble, was the motor. Move that, temporarily, move it to the front of the boat, and then the back would be higher and he could bail steadily for a while and maybe get ahead of this thing, at least until Doug and Kelp came back.

The important thing, he told himself, is not to drop the goddamn motor over the side. That would be tough to explain to the divers. He'd watched Doug install the thing, however, and it seemed to him he could uninstall it without disaster, so he set to work, at once, before the boat sank any lower.

First, release the gizmo on the side that permitted him to tilt the motor forward, bringing the propeller out of the water but, more importantly under these circumstances, also bringing some of the weight of the motor into the boat.

Then remove the fuel hose from the motor, in the front, just under the housing, where it attached by sliding on over a kind of thick bright-metal needle.

Then, one-handed, holding the motor with the other hand, very slowly and carefully loosen the two wing nuts holding the clamps on both sides.

Then, gripping the wet metal of the motor housing as tightly as possible, *lift* the motor out of the groove, *shift* it forward into the boat, *lose* balance on the wobbly unreliable bottom of the god-damn-it-to-hell boat, *lunge* away from the back and toward the front with the damn motor grasped tightly in both of one's arms to keep it inside the boat, and *sprawl* lengthwise on top of the motor as it lands heavily on the front part of the doughnut, fuel needle first. Fuel needle first.

What's that hissing noise?

• • •

Things were going so *well!*

Just as both Wally and Doug had said, from their different backgrounds and kinds of expertise, the bottom of the reservoir in the area of the field behind the library was so soft and mucky they didn't need any heavy complicated tools to do their digging for them. All they had to do was not mind getting their hands a little dirty.

And that's the way it worked, all right. They got their hands *very* dirty, but the water in which they worked constantly washed them clean again; and besides, it was kind of fun.

Floating just above the spot marked by the knot in the measuring cord, suspended on a slant with their heads lower than their feet, they kept reaching down into the muck, one hand after the other, and flinging the sludge backward like dogs preparing to bury a bone. The turbidity became *intense*, so that soon they could barely see what they were doing directly in front of themselves, even with both headlamps lit, but it hardly mattered. They could *feel* what they were doing: they were throwing mud, three feet worth of mud.

Boom-boom. They both hit it at the same instant, their grasping fingers jabbing down through the muck and running straight into something solid. Heavy. Wood. Didn't want to move.

Their pleasure made them both forget themselves for an instant, and they started to drift away from the spot, but both immediately compensated, kicking with their flippers, nosing down toward the messy muddy hole they'd made, reaching down into the mire, one on either side. Their questing fingers slid along the wood, then found the coffin rails. They pulled themselves right down next to the hole and spent awhile removing more and more mud, until the whole top of the casket was more or less clear and they could slip the cord connecting them beneath it, pulling up the slack. Then they added air to their BCDs and gripped the rails. Slowly, reluctantly, after so many years alone and asleep in the deep, the casket began to lift.

All they wanted to do at this point was get the casket up out of its hole and maybe drag it around to the firmer base of the steps or sidewalk in front of the library. Once they had it accessible, they'd tie to one of its handles the cord that linked them with the boat, and from there on it would all be easy.

First, they'd go up to the surface, attach the marker cord to the monofilament, then run back to shore where Tiny and Tom were waiting. They'd get the fresh scuba tanks, pick up the extra BCD and take the end of the rope from the winch. Then they'd go back out to the monofilament, find the marker cord, and tie it to the rope from the winch. Then Kelp and Doug would go back down to the casket, wrap it in the extra BCD, fill the BCD with air, and as Tiny winched from the shore, ride herd on the buoyant casket. Simple.

The first part was certainly simple, though not particularly easy. The casket was *heavy*, even with their buoyancy to help. They never did lift it clear of the mucky ground, so turbidity roiled and rolled in their wake, but they managed to haul it along as they followed the measuring cord back to the library, then worked their way around to the front of the building, where they put their burden down at last on the crumbling concrete between the old sidewalk and the library steps.

Doug removed the marker cord from his wrist and tied it to the coffin rail, then drifted up beside Kelp. They both looked down at the box, just lying there. Captured. Tamed. With a leash on it. They looked at each other again, smiling, elated with what they'd done, and a shoe drifted slowly downward between them.

A shoe? Naturally, they both looked down, following its descent, and so the shoe remained in the amber gleam of their lamps until it hit the casket, hesitated there, seemed to stumble over the box, and then fell slowly on down to the ground.

Doug moved first, swooping downward, snagging the shoe on the way by, bringing it back up to where Kelp hovered. They hung there together in the water, half a dozen feet above the casket, and studied the shoe as

Doug turned it slowly in his hands. Then they stared at each other again, wide-eyed.

Dortmunder. His shoe. No question.

• • •

"Taking them a long time," Tom said.

"Seems long cause we ain't doing anything," Tiny told him. "And because it's raining." Then he twisted around, seated on the damp ground in the rain-streaked dark, to peer into the sopping night and say, "How come you're behind me?"

Tom cackled. "You don't have to worry about me, Tiny."

"I don't worry about you," Tiny promised him. "Just come around and sit down here beside me."

"Too wet to sit down there."

"It's wet everywhere. Okay, *I'll* come back and sit beside *you*."

"Naw, never mind, here I come," Tom said, and Tiny heard the old bastard's bones crack as he got to his feet. Sounded like rifles being cocked.

In a minute, Tom slid out of the dripping darkness like a half-starved fox and sat down within Tiny's range of vision but just out of reach of Tiny's hands. "That better, Tiny?"

"I like you, Tom," Tiny lied. "I like to look at you."

Tom cackled, and then they were quiet awhile, the two of them sitting on the ground in the rather heavy rain beside Gulkill Creek, the reservoir spread out a murky gray-black in front of them, pebbled with a million raindrops.

"Hope everything's okay," Tiny said.

• • •

Now, *here* was a mess. Kelp and Doug followed the marker cord up to the surface, and when they got there, what did they find? A steady rain. The boat, deflated and empty, drooped down into the wet darkness of the reservoir, still attached to the monofilament but pulling it four or five feet lower below the surface than it had been before. The gas tank was floating around loose. The motor was gone. So was Dortmunder.

With full buoyancy in the BCD, Kelp could pull the mouthpiece out and cry, "Where's John?"

"I dunno." Doug was also at full buoyancy, paddling in a circle, trying to see in the dark.

"Jeepers, Doug," Kelp said, "what *happened* up here?"

"Rain swamped the boat," Doug told him. "I dunno what happened to the motor. Or John."

"He didn't *drown*," Kelp cried, staring all around, bobbing on the surface in his agitation, water from time to time lapping into his mouth. "We didn't see him coming down, Doug. Only the shoe, that's all."

"Well, no, he wouldn't drown," Doug said. "He's got a line here, the monofilament. All he has to do is pull himself along that until he gets to shore."

"Hey, you're right!" Kelp thrashed around in the water in his relief because, despite what he'd said, he'd been thinking privately that maybe John *did* drown.

"We'll catch up with him, help him," Doug said. "He can't have much of a start on us."

"Good idea!" Kelp looked left and right into two equally impenetrable darknesses. "Which way?"

Doug considered the problem. "I tell you what," he said. "You follow the line that way, I'll go this way. Go underwater, it'll be faster. And the light'll show on the monofilament."

"Right," Kelp said, and put his mouthpiece back in. Releasing a little air from the BCD, he sank a few feet below the surface, switched on the headlamp, and saw the gleaming silvery-white line stretch away through the black water. Kicking easily, he followed the line, really pleased at how good he was getting at this and looking forward to seeing John flounder along ahead of him like a wounded walrus.

But no such luck. Kelp went almost all the way to shore, close enough to see the railroad tracks emerge along the slanted bottom, and still no John. When he was in near enough to stand on the railbed with his head and shoulders out of the water, he even risked a quick flash of his headlamp at the tangled brush along the bank. "John?" he called in a half whisper.

Nothing. But John wouldn't have had time to get this far anyway, not as slow as he'd have to travel and as fast as Kelp had sliced through the water. So Doug must have found him in the other direction.

No. Doug was waiting again by the boat, head out of the water, and he was alone. When Kelp surfaced beside him, Doug said, "No?"

"Oh, wow," Kelp said.

• • •

Oh! May, suddenly awake, stared at a gray rectangle in the wrong place in the dark, and listened to a toilet flushing and flushing and flushing. Jiggle that thing! And what's the window doing over there?

Shifting in the bed, she suddenly realized she was alone, remembered where she was (that's why the window's *there* instead of *there*), and understood that the sound she could hear through the window was rain falling. Oh, those poor guys, out there at the reservoir, they're going to get soaked.

Well, Andy and Doug were going to get soaked anyway, but now the rest of them— May sat up, suddenly wondering what time it was and what had awakened her. A bad dream? A thought about John? Some sound? Were they back? Had they finally succeeded in getting the money? What time was it?

03:24.

She listened, but other than the rush of rain she couldn't hear a thing. Shouldn't they be back by now? Or soon, anyway?

In any event, she was absolutely wide awake. No chance to get back to sleep, not right away. Climbing out of bed, she found her robe in the dark, put it on, and stepped out to the hall, faintly illuminated by an ankle-height night light plugged into an outlet near the head of the stairs. She looked over the rail, but the downstairs was completely dark. She was about to start down when she noticed the line of light under the door of Andy and Wally's room.

Was Wally still up? May crossed the hall and knocked softly on the door. "Wally? You awake?"

There were scraping, rustling noises within, and then the door opened and there was Wally, as short and round and moist as ever, and fully dressed. Blinking wetly up at May, he said, "Are they back?"

"No. I just woke up, I thought I'd have a glass of warm milk. Want some?"

Wally smiled. "Gee," he said, "that sounds . . ." He looked around, at a loss for a simile. "That sounds like this *house*," he decided. "Gosh, I would. I'd like some warm milk, Miss May, thank you. I'll just switch off the computer, and I'll be right down."

He plays with that computer too much, May thought as she descended to the ground floor, switching on lights along the way. Then she thought, well, it could be worse. Then she thought: Wait. I'm not his *mother*.

It *is* this house. It's changing us. If we stay here much longer, we'll start buying one another birthday cards.

Before putting the milk on to warm, May opened the back door and looked out at the yard. Rain was steady, unrelenting, falling straight down through a world without wind. This isn't going to let up for days and days, she thought. The poor guys. I hope everybody's okay.

Two mugs full of gently steaming milk were on the kitchen table when

Wally came into the room, his wet smile gleaming in the overhead fluorescent light. "This is really nice, Miss May," he said, and sat across from her to cup both hands around the mug. "I was just thinking," he said, "how really nice this all is, everybody living together here like this. It's almost like we're a family."

"I was just thinking something like that, too," May told him.

"I'll miss it when it's over," Wally said.

May sipped milk in lieu of responding, and they sat in fairly companionable—but not familial, dammit—silence for a few minutes, until all at once Murch's Mom walked in, wearing big gray furry slippers, a ratty long robe, and a lot of green curlers in her hair. Squinting balefully in the light, she said, "I thought they were back."

"Not yet," May said.

"We're just waiting here," Wally told her happily. "We're having warm milk."

"Oh, that's what it is."

"I could warm you some," May offered.

"You'd waste it, then," Murch's Mom told her, and marched across the room to the refrigerator, where she got out a can of beer, popped the top, and took a deep swig. Wiping her mouth on the sleeve of her robe, turning to the table, she said, "Raining."

"I hope everybody's okay," May said.

"Rain never hurt anybody," Murch's Mom decided. "A little water's good for you." She came over and sat at the table between them, saying, "Might as well stay up till they get back."

May watched Wally watching Murch's Mom drink beer. She knew Wally was loving that, loved the two of them with their warm milk and the crotchety aunt—that would be Murch's Mom's role in the affiliation Wally was constructing—with her beer. If he says *like a family*, May promised herself, I'll pour bourbon into this milk. A lot of bourbon.

However, he didn't.

● ● ●

"I never did much like rain," Tiny said.

"Good for covering your tracks," Tom said.

Tiny wrung water out of his eyebrows. "*What* tracks?"

"When the dogs are after you."

Tiny was feeling the need to put his hands around something and squeeze. "Been on this job too long," he muttered.

"—*h*—"

Tiny frowned, making a lot of water cascade down his face. Wiping it away, he said, "You hear something?"

"The motor, you mean? No."

"Not the motor," Tiny told him. "Sounded like a voice."

"—*hehhh*—"

"You won't hear any voice," Tom said, "all you'll hear is—"

"Shut up," Tiny requested.

"What was that?"

Tiny was in no mood. "This ground's wet, Tom," he said. "Maybe I'll sit on *you* for a while."

"Well, we're all getting testy," Tom told him, forgiving him.

Tiny said, "Just be quiet, while I listen to this voice."

"Joan of Arc," Tom commented, sotto voce, but then he was quiet, and Tiny listened, and heard no voice.

Was it something he'd made up? Was it just something the rain did? But it had sounded like a voice out there in the water somewhere.

At last, restless and uneasy, Tiny lumbered to his feet and plodded down the soggy bank to the water's edge, listening, not even caring that Tom was behind him.

"—*eye*—"

By God, that *is* a voice. "Hey!" Tiny yelled.

"—*eye?*—"

"Over here!" Tiny yelled, and saw a dim light out there on the water.

Tom had come down to stand beside him at the lip of the reservoir. At this moment, neither was being wary of the other. Tom said, "What the hell is that out there?"

"The boogie man."

"No, it isn't," Tom said. "I'm the boogie man."

"*Tiny!*"

"Over this way!" Tiny shouted, and the light out there bobbled and disappeared.

Tom said, "Which one is it?"

"Couldn't tell. His voice was full of water."

Splashing sounded out there, and then the voice called again: "Tiny! Where are you?"

"Over here! Come this way! Can you hear me! Hey, here I am! We're both here! Can you—"

"They're here," Tom said quietly.

They were. Andy Kelp and Doug Berry came stumbling and wading out of the reservoir, still in their full diving gear. Berry said, gasping, "I thought we'd never find the right place."

"Where's the boat?" Tiny asked him. "Where's Dortmunder?"

Kelp and Berry stood panting in front of him. Berry said, "We were hoping he was here."

• • •

Driving around all night, *and* in the rain. Stan didn't mind driving usually—he was a driver, after all—but on tiny country roads, at night, in the rain, with no other traffic, nothing to look at or think about, no passenger in the vehicle, not even a destination, just driving aimlessly around until everybody else was finished work, that could get old. Very old.

Finally. *Finally*. Finally, at quarter to five in the ayem, when Stan made yet another pass by the bridge over Gulkill Creek, Andy Kelp appeared at the side of the road and gave him the high sign, and Stan pulled to a stop just past the bridge.

Sliding over to the right side of the seat, he opened the passenger door, stuck his head out in the rain, and watched Tiny and the others come up out of the woods and climb into the rear of the slat-sided truck. Too bad it didn't have a roof back there. He called back, "How'd it go?"

Andy came squidging forward through the rain. "Well, yes and no," he said. "Good news and bad news, like they say."

"You found the money?"

"That's the good news," Andy agreed. "It's still down there, but we got it dug up and we got a rope on it."

"Great," Stan said. "So that's the good news; you found the money. What's the bad news?"

"We lost John."

• • •

From the instant she saw Stan's face, May *knew*. She didn't know exactly *what* she knew, but she knew she knew. That much she knew; that she knew.

"Now, we're not giving up hope," was the first thing Stan said, when shortly after sunup he walked into the kitchen where May and Wally and Murch's Mom were still sitting around, bleary-eyed and weaving but unwilling to go to sleep before the word came. And now the word was *this*.

May said, "Stan? Not giving up hope about *what?*"

"Well, about John," Stan said.

His Mom said, "Stanley, tell us this second."

"Well, what happened, as I understand it—"

"This second!"

"The boat sank. John was the only one in it. Nobody knows where he is."

May leaped to her feet, spilling cold milk. "At the bottom of the reservoir!" she cried. "That's where he is!"

"Well, no," Stan told her. "At least, that's not the theory we're working on. See, there was this line stretched across the reservoir over the railroad track, up by the top of the water, and that's where John was, so the theory is, he held on to that line and followed it to the shore on one side or the other, and got out before Andy and Doug could catch up with him. So now Andy and Doug are going in along the railroad line from the road on one side, and Tiny and Tom are going in from the other side. And I come back to tell you."

"I'm going there!" May said.

"We'll all go," Murch's Mom said.

"Sure!" Wally cried, jumping up, eyes agleam.

"It's raining, May," Stan pointed out.

"I just hope it's raining where John is," May told him.

• • •

Of course, Bob couldn't drive a car yet, not just yet. Of course, he understood that completely, in fact, everybody understood that completely, and that's why Kenny the boss had said he'd drive Bob back and forth from now on, that is, just until Bob was ready to drive a car again. Kenny always drove Chuck anyway, because Kenny and Chuck lived right near each other over in Dudson Falls, and Kenny said it wasn't really out of the way much at all, and he didn't mind anyway, and in fact everything was perfectly fine about picking Bob up from his house in Dudson Center where he lived with that girl, whatsername, the one he was married to, and then dropping him off there again every morning after work. And Chuck said, "Hey, good idea. That's easy, man." So that's what was going to happen.

Bob was filing the *W*s, taking his time, feeling the texture of each sheet of paper, enjoying the even rows of words across all the sheets of paper—look at all those letters, making up all those words, filling up all those pieces of paper—and he was all the way to the *W*s when Kenny came by and said, "Hey, there, buddy, how you doin, pal, everything okay, Bob? Good, that's good. Listen, it's almost six and—"

BEEP.

Kenny jumped back, then nodded at Bob's watch, laughing nervously as he said, "Time for another pill, huh?"

"Oh, yes," Bob said. "We don't know what would happen to me, Dr.

Panchick and me, we don't know what would happen to me if I didn't take my pills."

"You take a lot of them, huh?"

"Well, we're going to taper off," Bob explained. "But not yet," he said, and went away to the bathroom for water and took his pill.

When he came back out to the office, it was after six o'clock and everybody was ready to go. "Here I am," Bob said, smiling happily at all these nice fellas, really liking how they all were just good pals together, working together, having all these nice times together. "All ready, Kenny," he said, and just beamed.

The crew went out to their cars, their usual exchanges of low humor with the day crew muffled a bit by the presence of this ethereal creature among them. Bob didn't notice any of that; he was noticing how pretty the rain was. When he looked up at the sky, raindrops fell on his eyeballs and made him *blink*. Nice!

"Ready, Bob?"

"Oh, sure, Kenny, here I come."

Chuck was in the passenger seat in front, so Bob got in the backseat with the naked man on the floor. "Hello," he said.

The naked man on the floor—well, he wasn't completely naked, he was wearing underpants and one sock—wasn't as happy as Bob's friends. In fact, he glared at Bob and shook his fist, and then he put his finger to his lips and pointed at himself with his other hand and emphatically shook his head.

Well, gee, all right. The naked man didn't want Bob to talk about him being there. Well, gee, that's okay. With the pill he'd just swallowed now stamping out every little brushfire of fear or excitement or panic in his entire neural network, Bob said, "Okay."

Kenny was just then getting into the car, slipping in behind the wheel. Pausing before putting the key in the ignition, he looked in the rearview mirror at Bob and said, "What's that, Bob?"

Giggling, Chuck said, "He's talking to his imaginary playmate back there."

Kenny gave Chuck a warning look. "Watch that."

But the naked man on the floor was nodding emphatically, pointing now in the direction of Chuck. So that was the true explanation after all. "That's right," Bob said placidly. "I'm talking to my imaginary playmate."

Kenny and Chuck exchanged another glance, Kenny exasperated and feeling his responsibility, Chuck guilty but vastly amused. Kenny shook his head, and irritably watched himself insert the key in the ignition. "Get well soon," he muttered.

As they drove away from the dam toward Dudson Center, Bob sat way over on his side of the backseat, his smile kind of raggedy around the edges, his eyes shooting out very teeny tiny sparks. His fingertips trembled. He didn't like looking at the naked man on the floor, but there he was, all the time, in the corner of Bob's eye.

Gazing straight ahead as the scrub forest ran backward past the windows on both sides, Bob could see the firm back of Kenny's head and a small segment of Chuck's profile. Chuck was giggling and smirking and at times pressing his palm to his mouth. Kenny's back radiated the lonely obligations of command.

Bob was very happy, of course, very placid, very content. All these little feathery feelings in his stomach and behind his eyes and in his throat and behind his knees didn't matter at all. It would be easier, of course, if the naked man weren't there on the floor next to him, but it wasn't *important*. It didn't change anything.

After a long period of silence in the car, Bob leaned forward a little and said, confidentially, to the back of Kenny's authoritative head, "I never had an imaginary playmate before."

This set Chuck off again, curling forward, collapsing against his door, various snorts and grunts squeezing out through the hands he held clamped over his mouth. Kenny, pretending Chuck didn't exist (the same way Bob pretended the naked man didn't exist), looked mildly in the rearview mirror and said, "Is that right, Bob?"

"Yes," Bob said. He felt as though there was more he wanted to say, but the words wouldn't come.

Kenny smiled in a big-brotherly fashion: "I bet it's fun," he said. "To have an imaginary playmate."

Bob smiled back at the face in the rearview mirror. Slowly he nodded. "Not really," he said. (The naked man's fist, in the corner of Bob's eye, was shaking again. The naked man's face, in the corner of Bob's eye, was enraged.)

Kenny hadn't actually heard Bob's answer. He'd gone back to concentrating on his driving.

Bob wanted to turn his head away so he could look out his side window and not see anything in the car at all, but it was hard to do. His upper body was made of one solid block of wood; it was hard to make one part of it turn separately from the rest. Slowly, very slowly, strain lines standing out on the sides of his neck, Bob turned his face away. He looked out the window. The first houses of Dudson Center went by. Very interesting. Very nice.

In the middle of town, Kenny had to stop for a red light. Bob gazed fixedly at the windows of a hardware store. The other rear door slammed. Kenny said, sharply, "What was that?"

Bob swiveled his head on his painful neck. Chuck said, "Bob's imaginary playmate just got out."

"Goddammit, Chuck!"

"That's right," Bob said. "He went away."

Chuck twisted around to grin at Bob. "He probably went on ahead to your house," he said. "Waiting there for you now, with Tiffany."

"Uh-huh," said Bob.

Through clenched teeth, Kenny said, "Chuck, your job is on the line."

Chuck gave Kenny an excessively innocent look. "Bob's happy," he said. But he faced front after that and didn't say any more.

Five minutes later, they reached Bob's house. "Here we are, Bob," Kenny said.

Bob didn't move. The lower half of his face smiled, but the upper half around the eyes had worry lines in it.

Kenny twisted around, frowning at him. "You're home, Bob," he said. "Come on, guy. I gotta get going."

"I'd like to go back to the hospital now, please," Bob said. And that was the last thing he said for three weeks.

● ● ●

The small-town habit of leaving doors unlocked had even begun to affect the residents of 46 Oak Street, and that was just as well. Reaching there at last, cold, wet, naked, in the downpour, and finding nobody even home to hear his complaints, Dortmunder might just have *bitten* his way through the front door if it had been locked.

He was feeling like biting his way through something, God knows. What a night! That reservoir was out to kill him, there was no question about that anymore. Every time he went near that evil body of water, it reached out damp fingers and dragged him down. If he so much as *thought* about that reservoir, waters began to close over his head. No more. He was through now. Three times and *out*.

This last time had been the closest shave yet. The goddamn rubber boat suddenly shrinking and deflating and sinking beneath him, and him sitting there not knowing what to do, the goddamn little 10hp motor clutched in his arms, resting on his lap. It wasn't till the boat had reduced itself to a two-dimensional gray rubber rag, dumping him into the reservoir, and he'd found himself heading straight for the bottom, that he finally got his wits about him enough to let go of the motor and let it proceed into eternity without him.

Then it was his own clothing that dragged him down. The shoes were pulled off first, one sock inadvertently going as well, then the jacket, then the trousers, then the shirt, taking the T-shirt with it.

By the time all that underwater undressing was done, he had no idea where he was, except in trouble; the boat, the line of monofilament, everything was gone. His head was above water, barely and only sometimes. Turning in ever more frantic circles, he'd finally seen the dim lights way over by the dam and had known that was his only hope. If he didn't have some target to aim for, he'd just swim around in circles out here in the dark and the wet and the rain and the deep and the horrible until his strength gave out.

So he swam, and floated, and swam, and floundered, and flailed, and at last staggered ashore down at the end of the dam near the little stone official structure and its attendant parking lot. An unlocked car there—nobody locks *anything* out in the sticks—provided some small shelter from the storm, and Dortmunder even napped in there occasionally, cold and wet and scared and furious as he was.

He'd been asleep, in fact, when the weird kid with the poleaxed smile came in and sat beside him and gave him a completely drugged-out look and just said, "Hello." He isn't going to turn me in, Dortmunder had thought. He isn't going to holler or get excited or do anything normal. He barely even knows I'm here.

And so he'd stuck tight, ignoring his first impulse to jump from the car and make a hopeless run for it, and the result was they'd given him a ride all the way back to Dudson Center. The last four blocks after he left the car, walking along almost completely naked, in daylight, with people on their way to work all around him, had not been easy. But anything was easier than being in the ————. (He wasn't going to say the R word anymore, wasn't even going to think it.)

But now here he was, home at last, and where was everybody? I don't even get a sympathetic welcome, Dortmunder thought, feeling very sorry for himself as he padded with his one bare foot and one socked foot to the kitchen, opened a can of tomato soup, added milk (no water!), heated it, drank the whole thing serving after serving out of a coffee cup, and packed crackers in around it in his stomach for body. Then, beginning at last to feel warm and dry, and *knowing* how tired he was, he went back through the empty house and slumped upstairs one heavy foot at a time and got into bed without even bothering to take his sock off.

The return, hours later, of the other eight residents of the house, cold, wet, discouraged, shocked, unhappy, and bickering, didn't wake him, but May's scream when she opened the bedroom door and saw him there did. Briefly. "Later, May, okay?" Dortmunder said, and rolled over, and went back to sleep.

FOURTH DOWN

CHAPTER SIXTY-ONE

Then they all blamed *him*. They all sat around in the living room on Oak Street after Dortmunder finally woke up and came downstairs, and they blamed *him*. Wouldn't you know?

"You had us very worried, John," May said, gently but seriously.

"I had myself a little worried, too," Dortmunder answered.

His foghorn voice more fogbound than usual, Tiny said, "I think I got a little head cold out there, walkin around in the rain while you were asleep in your bed here."

Murch's Mom sneezed and looked at Dortmunder significantly, but didn't say anything.

"Pretty dangerous," her son commented, "driving that borrowed truck around in the daytime, hour after hour. And then for nothing."

"You know, John," Doug said, "it's kind of hard to figure out how you missed that monofilament, that line stretching right across the lake, when it was right *there* and everything."

"That's right," Kelp said. "*I* saw it, no trouble."

Dortmunder lowered an eyebrow at him. "In the light from your headlamp?"

"Well, yeah."

Wally said, "John, while you were asleep up there, I asked the computer, and *it* couldn't predict you going to the dam either. That's the one direction nobody thought of."

"That's where the lights were," Dortmunder told him. "Mention that to your computer next time you run into each other."

345

Tom cackled and said, "Looks like everybody's sorry you made it, Al."

Then they all changed their tune, and everybody reassured him how happy they all were to see him under any circumstances, even home safe in his bed when they'd expected him to be either dead in the reservoir or half-dead beside it. And that was the end of that conversation.

It was late afternoon now, Dortmunder having slept most of the day, and outside the windows the rain still poured down. The weather forecast, full of stalled lows and weak highs, promised this stage of storms would, at the very least, even the score for the weeks of sunny days and star-strewn nights preceding it, and maybe even throw a little extra rottenness in for good measure.

After everybody got over the desire to be crotchety with Dortmunder for having saved himself from a watery grave, the next topic on the agenda was Tom's money, plucked at last from its own watery grave but not yet from the water. "From here on," Doug told the assembled group, "it's a snap. All we do is go back out to the res—"

"No," Dortmunder said, and got to his feet.

May looked up at him in mild surprise. "John? Where are you going?"

"New York," Dortmunder told her, and headed for the stairs.

"Wait a minute!"

"We got it beat now!"

"Piece of cake!"

"We know where the box is!"

"We got a rope on it!"

"We're *winning*, John!"

But Dortmunder didn't listen. He thudded upstairs, one foot after the other, and while he packed people kept coming up to try to change a mind made of concrete.

May was first. She came in and sat on the bed beside the suitcase Dortmunder was packing, and after a minute she said, "I understand how you feel, John."

"Good," Dortmunder said, his hands full of socks.

"But I just don't feel as though I can leave here until this is all over and settled."

"Uh-huh."

"It wouldn't be fair to Murch's Mom."

"Uh-huh."

"And if we walk away now, Tom might *still* decide he'd rather use that dynamite of his."

"Uh-huh."

"So you can see, John," May said, "why I feel I have to stay."

Dortmunder paused with his hands in a dresser drawer. "I *can* see that, May," he said. "And if you stop to think about it, you can see why I *can't* stay. When you're done up here, you'll come home. I'll be there."

She looked at him, thought it over, and got to her feet. "Well," she said, "I can see your mind is made up."

"I'm glad you can see that, May," Dortmunder said.

Tom was next. "Runnin out, eh, Al?"

"Yes," Dortmunder said.

Wally followed a couple minutes later. "Gee, John," he said, "I know you're not the hero, you're only the soldier, but even the soldier doesn't leave in the middle of the *game*."

"Game called," Dortmunder told him, "on account of wet."

Tiny and Stan and his Mom came together, like the farmhands welcoming Dorothy back from Oz. "Dortmunder," Tiny rumbled, "I figure you're the one got us this far."

"I understand it's a piece of cake from here on," Dortmunder said, folding with great care his other pants.

Stan said, "You don't want to drive to the city on a Wednesday, you know. Matinee day, there's *no* good routes."

"I'll take the bus," Dortmunder told him.

Murch's Mom looked insulted. "I hate the bus," she announced. "And so should you."

Dortmunder nodded, taking the suggestion under advisement, but then said, "Will you drive me to the bus station?"

"Cabdrivers don't get to have opinions about destinations," Murch's Mom snapped, which might have been a form of "yes," and she marched out.

"Well, Dortmunder," Tiny said, "I can't a hundred percent blame you. Put her there."

So Dortmunder shook his hand, and Tiny and Stan left, and Dortmunder's hand was almost recovered enough to go on packing when Doug came in to say, "I hear you're really going."

"I'm really going," Dortmunder agreed.

"Well," Doug said, "tomorrow or the next day, sometime soon, I got to go back to Long Island anyway, see to my business, pick up the stuff we need for the next try. You could ride along."

"I'm leaving today," Dortmunder told him.

"What the heck, wait a day."

"Well, Doug," Dortmunder said, "let's say I wait a day, a couple of days, everybody having these little talks with me. Then let's say I get into that pickup with you and we head for the city, and you just can't resist it, you gotta tell me the plan, the details, the equipment, you gotta talk about the res— the place there, and all that. And somewhere in there, Doug," Dortmunder said, resting his aching hand in a friendly way on Doug's arm, "somewhere in there, I just might be forced to see if I know how to do a three-sixty."

Dortmunder was just locking his suitcase when Andy Kelp came in. Dortmunder looked at him and said, "Don't even start."

"I've heard the word," Kelp told him. "And I know you, John, and I know when not to waste my breath. Come on over here."

"Come on over where?"

"The window," Kelp told him. "It's okay, it's closed."

Wondering what Kelp was up to, Dortmunder went around the bed and over to the window, and when Kelp pointed outside he looked out, past the curtain and the rain-smeared window and the rain-dotted screen and the rain-filled air over the rain-soggy lawn and the rain-flowing sidewalk to the rain-slick curb, where a top-of-the-line Buick Pompous 88 stood there, black, gleaming in the rain.

"Cruise control," Kelp said, with quiet pride. "Everything. You gotta go back in comfort."

Dortmunder was touched. Not enough to reconsider, but touched. "Thank you, Andy," he said.

"The truth is," Kelp said, leaning forward, speaking confidentially, "I think you're right. That reservoir *is* out to get you."

CHAPTER SIXTY-TWO

Well, at least there was a little more room at the dinner table, though no one said that out loud in case of hurting May's feelings. But it was nice, just the same, to have that extra inch or two for the elbow when bringing a forkful of turkey loaf mouthward.

On the other hand, when it came to discussing future plans, all at once Dortmunder's absence from the table became less positive and pleasant, though that wasn't obvious right at first, when Doug raised the subject over coffee, saying, "Well, it's easy from here on. We've *touched* the box. We know where it is."

"We've got a rope on it," Kelp added.

Nodding, Doug said, "And the other end of the rope is tied to our monofilament, which nobody's going to see."

"Especially in this weather," Tiny said, and sneezed.

"Another good thing," Tom added. "This last time, you birds didn't leave a lot of evidence around to alert the law."

Wally said, "The computer says there's a *million* ways to get it now. It's so easy."

Stan said, "Good. So let's do it and get it over with."

His Mom said, "I'll go along with that. I want to get back to where driving's a contact sport."

"So we'll just do it," Doug said, and shrugged at how easy it was.

"Be glad to get it over with," Kelp said.

Then there was a little silence, everybody drinking coffee or looking at the wall or drawing little fingertip circles on the tablecloth, nobody quite meeting anybody else's eye. The light in the crowded little dining room seemed to get brighter, the tablecloth whiter, the walls shinier, the silence deeper and deeper, as though they were turning into an acrylic genre painting of themselves.

Finally, it was May who broke the silence, saying, "How?"

Then everybody was alive and animated again, all looking at her, all suddenly eager to answer the question. "It's easy, May," Kelp said. "We just winch it in."

"We tie the rope to the rope," Doug explained.

"Naturally," Tiny added, "we gotta get a new winch."

"Oh, yeah," Kelp said, nodding. "And a rope."

Stan said, "Don't we need some kind of boat?"

"Not one that sinks in the rain," Tiny suggested.

Wally asked, "Well, when do we do it? Do you want to wait for the rain to stop?"

"Yes," Tiny said.

"Well, I don't know," Doug said. "Depends on how long that is. You know, the engineers in the dam put a little boat in the water every once in a while, run around the reservoir, take samples and so on, and if they ran over our line they'd cut it. Even if they didn't foul their propeller, even if *they* didn't find it, we'd lose the line."

Tiny said, "They won't do one of their jaunts in this weather, count on it."

"That's true," Doug agreed.

May cleared her throat and said, "It seems to me, John would point out right here that the instant the rain stops the people in the dam might go right out in their boat so they can get caught up with their schedule."

"That's also true," Doug agreed.

Wally said, "Miss May, what else would John point out?"

"I don't know," May said. "He isn't here."

Everybody thought about that. Stan said, "What it is, when John's around, you don't mind coming up with ideas, because he'll tell you if they're any good or not."

"Dortmunder," Tiny said, ponderously thoughtful, "is what you call your focal point."

With his patented bloodless lipless cackle, Tom said, "Pity he tossed in his hand just before the payout."

Everybody looked uncomfortable. May said, "I'm here to see to John's interests."

"Oh?" Tom asked mildly. "Does Al still have interests?"

Murch's Mom gave him a beady look. "I don't see what it matters to you," she said. "It doesn't come out of your half. You're just a troublemaker for the fun of it, aren't you?"

"As long as everybody's happy," Tom told her, "I'm happy."

"The question is," May insisted, "*when* are you going to do it, and *how* are you going to do it?"

"May," Kelp said, "I've touched that box now, with this hand." He showed it to her, palm out. "From here on, it's *so easy.*"

"Fine," May said. "Tell me about it."

Kelp turned to Doug. "Explain it to her, okay?"

"Well," Doug said. "We go out and tie the rope to the rope, and Tiny winches it in."

Tiny said, "Don't you have to do something to get the box lighter, so it'll lift up over the tree stumps?"

"Oh, right," Doug said. "I forgot that part."

"And *when*," May said. "And what kind of boat. And what are the *details*?"

"That's what we need John for!" Kelp exclaimed, punching the table in his irritation.

"We don't have John," May pointed out. "So we'll have to work out the details ourselves. And the first detail is, when do you want to do it?"

"As soon as possible," Stan answered. Turning to Tiny, he explained, "I hate to say this, but I think we're better off in the rain. As long as we get ourselves ready for it."

"And the boat doesn't sink," Tiny said.

"Well, a new boat," Doug said. "That's gonna be expensive."

Everybody looked at Tom, who gazed around mildly (for him) and said, "No."

"Tom," Kelp said, "we need a certain amount of—"

"No more dough from me," Tom said. He sounded serious about it. To Doug he said, "Who'm I buying all this equipment from? You. So donate the stuff."

"Well, not the boat," Doug told him.

"Steal the fucking boat," Tom advised.

Doug floundered a bit at that, but Stan rescued him, saying, "Okay, Doug, never mind, we'll work out the boat."

"Okay," Doug said, but he was getting those little white spots on his cheeks again, like when he'd been in shock.

Stan turned to May. "We'll work it *all* out, May. We're just not used to doing this, that's all."

May surveyed the table. "I'll make fresh coffee," she decided, and went away to the kitchen. She could hear them bickering in there the whole time she was away.

CHAPTER SIXTY-THREE

Dortmunder did not sleep like a baby, home in his own bed at last. He slept like a grown-up who'd been through a *lot*. He slept leadenly, at times noisily, mouth open, limbs sprawled any which way, bedclothes tangled around ankles. He had good dreams (sunlight, money, good-looking cars, and fast women) and bad dreams (water), and periods of sleep so heavy an alligator would have envied him.

It was during a somewhat shallower stretch that Dortmunder was slightly disturbed by the scratchings and plinkings of someone picking the lock on the apartment door, opening it, creeping in (these old floors creak, no matter what you do) and closing the door with that telltale little *snick*. Dortmunder almost came all the way to the surface of consciousness at that instant, but instead, his brain decided the noises were just Tom returning from one of his late-night filling-the-pockets forays, and so the tiny sounds from the hallway were converted in his dream factory into the shushings and plinkings of wavelets, and in *that* dream Tom was a giant fish with teeth, from whom Dortmunder swam and swam and swam, never quite escaping.

Normally, the interloper would have had trouble finding his way around the dark and almost windowless apartment, but Dortmunder's recent underwater experiences had led him to leave a light burning in the bathroom, by which illumination it was possible for the interloper to make his way all through the place, to reassure himself that the sleeping

Dortmunder was the only current resident, and then to go on and make himself a peanut butter and jelly sandwich in the kitchen. (The clinking of knife inside peanut butter jar became, in Dortmunder's dreams, the oars in the oarlocks of Charon's boat.)

The interloper was quiet for a long time after ingesting his sandwich and one of Dortmunder's beers; in fact, he napped a little, at the kitchen table. But then, along around sunup, he moved into the bedroom and threw all Dortmunder's clothing onto the floor from the chair beside the door so he could sit there, just beyond the foot of the bed, and watch Dortmunder sleep.

The faint metallic click as the interloper cocked his rifle caused Dortmunder to frown in his sleep and make disgusting smacking sounds with his mouth, and to dream briefly of being deep underwater and having his air tank suddenly fall off his back and separate from the mouthpiece hose with a faint metallic click just before his mouth and stomach and brain filled with water; but then that dream floated away and he dreamed instead about playing poker with some long-ago cellmates in the good old days, and being dealt a royal flush—in spades—which caused him to settle back down in contentment, deeper and deeper into sleep, so that it was almost two hours later when he finally opened his eyes and rubbed his nose and did that sound with his mouth and sat up and stretched and looked at the rifle aimed at his eye.

"GL!" Dortmunder cried, swallowing his tongue.

Rifle. Gnarled old hands holding the rifle. Wrinkly old eye staring down the rifle's sights. The last resident of Cronley, Oklahoma, seated in a chair in Dortmunder's bedroom.

"Now, Mr. Department of Recovery," said the hermit, "you can just tell me where Tim Jepson is. And *this* time, ain't nobody behind me with no bottle."

CHAPTER SIXTY-FOUR

No bottle . . .

. . .

When dawn's sharp stiletto poked its orange tip into Guffey's eye through the windowless opening in the Hotel Cronley's bar's front wall, he awakened to a splitting headache and a conundrum. Either the infrastructure man's partner had hit him on the head with three bottles, which seemed excessive, or something funny was going on.

Three bottles. All broken and smashed on the bar floor, all with their corks still jammed tight in their cracked-off necks. And all absolutely *stinking*. They were dry inside, so it wasn't merely that the wine had gone bad after all these years; and in any event, the stench seemed to come more from the crusted gunk on the bottles' outside.

Plumbing. The second invader had gone to the basement to look at the plumbing. So did Guffey, reeling a bit from the aftereffects of the blow on the head, and when he found the dismantled trap he *knew*. By God, it was Tim Jepson after all! Come back for his fourteen thousand dollars, just as Mitch Lynch had said he would. Fourteen thousand dollars hidden all these years in those wine bottles in this dreadful muck river; wasn't that just like Jepson?

In my hands, Guffey thought inaccurately, and I let him get away. But perhaps all hope was not yet lost. There was still one slender thread in

355

Guffey's hand: the license plate of that little white automobile. Could he follow that thread? He could but try.

Before noon on that same day, Cronley became at last what it had for so long appeared to be: deserted. Guffey, freshly shaved, garbed in the best of the professors' stolen clothing, dismantled rifle and more clothing stowed in the knapsack on his back, marched out of Cronley and across the rock-strewn desert toward his long-deferred destiny.

By early evening, he'd walked and hitchhiked as far as a town with a state police barracks, where he reported the hit-and-run driver, offering a description of the car and its license number, plus the welt on the back of his head for evidence. They took the license number and description and ran them through their computer, and they took the welt on the back of his head and ran *him* through the hospital, giving him the softest night's sleep and the best food of his entire life, and almost making him give up the quest right there. All a fella had to do, after all, to live in the lap of luxury like this, was step out in front of a bus seven or eight times a year.

But duty called, particularly when the cops came around the hospital next morning to say they knew who'd hit him but there wasn't much to be done about it. (He'd been counting on this official indifference.) The car, it seemed, was a rental, picked up at the Oklahoma City airport the same day it hit Guffey and turned back in the next day. The miscreants—"New Yorkers: you might know"—were long gone. There wasn't the slightest mark on the car, nor were there any witnesses, nor had the hospital found anything at all seriously wrong with Guffey (amazingly enough), so there simply wasn't enough of a case to warrant an interstate enquiry.

Guffey, humble as ever, accepted everything he was told, and asked only one thing in return: Might he have, please, the name and address of the person who had rented the car?

One of the cops grinned at that request and said, "You wouldn't think of taking the law in your own hands, would you?"

"I've never been out of Oklahoma in my life!" Guffey cried, truthfully. "I just want to write that person and tell him I forgive him. I'm a Christian, you know. Praise the Lord!"

When it looked as though Guffey might intend to start preaching in their direction nonstop, the cops gave him *two* names—Tom Jimson, who'd rented the car, and John Dortmunder, who'd driven it—plus one address in New York for both of them. (Tom Jimson, huh? Tim Jepson, Tom Jimson, huh? Huh? *Huh?*)

There was a little glitch when the hospital said they wanted to keep Guffey a few days longer for observation, but when they discovered he didn't have any insurance they realized they'd already observed him long enough, and he was let go. And then, for the first time in his life, thumb extended, Guffey left Oklahoma.

The trip northeast was fairly long and adventurous, punctuated by a number of crimes of the most cowardly and despicable sort: church poor-boxes rifled, cripples mugged for their grocery sacks, things like that. And here at last was New York. And here was the address. And here was John Dortmunder.

Tim Jepson wasn't here right at this minute, unfortunately—killing him in his sleep would be the safest way to go about it, after all—but that was all right. John Dortmunder was here and John Dortmunder could tell Guffey how to find Tim Jepson.

And he would, too. Oh, yes.

CHAPTER SIXTY-FIVE

W ell, no," Dortmunder said, trying to sound like a reasonable person in control of himself and his environment, rather than a terrified bunny rabbit who's just been awakened by a madman with a rifle. "No, I don't know where Tom—Tim is."

"Lives here," the madman corrected him. "Said so when you rented the car."

Dortmunder stared, astonished at the madman's information, and the madman cackled, rather like Tom himself, except that his mouth opened plenty wide enough to see the shriveled and darkened toothless gums. "Didn't know I knew that, did you?" he demanded, the rifle as steady as a courthouse cannon in his wrinkled old hands.

"No, I didn't."

"Oh, I know all sorts of stuff, Mr. Department of Recovery. Tim Jepson calls himself Tom Jimson now. He paid for that rental car. You drove."

"Well, gee, you're pretty good," Dortmunder told him, thinking like mad.

"You know what I'm *really* good at?" the madman asked him.

"No, what's that?"

"Shooting." The maniac grinned, cheek nestled against the cold rifle. "I been shooting for the pot for years now," he explained.

"Don't you ever hit it?" Dortmunder asked him.

Which made the old guy mad, for some reason. "Shooting for the *pot!*" he repeated, with great emphasis. "That means shooting food! Coyotes and

358

rabbits and gophers and snakes and rats! That you put in the *pot*! And *eat*!"

"I'm sorry, I'm sorry," Dortmunder told him, very sincerely. "I'm a city person, I don't know these things."

"Well, *I* do," the touchy countryman said, "and let me tell you, Mr. City Person, I'm goddamn good at shooting for the pot."

"I bet you are," Dortmunder told him, filling his voice to the gunwales with admiration.

"You get a little squirrel out there," the madman told him, "it don't stand still and let you aim, like how *you* do. It keeps moving, jumping around. And yet, every blessed time I pull this trigger, I hit that squirrel just exactly where I want. I *never* spoil the meat."

"That's pretty good," Dortmunder assured him.

"It's god*damn* good!"

"That's right! That's right!"

"So, then," the madman said, settling down once more, "what do you think the chances are, if I decided to shoot that left earlobe offa you, that I'll probly do it?"

"Well, uh," Dortmunder said. His left earlobe began to itch like crazy. His left hand began to tremble like crazy, thwarted in its desire to scratch his left ear. His left eye began to water. "Uhhhhh," he said, "I don't think you ought to do that."

"Why not?"

"Well, uh, the noise, the neighbors, they—"

"What I hear about New York City," the madman informed him, "when the neighbors around these parts hear a gunshot they just turn up on the TV and pretend it didn't happen. That's what *I* hear."

"Oh, well," Dortmunder said, "that's just people out in the sticks knocking New York the way they do. This city's really a very warm-hearted, caring, uh, for instance, people from out of town are *constantly* getting their wallet back that they left in the taxi."

"Well, I don't leave no wallet in no taxi," the madman told him. "I only know what I hear. And I figure it's worth the chance."

"Wait a minute!" Dortmunder cried. "Why do you, why do you want to *do* such a thing?"

"For practice," the madman told him. "And so you'll take me seriously."

"I take you seriously! I take you seriously!"

"Good." The madman nodded agreeably but kept the rifle aimed at Dortmunder's ear. "So where's Tim Jepson?" he said.

CHAPTER SIXTY-SIX

U h," said the man on the bed. Guffey frowned at him. "Uh?"

"I don't know!"

"If you really don't know," Guffey told him, in all sincerity, "that's a pity, because you're about to lose an ear."

"Wait a minute!" the man called John Dortmunder cried, waving his arms around, kicking his legs under the blanket. "I *do* know, but wait a minute, okay?"

Guffey almost lowered the rifle at that, it was so astonishing. "You do know, but wait a minute?"

"Listen," John Dortmunder said earnestly, "you know Tom Jimson, right? Or Tim Jepson, or whatever you want to call him."

"I surely do," Guffey agreed, hands squeezing the rifle so hard he almost shot the fellow's ear off prematurely.

"Well, then, think about it," Dortmunder invited him. "Would anybody on this Earth *protect* Tom Jimson? Would anybody risk their own ear for him?"

Guffey thought that over. "Still," he said, "Tim Jepson lives here with you, and you know where he is, but you don't want to tell me. So maybe you're just crazy or something, and what you need is shock therapy, like me shooting off your ear and then a couple of fingers and then—"

"No no no, just give me a chance," Dortmunder cried, bouncing around on the bed some more. "I don't blame you, honest I don't. I know what Tom did to you, he told me all about it."

Guffey growled, low in his throat. "He did?"

"Getting you stuck in that elevator and the whole thing." Shaking his head sympathetically, he said, "He even *laughed* about it. I could hardly stand to listen."

Nor could Guffey. "Then how come you hang *out* with this fella?" he demanded. "And *protect* him?"

"I'm not protecting Tom," Dortmunder protested. "There's other people in it that I *do* care about, okay?"

"I don't care about nobody but Tim Jepson."

"I know that. I believe it." Dortmunder spread his hands, being reasonable. "You waited this many years," he pointed out. "Just wait another day or two."

Guffey gave that suggestion the bitter chuckle it deserved. "So you can go *warn* him? What kinda idiot do you think I am?"

Dortmunder stared around the room, brow corrugated with thought. "I tell you what," he said. "Stay here."

"Stay *here*?"

"Just till I get my phone call."

"What phone call?"

"From the friends of mine that'll say they're done doing what they're doing, and then—"

Guffey was getting that lost feeling. He said, "Doing what? Who? What are they doing?"

"Well, no," Dortmunder said.

"By God," Guffey said, taking a bead, "you can kiss that ear good-bye."

"No, I don't think I could, really," Dortmunder told him. "And I don't think I can tell you who's doing what, or where they're doing it, or anything about it. But if you shoot my ears off, I won't be able to answer the phone, and then you'll *never* get your hands on Tom Jimson."

Guffey nodded and said, "So why don't I forget about your ear and just drop a cartridge into your brainpan there and wait for that phone call myself?"

"They won't talk to you," Dortmunder answered. "And what do you want to sit around with a dead body for?"

"They'll talk to me," Guffey said. "I'll tell them I'm your uncle, and they'll believe me. And the reason I want to sit around with a dead body is, if you're alive I won't be able to sleep or turn my back or go to the bathroom or *nothing* for two, three days until the phone rings. As a matter of fact," he added, having convinced himself with his own logic, "that's *just* what I'm gonna do." And he adjusted his aim accordingly, saying, "Good-bye."

"Wait!"

"Quit shoutin things," Guffey told him irritably. "You throw off my concentration, and that could spoil my aim. I'm givin you a nice painless death here, so just be grateful and—"

"You don't *have* to!"

Guffey knew it was rude to sneer at a person you're about to kill—it adds insult to injury, in fact—but he couldn't help it. "What are you gonna do? Give me your word of honor?"

"I got handcuffs!"

Guffey lowered the rifle, intrigued despite himself. "Handcuffs? How come you got handcuffs?"

"Well, they kinda come in handy sometimes," Dortmunder said with a little shrug.

"So your idea is, I should cuff you to the bed there—"

"Maybe to the sofa in the living room," Dortmunder suggested. "So it's more comfortable and I could watch television if I wanted."

Was this some sort of trick? In Guffey's experience, *everything* pretty much was some sort of trick. He said, "Where's these cuffs?"

Dortmunder pointed to the dresser along the wall to Guffey's left. "Top drawer on the left."

By standing beside the dresser, back against the wall, Guffey could keep an eye on Dortmunder while he pushed the drawer open and studied its contents by means of a number of quick peeks. And what contents! Mixed in with gap-toothed combs and nonmatching cufflinks and broken-winged sunglasses and squeezed-out tubes of various lotions and ointments were worn-looking brass knuckles, a red domino mask, a Mickey Mouse mask, a ski mask, three right-handed rubber gloves, a false mustache mounted on a white card in a clear plastic bag, a sprinkling of subway slugs, and as advertised, a pair of chrome handcuffs with the key in the lock.

One-handed—the other hand keeping the rifle trained on Dortmunder— Guffey removed the handcuffs, dropped them on the dresser top, and pulled out the key, which he pocketed. Then he tossed the handcuffs at Dortmunder and said, "Good. Put em on, why doncha?"

"Well, hey, you know," Dortmunder complained. "I just woke up. Could I get dressed? Could I at least go to the bathroom?"

"Just a minute," Guffey told him. "Don't move."

So Dortmunder didn't move, and Guffey stepped sideways to the doorway, then backed through it and looked to the left (apartment door) and right (kitchen, with stove visible) before saying, "Okay, Mr. Dort-munder. I'm gonna go in the kitchen there and make me some coffee. And I'll keep an eye down this way. And if your head shows past this door before I say okay, I'll blow it off. You got that?"

"Oh, sure," Dortmunder agreed. "I'll just stay in here until you say."

"Good." Guffey started to back away toward the kitchen, then stopped. Grudgingly, he said, "You want coffee?"

"Yeah, thanks."

"Okay." Guffey started to back off again, but Dortmunder raised his hand like a kid who knows the answer. Guffey stopped. "Yeah?"

"If it isn't too much trouble," Dortmunder said, "uh, orange juice?"

CHAPTER SIXTY-SEVEN

Shoulders hunched against the steady rain, Myrtle leaned her chest against the side of the house on Oak Street and stood up on tiptoe. Watching through the kitchen window, she could see Doug standing next to the refrigerator, telephone to his ear. Across the back yards and across Myrtle Street, she could hear faintly the sound of her own phone ringing.

When *will* he give up? she wondered, and at last he did, the ringing sound from the next block cutting off at the same instant. Shaking his head, Doug turned from the wall phone to say something bewildered—"She's *never* home!"—to Gladys, who had just marched into the kitchen, wearing a zipper jacket and a cloth cap. But Gladys gave him an unsympathetic shrug, opened the refrigerator, took out a can of beer, and was just popping the top when someone tapped Myrtle on the shoulder.

That touch made Myrtle jump so high that both people in the kitchen turned to look out the window at the movement, and when she landed she sagged back against the rain-wet wall of the house like an overwatered clematis. In growing horror she stared upward at what appeared to be the Abominable Snowman standing before her in a yellow slicker and rainhat that made him look like a walking taco stand. This creature, spreading out massive arms with catcher's-mitt hands at the ends of them to pen her in and keep her from running away (as though her legs had the strength to run or even, without the help of the house, to hold her upright!), growled low in his throat and then said (in English! like a person, a human being!), "You don't look like *my* idea of a peeping Tom, lady."

"I'm not, I, I, I, I, I—"

The monster lifted one of those hands and waved it back and forth, and Myrtle's voice stopped. Then he said, "You, you, you, I got that part. Now try me on the next word."

Never had Myrtle felt so thin, so frail, so vulnerable and defenseless. She stammered out the only words that seemed to suit the case: "I'm sorry."

"That's nice," the giant said. "That's good. That counts on your side. On the other hand, 'sorry' isn't, you know, an *explanation*."

While Myrtle's brain ran around inside her skull, looking for a bouquet of words that might placate this monster, the monster looked up at the window, raised his monster eyebrows, pointed at Myrtle a monster finger with the girth and toughness of a rat's body, and mouthed elaborately, "You *know* this?"

Myrtle turned her head, looking up, and at this extreme angle Doug's face, seen through the rain-drenched window, looked as scared as she felt. *He* was scared? Oh, good heavens! And when Doug nodded spastically at the monster, it seemed to Myrtle that her last hope, not even noticed till now, had just fled.

"Okay," the monster said, and lowered his cold gaze on Myrtle once more. "It's raining out, little lady," he said. "Let's us be smart. Let's get in out of the rain."

"I want to go home now," Myrtle said in her tiniest voice.

For answer, the monster lifted his right hand and made a little move-along gesture. Myrtle, not knowing what else to do, obeyed, preceding the monster around to the back of the house and through the door and into the kitchen, where Doug and Gladys both looked at her with surprised disapproval.

The monster shut the door, and Doug said, "Myrtle, what are you *doing* here?"

Desperate, betrayed, feeling that *Doug* at least should be on her side, Myrtle said, "What are *you* doing here? You and the computer man and the so-called environment protection man and Gladys and my f-f-f-f—everybody else? You were here all along, lying to me, waiting for rain!"

The looks these three people gave one another at that outburst suggested to Myrtle, somewhat belatedly, that she might have revealed a bit more knowledge there than she should have. (At least she'd had sense enough not to mention her father.) Confirming this fear, the monster said, "This friend of yours knows a lot about us, Doug."

Doug shook his head, protesting with a tremor in his voice. "Not from me, Tiny! Honest!"

Tiny? Myrtle stared, but was distracted from this exercise in misapplied nomenclature by the sudden appearance in the kitchen of her father.

Yes. No question. She knew it at once. And almost as quickly she also knew, after one look in those icy eyes and at that gray, fleshless, hard-boned face, that this wasn't a father into whose arms one threw oneself. In fact, as instinctively as she'd grasped their relationship, she also grasped that it might be a very bad idea to inform him of it.

It was already a bad idea merely to have attracted his attention. After a quick but penetrating glare at Myrtle, her father swiveled his eyes to the monster and said, without moving his bloodless lips, "Tiny?"

"Peeking in the window," Tiny told him succinctly. "Doug's girlfriend, only the idea was she didn't know about this house or we're here or what's going on. Isn't that right, Doug?"

"I *thought* so," Doug said, sounding desperate. Spreading his arms in a gesture of appeal, he said to Myrtle's father, "Whatever she knows, Tom, she didn't know it from me. I swear!"

"And she knows a lot," the monster called Tiny said. "Including we been here waiting for weather."

Surprised, her father looked full at Myrtle (*now* she could see why Edna's reaction had been so extreme when she'd seen this man again after so many years) and said, "Know everything, do you? Where'd you learn it all?"

"I, I saw you all come out on the lawn," she told him in her little voice. "You were so happy when the clouds came."

Tiny said, "She's been keeping an eye on us, this girl."

Myrtle's father gave Doug a look of icy contempt, saying, "You gave it away, all right. You *are* as stupid as you look."

While Doug was still trying to decide what if any answer to give that, her father turned back to Myrtle and said, "Who else knows about us?"

(Keep Edna out of this!) "Nobody!"

Doug said, "That's gotta be true, Tom. She wouldn't tell her mother, and there's nobody else she hangs out with. She's just a librarian here in town!"

(How empty he makes my life sound, Myrtle thought. And how little he cares about me, really.)

Her father nodded slowly, thinking things over, and then he said, "Well, the back yard's nice and soft after all this rain. We'll plant her when it gets dark."

Everyone else in the room got the import of that remark before Myrtle did, and by the time she'd caught up they were all making objections, every one of which she heartily seconded.

Gladys spoke first, in tones of outrage: "You can't do that!"

Then Doug, in tones of panic: "I can't be involved in anything like that!"

And then Tiny, calm but persuasive: "We don't need to do that, Tom."

"Oh, yeah?" Her father—Tom Jimson—shook his head at all three of them. "Where does she go from here, then? Straight to the law."

"We keep her," Tiny said. "We're making our move tomorrow night, anyway. After that, what do we care what she says or where she goes?"

"Then her *mother* goes to the law when she doesn't come home," Tom Jimson said. (It was easier to think of him by his name, and not as father at all.)

Gladys said, "She can phone her mother and say she's gonna spend the night with Doug."

Myrtle gasped, and Doug had the grace to look embarrassed, but Gladys turned and gave her a jaundiced look and said, "It's better than not spending the night anywhere," and Myrtle knew she was right.

But Tom Jimson hadn't given up his original plan. "Where do we keep her?" he demanded. "Who's gonna stay up with her all night? Anywhere we put her she'll go out a window."

"Not the attic," said a voice from the door, and they all turned, and Wally was there (if that was his name).

How long had he been there? *Was* he the criminal mastermind Myrtle had been imagining, or merely the inoffensive little round man he seemed? Or something between the two?

Myrtle stared at him, but Wally didn't meet her eye. Instead, he came farther into the kitchen, saying to Tom Jimson, "There's a room up in the attic with a door we can lock. And I kind of stay up all night anyway, so I can check from time to time, make sure she isn't trying to break out or anything."

"She can yell out the window," Jimson objected.

Wally shrugged that away with a little smile. He *must* be the mastermind, he was the only one who didn't exhibit any fear of Tom Jimson. "In this rain?" he said.

Gladys said, "Wally's right. Nobody's out there, and if they were they couldn't hear her." So Wally was his real first name, at least.

Tiny said, "Look at it this way, Tom. Up to now we haven't done anything that's gonna get the law all excited about finding us. But if we start bumping off local citizens, everything changes."

"I don't *do* things like that," Doug said with shaky insistence. "I'm a diver. That's all I came here for."

A brisk discussion ensued, everybody arguing against Tom Jimson's bloodlust, and under it—behind the conversation's back, as it were—Wally kept staring fixedly at Myrtle, as though trying to convey some private message to her. But what? Was he threatening her? Warning her? Maybe he didn't want her to tell the others she'd met him before.

Well, that was all right. She didn't want to tell anybody anything. Every one of these people scared her, even Gladys.

The discussion was still raging when three more people crowded into the kitchen, demanding to know what was going on, and the story of Myrtle's capture and the controversy over her disposal was told all over again. These were two men and a woman, but neither man was the one who'd come raging and angry to pull Doug away from Myrtle's front porch that time. So how many people were there in this . . .

. . . gang.

It's a gang, Myrtle thought. I've been kidnapped by a gang. But what in heaven's name is a gang doing in *Dudson Center*?

The woman who'd just arrived, a taller and younger and friendlier-seeming person than Gladys, said at one point, "I wonder if I should phone John, see if he has any ideas for what to do."

"*My* idea is," Tom Jimson told her, "Al's out of this story,"

"The attic," Tiny said, quiet but emphatic. "Wally's right."

There was general agreement on this, except of course for Tom Jimson, who said, "I'll tell you one thing, and listen with all your ears. If she gets away, it's dynamite. *Now*."

"Okay, okay, okay," everybody said, and then they all gestured to Myrtle, a little impatient and irritated with her. "Come on, come on," they all said, and the whole crowd escorted her upstairs.

CHAPTER SIXTY-EIGHT

The warlord and the princess do not recognize each other!

The princess, stolen by gypsies/crows/Merlin/the childless peasant woman, will have a birthmark in an intimate location.

Not in Real Life. Or, even if she does, it doesn't matter, because there isn't any inheritance.

A princess has her father's realm. A warlord has a cache of valuables.

Oh, the money in the reservoir. I think Tom intends to take that with him. The point is, the princess is in peril!

Naturally.

I arranged to have her placed under my protection.

Naturally.

And now I wait, and I'm patient, and I see what transpires, isn't that right?

Naturally.

CHAPTER SIXTY-NINE

When Dortmunder opened one eye, *everything* was wrong. Opening the second eye didn't improve the situation. He was still in the same condition, lying on the floor in the living room, facing a television set on which Raquel Welch wore a lab coat and discussed microbiology. Raquel Welch. Microbiology. *Micro*biology.

Feet. Feet entered the living room, dressed in scuffed old brown boots and raggedy-cuffed faded blue jeans. Seeing the feet, Dortmunder realized it had been the opening of the apartment door that awakened him, and then he remembered it all: 1) Guffey. 2) Tom/Tim Jimson/Jepson. 3) Handcuffs. 4) Pizza, which Guffey had gone out for.

"Got it," Guffey announced from way up there above the feet.

"Great." Dortmunder used his left hand to push himself to a seated position, since his right wrist was through a loop of the handcuffs, whose other loop was closed around a segment of the radiator. Dortmunder felt dizzy, woozy, and now he recalled that the reason Guffey had gone out for pizza in the first place was because they both had begun to feel they'd put somewhat too much beer into empty stomachs.

Companionably, Guffey opened the pizza box on the floor, within easy reach of Dortmunder's left hand, and then said, "I got us some more beer, too."

"Good."

Guffey also sat on the floor, democratically, and they both rested their backs against the sofa while they ate pizza and drank beer and watched

370

Raquel Welch run around inside somebody's bloodstream. She was in a jumpsuit now, more sensibly, but she was still talking about microbiology.

After a while, Guffey said wistfully, "You know, John, this is about the nicest party I've been to in, oh, forty, uh, lemme think, forty-four years."

"Well, it's not a real party, Guffey," Dortmunder pointed out. "It's just the two of us."

"For me," Guffey told him, "two's a crowd."

"Yeah, I guess so."

They sat in easy silence together awhile longer, and then, during a National Guard commercial—it was really very late at night, damn near morning already—Guffey said doubtfully, "Maybe it's Matt."

"You think so?"

"I dunno. Try me on it."

Filling his voice with enthusiasm and good cheer—or at least giving it the old dropout try—Dortmunder said, "Hey, Matt, whadaya say? How ya doing, Matt? Hey, look, fellas, it's Matt Guffey!"

Guffey listened to all that, listened to the echoes, thought it over, then shook his head. "Don't think so," he said.

"It'll come to you," Dortmunder assured him.

"Yeah, sure it will."

That had been a kind of embarrassing moment, much earlier this evening, when Dortmunder, in a psychologically clever ploy to get Guffey to relax his vigil and lower his guard, had said, "Listen, if we're gonna be stuck together a couple days, let's at least be friendly. My name's John." And it had turned out that Guffey couldn't remember his first name.

Well, you couldn't blame the guy, really. For the last couple of decades, nobody had talked directly to Guffey at all, and during the prison years prior to that people all called one another by their last names to demonstrate how manly they really were despite whatever sexual practices incarceration might have reduced them to, so it had probably been some time in the waning days of the Second World War that anybody had last addressed Guffey by his first name.

Guffey had been embarrassed, of course, at this lapse in his memory, and Dortmunder had volunteered to help him find the missing name, so now Guffey spent a part of his time—that part not learning about microbiology—thinking about potential names, and whenever he came across one that seemed a possibility Dortmunder would try it out on him. So far, no success.

A while later, the microbiology movie came to an end and Guffey managed to get to his feet on the second try and go over to switch around the channels till he found Raquel Welch again, this time not discussing anything at all because she was a cavewoman.

The lack of discussion didn't seem to harm the impact of the picture. "Sam. Try Sam."

"Hey, Sam! Sam Guffey! Come over here, Sam!"

"Nope. Makes me sound like a dog."

After another little period of time, Dortmunder came out of a half snooze to realize he had to make room for more beer. (The pizza was all gone, but a couple beers were left.) "Guffey," he said.

Guffey looked away from the prehistoric landscapes. "Nurm?"

"Listen, Guffey," Dortmunder said. "I gotta go the bathroom."

"Gee, so do I," said Guffey.

"Yeah, but I'm, uh, I got this, this *thing* here. The whatchamacallit."

"Oh, *that* thing," Guffey said, and frowned.

In previous similar circumstances, Guffey had sat across the room and tossed the key to Dortmunder, who'd unlocked the cuffs and tossed the key back before Guffey permitted him to go away to the bathroom. Then it had been Dortmunder's responsibility, under Guffey's watchful gaze and steady rifle, to lock himself to the cuffs again on his return.

But this time, Guffey made no move to get up and cross the room to where the rifle leaned against an armchair. "Listen, Guffey," Dortmunder said. "It's kind of urgent."

Guffey frowned at Dortmunder, doubling every wrinkle on his wrinkled face. He said, "You won't try to run away, will you?"

"Run? I can barely walk."

"Here, take the goddamn thing," Guffey said, and yanked the handcuff key from his pocket and slapped it into Dortmunder's palm.

"Thanks, Guffey," Dortmunder said, the gravity of the occasion causing him to pay insufficient attention to what Guffey had just done. So he simply unlocked the cuffs, climbed the sofa and the wall to his feet, and lurched a circuitous route to the doorway and the hall and the bathroom.

While he was in there, Guffey's voice sounded from the other side of the door: "Try Jack."

"Hey, Jack!" Dortmunder yelled, trying to keep his aim true on a sneakily shifting bowl. "I'm fulla beer, Jack! Hey, Jack Guffey, you fulla beer?"

No answer. Dortmunder finished, flushed, washed, opened the door, and Guffey was standing there, nodding slowly, his eyes at half mast. "No," he said, "and yes."

Dortmunder went back to the living room and sat on the floor in front of the sofa but didn't put the cuffs back on. He gazed at the Neanderthals—what casting!—and then at the rifle leaning against the armchair beside the television set, and thought things over. He *could* move, if he wanted to, no question about that. He just didn't want to, that's all.

After a while, Guffey came back into the room, bouncing off the doorposts. He gazed blearily at Dortmunder. Sounding maybe worried, maybe dangerous, certainly drunk, he said, "You didn't put the cuffs on."

"No, I didn't," Dortmunder told him. "And I didn't grab the rifle either. What the hell, Guffey. Any enemy of Tom's is a friend of mine. Come over here and watch the movie."

CHAPTER SEVENTY

What Doug was, was terrified. Petrified. He had so many things to be terrified about that it petrified him just to try to list them all. That after they let Myrtle go she'd report him to the authorities, for instance. Or that they wouldn't let her go, but instead would do something dreadful to her and he'd be a party to it. Or that Tom would do something awful to everybody else at the last minute in order to keep all the money for himself. Or that after all these assaults on the reservoir the authorities would have the place staked out and would arrest everybody the minute they showed up for the fourth and final attempt. That Stan Murch, once more at the wheel of Doug's pickup (because Doug was too nervous to drive), might take it into his head to do another three-sixty just for the high-spirited fun of it. That Andy Kelp, seated on Doug's other side in the pickup on this run to Long Island, would realize he was proficient enough now to do the rest of the job himself and didn't need Doug anymore, and so would unload him profitless from the job, via methods ranging from telling him to get lost to killing him.

But all of these paled into insignificance beside the big one, the main fear, the thing he was at this particular moment the most terrified about, which was: he was going to steal a boat.

A crime. A felony. An active robbery or theft, in which he was *the principal figure*. Or at least that's the way it would look to the law. True, his companions in crime were hardened criminals while he was still so soft he was practically runny, but in fact *his* expertise was necessary to the selection of just the right boat; *his* equipment from *his* shop would fill out the required gear; *his* pickup truck would tow the stolen boat halfway across New York State; and *he* would be *present* throughout the entire event.

Not that he wanted to be, God knows. He didn't want to have anything to do with this entire operation. And yet, here he was. At just around the same time that—unknown to those in the pickup—Dortmunder and Guffey were sociably and comfortably observing Raquel Welch in that cozy living room in Manhattan, here was Doug in the middle of the seat of his pickup, flanked by these hardened criminals here, and heading toward his first major crime through a pelting rain that even *sounded* like doom, thundering on the pickup's tin roof.

Somehow or other, by a wandering and purposeless journey he barely remembered and had never understood, Doug's very first purchase of off-the-back-of-the-truck merchandise from Mikey Donelli (or Donnelly) had led, by minuscule gradations and unnoticeable slippages and the tiniest of forward steps, to *this*: piracy. On dry land.

Well, not that dry, really; it was raining just as hard here on Long Island as back upstate. "This is good for us," Andy announced. "Nobody's gonna be out and about to observe us."

"It's a well-known fact," Murch added, racing them along a Long Island Expressway that was virtually empty for almost the only time in that clogged roadway's existence, "that cops are afraid of water. They never come out in weather like this. That's why we can make such good time."

Very good time, unfortunately. The sign for the Sagtikos Parkway loomed out of the wet dark, and Murch took the ramp and swung them around onto the southbound highway without in the least slackening speed, leaving a double wake and a million dancing water specks in the oversoaked air behind them.

From there it was a quick run down to the south shore, Doug's home area, where they would find their boat. (In one way, it seemed kind of dumb to do his first major criminal act in his own back yard, but on the other hand it would be even dumber to do it where he didn't know the territory. Also, this way he could get back at a boat dealer who'd shafted him half a dozen years ago, too far back for anybody to think of Doug in connection with that dealer now.)

The Sagtikos took them to Merrick Highway, and then Doug directed them along that shopping artery through its various name permutations in several identical little south shore towns (identical even by day, when it wasn't raining) until at last he pointed to the left, across the empty road, and said, "There's the son of a bitch, right there."

It was a revelation to see how professionals handled themselves in this situation; much, he supposed, as he handled himself when working underwater. The danger simply made you more methodical.

While Murch waited in the pickup, Andy and Doug got out into the pouring rain and Andy collected the short stepladder from the bed of the pickup. Then he and Doug approached the boat dealership, a long two-story building with large showroom and repair shop downstairs and offices up, plus a good-sized yard down at one end containing a number of new and repaired boats and enclosed by a chain-link fence with razor wire on the top.

Stopping in front of the triply bolted double gate in this fence, Andy peered into the darkness of the yard and said, "Where's this dog, do you suppose?"

"Maybe he's afraid of water," Doug suggested. "He's a police dog."

"Well, he'll be along," Andy said, and opened the stepladder and climbed to its top. While Doug watched, he used the rubber-cowled alligator clips on the long length of wire to bypass the alarm system and make it possible to open the gate.

The dog, half German shepherd and half crocodile, came trotting out from under a large boat as Andy started picking the first of the padlocks. He didn't bark, but simply looked at Andy and Doug the way heavyweight boxers look at each other. "Nice doggy," Andy said, and took the aluminum foil package from his pocket. "Here's a nice gift for you from Mickey Finn," he said, opening the foil. Putting it on the pavement and using his boot-shod foot, he nudged the hamburger patty on its foil bed under the bottom of the gate and into the dog's realm.

The dog sniffed once, chomped once, and the meat and half the aluminum foil disappeared.

Doug winced. "How can he do that?" he said, "D'jever get aluminum foil on your teeth? It's *terrible*."

"You know what's worse than that?" Andy asked, returning to the padlock. "Eating a grapefruit and drinking milk at the same time."

Oog; that *was* worse. Doug decided not to try to outgross Andy, and so the lock-picking was finished in silence, during which the dog wandered unsteadily back under the large boat and went to sleep.

What a complex moment it was for Doug when at last Andy pulled open the swinging gates! Mad elation swirled in tandem with redoubled terror in his brain, leaving him so shaken he almost lost his balance and fell when he stepped onto the boat dealer's property. But he clutched at the breached gate for support, regained control, and went on to study the available boats while Andy put the stepladder back in the bed of the pickup, which Murch then backed into the yard.

"This one," Doug had decided when Andy rejoined him.

Andy looked up at it. "Gee, Doug, we don't wanna go to *Europe*."

"This boat won't sink in the rain," Doug told him. "It's quieter than an outboard. We can do the winching right *on* it."

Andy said, "You mean, bring the box up and put it on the boat?"

"Yes. Much easier, Andy."

"Gee, Doug, I think you're right," Andy said. "At night, in the rain, nobody's gonna see us anyway. So why not be comfortable, right?"

"Sleeps two," Doug told him, and couldn't repress a giggle. The mad elation combined with a completely unexpected exhilaration were beginning at last to conquer his fear.

"Is that right? Sleeps two?" Andy stepped back and surveyed the boat with a kind of proprietary pride. "Pretty good, Doug," he agreed. "Pretty good."

And it was. The boat Doug had selected, already strapped to a three-wheel hauler, was a twenty-four-foot Benjamin inboard cabin cruiser with a Fiberglas top and Lucite sides around the wheelhouse amidships, an open deck at the rear, and a narrow cabin below in front containing two single-person sleeping sofas, minimal kitchen facilities, and a very basic head. In comparison with the *QEII*, say, it was merely a tiny pleasure craft for weekend fishermen, but in comparison with their previous rubber raft it was the *QEII*.

Nodding happily in the rain, Andy said, "Stan's gonna have a lot of fun towing this upstate."

Startled, Doug said, "Andy? Stan, he won't, uh, my truck . . ."

Andy reassuringly patted him on the arm. "Don't worry, Doug," he said. "Stan'll be good. I'll *tell* him to be good."

"Uh," said Doug.

CHAPTER SEVENTY-ONE

Myrtle awoke to a scratching sound. She opened her eyes and saw that it hadn't been just a bad dream, after all. It had been true and real. The monster called Tiny, the tough gang members, her own icy-eyed father, all real, and she in their grasp, imprisoned here on this narrow old canvas cot in the attic of the house on Oak Street, under one holey sheet and one threadbare blanket, with a lumpy pillow under her head and a lock on the door.

It was amazing, really, that she'd been able to sleep at all. The cot was so *lumpy*, with one giant hard bump in particular, in the small of her back, that she just hadn't been able to either prod out of the canvas or ignore. And there was also her situation, of course, as desperate as it could be, with the gang downstairs including among its members two people—Doug and Wally—that she'd thought of at one time as her friends, in their very different ways. Friendly, in any case.

So the fact that sleep had come to her at *any* time in the course of this night was just a proof of her exhaustion in the face of all this peril. And now, some sort of scratching noise had awakened her. Rats? Ooo!

Staring around at the bare wide-planked floor, Myrtle saw no rats, saw nothing alive or moving at all. Then she realized what it must be: rain. Very dim light showed at the one window in the end wall, meaning it must now be very shortly after dawn, and in that gray light she watched the raindrops pelt the window glass as hard and unceasing as ever.

So it was the rain, that's all; too early to wake up. Myrtle closed her eyes again, and listened, and heard the scratching sound once more, and it came *from the other direction*. Not from the window at all. From the other way.

Reluctantly, Myrtle opened her eyes and looked the other way. Down there was the unfinished interior wall, closing off this room at the end of the attic. Centered in the wall was the old wooden door with its old worn brass round knob.

Skritch. Skritch. Someone was at the door.

Myrtle sat up on the creaky old cot. Though she'd slept in all her clothes—wouldn't you?—she held the ragged sheet and blanket up to her throat as she stared wide-eyed toward the door.

Who is it? She whispered that: "Who is it?"

Skritch. Skritch.

Well, she hadn't slept in *all* her clothes. Tentatively putting her legs over the side of the cot, she felt around with her toes, found her shoes, slipped them on, and *now* was completely dressed. As armored as possible under the circumstances, she crept across the rough wood floor and bent her ear to the door. "Hello?"

"Myrtle!" An excited but unidentifiable whisper.

"Who is it?"

"Wally!"

She recoiled. The mastermind! Her own whisper became increasingly sibilant, with falsetto breakthroughs: "What do you want?"

"I don't dare rescue you yet!"

She frowned at the wood panel of the door: *"What?"*

"Tonight," his faint whisper came, "when they've all gone— Myrtle?"

"Yesss?"

"Can you hear me?"

"I think so," she whispered.

"Get down by the keyhole!"

Poison gas. Pygmy dart in her eye. Bending nearer the keyhole but not all the way in front of it, she whispered, "I can hear you."

"Tonight," came that rustle of his whisper, "they'll all be going to the reservoir."

Devil cults, black masses. Mass poisonings. "Why?"

He ignored that (of course!). "Only May and Murch's Mom and I will be here. The compu—"

"Who?"

"The two ladies." Then, his whisper somehow closer, more insinuating, as though his astral person had shinnied through the keyhole and up onto her shoulder, he asked, "Is her name really Gladys?"

"I don't know anything anymore," Myrtle wailed, half whispered and half in that screechy falsetto. "I don't know what anybody's *doing*, I don't know anybody's real name—"

"You know *my* real name."

"Do I?"

"And I know yours."

That brought her up short. She leaned her palm against the door, its wooden surface surprisingly warm and comforting to her touch. Her mind ran like watercolors.

"Myrtle?"

Nobody can be trusted, she thought hopelessly. Not even me. Bending closer to the keyhole, she whispered, "No, you don't."

"I don't what?"

"Know my real name. My real name is Myrtle Street."

"That's where you *live*."

"That's partly why I lied. And partly, just before I met you, I just found out Tom Jimson's my, my, my . . . father."

"You just found out?"

"You're the only person I ever said that name to. And now that I've *seen* Tom Jimson . . ."

His whisper awash in sympathy, Wally told her, "I guess he's not much what people think of when they think 'father.'"

"I sure hope not," Myrtle whispered back.

"Well, listen. The computer says we can rescue each other!"

"Wally," she whispered, bending closer and closer to the keyhole (oh, chink!), "who do you talk to when you use the computer?"

"What do you mean?"

"Where is it *connected*?"

"It's just plugged in," he whispered, sounding baffled. "Like any computer."

"You aren't giving orders to a gang? Or getting orders from a boss? Or anything like that?"

"Well, gee, no. Myrtle, it isn't a VDT, not like your terminal at the library, it isn't connected to a mainframe anywhere."

"It isn't?"

"No, honest. It's my personal personal computer."

Could she believe him? *What* could she believe? What *could* she believe? And, given her present circumstances, what did it matter what she did or did not believe? She whispered, "Wally, I don't know what's going on."

"I'll tell you," he promised. "Tonight, they're all going out to the reservoir to get some money that's hidden there. I think Tom's going to try to cheat everybody once they get the money."

Well, *that* sounded believable. Myrtle whispered, "Then what?"

"Tom might come back here to, uh, make trouble."

Myrtle had the feeling she knew what he meant. She had a quick vision of herself pleading for mercy—*I'm your daughter!*—and she pressed herself closer to the door, imagining the little, squat, round, moist, *reliable* form of Wally Knurr on its other side. "What should I do?"

"After everybody else leaves," he whispered, "I'll get you out of there and we'll go over to your house. We'll be able to see what happens from there."

My house. *My* house. No other part of the plan mattered. "That's wonderful, Wally," Myrtle whispered, patting the door. "I'll be waiting, whenever you say. I'll be right here."

CHAPTER SEVENTY-TWO

M ore coffee?"

"Yeah."

"Another English muffin?"

"Yeah."

"Marmalade again?"

"Yeah, yeah. Okay? Yeah!"

"Fine, fine, fine. Listen, try Frank."

"Frank? You think so? Okay: Hey, Frank! I *always* want marmalade on my English muffin, Frank! Hey, Frank Guffey, you got that?"

Guffey, watching the English muffins in the toaster oven little by little turn brown, like Larry Talbot becoming the wolfman, pondered and pondered and then shook his head. "No," he said. "I wouldn't be a Frank."

"I didn't think so, either," Dortmunder admitted.

"I might of been better off if I *was* a Frank," Guffey decided, taking out the English muffins and going to work on them with the marmalade. "More self-assertive. Not so much of a patsy."

"Hey, Patsy!" Dortmunder called. "Give me more marmalade, Patsy! Hey, Patsy Guffey, bring that English muffin over here."

"Could be my sister," Guffey said, bringing the plates over to the kitchen table, where Dortmunder sat hunched over his planted elbows, contemplating his hangover. Guffey went back to the counter for the coffee cups, brought them over, and placed them on the Formica with two loud *ticks* that made Dortmunder flinch.

They sat in silence together while the kitchen clock moved from three-twenty P.M. to three-forty P.M. without anybody noticing or caring. Then, Dortmunder, lifting his head and his eyes while draining the last of his now lukewarm coffee, noticed the clock and found himself thinking about what was or was not going on upstate. Putting down his cup (*tick*, flinch), he said, "I think I'm gonna phone them."

Guffey looked semialert. "Oh, yeah? Oh, yeah?"

"*You* make more coffee," Dortmunder told him. "I go to the living room and make my phone call."

"Hey, come on, Dortmunder," Guffey said. (He wouldn't use Dortmunder's first name, he'd announced, until he found his own.) "That isn't fair."

"I'm not trying to be fair," Dortmunder said, getting with some difficulty to his feet. "I'm trying to protect my interests."

"Well, *I* got interests, too," Guffey exclaimed.

"Not that *I* am trying to protect," Dortmunder told him. "I don't want you listening when I make my call." Then, seeing Guffey try to be surreptitious about looking around the kitchen, he smirked a little, as much as his hangover would permit, and said, "No, there aren't any extensions, though a particular friend of mine keeps trying to load them on me. I always said no, I didn't want the goddamn things, and now I'm gonna be very happy to tell him I know *why*."

Sitting at the table, Guffey shook his head and said, "Somehow or other, I lost the advantage around here. I mean, I *had* it. I had the rifle in my hands, I had the drop on you, I had you scared shitless, I had—"

"Well."

"Never mind 'well,'" Guffey told him. "I had you scared shitless, admit it."

"You had me worried for a while," Dortmunder allowed. "But we're both reasonable men, so we worked things out. Or we're *working* things out. Like right now, I'm gonna make my phone call and you're gonna make more coffee."

"It isn't that I'm reasonable," Guffey was saying, as Dortmunder left the room, "it's that it always happens that way. I *always* lose the advantage. It's a hell of a thing to live with."

In the living room, Dortmunder called the number up in Dudson Center, hoping May would answer, and astonishingly enough it was May who answered. Recognizing her voice, he said, "May, it's me."

"John! Where are you?"

"Home, like I said I'd be."

"Safe at home," she said, sounding wistful.

Looking at the rifle, which still leaned against the wall beside the television set, Dortmunder said, "Well, kinda safe. Safer now, anyway. What's happening up there?"

"John," May said, all at once sounding excited, even admiring, "Stan and Andy and Doug came back with a *boat*! It's *huge*! You wouldn't believe how big it is!"

"Oh, yeah?"

"John, it sleeps two!"

"Sleeps two!" Dortmunder, visualizing the *QEII*, said, "What are they gonna do with it? Is it gonna go in the reservoir?"

"John," May said, "it's going to look like a toy boat in a bathtub. But Doug says it's better, it's quieter than an outboard motor and they can put the winch right on the boat and winch the box straight up out of the water and take it to shore on the boat."

"Well, that part sounds okay," Dortmunder admitted.

"On the other hand," May said, lowering her voice, "we've had a little trouble around here."

"Tom?"

"Not yet. He *will* be trouble, but not yet."

"What, then?"

"There's a girl," May said. "Tiny found her peeking in the kitchen window. Turns out, she's the girl Doug's been seeing up here, and she was spying, and she knows a *lot* about us. And her mother's the one Murch's Mom's been playing canasta with. John, did you know Murch's Mom's name was Gladys?"

"Go on."

"No, it really is. Anyway, that's what she told this girl's mother that she plays canasta with."

Dortmunder said, "Wait a minute. Tiny found the daughter spying?"

"Looking in the kitchen window."

"Then what?"

"Well, one thing led to another, and now she's locked in the attic until we're finished."

"And then what?"

"Well, *we* say we let her go. I don't know what Tom says."

Dortmunder could guess. He said, "What about her mother? Won't she call the cops when her daughter doesn't come home? Won't they *first* look around the neighborhood?"

"We made her call home last night," May said, "and say she was going away overnight with Doug. I listened on the extension, and—"

"Huh," Dortmunder said.

"What?"

"Never mind, something I'll tell you later about extensions. What happened next?"

"Well, John, I was *astonished* at that mother, let me tell you. The daughter—her name's Myrtle *Street*, would you believe it?"

"Why not?"

"Because she lives on *Myrtle* Street."

"Oh. No kidding."

"Anyway, her mother said, 'Good. About time you got your blood moving.' Did you ever hear such a thing?"

"Weird," Dortmunder agreed.

"*Then* she wanted to talk to Doug. The mother did. So Doug got on, expecting to have to say how he was going to respect the daughter and all that, and the mother wanted to talk to him about *condoms*."

"Ah," Dortmunder said.

"I don't know who was more embarrassed, the girl or Doug. Particularly since, you know, nothing like that was going on anyway. Apparently, Doug hasn't been too successful with this girl. So she wasn't even spending the night with him, she was spending the night locked in the attic."

"I don't know, May," Dortmunder said. "That doesn't sound to me like a good situation up there."

"Well, it'll be over soon," May said. "And John, I do understand your feelings about all this, I'm not going to argue with you or try to change your mind or anything, but we sure could use you up here."

"What *I* think is," Dortmunder said, "I think everybody should just walk away from it right now."

"That's impossible, John, you know that. Besides, they're going to go do it tonight, and then it'll be all over with. One way or the other."

"It's the other that bothers me," Dortmunder said. "You keep your back against the wall, May."

"I will. And I'll see you tomorrow, John."

Dortmunder was very thoughtful when he went back to the kitchen, where Guffey offered him a fresh cup of coffee, plus two more names to try: Harry and Jim. Neither did the trick, and then Dortmunder said, "Guffey, I'm gonna have to go up there."

Guffey looked alert. "Up where?"

"Not near the water," Dortmunder said. "Just to the town."

"What town?"

"Now, here's the deal," Dortmunder went on. "If you wait until Tom's got his money, then maybe Tom gets away and you don't get to meet up with him at all. Which is maybe just as well."

Guffey rested a scrawny fist on the kitchen table. "That man ruint my life," he said. "And I mean that, Dortmunder. I was just a young fella when he got his hooks into me, and he ruint my entire life. My *destiny* is to catch up with that son of a bitch, or why would you and him come all the way out to Cronley, Oklahoma? What happens after I catch up is between him and me, but I *got* to have him in my sights one time before I die."

"I guess I can understand that," Dortmunder said. "So this is what I offer. You give me your solemn word you won't make a move on Tom until this other business is over with, and you can come along with me upstate."

"Where to?"

"But you have to swear you won't do anything till I say it's okay."

Guffey thought about that. "What if I won't swear?"

"Then I go out to the living room and get your rifle," Dortmunder told him, "and bring it back in here, and wrap it around your neck, and go upstate by myself."

Guffey thought about *that*. "What if I swear, only I'm lying?"

"I got a lot of friends up there where I'm going, Guffey," Dortmunder said. "And all you got up there's one enemy."

CHAPTER SEVENTY-THREE

It hadn't been easy for Andy Kelp to find a large station wagon with *both* MD plates and a trailer hitch, but he'd persevered, not settling for second best, and so it was a big solid Chrysler Country Square with woodoid trim that he sat in the front passenger seat of as Stan Murch steered off the county road an hour after alleged sunset that wet evening, towing the big boat (containing Doug, back there familiarizing himself with the controls) onto the same dirt lane they'd used for their very first assault on the reservoir, months ago. "*This* time we get it!" Kelp said. "I can feel it!"

Tiny got out of the backseat he was sharing with Tom. Carrying the wire cutters through the pouring rain, he lopped the new padlock at the same old barrier, then lifted the barrier out of the way. "*Another* déjà vu," he muttered as he put the barrier back in position after car and boat had passed, then returned to his place in the wagon.

Last time on this road, in the motor home, Kelp had been the driver, mostly by ear, keeping the lights off and the windows open so he could listen to the bushes as they scraped past. This time, the downpour meant not only that no one in the car had any desire for the windows to be open, but also that Stan felt he could safely drive with the parking lights on. The rain both obscured the lights and lessened the likelihood of observers wandering the nearby vicinity. So the windshield wipers slashed back and forth, flinging water left and right, and through the sporadically clear glass they could dimly see the rutted dirt road and its surrounding trees and shrubbery, all muddily illuminated in a smoky amber glow.

After a while they reached, and this time saw, the second barrier, at the reservoir property's perimeter fence, the one Kelp had not quite driven into the first time. Tiny climbed out again and cleared the way again, and when he got back into the car, dumping the wire cutters onto the carpet-covered storage space in back, he said, "I might as well *go* underwater this time. I couldn't get any wetter."

"Soon be over," Kelp told him.

"That's right," Tom said mildly.

● ● ●

"According to the computer," Wally said, "as soon as they get their hands on the money, Tom is going to try to betray everybody."

"I'm afraid that's true," May agreed.

Murch's Mom sniffed. "You don't have to be a machine smarter than a human being to dope *that* out," she said.

May said, "The guys out there with Tom know he's got something in mind. They'll keep an eye on him."

"That's right," Murch's Mom said. "They aren't creampuffs, you know. My boy Stanley can take care of himself."

"And Tiny," May said. "And Andy."

Wally cleared his throat. "Just in case," he said.

Murch's Mom gave him an irritable look. "Are you talking against my boy Stanley?"

"What I'm saying is," Wally assured her, "we ought to think about all the possibilities. That's what the computer says we should do, and I agree with it."

"You always agree with that computer," Murch's Mom told him. "You got a real mutual admiration society going there, that's why you keep it around."

May said, "Wally, what are you getting at? What possibilities?"

"Well," Wally said, "let's just say Tom does something really underhanded and nasty—"

"Sounds right," Murch's Mom said.

"And let's just say," Wally went on, "that he *wins*. He's got the money and he's, you know, harmed our friends."

"Killed them, you mean," May said.

"I don't really like to *say* that."

"But it's what you mean."

Wally looked pained. "Uh-huh."

"Hmp," said Murch's Mom. But then she shook her head and said, "All right, go ahead, what then?"

"Well, that's the question," Wally told her. "Is Tom just going to take the money and run? Or is he going to say to himself, 'I don't want any witnesses left behind?'"

May looked at the storm-battered front windows. "You mean he might come back here."

"The computer thinks so."

Murch's Mom said, "And you agree with it."

"So do I," May said. She looked very worried.

Wally said, "And then there's Myrtle."

Both women were taken aback by this abrupt change of subject. Murch's Mom said, "Myrtle? That little ninny upstairs? What's she got to do with anything?"

"Well, that's just it," Wally said. "Nothing."

"That's what I figured," Murch's Mom agreed.

"What I mean is," Wally told her, "the rest of us got into this because we wanted to, we *chose* to be here. But Myrtle didn't. And if her father comes back and—"

May said, "Who?"

"Tom's her father," Wally said. Nodding at Murch's Mom, he said, "That lady Edna you play canasta with—"

"The girl's mother. I know."

"She worked in the library in Putkin's Corners when Tom buried the casket behind it. She was the one told him they weren't going to put in the parking lot after all. And her father was the town undertaker; it was from him that Tom got the casket."

May said, "Why didn't Tom *say* anything when Tiny caught her?"

"He doesn't know. And I don't think he'd care."

Nodding thoughtfully, Murch's Mom said, "Not a sentimental kind of guy, Tom."

May said, "Wally? Do you and your computer have an idea what we should do?"

"Go to Myrtle's house."

They stared at him. May said, "For heaven's sake, why?"

"It's just one block over," Wally explained. "We can *see* this house from there. If we turn off all these lights and go over there, then we can keep an eye on this house, and when the lights turn back on I'll come over and look in the window and make sure everything's okay."

May said, "Doesn't this mean letting Myrtle and her mother in on the whole thing?"

"Well, Myrtle's already in on a lot of it," Wally pointed out. "And her mother already knows Gladys, and—"

"I don't particularly," Murch's Mom said through gritted teeth, "like that name."

"Oh." Wally blinked. "Okay, sorry. Anyway, you know Myrtle's mother, and *she* knows Tom's in town. She saw him go by in a car, and that's what started Myrtle trying to find out things."

May and Murch's Mom looked at each other. Murch's Mom said, "Well? What do you think?"

"I think I wish John was here," May said.

• • •

"There's *never* anybody home in this goddamn place," Dortmunder said, fifteen minutes later, as he and Guffey pulled to the curb in front of the darkened 46 Oak Street. Sitting behind the wheel of the Peugeot Dormant he'd borrowed three hours ago from a cross street in the theater district back in New York, Dortmunder gazed discontentedly through the rain at the house where half the people he knew were supposed to be in residence, and where not one light was shining. Not one.

"Something wrong?" Guffey'd been getting increasingly nervy over the course of the trip, which could only be partially explained by the miserable highway conditions and Dortmunder's less than professional driving skills. He hadn't offered any first names for Dortmunder to try since way down by exit 2 on the Palisades Parkway. (George: No.) And now he sat hunched beside Dortmunder, chin tucked in as he blinked out at the night and the rain and the old dark house. He looked like one of the three little pigs watching for the wolf; the straw-house pig.

"Well, I suppose something's wrong," Dortmunder answered. "Something's *usually* wrong. So what we're gonna do, you stick close to me, and we're gonna go in there and *not* turn on any lights."

"Uh-huh."

"And we'll see what we see."

Guffey frowned. "With the lights off?"

"Yes," Dortmunder said. "We'll see what we see with the lights off. Out."

They got out of the car into the downpour and ran to the comparative safety of the porch. Guffey shied at the sight of the glider swinging back and forth with nobody on it. Approaching the door, Dortmunder muttered, "*Last* time they left the place a hundred percent unlocked. Quiet, now."

Guffey, who hadn't been saying anything, remained quiet.

Dortmunder gently opened the screen door, gently turned the knob of the inner door, gently pushed, and the door yawned open. Dortmunder slid silently in, followed by Guffey, and they quietly closed both doors.

"Stick close to me," Dortmunder mouthed into Guffey's ear, and Guffey nodded, a movement barely visible in the faint glow that was all that could reach here through the rain from the nearest streetlight.

They moved through the house, found nothing, found nobody, and found no explanation. "I should have known this," Dortmunder said aloud, back in the living room, Guffey still so close to his right elbow it was like wearing a sleeve guard.

"You should have?" Guffey asked. "Should have known what?"

"That I'd have to give that reservoir one more whack at me," Dortmunder said.

• • •

Soft ground. Heavy boat. Stan finally got the station wagon and boat turned around in the restricted area of the clearing at the end of the access road, but when he tried to ease down the muddy slope into the water everything immediately bogged down. The two rear wheels of the hauler virtually disappeared into the mud, and the rear wheels of the station wagon spun messily in place.

"Well, hell," Stan said. "Everybody out."

"Hell it is," Tiny agreed, and everybody but Stan climbed out into the rain and the dark and the mud and the mess and a kind of nasty little needle-tipped wind.

The station wagon was lighter now, but the boat was still heavy and all the wheels were still stuck. Kelp and Tiny pushed against the front of the wagon while Tom stood off to the side and observed. The wagon's big engine wailed and whined in competition with the wailing and whining of the storm, but nothing happened except that the pushers got extremely muddy.

Finally, Stan put the wagon in neutral, opened his window, and called Kelp and Tiny over. They slogged around to talk to him, looking like the defensive line in the final quarter of a particularly hard-fought football game, and Stan said, "We aren't getting anywhere."

Tiny said, "You noticed that, too, huh?"

"What we gotta do," Stan said, "is get up on dry land and start again."

"There isn't any dry land," Kelp told him.

"Drier," Stan explained. "A little more solid, I mean. If I get up there all the way to where the road comes in, up at the top of the clearing, then I can get up some speed, run it backward fast as I can, get some momentum on shoving that goddamn boat into the water."

"Without jackknifing," Kelp pointed out.

"I gotta give it the try," Stan said.

"Very tricky on this messy surface," Kelp suggested.

Tiny said, "I hate having ideas like this, because I know who they make work for, which is me, but I think maybe we oughta drag it up to the end of the clearing like you say, and then turn this blessed *car* around and put the trailer hitch on the front bumper instead of the back, so you can drive *frontward* in low-low."

"Now *that* is an idea," Stan told him.

"I was afraid it was," Tiny agreed. "And now I got another one. Doug can get down off that boat and help push."

Kelp grinned at the idea. "Doug'll love that," he said.

"We all will," said Tiny.

They went around to the prow of the boat and yelled at Doug for a while, and after he gave up pretending he didn't understand what they wanted, he very reluctantly came down off his high boat and helped.

At first the station wagon didn't want to move forward either, but then its rear wheels came struggling up out of the holes they'd dug, and the hauler's wheels grudgingly began to lumber along through the mire, and movement took place. At the top of the clearing, Stan brought the wagon and the boat to a stop. The *V* tongue on the hauler was removed from the trailer hitch, and then Tiny lay down in the mud and Kelp stood by to hand him tools while Tiny, his work illuminated by the station wagon's back-up lights, with some difficulty removed the muddy hitch from the muddy bumper. Then Stan turned the wagon around and Tiny bent over the front bumper with the trailer hitch in his hands and studied the situation. "It doesn't want to fit," he decided.

"Make it fit," Kelp advised.

"Yeah, that's what I figured."

Doug, sounding scared, his voice cutting through the ongoing roar of the storm, said, "Stan, turn off your lights!"

Stan didn't ask questions. The heel of his hand slapped the headlight control on the dashboard. Their clearing became abruptly black, pitch black, and they all turned their heads to watch the bright lights approaching down the access road through the rain and the night and the sopping trees.

• • •

"Still no light," Myrtle said, coming back down to the living room from her own bedroom, where she had the best view past the intervening buildings to the house on Oak Street.

"Oh, I think they'll take another hour, maybe even more," Wally told her.

"Plenty of time," Edna said, "to tell me what's going on. Myrtle, you begin."

• • •

"I think I see a car," Dortmunder said, peering through the windshield and out at the storm-tossed night. "They're probably all out on the reservoir in that big boat May told me about."

He braked the car to a stop at the beginning of the clearing. It was hard to see anything at all through the sheets of rain, even with the headlights on; the zillion raindrops just bounced the light right back at you.

Guffey said, "What's three thousand, seven hundred fifty dollars compounded at eight percent interest for forty-three years?"

"I give up," Dortmunder said. "What is it?"

"Well, *I* don't know." Guffey sounded surprised. "That's why I was asking you."

"Oh," Dortmunder said. "I thought it was one of those puzzle things."

"It's what Tim Jepson owes me," Guffey said grimly. "So I figure a lot of that money you say is down there in that reservoir comes to me."

"You can discuss that with Tom," Dortmunder advised him. "And remember, half of it belongs to the rest of us."

"Sure, sure. Sure."

Dortmunder switched off the headlights. "Can't see a goddamn thing," he said.

"Sure you can't," Guffey said. "You turned the lights off."

"I'm looking for *their* lights," Dortmunder told him. "We better get out of the car."

The interior light went on when they opened the doors, illuminating the inside of the car but nothing else, and only making the surrounding blackness all the blacker once the doors were shut.

Dortmunder and Guffey, two bulky huddled figures in the night, met at the front of their car, and Dortmunder pointed past Guffey's nose, putting his hand up close so Guffey could see it. "The reservoir's that way, and I thought I saw a car over there. That's where we'll look."

"Uh," Guffey said, and fell down.

"Uh?" Dortmunder turned, bending, to see what had happened to Guffey, and therefore spoiled Tiny's aim. The sap merely brushed down the side of his head, not quite removing his ear, and bounded painfully off his shoulder. "Ow!" he yelled. "Goddammit, who is that?"

"Dortmunder?" came Tiny's voice out of the dark. "Is that you?"

"Who the hell did you *expect*?"

"Well, we didn't expect nobody, Dortmunder," Tiny said, sounding aggrieved. "Who's this with you?"

Out of the darkness, Tom's voice said, "So you couldn't keep away, huh, Al?"

"Looks like it," Dortmunder admitted.

"Who *is* this guy?" Tiny wanted to know, prodding the fallen Guffey with his toe.

Aware of Guffey's helplessness and of Tom's presence, Dortmunder said, "Um. A hitchhiker."

The others had gathered around now, and it was Kelp who said, "John? You brought a hitchhiker to the caper?"

"Well, I couldn't leave the poor guy out there in the rain," Dortmunder said. At the same time, he was inwardly furious with himself, thinking: Why did I say *hitchhiker*? Well, what else would I say? Aloud, he said, "It's okay, Andy. Trust me, I know what I'm doing. You guys finished already?"

That changed the subject, with a vengeance. Everybody vied to tell him how much fun they were having, even Tom. "Uh-huh, uh-huh," Dortmunder said. "Let's see this monster boat."

After all the build-up, when he finally got face-to-face with the leviathan, it wasn't really that big. On the other hand, it did look as though a person could survive a voyage on it. Looking at it in the splattered gleam of the station wagon's headlights, while Tiny banged the trailer hitch into a shotgun wedding with the front bumper, Dortmunder said, "A lot of boats like this have funny names. Does this one?"

There was a brief awkward silence. Dortmunder turned to Kelp, who was nearest. "Yeah?"

"It has a name," Kelp agreed.

"Yeah?"

Tom, on Dortmunder's other side, did his cackle thing and said, "It's called *Over My Head*."

"Uh-huh," Dortmunder said.

Doug came over and said, "Uh, John, that hitchhiker of yours."

"Yeah?"

"Well, he isn't dead."

"Course not," Tiny said. "I just gave him a lullaby."

"But he is unconscious," Doug said, "and I'm afraid he might drown."

Dortmunder frowned at that. "In the water?"

"In the rain. What should we do with him?"

Kelp said, "Leave him. He'll wake up."

Tom said, "And go straight to the law before we can get finished and outta here. I don't know about you sometimes, Al. Maybe we should just help him drown."

"Aw, hey," Doug said.

Dortmunder said, "He can come with us."

Everybody hated that idea. Dortmunder listened to all the arguments, *wishing* he'd thought of some other explanation for Guffey, and when they were all finished yammering he said, "Put it this way. I don't wanna kill him. We can't leave him. So we'll take him with us. I got reasons with this guy, and I'll explain them later. Tiny, how you coming?"

"Done," Tiny said, lumbering to his feet. "Dortmunder," he commented, "you get weird notions sometimes."

"Maybe so," Dortmunder said. "We'll put him in the boat now, with Doug."

So Guffey's limp light body was picked up by Tiny and handed up to Doug, who would ride the boat out into the water so they wouldn't lose it once it was finally launched.

Which this time at long last happened. Dortmunder, Kelp, Tiny, and Tom all stood to one side; Doug braced himself against the wheel of the *Over My Head*; and Guffey lay like a bag of laundry on the floor around Doug's feet. Stan put the station wagon into low-low, tromped the accelerator, and the double vehicle lunged down the slope. The hauler wobbled left and right, slowing down as it hit the muck, wanting to jackknife, but Stan kept correcting with tiny movements of the wheel, and steadily and inexorably the boat backed down through the mud and the ooze and into the reservoir.

Stan never let up on the accelerator till the headlights were underwater and wavelets were breaking on the hood, and the instant he lifted his foot the engine died; probably never to live again. But the *Over My Head* was, just barely, in water deep enough to float.

Now Doug went to work unattaching the straps that held the boat to the hauler, and Stan climbed through the foundered wagon to exit out the tailgate and go wait in Dortmunder's car. At the same time, Kelp and Tiny and Tom waded out to climb aboard. Halfway there, Kelp looked back: "John? Aren't you coming?"

The rain beat down. The nasty little wind pressed wet clothing against cold flesh. You couldn't even *see* the reservoir out there. But a man's gotta do— Well, you know.

"Shit," said Dortmunder, and waded into the water.

• • •

Edna said, "When I think of the foolish young girl I was then, I could slap my face. And when I think, Myrtle, of the foolish young girl you've *never* been, I could slap both our faces. I know it's partly my fault for stifling any impulse you ever might have had to fly from the nest, and I know it's partly Tom Jimson's fault for turning me into a bitter old woman before my time, but good heavens, girl, don't you have one single rebellious bone in your *body*? Whatever happened to heredity? Don't interrupt when I'm talking. The *point* is, Tom Jimson may, just may, be doing some good for once in his life, even if he didn't intend it and doesn't know about it. If all this hadn't happened, you and I could have just drifted along the same way, day after day, year after year, all the way to the grave, you just another dim little obedient country spinster taking care of her bad-tempered nasty old mama—now just let me *finish*, if you don't mind—but we've been shaken out of that, the two of us, and that's *good*. That diving fella's no good for you, Myrtle, and you know it as well as I do. He's just a paler Tom Jimson, that's all, less coldblooded but just as untrustworthy. If you're going to have your head turned by a pretty face, go right ahead, but *please* try to reassure yourself that there's some sort of reliable brain behind it. Which brings me to you, Wallace. I know your type, and don't think I don't. I used to see little boys like you *all the time* when I ran the library at Putkin's Corners. Intelligent little boys who weren't any good at sports, boys the other children used to make fun of, and they'd come into the library for a refuge and a fantasy. But you aren't a child anymore, Wallace. It's true you're still funny-looking, but most adults are; it's time for you to come out of your shell. Fantasy has led you into dangers you can't possibly deal with, and you know it. Never mind, never mind, there are things that computer of yours doesn't know, either. *I* say it's New York City did it to you, having to lock yourself away for protection all the time, and what *you* should do is move to a *real* place, a good small town where you could get to meet people and know people and be part of the real world. Now, we have that spare room upstairs. Myrtle and I have been talking forever about fixing it up and renting it, and—yes, we have, Myrtle, don't be a goose—and I know Mr. Kempheimer at the bank, I'm *sure* they could use a computer expert there, he's always complaining about modern times, you know how men get. Well, you'll look into that when you make your mind up."

Murch's Mom said, "Edna—"

Edna said, "Now about the money. It's dirty money. I don't care how long it's been in the water, it's still dirty. Myrtle and I don't want any part of it, and you shouldn't want it either, Wallace, and you certainly won't *need* it if you're working at the bank, and however would you report it on your income tax? Gladys, I understand your son is a professional in this sort of thing and therefore he *would* want his share of the money, and I accept it if you say he isn't a vicious monster like Tom Jimson but simply a very good professional driver, but I'm really afraid he should never have gotten involved in this. Tom Jimson will be going to Mexico, all right, and glad to see the back of him, but he'll take *all* that money with him when he goes. Miss Bellamy's friend John was right when he left, and I think your son Stanley should have gone with him, because there is simply no depth to Tom Jimson's wickedness. I'm *sure*, by now, out there on that dark water, he has started doing something terrible."

• • •

Tom went down into the cabin of the *Over My Head* to have a look around. The curtains had been shut over the windows down here and one dim light over the sink switched on, in which glow he saw they'd put Dortmunder's hitchhiker, still out cold, on the sofa where Tom had stashed the Ingram Model 10 when he'd left the house briefly and surreptitiously much earlier today. That was all right; when the time came, the hitchhiker could be target number one.

The Ingram Model 10, named for its designer, Gordon Ingram, was manufactured from 1970 in the United States by the Military Armament Corporation. A machine pistol less than a foot long and weighing only 6.5 pounds, the Model 10 fires .45-caliber ammunition from a 30-round magazine that fits into—and juts down from—the pistol grip. It fires in fully automatic mode, using the blowback principle, has fixed sights fore and aft, and the cocking handle, mounted on the top (convenient for both right- and left-handed shooters), is grooved down the middle so as not to interfere with sighting. It is factory-fitted with a suppressor to reduce noise.

Tom had removed from his copy of the weapon its usual retractable metal-pipe shoulder butt that, when extended, just about doubled the weapon's length. After all, he didn't expect ever to use it for targets more than a couple of feet away, so he would never have to aim from a shoulder stance. Like tonight, for instance; how far can a target go on a boat?

Tom gave off contemplating the unconscious hitchhiker, and the equalizer concealed beneath his sleeping head, when Doug came bounding down the narrow steps, filling the cabin as much by his energy and sheer physicality as by his simple presence. "Gotta suit up," he explained.

"I'll get out of your way then, Popeye," Tom said.

"Naw, that's okay, Tom," Doug said. "It's miserable up there on deck, not enough room for everybody to get in under the tarp. Sit on the other bunk, why doncha?"

"Good idea," Tom said, and did so.

Doug frowned at the sleeper. "He's been out a long time," he commented. "Tiny doesn't know his own strength."

"Oh, I think he does," Tom said.

"Think he'll be all right?"

"We'll all be all right, Popeye. Very soon, now."

If Doug minded this nickname Tom had recently found for him, naming him after a blowhard comic-strip sailor, he hadn't yet said so. Of course, it was possible he didn't get it; Tom had found, in his long life, that an astonishing number of people had just about no sense of humor at all.

Doug was still frowning in worry at Dortmunder's unconscious friend. "See, the thing is," he explained, "up till now, we maybe broke a few laws and all, trespassing and stealing this boat and like that, but nothing really *major*, you know? If we got caught—"

"You won't get caught," Tom told him. "I guarantee it."

"Hope you're right," Doug said, and turned his attention to the wetsuit and other gear he had to change into, stowed in the forward storage area beyond the bunks.

Meantime, up on deck, Dortmunder had been left by Doug in charge of the wheel, with somewhat more assistance from Kelp and Tiny than he felt he absolutely needed. "Remember," Kelp said, for about the thousandth time, "you don't want to run across that monofilament and bust it."

"The boat isn't even *moving*," Dortmunder pointed out.

Tiny said, "Well, Dortmunder, it's not exactly *not* moving, either. Up and down and side to side count."

"I'm holding the position," Dortmunder answered, with just a soupçon of asperity in his voice. "Doug said hold the position, I'm holding the position."

"We're only saying," Kelp said.

Doug came flap-footing in his flippers up from below at that point. He was changed into his diving gear, which made him the only person here properly dressed for the weather. He said, "Holding the position?"

"Yes," said Dortmunder, in lieu of a lot of other things.

"Good. Might as well get it over with."

Doug picked up a coil of line, one end of which was knotted to the side rail. Seating himself on that rail next to that knot, he used his free hand to adjust the mask and mouthpiece over his face, waved sideways like Queen Elizabeth, and flipped backward over the side.

"Gee," Kelp said. "Just like that."

"I see his light down there," Tiny said, leaning his head briefly out into the full blast of the rain. "Nope; now it's gone." And he crowded back in with Dortmunder and Kelp and the wheel.

The position that Dortmunder was holding was into the wind, somewhere between where the monofilament line should be and where the dam should be. So long as he faced the *Over My Head* into the wind this way, the canvas-and-Lucite temporary wheelhouse provided a certain amount of protection from the elements.

The idea was, they would stay here while Doug moved along just below the surface of the reservoir, shining his forehead lamp out ahead of himself, looking for the thin white line of monofilament to glow back at him from out of the watery dark. Once he'd found it, he would search along it until he came to the marker rope leading down to the casket at the bottom of the reservoir. The line he'd carried with him, which he would have been unreeling all along, would be tied to the monofilament at the same place as the marker rope, and then Doug would swim back to the boat and guide them very slowly to the proper place.

Once boat and marker rope had been brought together, the rest would be easy. They would use the *Over My Head*'s own power winch to raise the casket from the bottom of the reservoir up out of the water, where they'd be able to wrestle it aboard like Moby-Dick; Tiny's particular skills would come strongly into play at that point. Then it would be back to the clearing where Stan awaited; run the *Over My Head* aground, prow in; shlep the casket ashore; carry it home, divide the money, get into warm clothes, and have a beer.

A definite plan.

* * *

There. The nearly straight line of monofilament, just a foot below the surface of the reservoir, gleamed with a ghostly pale radiance where Doug's lamp beam touched it. He ranged along that shimmery line and soon found the marker rope, still in place.

He quickly tied the new line from the new boat to the monofilament, then looked down at the marker rope, extending away into the murk below, and he just couldn't resist. Flippered feet kicking strongly, he swooped down through the dark, headlamp picking up the marker rope along the way, and there he was at the bottom, and there *it* was, waiting.

Standing on end, a casket has a less restful, more problematic appearance than in its more usual lying-down posture. Standing on end in fifty feet of mucky water, in front of a slime-covered brick wall, its own once-glossy surface dulled and dirtied and covered with goo, a casket looked like a doorway to a different world. Not a better one.

He could imagine that door opening.

Superstition, Doug thought, ignoring the little chills running through his body, inside the warm wetsuit. There are no premonitions, he told himself. The whole thing's a piece of cake. Taking the light with him, leaving the blackness, he swam powerfully toward the surface.

● ● ●

Tom sat on the narrow bunk in the gently rocking boat, back against a pillow against the wall, and listened. Doug wasn't back yet. It was nowhere near time to make the move.

Beside him on the bunk, nestled against his bony hip, was the hammer he'd found in a storage drawer beside the sink, for use in case the hitchhiker regained consciousness before Tom was ready. But he doubted now that he'd need it; the hitchhiker's even breathing and relaxed face suggested he'd moved on from unconsciousness to sleep. He was probably good till morning, if nothing disturbed him.

Tom shifted position on the bunk, fluffing the pillow behind his back. He figured he had half an hour or more to wait. And then the timing would have to be perfect.

The thing was, Dortmunder and his pals would expect Tom to make a move. Everybody always did, that was written into the equation. Tom's job was to figure out the earliest point at which they'd expect something from him, and the earliest point before that when he *could* usefully make his move, and then pick his spot between the two.

This time, it seemed to him, they wouldn't really expect much trouble before they got the loot ashore, but they would probably start being tense and wary once the casket was actually inside the boat. But now that they had a boat with its own winch attached to its own motor, so that Tiny was no longer needed to drag the casket up out of the reservoir, Tom's actual first potential moment was much earlier than that.

Not when Doug found the marker rope.

Not when he led the boat to it.

Not when he untied the marker rope from the monofilament and handed it to someone in the boat.

When the marker rope was attached to the winch: *then*.

● ● ●

Dortmunder and Kelp and Tiny huddled their heads together over the wheel so they could hear one another above the storm without having to shout loud enough to be heard by Tom down in the cabin. "Once we get that box ashore," Kelp was saying, "we've got to keep a very close eye on Tom because you just *know* he's gonna pull something."

"Before that, if you ask me," Tiny growled. "Once we get that box in the boat, once he *sees* it, there's no way he's gonna control himself. He'll make his move. That's when we gotta be on our guard."

"You ask me," Dortmunder said, "the time to be on your guard with Tom is all the time."

"*Pflufh!*" said Doug, appearing at the rail, spitting out his mouthpiece.

They all turned to watch as Doug, who had hoisted himself up out of the water onto the narrow platform jutting out from the stern of the boat, climbed over the rail and stood on the exposed rear deck for a second, face mask still on, dripping in the rain. Then he pulled off the face mask and grinned and came over to speak to Dortmunder, his large wet presence forcing Tiny to back down two steps into the cabin.

"I got it," Doug said. "So all you do is keep us moving just barely forward, okay?"

Doug had given Dortmunder a quick orientation course in operating this vessel on their way out from shore, not enough to take it on a round-the-world cruise, but maybe enough to keep it moving just barely forward for a few minutes. "Sure," Dortmunder said.

"I'll be up on the prow," Doug told him. "You'll be able to see me up there through the windshield. If I want you to steer to the right or the left, I'll wave my arm out like this."

"Got it," Dortmunder said.

"Forward, I point that way. Stop, I hold my hand back to you like this."

"Got that, too."

"Now, take it real slow and easy," Doug told him, "because I'm going to be bringing in the line while we move."

"Very slow, very easy," Dortmunder promised.

Tom, sitting up on the bunk, heard the conversation through the narrow open doorway where the bottom half of Tiny now stood. He heard Doug's footsteps move forward on the deck just above his head, and saw Tiny's legs recede back up to the wheelhouse level. One on the prow, he thought. One on the bunk down here. Three around the wheel.

Doug, seated cross-legged on the prow, waved for Dortmunder to ease them forward, and then began to draw in the line as they moved, coiling it in his lap so it wouldn't drift under the boat. Getting fouled on one of their lines was, as he saw it, their greatest danger at this point.

They were less than ten minutes easing their way across the rainswept reservoir, and then Doug, still tugging gently on the line, saw the knot rise dripping and swaying out of the water dead ahead. The monofilament was invisible in these conditions, so the white knot of rope seemed to be levitating itself. He waved to Dortmunder to stop, looped the rope in a quick knot over the davit on the prow, and went back to the wheelhouse.

(One down here, four around the wheel.)

Dortmunder said, "Now I hold the position, right?"

"You bet," Doug told him. "Tiny, let me show you the winch."

Tiny said, "That includes going out in the rain, huh?"

Doug went to the rear, and Tiny followed. (One down here, two at the wheel, two at the stern.) Opening a floor panel at the stern, Doug shone his headlamp in and pointed out the machinery. "There's the switch. That's the spool. It runs off the same shaft as the propeller, so John can make it go slower or faster up there at the wheel."

"Gotcha," Tiny said.

"Be right back with the rope," Doug told him. Straightening, he adjusted face mask and mouthpiece and then backflipped out of the boat.

Tom shifted on the bunk, putting both feet on the gently rocking floor. One down here, two at the wheel, one at the stern, one in the water. That one's the duck in the barrel.

Doug swam to the monofilament, untied the marker rope, tied it to his wrist instead, and made his way back to the boat. He came up on the small platform at the rear, but Tiny was looking the other way. "Tiny!" he called. "I got it here!"

Right, Tom thought. He stood, leaned forward, reached over the sleeping hitchhiker, slid his hand in under the mattress, and it wasn't there.

What? Tom moved his hand left, right . . .   Cold on wrist. *Click.*

Tom blinked, and the hitchhiker sat up, the Ingram just visible beyond him under his pillow. Wild-eyed, glaring in triumph, raising their right wrists handcuffed together, the maniac cried, "*Now*, Tim Jepson! Now!"

• • •

"Oh, *shit!*" Dortmunder cried. "It's started!"

Kelp yelled, "What—" But the rest of his words were blotted by a sudden chatter of automatic gunfire.

Everybody stared at everybody else. Doug looked ready to jump back into the water. In fact, *everybody* looked ready to jump into the water, even Dortmunder.

"Al?"

The wheel forgotten, Dortmunder concentrated on keeping well away from the opening into the cabin. "Yeah, Tom?"

"It's a wash, Al," Tom's voice called. "You were cuter than I thought."

Dortmunder had no idea in what way he'd been so wonderfully cute. He said, "So now what, Tom?"

"I'm coming up," Tom called. "I won't bother none of you, none of you bother me."

"Hold it a second, Tom."

Dortmunder pushed frantically at Kelp, gesturing to him to get up on the forward deck, above the cabin and ahead of its entrance. Tiny handed the end of the marker rope back to Doug and moved swiftly to the opposite side of the cabin entrance from Dortmunder. Doug, clutching the marker rope in one hand and the rail in the other, crouched down on the platform sticking out behind the boat at the stern.

"Jesus Christ, Al," Tom called, "how much time do you need? I told you, I'm no threat."

"You kinda sounded like a threat a minute ago," Dortmunder called back. "Why don't you toss that Uzi or whatever it is out ahead of yourself?"

"You're still a joker, Al," Tom said. "Here I come."

Here he came, moving in an odd crablike fashion like Quasimodo on his way up to his bells. The Ingram, looking like a particularly mean example of plumbing supplies, was grasped in his left hand, held out in front of himself for balance. His right hand was down behind him at his ankle, as though he were dragging something.

And, in fact, when he came farther up out of the cabin, it could be seen that he *was* dragging something. Guffey, a dead weight, bleeding onto the steps, his blood then swirling away once Tom had dragged him out into the rain.

Tom, at a fast scuttling lope, rushed past Dortmunder and Tiny, dragging Guffey behind him. Then he turned around, already drenched, and stared back at Dortmunder and Kelp and Tiny, in a triangle facing him. "Where's Popeye?" He had to shout over the storm.

"Diving," Dortmunder yelled back. "Over to the monofilament."

Tom waved the Ingram in the air like a terrorist announcing a victory, but in his case he was only showing it off, because he said, "A trade, Al. This for the key."

That was when Dortmunder saw that it was, in fact, his own handcuffs that Guffey had brought along, without Dortmunder's knowledge, and had used to attach himself to Tom. But Guffey had the key. Wishing Doug would use the advantage he had that Tom didn't know there was anyone behind him—but knowing damn well Doug would never do one blessed thing—Dortmunder said, "What if it's no trade, Tom?"

Raging, Tom grimaced, his teeth shiny in the rain. "I'll kill the bunch of you!" he snarled, "and use the bread knife down there to cut this idiot's hand off!"

"You won't get your seven hundred thousand," Dortmunder pointed out.

"That's right, Al," Tom said. "And neither will you. But I'll be the only one worried about it. Goddammit! Get this idiot off me! Half the money's yours, Al, it's yours, I don't *care*, just get this—"

And Guffey, not dead yet after all, suddenly came surging up off the deck, left hand reaching for Tom's scrawny neck, closing around it. The Ingram in Tom's hand spattered once more, spraying bullets as he pounded its butt against Guffey's head, and Dortmunder and Tiny both dove down into the cabin as Kelp jumped headfirst into the reservoir.

Doug, terrified, reared up on the little platform as Tom and Guffey, struggling in each other's grasp, toppled over the rail and crashed into him. All three flailed and toppled and splashed into the water, Tom losing the Ingram, Doug losing the rope.

Guffey, weak, swallowing water, slumped down below the surface, unable to keep afloat. Tom, tangled with him, hoarsely screamed out, "Al! The key! For Christ's sake, the key!"

"The *rope!*" Doug shrieked, and dived, jamming his mouthpiece in, face mask on. Kicking hard, he reached up, and when his fumbling hands found the headlamp's switch and turned it on, he could see nothing around him but dirty water. Ahead, it must be; lower; out there ahead. He dived.

Dortmunder and Tiny came stumbling up out of the cabin. "Where—" Tiny said. "Where is everybody?"

"Help!"

They rushed to the side rail, and there was Kelp floundering in the water. Tiny bent down, grabbed one of Kelp's wrists, and yanked him aboard. Then, while Kelp sat on the wet deck wheezing and coughing and gasping, Dortmunder and Tiny looked out at the speckled black surface of the reservoir.

Nobody.

• • •

Can't lose the rope, can't lose the rope, can't lose the rope. Doug quartered like a hungry fish, slicing through the murky water, straining to see that rope, floating somewhere, nearby, drifting, attached to seven hundred thousand dollars, the only link to seven hundred thousand dollars.

And I was just *there* with it, he thought.

Movement in the water. Doug turned and saw a leg descending, then another, then a cluster of limbs.

The two bodies floated down past him, entwined, Tom's face almost unrecognizable with those staring eyes and wide open mouth.

Shuddering, Doug turned away. More money for the rest of us. More money for the rest of us. The rope, the rope, the rope.

● ● ●

"Dortmunder," Tiny said, "this is a mess."

"I never expected anything else," Dortmunder told him.

The two stood over the wheel, rain beating down all around them as Dortmunder held the position, waiting for Doug to reappear. He was, they'd realized, off looking for the rope to the money, which he'd managed to lose in the general excitement. Kelp was lying down in the cabin, recuperating from his unexpected plunge. And Tom and Guffey were gone, no question about that.

Dortmunder had explained to Tiny who Guffey was, and Tiny commented, "I guess it was only a matter of time, with Tom, till *one* of his pasts caught up with him."

"He was safer in jail," Dortmunder agreed. "But what bothers me, Guffey never did find his first name."

"Tom must of known it," Tiny said. "Maybe he told him on the way down."

Kelp came up from the cabin then, looking a lot greener than usual. "Listen," he said. "Is it okay for the floor down here to be full of water?"

● ● ●

Find the railroad tracks. Then you find the town. Then you find the railroad station. Then you find the casket and the rope.

For the first time in his diving life, Doug was being stupid underwater. Greed and panic had combined to make him forget everything he knew. He was down here alone, an incredibly dangerous thing to begin with. He was improperly equipped for the kind of search he'd suddenly started to undertake. And, most stupid of all, he was paying no attention to the passage of time.

He'd had an hour of air when he started.

● ● ●

"The fucking boat is sinking," Dortmunder said. "I'm not going to stand here and have *conversations*."

"John, John," Kelp said, "all I'm saying is, think about it. You hardly know a thing about how to run this boat, and—"

"Of course I do."

"You know how to hold the position. And how to ease it forward a little bit. Doug knows the *whole thing*. Even if we're sinking—"

Bitterly, Tiny said, "Tom and his goddamn machine gun, shot the bottom full of holes."

"Even so," Kelp said, "we're sinking *slowly*. We can wait for Doug."

"No way," Dortmunder said.

"He needs us."

"He's a pro," Dortmunder insisted. "He's dressed for what he's doing. When he comes up and we aren't here, *he* can swim to shore. *I* can't swim to shore, not again."

Then, to cut through all the crap and get *out* of there, Dortmunder stepped to the wheel and pushed the accelerator level hard forward. The boat surged ahead and cut through both the monofilament and the rope Doug had been coiling so carefully on the prow. That's the rope that now wrapped itself tightly a dozen times around the propeller and shaft and stopped the *Over My Head* dead in the water.

• • •

Standing in the heavy rain, Stan listened and listened but heard no more gunshots. What's happening out there? He rested one hand on the rear window of the station wagon, looked out over its forward-slanted roof and submerged hood and saw nothing. But nothing.

So Tom made his move before they got ashore, did he? And did it work?

Whoever came out ahead out there, the winner or winners will want wheels. For themselves, and for the money. Not this station wagon, this heap will never go anywhere on its own again, but Dortmunder's car, the Peugeot.

Just in case; okay? Just in case Tom managed to catch everybody by surprise out there, Stan should do something to defend himself. So he turned and walked upslope to the Peugeot, got behind the wheel, and started the engine. Better than half a tank of gas; good. He switched on the headlights, then got out of the car and splashed through the rain over to the right side of the clearing and in among the trees.

There were no dry places out here, not after two days and nights of steady rain. Wet and cold but unwilling to make a sitting duck of himself, Stan hunkered down against a tree where he could see the Peugeot's lights, the clearing, even a bit of the station wagon.

Hell of a position for a driver.

• • •

"Got it!" Tiny cried. "Pull me up outta here."

Dortmunder and Kelp heaved on the rope. The other end of it was tied around Tiny under the armpits, and Tiny was lying half on and half off the platform at the rear of the *Over My Head*. He'd been reaching farther and farther down under the boat, trying to find an end of rope or—for preference—monofilament, and now at last he'd done it, and once Dortmunder and Kelp's combined efforts got him completely back up on the platform he rose and held up a jumble of monofilament in his left hand like a serving of angel hair pasta.

"Beautiful stuff," Kelp prayed.

Tiny tied the monofilament to the rail, then climbed over onto the deck and removed the rope from around himself.

"Tiny, I'm sorry," Dortmunder said.

Tiny pointed a fat finger at him. "Dortmunder," he said, "I want this to be a lesson to you. This is what happens to a person that's rude. You break off a little discussion before it's finished, before everybody's done talking, maybe there's something you oughta know that you *don't* know."

"I just didn't like," Dortmunder explained, "the idea of being on a sinking ship."

"How about," Tiny asked him, "being on a sinking ship that can't go nowhere?"

"That's worse," Dortmunder admitted.

Kelp said, "But we'll go now, won't we? We got the monofilament, right?"

"*I* got the monofilament," Tiny reminded him.

"That's what I meant," Kelp agreed. "And the other end of it's tied to the railroad track in by shore, right? Over where we tried the first time. So now all we do is just tow ourselves in."

"If it doesn't break," Tiny pointed out. "It's awful skinny stuff."

"It's supposed to be very strong," Dortmunder suggested. He was feeling unusually humble. "For bringing in big fish like tunas and marlins and things," he said.

"Well, let's see." Tiny reached over the side, lifted the monofilament, wrapped it once around his fist, and tugged gently. Then he stopped. "Not bare-handed," he said. "This stuff'll take my fingers off."

"I'll get you a rag or something, Tiny," Dortmunder offered, and went away to the cabin, where the water was almost knee deep now, despite the laborings of the boat's automatic pump. Ignoring that, or trying to, Dortmunder searched around and found two oven mitts hanging from hooks beside the stove. He waded back up on deck and offered the mitts. "Try these."

With some difficulty, Tiny jammed his hands partway into the mitts, then picked up the monofilament and pulled with a slow and even pressure. "Much better, Dortmunder," he said.

"Thank you, Tiny."

A sound of sloshing was heard from the cabin. Sounding surprised, Kelp said, "I think we're moving."

"So far," Tiny said. Hand over hand, he reeled in the monofilament.

Kelp looked over the side. "You'd think Doug would of come up by now," he said.

• • •

Tree stumps, tree stumps, tree stumps. Doug flew back and forth like an underwater bat over the drowned hillsides, his meager light playing in sepia tones across the devastation. There had to be some sort of landmark around here *somewhere*, but all Doug could see, every which way he turned, was these rotting tree stumps.

His turns, in fact, were slower now, less coordinated, as the strain of constant underwater exertion began to take its toll. These are signs he would normally have heeded, but at this moment there was no room in his brain for anything but this:

I saw the casket full of money, I saw it tonight, I swam down to it, just a little while ago. I held the rope in my hand. I have to be able to get it all back. It wouldn't be fair otherwise. I have to get it all back.

No tree stumps. Doug in his weariness almost flew on over the spot, but then his laggard brain caught up with his eyes and he reversed, awkwardly, like a manatee, and shone his light on the spot again, and it was true. A clear swath cut through the forest of decayed stumps.

A road; it must have been a road. So it has to lead somewhere, and once there I can orient myself.

This way, or that way? I think it should be that way. Doug set off along the faint line of road, kicking doggedly.

• • •

Stan didn't hear anybody coming, and then all at once people were moving around in the Peugeot's headlights. People. The boat hadn't come back, he knew *that* much for sure. So who were these people?

Maybe the law *did* have the reservoir staked out, after all. Cautious, doubtful, apprehensive, Stan straightened stiffly from his hunkered-down position and stalked the people moving around out there in the clearing. Who were they? What were they up to?

It was Tiny's shape he recognized first, and right after that the sound of John's complaining voice: "Now, where the *hell* is Stan?"

"Here," Stan said, stepping forward into their midst and causing all three to jump like little kids in a haunted house. "What's going on?" Stan asked them. "Where's the boat?"

"Down there by the railroad tracks," Andy told him, pointing vaguely away along the shoreline. "We walked here from there."

"*Waded* here," Tiny corrected. He was holding his hands in his armpits, pressing his arms against his sides as though the hands were cold or sore or something.

John said, "Can we go now?"

"Go?" Stan looked around. "Aren't we missing a couple people?"

"*And* seven hundred thousand dollars," Tiny said.

Andy said, "It's a long story."

John said, "Let's tell it tomorrow, okay? Today is finished."

CHAPTER SEVENTY-FOUR

The lights are on!" Myrtle cried, in great excitement.

So then Wally crept over to see what was happening, and after that everybody including Myrtle and Edna had to go over to Oak Street, and the whole long story did have to be told tonight, after all. But at least they were all indoors and warm, and the stay-at-homes were willing to wait until the returnees had changed into dry clothes. By then, May had made soup, Myrtle had made toast, and Edna had made a pitcher of what she called "Bloody Marys that'll iron your socks." Under those conditions, it was possible to recount the night's events without too many qualms or expressions of disgust. Kelp did most of the talking, with amplifications by Tiny and occasional color reportage from Dortmunder.

Tom Jimson's lady friend and daughter bore up very well under the news of his death. "Well, *that* was overdue," Edna commented. "I thought I was done with that man years ago, and now I am."

"I so wanted to meet my father," Myrtle said with a little shiver, "and then I did. He'll be much better as a memory."

The news about Doug was a little harder to take. "Well, I don't hold much brief for that young man," Edna said, "as Myrtle well knows—"

"Mother!"

"—*but* I certainly don't wish him ill."

"Doug's a pro," Dortmunder said for about the thousandth time. "He'll be okay. But there was no point our hanging around. He wouldn't of found us anyway."

"That's really true," Kelp said.

"And John did get back by himself last time," May said doubtfully.

"Darn right I did," Dortmunder said. "Without wetsuits and air tanks and *all* of that."

"We'll hope for the best," Edna said.

"*I* hope for the best," Myrtle agreed.

"We all do," Wally said, but his eyes were on Myrtle.

CHAPTER SEVENTY-FIVE

Gray day was returning, seeping back into a sopping world, and still they hadn't gone to bed. Dortmunder was ready, more than ready, but now everybody else wanted to talk about the *future*. "There isn't any," Dortmunder stated, as definitively as he could. "Not between me and that reservoir."

"The thing is, Dortmunder," Tiny said, "we invested so much in this already."

"Including," Dortmunder pointed out, "two, maybe three people. I'm in no hurry to go with them."

Kelp said, "I've touched that box with these hands. That's what gets me."

"And," Stan said, "we don't have Tom to worry about anymore."

Dortmunder said, "We don't have anything else, either. Doug lost the rope that leads down to the casket, and *I* lost the monofilament. Also, we don't have a boat. Also, we don't have a professional diver anymore."

"He could still show up," Murch's Mom said.

"Even so." Dortmunder spread his hands. "The only reason I got into this was to keep Tom from blowing up the dam and drowning everybody—"

"*So* like him," Edna said.

"Well, that danger's past," Dortmunder said. "It's Tom's money. He's down there with it. Let them stay together. *I'm* going to sleep. And then I'm going to New York. And then I'm gonna think about something else for the rest of my life."

• • •

The Batesville Casket Company is quite properly proud of its Cathodic System® steel casket. A bar of magnesium is welded to the bottom of the casket with a resistor attached that detects rust as it develops anywhere on the casket surface and *sends* the magnesium to that spot. Eventually the magnesium will degenerate, but Batesville still guarantees the internal integrity of its Cathodic System® caskets in air or ground for a minimum of twenty-five years.

In air or ground. In water, who knows?

CHAPTER SEVENTY-SIX

Morning. All morning the rain poured down, as before. The night shift left the dam with heads down and chins tucked in, running for their cars and climbing in and driving away with none of the usual horsing around. The day shift, arriving, ran the other way, crowding into the dry safety of the dam with nothing on their lips but curses. The weeks of beautiful weather were forgotten: "Won't this crap *ever* let up?"

In the course of the morning, only three cars passed by on the road over the dam, and Doug opened his eyes in time to see the third go by just above him. I'm alive, he thought, lying there on the rocks at the east end of the dam, barely clear of the water and a little below the roadway, and he was amazed.

He was right to be amazed. His last clear memory from the night before was that exhilarating moment when he had *seen the railroad tracks!* Exhilarating in part because, he now realized, his brain had already begun to suffer oxygen starvation. But exhilarating anyway, after all his desperate searching, when the road he'd been following had suddenly crossed those two rusty black lines leading toward seven hundred thousand dollars.

And death.

He'd actually started to follow the tracks, he remembered that now. Even though in some still-rational corner of his brain he'd realized he was running out of air, that he didn't dare stay down one second longer, he had turned and obstinately kicked himself not upward but downward at a long slant, closer to the tracks.

That's all he could remember. Somewhere in there, he must have blacked out, or partially blacked out, and once his greedy stupid conscious mind had gotten out of the way his professional knowledge and diver's instincts had taken over and, at long last, he had started doing the right thing.

A diver out of air is only out of air at his current depth. Ascending alters pressure, and more air becomes available; not much, but every little bit helps.

Still, at some point Doug must have done an emergency ascent, because he no longer had either his weight belt nor his air tank. In an emergency ascent, the diver simply tries to get to the surface as rapidly as possible, slowly exhaling into the water along the way to prevent injuries caused by his lungs expanding too rapidly with the decreasing pressure. The partly inflated BCD would have helped speed his ascent, and would have kept him afloat and alive once he'd made it all the way up to air. And some remaining flicker of intelligence had made him swim toward the dam's lights (as John had done the last time), and had helped him drag himself up above the water line, where he'd been lying ever since.

The wetsuit had kept him from hypothermia, but he was incredibly weary and achy and hungry and cold and, now that he stopped to think about it, scared. I could have died down there!

I *should* have died down there. How could I have been so dumb?

Slowly Doug sat up, moaning in pain. Every joint and muscle in his body ached. Despite the wetsuit, he felt cold, chilled to the bone. Warmth, he thought. Warmth, food, bed. Too bad he'd never really connected with Myrtle; bed with a woman right now would be *exactly* what the doctor ordered.

Moving as stiffly as the Tin Woodman when he needed oil, Doug bent down over his knees and removed the flippers from his feet. Then he crawled up the rocks and boulders to the parking area beside the dam entrance. After a couple of minutes of limbering-up exercises there, bending and twisting and kicking (all the time hoping a car would come by so he could thumb a ride), he started walking along the road. Too bad he didn't have Andy Kelp's skill at commandeering cars.

At least with movement he wasn't so cold. On the other hand, his bare feet didn't like the rough road surface at all. Still, he was alive, and that counted.

He'd walked a bit more than half a mile when he heard the car coming along behind him. Turning, trying his best to smile like a friendly and innocent hitchhiker, he stuck his thumb out and was quite surprised when the car, a Chevy Chamois, actually came to a stop.

His surprise was doubled when he opened the passenger door to climb in and saw that the driver was a good-looking girl. A *very* good-looking girl. "Thanks a lot," he told her, shutting the door. "Pretty bad out there."

"Well, you're dressed for it," she commented, giving his wetsuit a crooked grin as she shifted into gear and the car rolled forward.

Oh, it was nice to watch the countryside go by at forty miles an hour instead of four. Doug said, "*Nobody* should be out in this stuff."

"You bet," she said. "I wouldn't be out here, believe me, if I wasn't such a good little wifey."

The word *wifey* sent one signal to Doug, but the ironic tone sent another. Looking at her more closely, he said, "Your husband sent you out in this weather? For what? Get him a sixpack?"

"He didn't *send* me," she said. "He doesn't send anybody anywhere, believe me. I was just visiting him in the hospital."

"Oh, I'm sorry."

"The bug hospital," she said, not sounding sorry at all. "He's wiggy, you know?"

"That's terrible," Doug said. "A good-looking girl like you, stuck with a nutcase?"

She gave him a gratified smile. "You think I'm good-looking?"

"You *know* you are."

"Would you believe I'm pregnant?"

"No! Really?"

"I don't show, do I?"

"Not a bit," Doug told her truthfully, wondering if he dared pat her belly. Probably not. A ride was more important than anything else at this point.

The girl sighed theatrically. "I should have listened to my mother," she said. "*She* knew there was something wrong with him from the beginning, but I just never listened."

"Why not?"

Another sigh. "I guess I just like sex too much," the poor girl said.

"Mmm," said Doug, in sympathetic understanding. "Uh, what's your name?"

CHAPTER SEVENTY-SEVEN

Dortmunder raised his cup. "My last coffee for a year," he said, and drank.

May, with him in the kitchen of the house on Oak Street, said, "Why's that?"

"Because I'm going back to the city," he explained, "and I won't be drinking anything out of a faucet there for a good long time."

"What about taking showers?"

"I haven't doped that out yet."

May said, "John, they do all kinds of things to purify that water before it ever gets to the city. Animals and birds and fish and things die in it all the time."

"Still," Dortmunder said. "Every time I turn the faucet and the water splashes in the sink, you know what it's gonna sound like? '*Al.*'"

Murch's Mom came in and said, "Wally's off."

Dortmunder and May went out to the living room, where the front door was open, letting in cold damp air and giving a great view of the rain-drenched world outside. Tiny carried the components of Wally's computer in white plastic trash bags to protect them from the weather, and Wally carried his bulgy green vinyl bag. He was grinning from ear to ear, which made him look more than ever like a novelty item for sale on the Jersey shore. "Miss May, John," he said. "It's been wonderful. I learned so much from you all."

"It was nice to meet you, Wally," May said.

"You and the, uh, computer," Dortmunder said, coughing slightly, "were a real help."

"I hate long good-byes," Tiny said. "Especially when I'm carrying three hundred pounds of shit."

So they had a short good-bye, and Wally and his equipment went out to Murch's Mom's cab for the run around the corner to Myrtle Street. Uh, Myrtle Street. *On* Myrtle Street.

A little later, Kelp and Stan Murch came back with transportation for the trip back to the city; Stan a Datsun S.E.X. 69 for his Mom and himself, Kelp an MD-plated Pontiac Prix Fixe for himself and Dortmunder and May and Tiny. They packed the two cars, running back and forth in the rain, and when they were about to leave, Dortmunder shut the front door and turned to see May frowning in worry at Doug's pickup, still parked on the gravel drive beside the front lawn. Dortmunder said, "What's up?"

"I wish I knew Doug was all right," she said. "And don't say, 'He's a pro.'"

"I wasn't going to," Dortmunder lied. "I was going to say he's a big boy. Come on, May, it's raining."

FIFTH DOWN?

CHAPTER SEVENTY-EIGHT

February 11. It had been months since Dortmunder had even thought about the failed reservoir job. . . .

"It's too awful to go out tonight," May said.

"You're right," Dortmunder said, and she was. A winter storm, high winds packing an overload of wet snow, swirled through the canyons of New York City, hunting for victims.

"There's a special on TV tonight about Caribbean vacation places," May said. "We can stay in and watch."

"I wish we could *go* there, May."

"We've been before," she pointed out, "and we'll go again. This year, we'll just watch."

So they watched. And twenty minutes in, half asleep, distracted, barely paying attention at all, they were both snapped awake by—

Doug.

"Jesus *Christ!*"

"Ssh, John!"

"—new owner Douglas Berry, a transplanted New Yorker, has big plans for his resort hotel and dive shop, right on the beach, with easy access to the reef."

Doug, grinning big, tanned, in a bathing suit, stood on the sand with a low white resort hotel behind him, his left arm around a beautiful young woman holding a tiny baby. "It's gonna be great for little Tiffany, to grow up here. It's a terrific place to be a kid. I'm a kid myself. Love it!"

Then there was a shot of Doug wind-surfing, grinning like a baboon, huge ocean, huge blue sky, fantastic yellow-white sun. The off-screen announcer said, "Berry himself, a qualified professional dive instructor, leads the snorkel and scuba-diving classes. His emphasis is on active vacation life."

And now a shot of Doug bursting out of the ocean into close-up, in full scuba gear, pulling off the face mask and mouthpiece, giving that *shit-eating* grin right at the camera. "Come on down!"

"You're goddamn right I will!" Dortmunder raged, on his feet, about to jump headfirst into the TV.

"John, John, John!" May leaped up and stood in front of him, patting his chest as though he were a spooked horse. "John, no."

"He *got* it, the son of a bitch! He got the seven hundred thousand! New *ooooow*-ner!"

"John, *forget* it," May begged him.

"Where was that place?" Dortmunder demanded. "What island was that?"

But the TV was showing a commercial now, for a timed-release cold remedy. May said, "John, what can you do about it? Nothing."

"Nothing! I can go down there, I can—"

"And do what? John, if he bought that hotel, he's figured out how to make the money look legitimate. Said it was an inheritance, or gambling winnings, or something. Paid taxes on it, and bought that place with the rest."

Dortmunder didn't want to calm down, but he didn't seem able to stop himself. "Yeah," he agreed, "that's the way to do it. But *still*, May—"

"It wasn't ever your money," May pointed out. "You can't take him to court. If you go down there, if we even find out where it is, he won't have to give you a thing." She looked at the TV set, now showing a nasal spray commercial. "We gave up too soon, that's all."

Dortmunder gnashed his teeth. "His own hotel." He started out of the living room, snarling, "You want a beer?"

"At least," she said.

As he went through the doorway, the phone rang. He stopped, turned, pointed at the phone. "You tell Andy," he said, "I don't want to talk about it."